Graham's Reso.

Book 1
The China Pandemic
By
A. R. Shaw

Liberty Lake, Washington

Publisher's Note: This is a work of fiction. Names, characters, places, and incidents are a product of the author's imagination. Locales and public names are sometimes used for atmospheric purposes. Any resemblance to actual people, living or dead, or to businesses, companies, events, institutions, or locales is completely coincidental.

ISBN-10: 1494368552

ISBN-13: 978-1494368555

Cover Design by Keri Knutson of Alchemybookcovers.com

Dedicated to Thomas
For all your faith in me.

Contents

Some said that China's intent to develop the H5N1 virus merely came about as an attempt to culture a vaccine, knowing the nation's dense population would be at catastrophic risk if attacked by such a virus. Others said that China's motives had always been sinister, and that they had developed a weaponized form of the virus. In the end it didn't matter what the intentions had been; having tinkered with Pandora 's Box, and without safeguards in place, they had unleashed it. And not only on their own people; it spread like wildfire across the globe, exterminating more than six billion souls. The million or so who were still alive were somehow immune, but they were carriers. As for the virus itself, it became known simply as the China Pandemic.

Shivering in the pounding Pacific Northwest rain, Hyun-Ok needed to see for herself what threat the grim man in the distance posed. She'd heard him yelling before, followed by a gunshot blast and then a terrible scream. Having already counted him an unsuitable candidate to offer her the aid she needed, she had to be certain he wasn't an immediate threat to her and her son.

With a death grip on the bed of the parked black pickup truck behind which she had taken refuge, Hyun-Ok gasped in horror as the crazed man powered up a small, worn backhoe. He scooped his victim up with the bucket, then spilled him, still alive and screaming, into a massive fire he had kept burning all day in a Dumpster.

She slinked away, her broken sobs bringing on a coughing fit from her own infected lungs. The agonized screams finally stopped, and Hyun-Ok grieved in silence for the unlucky man's soul as sparks flew skyward. She must escape this part of town! The grim man, Campos, had posted NO TRESPASSING signs, and his actions told her he meant it.

She was her son's only hope, and there was little time left to ensure his future. The disease weakened Hyun-Ok more each day, and she knew she would soon die. She could not leave her five-year-old to fend for himself with the likes of Campos around. Her days of scouting had told her there was only one person left to consider; the search had already taken up too much valuable time and energy, and Bang had to be in caring hands soon.

The one she was thinking of had one more to bury anyway. She might as well spend what little time she had left with her son.

Hyun-Ok recovered from her coughing fit as best she could and continued her journey home. She would need to make the trip in silence through the forested night, hidden from the few remaining people. Since coming to the realization that Bang showed no signs of the virus she had been venturing out like this, into the dark, every night.

One by one those around her had died off as she cared for them, Bang always at her side. Her elderly mother had been the first to go, followed closely by her father. Shortly after that, her husband, though he desperately clung to life, not willing to abandon his wife and son.

Covered in the sweat of fever, and her words rasping, Hyun-Ok had assured him his son would be fine and urged him into a peaceful beyond. "I will be with you soon, my love," she'd told him with tears streaming down her face. As weak as she was at the time, the tears had surprised her.

The endearment, and the true meaning of her words, had sparked something in her dying husband. His eyes darted from Hyun-Ok to Bang, who was standing at the bedside. In brutal agony he drew himself up to gaze at his son's face. "He must not be left alone and defenseless in this world gone mad!"

Hyun-Ok tried to comfort her husband with words, pushing him gently back toward the mattress, and she revealed her plan to safeguard their son. Her husband held them both close, praying aloud to an unhearing god that he could draw them with him as he slipped away.

That was just a week ago, and that night, after Bang drifted off to sleep, Hyun-Ok had gone out canvassing for the few remaining survivors in the neighborhood. Cloaked in black and defying the many dangers, she spied on the others and assessed them based on instinct alone. She estimated six hundred had originally occupied this immediate area in the Seattle suburb of Issaquah, and with only a 2 percent survival rate there should be twelve survivors—now known to be carriers. Of those, she had only found seven.

Tonight she immediately discounted the first person she came across, two streets over, as being too elderly to be the guardian of a child of five. This lady only had a year left in her, if that. Hyun-Ok's boy needed someone younger to carry him through life, at least into his teens.

The man she found next made her uncomfortable. She observed him decidedly grieving for his lost family, sitting out in a lawn chair in the night, yelling obscenities. He taunted and waited for the starving dogs, now gone wild, to smell him out. He shot at them, but it seemed to her that he was only trying to provoke an attack. She could sense his massive sorrow and knew his intentions were suicide by mauling if he could manage it. If not, he would likely soon take his own life. Sadly, she suspected that happened a lot with survivors.

Hyun-Ok crossed the highway unseen and found a scantily clad woman picking apples from a tree in a vacant lot. She knew the woman would attract the wrong kind of attention and wouldn't be a good choice for her son's welfare.

The man she had finally chosen seemed the only one capable of being her son's guardian. Not only that, but something about him— either the way he carried his tall frame or the thoughtful dignity with which he buried his loved ones—assured Hyun-Ok that the neighbor named Graham would prove himself the best guardian. She knew that she could trust him with her boy. Knowing that as soon as Graham's father passed away he'd have no more to bury, she could take her boy to him going on her own journey into death. *One more day*, she thought. *But before then, I need to write to him about Bang.*

With a sad smile, she stepped through the maze of parked vehicles, listening attentively to all sounds and alert for any dangers. She glanced back at the glow in the distance one last time. The last remaining obstacle would be to make Graham understand that he needed the boy as much as the boy needed him. She knew that would be the greatest challenge. She had to convince him of that or her son would be doomed.

The frail man reached out to his son. Through tears, Graham gently grasped his father's shaking hands as he lay dying. He knew it was the closest they had ever been.

Graham reaffirmed that he would go on as they had planned, that he would always keep the rifle beside him. Through drowning coughs his father reminded Graham that taking his own life was not part of God's plan; it would only ensure a soulless wandering in the afterlife and would prevent him from ever again joining his departed family.

Having seen the signs so many times before, Graham knew the end was drawing near. He became desperate, knowing that the difference, this time, would be him standing alone without a soul known to him. His father's wheezing came in shorter gasps, his eyes drew quiet, and his face sank into itself. Graham went from the desperation of losing his father to praying for mercy and a quicker end; he could take no more of this torment. Just like all the others, one by one, they all died in anguish.

Graham could not understand why he still lived. He had watched helplessly as his wife Nelly had died, taking their unborn child with her. Then his dear mother left him, followed by his sister and four-year-old niece. And now his father.

"What will I do without you?" he asked.

"Do what I have taught you, Graham. Make good decisions along the way, and don't regret anything. You'll do fine. Always know that I'm proud of you."

Graham wiped spittle from his father's lips and clutched his hand.

When death finally came, his father assumed a peaceful demeanor and said for the last time, "I love you, son."

Exhausted from the night's endless vigil, Graham rubbed his face. Tears of frustration, fear, and loss streamed down through his light brown whiskers. He had not shaved since way back when things were normal, and he did not care if he ever shaved again. Food, and even the very air he needed to breathe, had lost all importance. He could only wonder how he could possibly go on without his father's strength and guidance.

With his last racking sob, Graham took a deep breath. "Buck up," his father would have said sternly. And that's what he decided to do. He was now the father of the clan, and he continued as if there was a family to lead.

There was only the one last grave, though this one would be the hardest to dig. Such little consolation would have to do at this moment. Everyone he'd ever known was now gone: all of his family, friends, and acquaintances. From the lowliest beggar to the wealthiest tycoon, no class had gone untouched; even the president had died. This was an equal opportunity pandemic; no one could be accused of racism or class warfare.

With only the blue shadowy morning light peering in on them, Graham reached over to close the blue-veined eyes of the man he loved and admired.

"Good-bye, Dad," he whispered, kissing him on the forehead. He wrapped the edges of the white bedsheet slowly around his father's body; it was a skill he had learned through repetition. Then he left the room, walking lightly so as not to disturb the peace.

~ ~ ~

His father had asked Graham to leave space in the middle of the other four graves in his mother's prized rhododendron garden. On one side lay his mother and Nelly, and on the other his sister and niece. His father had wanted it that way so he could "safeguard the ladies." Graham had known that his dad, always the gentleman, would hold out to the very last, until after the ladies had gone.

In October the soft loamy ground would still shovel easily, though it would freeze soon enough. The autumn rains were often misty, but this morning it rained as if it meant it. The digging would have to wait.

Graham dreaded this final act almost as much as when he'd buried his beloved Nelly. He slumped down in his father's living room chair and sobbed uncontrollably. "Where do I go from here?" he yelled, grabbing his water glass and flinging it across the room, where it crashed against the wall.

But he already had his answer; his father had already made him commit to certain plans. Graham remembered this but asked aloud, "What for?" He continued to sob, frustrated by the lack of answers.

He left the bedroom, walking to the dining room window to peer out into his mother's garden. He saw the fading leaves of the rhododendrons, and the memory of their spring flowers made him wish he could somehow share his grief with Nelly.

After the pandemic had started, he and his wife had fled to his parents' isolated home from the chaos that had come to Seattle. With Nelly's teaching job suspended due to futile quarantine efforts and Graham's job as a math professor gone, it only made sense to get the hell out of their apartment in the city. The decision became final when shots rang out one night, waking him from his sleep and causing him to clutch his pregnant wife securely against him. The next day they learned their neighbors had been murdered for their food supply. Fearing that he and Nelly were next, he packed the car and they left.

As humanity died off, people turned on one another. Fresh food was at a premium, and even preserved foods were running short. The immune preyed on the living; they desperately searched for dwindling food supplies because the grocery stores were no longer being stocked. To make things worse, counties had implemented quarantine roadblocks in an ill-fated attempt to lock infected populations out, thus making residents prisoners within their own communities.

Even though Graham had been raised by a Marine Corps father, he staunchly believed in gun control. He blamed easy access to guns for the various school shooting tragedies and railed against the ongoing wars fought abroad. These views had been furthered in the liberal-minded schools and universities he'd attended and subsequently taught in.

Having grown up in the Northwest, Graham embraced its culture and ideals, unlike his mother and father, who had kept their worldly views to themselves. They had never taken sides publicly nor

15

tried to push their own views on their children. They had wanted Graham to become his own man in their troubled world.

Though Graham's dad had insisted that he learn to hunt at a very early age, Graham had never owned a gun of his own. His father often tried to convince him to have a pistol with him for protection, especially since he was married and lived in what his dad thought a dangerous neighborhood. Graham had always refused, and had even tried to convince his father that those were the old ways of thinking and that every situation could be reasoned out peacefully.

His father, of course, doubted this based on his own experience. While he worried about his son's attitude, through the years the older man's subtle teachings provided Graham with the skills he needed to survive. He wanted the boy to be prepared regardless of personal ideals or political affiliation. They spent a lot of time in the wilderness. Even at their family cabin, where all manner of survival skills were keenly disguised as camping or hunting lore, he tricked his son into learning.

They would sometimes arrive at the old cabin that had been retrofitted over the years with running water and electricity to find both unavailable. Graham's father would then show him how to set up solar panels for power and how to sterilize the nearby lake water. He also taught him how to hunt and cook outdoors over a wood fire. Graham now realized how clever the man had been in those early days to teach him so well.

Before it all came apart, Graham and Nelly had been happy and enjoyed healthy lives; they had just celebrated their second year of marriage. She was a planner and a list maker and, not surprisingly, had their futures all mapped out.

Graham usually arrived home first and got dinner ready for them. On one particular day, Nelly had been down with a cold, so he'd planned to make her favorite knockoff of a soup they both enjoyed from a local Italian restaurant, the one with sausage and kale. He was startled that evening when he found her home from work early, balled up and crying on their bed. She was not one for weeping fits, so he knew something terrible must have happened to her as he bent down to comfort her. She resisted, and sat up to face him. "I'm pregnant!" she blurted out through tears.

"You're *what*?" he asked, stunned.

"I'm pregnant. We're going to have a baby, and it's way too early. It's not part of the plan. Now I won't be able to get my masters degree."

He pulled her toward him, even though she struggled and kissed her swollen red lips. "You're so silly, Nelly. We're going to have a *baby*! It'll all work out. I love you!"

But nothing did work out. Soon the pandemic came, and it took Nelly and their unborn child.

Now that he was all alone, Graham wondered how many in the neighborhood were still alive and how many would, as his father had warned, have "evil intent."

The pelting rain had dwindled to a light mist. Graham retrieved his slicker and shovel from the garage, and his rifle from beside the door. A rifle: it felt as natural to him now as carrying his keys. Anytime he ventured outside he had it slung over his shoulder; indoors it was always within arm's reach. "At all times," his father had insisted.

Graham knew it was time. His throat tightened as he tried to suppress more tears. Out among the rhododendrons he leaned the rifle within reach against the garden shed. The wind picked up as he stood and listened. He and his father had made a practice of this early on; the act of listening had become one of the rituals of survival. The silence should be filled with familiar sounds, and the total absence of them could mean trouble. There were very few familiar sounds now.

No distant train could be heard, no planes overhead. No lawnmowers, or cars' squealing belts, or the ever-present roar of Interstate 90 passing through town. Neighborhood chatter and children at play were now only past memories, but they were the sounds that Graham missed.

What he did hear was often met with the natural instinct of fight or flight: the howling of a dog (or was it a wolf?); the noise of dogs fighting over prey, as fear-inducing as any distant gunshot; the occasional scream, though in recent days these had become less frequent. This was what Graham chose to distract himself with while bending over the soaked loam next to the mounded grave of his mother; the ruminations of a world gone silent.

As sweat dripped from his nose he heaved each shovelful with vengeance, using the activity to release some of his anger. He continued to toss shovel after shovel of dirt, ignoring the pain in his back and shoulders.

Then he could not help it. Graham broke down again as an image of tossing a ball with his father in that very spot crossed his mind. He dropped the shovel and put his hands on the back of his neck. He fell to his knees in the damp grass. "No, this cannot be happening," he cried, lifting his face toward the sky.

At that moment, out of the corner of his eye, Graham spotted a form in gray next to the barberry bush. It was so slight that he nearly missed it altogether. In one fluid motion he quickly retrieved his rifle, cursing himself for not noticing something sooner.

Graham leveled the rifle and aimed, grief fueling his anger. "Get back! I will shoot you!" The shape slipped back around the corner, but he knew it hid there. He could sense its presence, but had no idea of who or what it could be.

"There is nothing for you here, so please leave," he added more calmly.

Then a muffled coughing signaled someone around the corner. Graham knew it was not his imagination; he took several wide side steps to view the hidden space, then adjusted his aim to get a visual of the one who dared intrude upon his private grieving.

A slight female form stood against the house, hooded, bent over in a futile attempt to restrain a persistent cough. When the cough lessened, she lifted her head to gaze at Graham. Her eyes pleaded with him as she raised her hand up in a gesture to show she meant no harm.

The frail woman limped forward, stopped, and raised her hands again. Graham could tell she was weak with the disease, and after she took a couple more steps he could clearly see she would not last more than an hour or so. Her face showed all the signs he'd seen before, and the fact that she was able to stand was a miracle alone. Her whole body rattled with the endless coughing. Graham walked within fifteen feet of her and lowered the business end of his rifle. He met the woman's pleading gaze with his own, knowing her dying breath might come at any minute.

She must be one of the few still alive with the virus. But not for long.

"I am Hyun-Ok," she said, barely audible; it was the voice of a woman weakened and scarred. She gestured vaguely behind her. "This is my son Bang."

Graham took several steps back and held up his hand, knowing right away what she wanted from him. He shook his head. "No, I can't take on someone else."

She shuffled forward a few steps and pleaded again. "I have watched you, you're a good man. Please, you're the only one. He is immune, like you."

Before she could say any more, she stumbled on the rocky driveway, falling to her knees and coughing again. Bang ran to her side.

Surprised at seeing such a small child, Graham slung his rifle over his shoulder and took several steps closer to her. He'd never taken any notice of the danger the virus might cause him. Hell, he'd even tried to catch it once Nelly had passed away.

Graham lifted the dying woman's small frame into his arms while the boy watched his every move. The child trailed him closely as he moved toward the house.

He had few choices here. He could not watch this woman die right in his driveway, especially with her child there; he doubted his father would have allowed this either. He opened the sliding glass door with one free hand while the lady continued to cough in his arms. He could not see the boy, but knew he was close behind. He laid her down on the living room sofa and heard the boy slide the door closed. Graham pulled his mother's red floral quilt down from the back of the sofa and laid it over the tiny woman.

He watched as the little boy ran to his mother's side. She reached for him, and once she regained control she reached for Graham's hand as well. She looked at him with desperate eyes.

"Please, Graham, you must take him, there is no other," she said.

He wondered how she knew his name. "Let me get you some water," he said, trying to stall the conversation. It dawned on him how cruel her plight must feel, knowing she would leave a young child alone and helpless in this new world.

"No, there is so little time now," she mumbled. "Please don't bother."

Graham no longer felt so sorry for himself; he knew the boy's predicament was much worse than his own, but still he felt unprepared to take him on as a responsibility.

Hyun-Ok grabbed his hand to keep him close.

Before she uttered another word, she joined her son's small hand with Graham's. "You need him as much as he needs you. Please, take him," she continued, crying.

Graham found himself nodding as he became more aware of her desperation. At any second she would perish right there on the couch in front of her son. He could not take any more heartbreak.

He gave in.

"I'll take him. I'll take care of him."

To bring her peace, he lifted the child onto the couch next to his mother. As Bang cried, Graham's voice cracked. "It's okay. I promise to take good care of him."

He wanted to give her this gift. He'd had no control over the loss of his loved ones, but he could at least give this stranger peace. He wanted to show her some humanity in her dying moments. He missed the kindness of the living.

Hyun-Ok looked up at him, and Graham saw that the same peacefulness that had come over his father just before dawn was now coming to her. Her face softened and she managed a weak smile, moving her eyes from Graham to her son. She blinked away tears and her smile faded. Then her mouth fell open. The spark of life was gone just like that. She had completed the transfer on borrowed time.

Graham stared at her for a few moments in silence. He heard a low, muffled cry starting deep in the boy, who remained curled up next to his mother. Graham could understand his sorrow; the boy, too, had seen too much death—and so early in his life. He stroked Bang's head as the boy clung to his mother's side, sobbing.

Graham gently closed Hyun-Ok's eyes and laid his hand on the boy's shoulder. "It's going to be all right," he said, but Bang pulled away from him and clung to his mother.

Graham stepped back. He shook his head, cursing himself for the promise he'd just made. He walked away, leaving the little boy there. He now had another grave to dig before sundown.

Graham dug the dead woman's grave next to his beloved Nelly's; he wanted to think that the two would have gotten along in the living world. They both loved children, and he didn't think he wanted this brave little lady to be alone. This just seemed like the right thing to do.

Exhausted, he trudged back inside, stomping the dirt off his boots at the door. The boy still lay at his mother's side. Graham knew this wasn't a good sign. *What if I can't get him away from his mother's dead body?*

He walked over to the boy and shook him awake. Eyes just like his mother's, but now rimmed in red, looked up at him.

Hey, kid, what's your name again?" Graham asked. The boy hesitated.

"Look, my name's Graham. What's yours?"

"Bang."

Graham wasn't sure he heard it right. "What?"

"Bang!" the boy said and rolled over, weeping.

"Come on, Bang, I need your help," Graham said.

The boy closed his eyes and buried his face in his mother's side.

"Hey, come on. We have work to do," Graham insisted, pulling him away from his mother and off the couch. Bang began to kick and scream, landing a lucky strike against Graham's shin.

"God dammit, kid!" He held Bang firmly by one arm, and pulled him, kicking and screaming, into his father's bedroom.

"Look!" Graham said, pointing to his dead father and yelling over the crying. Bang quieted and looked up at Graham, terrified. His eyes and nose were running, and he tried to stop his sniffling.

"We have to bury him, and then we'll bury your mother," Graham said in a stern voice. "But I need your help."

Graham let go of the boy's arm, and Bang took hold of the dead man's sheet. Graham took a deep breath.

"All right, Dad, here we go." Graham worked his arms under his father's lifeless body, which had already begun to stiffen. It was easier to lift than he had thought it would be, and he cradled his father against his chest.

"You follow me," he told the boy. He didn't expect him to be happy, or even quiet; he just wanted to give him a part in the task to keep him busy. Bang followed him through the house and out the door. Once outside, Graham stopped for a moment and buried his head in his father's shoulder. "I'm so sorry, Dad," he said, wishing he knew of a more dignified way of transporting him.

The late afternoon sky was gray, and more rain was on the way. Graham laid his father at the edge of the grave, then jumped down into the hole and looked up at Bang. Somehow the boy had quieted, maybe because he had something to do, or maybe because he was stunned with so many dead people around. Whatever the reason, Graham was grateful.

"Okay, you help me get him in here," Graham said, struggling to hold back his own emotions. "Try to give him a little push."

Graham dragged his deceased father over toward him. The boy helped push as much as he could, which was barely at all. The body started to sink to the bottom too quickly in what ended up in more of a controlled fall. Graham couldn't help but cry. He settled his father neatly within the grave and started to climb up. As he climbed out, the first thing Graham noticed was that the kid had disappeared. He looked all around the yard but saw no sign of him.

"Shit!" Graham said, followed by, "Hey, Bang!"

Graham ran to the back door of the house, thinking that perhaps Bang had gone back to his dead mother's side. But looking through the glass door he couldn't see the boy. Then he heard a yell and a dog barking from the front of the property.

Graham grabbed his rifle and ran to the front of the house to see Bang running down the street with a pit bull at his heels. He yelled and ran toward the dog, startling it enough that it turned in his direction. Graham aimed and fired, killing the attack dog instantly.

Knowing they had caused a commotion enough to attract other predators, Graham didn't delay; with one arm he grabbed Bang, who was crying and kicking, and ran home, closing the gate behind them. He then sat Bang down in the grass and knelt next to him.

"Okay, okay, be quiet! It's done now. The dog is dead," Graham said. He felt guilty for forcing the kid to behave, but he needed him to quiet down. Graham went to the front gate to look for more dogs; so far there weren't any.

"You need to be quiet or the other mean dogs will find us," he said, rubbing Bang's head. The boy tried to stifle his crying. "Are you okay? Did he bite you?"

Bang shook his head. Graham took a rag out of his pants pocket and wiped the tears and snot away. The little boy's chest heaved with his effort to hold back his sobs.

"I know this is tough, but you can't run away from me. Your mom wanted you to stay with me so I could take care of you. I promised her. Please don't do that again. Now, come on, let's finish our job." Graham got up and headed back to the graves, taking his rifle with him all the while keeping an eye on the street for more dogs. If he were lucky, the dead, rather than he or Bang, would attract predators.

"We need to be quiet out here, okay?" he said to Bang. The boy followed slowly behind him at a slight distance.

Graham knelt at the edge of his father's grave, as if in a moment of prayer or meditation, then stood up and grabbed his shovel. When Bang walked over, Graham handed him a smaller shovel.

"Here, you can use this one," but the boy just started shaking his head and crying again. "Fine," Graham muttered in frustration. "Just sit down there, then."

He reluctantly picked up a shovelful of dirt and slowly swung it over the hole. He started at his father's feet and carefully dropped in the soil. He grabbed another shovelful, and another, but when it came time to cover his father's face he was reluctant. He didn't cry, but still he shook with grief.

The next thing he knew, the boy shouted out as a dog snarled close behind them. Graham looked up and saw two more. He reached for Bang and pulled him away just as the dog bit into the kid's jacket. He flung the boy behind him, toward the edge of the grave. Bang scrambled away from the edge, bawling. Graham swung the shovel at the attack dog and smacked it in the head. He then grabbed his rifle, putting a bullet into the skull of the stunned dog.

"Get out of here!" he yelled at the other two.

With its teeth bared, head down, another dog came at him. The third tried to edge around him toward the boy. Graham shot the closest dog squarely in the forehead, so close that he felt the misty splatter of blood on his face.

The last dog tried to take advantage by lunging at Graham, but it was too little too late. Using the gun barrel as a club, he knocked the dog to the side. He had just enough time to squeeze off a shot, wounding the dog in the hip. He cocked the rifle one last time and fired.

Nothing happened. He was out of ammunition, right when an enraged and wounded beast was coming after him. He tossed the rifle down and grabbed the shovel again, slipping in the mud and falling on his side. The injured dog locked its teeth into Graham's pants leg.

He swung the shovel with all his might. There was a clang and a yelp, but he still felt the dog pulling on his pants. He swung again and finally heard silence. He scrambled to his feet.

Bang just stared at the dead animal. The growling had stopped, but the boy's bawling did not; he was nearly hysterical. Graham dropped the shovel and grabbed him by the shoulders. "Shhh, be quiet, or more will come," he told him in a harsh whisper. He left him there and quickly filled in his father's grave, mounding the dirt deeply and looking all around him as he did.

He tossed the dogs' bodies in a wheelbarrow, and then went back to kneel again at his father's grave. Though Graham had never been a religious man, he hoped now that all of his loved ones were in a better place. His heart ached as he smoothed the mounded dirt with his rough hands to level it out.

"It's so hard to say good-bye, Dad. I don't know what I'm going to do without you." Then he remembered what his father would expect of him. He stood, grabbed his rifle, and led the sobbing boy inside the house.

There was still the boy's mother to bury, and dusk was quickly falling, so he knew he had to hurry. Bang immediately ran to the body, and Graham could tell this was going to be a battle.

He used a rag to wipe mud from the rifle quickly and reloaded it. "We have to bury her now," Graham said when he was done.

"No!" the boy cried.

"We can't leave her here. It's getting dark, and we have to do it now," Graham said gruffly, walking over to the couch. Bang put his arms around his mother as if to guard her. Graham pulled him back by the shoulders and said, "Look, kid, we have to do this right now. You can either help or you can stand back. Don't make me lock you in a room. The least you can do for your mother right now is be strong and help me."

Graham wrapped the red floral quilt around Hyun-Ok, much as he'd done with the others. At first Bang just stood there sobbing; then he began patting her wrapped legs. As Graham started to cover the rest of Hyun-Ok, he noticed a necklace with a medallion. He took it off her body as the boy watched. He then reached for Bang, who pulled back, clearly untrusting until he realized what Graham was trying to do. He let Graham put the chain over his head. The medallion landed with a thump against Bang's narrow, bony chest.

"She has a book in her pocket there," the boy said, pointing to her gray jacket. They were the first words he'd spoken other than his name and "no."

Graham felt in her coat and found a small journal in a leather sleeve.

"Is this for you?" Graham asked Bang, who just shrugged, not knowing the answer.

"Well, you hold on to it for now," Graham instructed. He continued to wrap Hyun-Ok but stopped when he got to her face.

"Go ahead and say good-bye," he said to Bang.

The boy sniffled, and then kissed her on the cheek. He hugged her one last time and stroked her long silky hair.

Graham looked outside and realized the night was coming quickly. He pulled the boy back gently from his mother. "Okay, it's time. We need to get her buried now."

The boy watched as Graham covered her face with the quilt. "No, no, no!" he cried again. Bang tried to tear the quilt off, and Graham had to pull him away, restraining him. He knew this was heartbreaking for the boy, but he didn't have a choice.

"Look," he said, "we have to bury her now or we'll have more trouble with the dogs. Do you want that? Your mother wants you to be safe and stay alive. We can't do that if there are dogs attacking us."

Bang looked miserable and confused and just shook his head again.

"All right then, let's get this done before dark," Graham said, slinging his rifle over his shoulder.

He picked up Hyun-Ok's light frame and led the small procession out to her last resting place. The boy followed, unable to suppress his grief. The closer Graham got to the grave, the more Bang struggled to pull the quilt away, and Graham ordered, "Knock it off!"

When they reached the grave, Graham lowered Hyun-Ok's body to the grass at the edge of the hole. Bang pulled more of the quilt off, exposing her feet, and Graham pushed him away, landing him on his rear.

Looking around first for any more predators, Graham jumped into the hole. "Give me a hand, kid," he whispered, but the boy ignored him.

Graham pulled Hyun-Ok's body into the grave and gently lowered her to the bottom. Bang scrambled over to the grave's edge, again yelling, "No, No!"

Graham quit worrying about the kid and instead shoveled dirt into the grave as quickly as he could with Bang crying all the while. He felt awful having to do it this way, but the circumstances left him with no choice. Nightfall meant predators.

By the time Graham finished it was nearly dark, and Bang's sobs had faded to whimpers. Graham, exhausted both emotionally and physically, began to smooth the mounded dirt atop the grave. To his surprise, Bang shoved his hands away and began smoothing it himself. Graham let him do it.

Another howl pierced the backyard silence, sending a chill up Graham's spine. Not knowing the kid's religious beliefs, he said, "Okay, kid, hurry up and say good-bye."

The boy said something in what Graham assumed must be Korean, but he wasn't sure. He knelt beside the boy and bowed his head. He hoped that bringing Hyun-Ok into his home had allowed her to pass peacefully. Out loud, so the boy could hear him, he said, "Just like I promised, I will look after your son." Graham heard another howl, then reached over and picked up Bang, who leaned, now spent and tearless, against his shoulder.

They were the lucky ones, able to bury their dead. Most families without members among the 2 percent still alive were left unburied; they lay in hospital beds, their own beds, and sometimes in vehicles, trying to reach a destination or escape from what had become a travesty of the life they had once known.

Early on, ailing and dying people had overrun the hospitals; after attempting to encase every single dead body in plastic body bags, workers soon ran out of them. As the disease spread they resorted to simply burning bodies in parking lots. Many bodies were left to decompose; depending on daily conditions, nature, either sped up or slowed down the process of decay.

This caused wild animals to descend in droves out of the forests and into the normally forbidden land of man. They appeared around houses and on the black asphalt-topped roads, lining the maze of streets beyond their natural borders. Drawn in by the lack of human sounds that had formerly kept them at bay, they now were enticed by the aroma of rotting flesh. Neglected family pets soon either became prey or turned into semiferal predators, forming large packs and often tangling with the wilder animals.

Coyotes, wolves, bears, and bobcats chased their natural prey, the deer, which were once only seen at dusk and dawn, but the sound of the ruminants' clip-clopping hooves on the hardened road surface and concrete sidewalks was heard by few people now. Those humans who did hear them would just as often witness the sound of savagery as they suffered death by fang and claw. This left those who endured with an intense fear of being hunted by wild beasts, so they remained in their shelters, slowly running out of resources.

~ ~ ~

Graham put the boy down and locked the door. The wind picked up and the rain started again. Bang just stood there, dazed, as Graham looked out at the graves, which now totaled six. He leaned his head against the cold glass, fighting back the pain. He thought about the answer his father had given when Graham had asked, "Why should I go on?"

"You'll find a reason, or the reason will find you," the old man had replied. Graham now looked down at the boy. *Great! My reason's a pissed -off kid?*

Graham sighed and looked down at his boots, caked in mud. He began to wipe them off on the mat but saw how useless that was. He removed them instead and glanced at the boy's tennis shoes, which were filthy as well; too filthy to track around Graham's parents' house.

"Hey, Bang, take off your shoes," he said.

"I want to go home," the boy whined.

Graham spun him around to face him. "Listen, your mother spent the last moments of her life trying to save yours. She brought you to me and I promised to take care of you. I'll do that until you manage to get yourself killed. Until then, you will do what I say, when I say it; and if you leave my sight again, you won't get two blocks before you're attacked by big, mean dogs. Only this time I won't save your ass because you didn't listen to me. Got it?"

Bang cried, but he also took terrified glances at the darkening outside; Graham hoped the warning was enough to keep him from running off again. The truth was that he could have easily been mauled to death earlier.

"Now, take off your shoes," he ordered again.

Bang sat down on the carpet and untied his shoes. He still sniffled, but at least complied.

"Are you hungry?" Graham asked, trying for a kinder tone.

The boy didn't look up at him.

Graham didn't feel like eating now, either. He looked down at his dirt-covered hands. He was concerned that Bang might try to run off if he turned his back. "Okay, listen. I've got to go shower. You have two choices. You can either promise me you'll stay here and behave, or get eaten by the dogs outside—what's it going to be? Because I don't have time for this."

Between sobs the boy said, "Stay."

"All right," Graham said. "It's getting dark in here. Let's go in back." Bang picked up his backpack from beside the door, and Graham realized he hadn't even noticed it there before. The kid followed him.

Since the illness had come, Graham's family had kept the house mostly dark at night. He used a flashlight to light the way to the back of the house, where he opened a bedroom door, revealing a pair of twin beds.

"That's my bed, by the window. And you can sleep there," Graham said, pointing to the one nearest the door. He pointed again. "That's the bathroom, across the hall. I want you to go do your business and wash your hands."

The boy looked up at him. Graham started to feel guilty for being so harsh with him, but it was for his own good. The kid walked into the bathroom, where a small nightlight cast a soft glow, and closed the door behind him.

Graham heard the water running, so he waited in the hall for the boy to finish. In the meantime he leaned his head back against a closet door. He hadn't eaten anything today, but he knew that if he tried he wouldn't be able to keep it down anyway.

His thoughts wandered back to dawn and his father's death. He bowed his head, and when he looked down, Bang was standing there, gazing up at him.

"Are you all done?" The boy nodded. Graham walked him into the bedroom and pulled back the blankets on the bed for him. "Okay, climb in," he told him.

The boy climbed up and Graham pulled the covers over him. "I've got to take a shower. You're going to stay right here, right?" Bang nodded, but his lower lip quivered. Graham patted him on the head, but the boy jerked away from his touch.

Graham closed the bedroom door, but left the door to the bathroom open so he could listen for any noise. He looked at himself in the mirror, still holding his rifle over his shoulder, and saw a man he didn't recognize. He was filthy and utterly spent—both of energy and of emotion. He peeled off his dirty clothes and turned on the shower, then propped the rifle nearby. He kept the shower curtain partially open so he could see out. He let the hot steamy water run over his worn body, watching it turn brown as it drained away. After showering off the dirt of graves, he emerged and checked the bedroom to find Bang asleep.

Graham stopped at the door and watched the sleeping child, then noticed the leather-sleeved book lying atop the kid-size backpack. He picked it up and sat down on his own bed. Under the golden glow of the flashlight he removed the book from its sleeve. The first two pages showed a genealogical tree; a photo of Bang rested on a top branch. Photos and names of ancestors were in the lower branches, delicately translated into English below what he guessed were Korean names. The brave lady whose likeness Bang bore had been a beauty. Graham's stomach knotted at the pain of losing his own mother. He turned the pages slowly until a loosely folded letter addressed to him came into view.

Dear Mr. Graham,

I'm writing you this letter with a happy heart. I know you are a good man and will take good care of my son Bang. Please keep him safe and remind him of his father and me. When he is sad, ask him to tell you of his whole family and the people we were. We will be with you both in spirit.

I will tell you a little about Bang so that you will know how to care for him.

We are Korean American. My father bravely escaped the death camps of North Korea, Bang knows of the story. He is five years old and his birthday is July 15th. He was born in Seattle.

He loves cars and animals. He is scared of the dark and sometimes has bad dreams. I taught him he must be brave for you. He is a good hunter of small game.

Reading this, Graham lifted his head and looked over at the boy, then turned back to the journal.

His father and I trained him well to fish and hunt duck, rabbits, and squirrels. He knows how to set small snares and traps for them. There is a slingshot in his backpack, and he is good with a bow and arrows.

Bang is quiet most times but can read and write well for his age. Most important, I believe you need him as much as he needs you. You are both alone now. That is why I chose you over the others.

There it was, as if the answer to Graham's father's premonition: *You'll find a reason, or the reason will find you.* Obviously Hyun-Ok had written the next part later, because the handwriting wasn't as smooth or as calm.

Please heed my warning!

I must warn you about a very bad man named Campos in case you take Bang and leave this place, I watched all the living here at night to make my decision. Campos has killed two of the few that walked into town. If you leave, please go at night, away from the highway exit. Campos stays at the gas station there by a small blue-trimmed house. He seems like his mind is gone and he speaks to himself out loud in different voices. He's very dangerous and you should avoid him. He has guns and carries a hatchet on his belt at all times. He keeps the fires in the Dumpster going and he even threw one of the survivors into it alive. When you leave, don't make any noise with a car, or I fear Campos will find you. Stay hidden from him.

Do not be sad for those you lost, Mr. Graham. You now have someone to live for.

With my deepest gratitude as a mother,

Graham refolded the letter and placed it back into the book, then slipped the journal back into its leather sleeve. He wasn't sure what to think of the boy. He wasn't surprised by the warning, since he'd often heard the distant sound of gunfire and had seen the black smoke drifting this way from afar almost every evening. He'd had no reason to venture that way because his dad had issued the no-contact order. The family members had always stayed close to the house, and then they had started dying off, one by one, so Graham certainly hadn't thought of going anywhere before now. But there was the family's cabin, as he and his father had planned—far away, Graham hoped, from all this madness, disease, and death. Now that he knew of Campos he would have to devise a plan so that he and Bang could get away safely.

Unfortunately, the route he needed to take to get to the cabin led him right through the trouble spot; they were locked in by man and nature both. To get to the other side of the highway, raised above the neighborhood like a causeway and lined with stone walls on each side, they needed to cross under the bridge right where this Campos fellow resided. This guy sounded pretty bad. Regrettably, the immunity to the virus wasn't confined to good people alone, as Graham's dad had warned him.

Then, like most nights before he went to sleep, Graham cleaned his rifle, taking pleasure in the familiar routine. This act had recently taken precedence over his bedtime ritual of reading a chapter or two of a dystopian novel; in the last few days the world around him mirrored the novels too closely for Graham to be able to enjoy them.

Having finished cleaning the rifle, Graham lay down on his bed. Despite everything that had happened that day, it took only minutes to fall asleep.

Just before he woke, Graham's father's death replayed in his dreams. The desperate pleas, and the last-minute imparting to Graham of every bit of advice he would need to survive, remained with Graham as he awoke. Rubbing the sleep from his eyes and yawning, Graham suddenly noticed the sleepy little boy sitting atop the adjacent bed, leaning against the headboard. For a moment Graham couldn't make the connection. Then it all came back to him from the day before: losing two and gaining one. This new day brought with it a new purpose, one Graham could look forward to because now he had a boy to look after and that meant he needed to keep him safely away from harm. He felt the burden of the promise, but he did not resent it, even though it had come unexpectedly.

Time to get the hell out of here, especially considering Hyun-Ok's warning.

"Morning, Bang. You sleep well?" he asked. The boy nodded. Graham could see from Bang's sad little face that yesterday's facts were shaping into reality for him as well. Bang let himself drop back down to his pillow.

"I'm going to take another shower this morning, because we're headed off on a journey and we probably won't be able to get clean for a while—until we get to the new place. After I'm done, you can take a shower or a bath, too—whatever you'd like to do. You do know how to take a shower, right?" Graham asked him.

Bang nodded, then asked, "Where are we going?"

"Away from here. Someplace safe. You'll see in due time."

Hell! I don't know what to do with a five-year-old. Guess I better let him figure the shower thing out, and if he comes out clean then that will do. A stinky little boy will be the least I have to worry about. Heck, we're both going to be pretty ripe soon enough.

Graham grabbed a change of clothes, went back to the bathroom and turned on the hot shower. He tried to wash away his grief and the uncertainty of what lay ahead. *It looks like I'm going to have to find a way out of town tonight, sans engine, according to Hyun-*

Ok's warning, he thought. His truck was out of the question. Then it hit him: maybe they could take the bikes in the garage and make a quiet escape. He did not know if Bang could ride a bike. His niece's bike was about the right size, and it would have to do, even if it was a bit girly.

Graham hoped the boy knew how to ride; teaching him out front in the driveway would be too risky. As he thought about it, teaching a kid he hardly knew hit right up there with experiencing parenthood. Graham was a novice guardian at best and felt severely unprepared; he wished he could just go into the next room and ask his dad, but instead he'd have to rely on what he remembered of his own experiences as a kid. His parents had been pretty decent with him and his sister, so he would just ask himself what his mom or dad would do as each case presented itself. He'd made a promise to Hyun-Ok and, as best he could, he intended to keep it.

The day had come where he would set into place what he and his father had planned, though now these plans also included a young boy. It would certainly slow him down, but he'd never been a loner in life and started to warm to the idea of having the kid along. At least it gave him a legitimate reason to talk—to someone other than himself.

After showering, Graham contemplated shaving, but somehow just couldn't bring himself to do it. Looking at his reflection in the mirror he saw a worn man full of grief, someone he did not know at all.

He headed into the bedroom, where he found a neatly folded solid blue comforter but no boy. "Bang?" he called in a panic, cursing himself for not leaving the bathroom door open this time. He did not have to look far; Graham found Bang in the kitchen, staring out the glass door at his mother's grave.

The boy's eyes had still not lost their sleepy morning gaze. "All right, buddy, it's your turn," he said with relief. "You do know how to turn on the shower, right?" Bang grabbed his backpack without looking up at Graham and stomped past him, heading down the hall and into the steamy bathroom. Graham watched him as he closed the door; somehow he did not quite believe the kid could do it all by himself, as tiny as he was.

Graham turned on the Keurig coffeemaker one last time and leaned against the counter. He and his father had joked many times about who would be the first to die and who would get the last K-cup. His dad dubbed it the "last stander" trophy. Graham flipped the white cup around a few times and opened the Keurig's hatch, popping the cup in with its familiar snap; this single cup of coffee, the last that remained, seemed a morbid symbol.

He let the machine go through its routine. The pleasing aroma filtered through the room, which made the first tears of the day slip gently down his sunken cheeks. Graham lifted his steaming cup in a toast to his departed father and sipped down the black brew. He needed this caffeine jolt to begin this day. His father had been right. If it were not for the well-planned escape, Graham would not make it for long here in such silence.

Bang emerged from the bathroom and walked back down the hall toward Graham, dragging his feet and his backpack. He looked and smelled fairly clean.

"Good job, buddy," said Graham. "Lookin' good. Let's get some breakfast and start packing up this place. We have got a lot to do before we head out tonight."

Graham reached down and lifted the boy easily onto the granite countertop. He needed to talk to him while reheating some leftover beans and rice he'd made a few days earlier. Initially it was intended to be enough to last Graham and his dad a few days. Now they'd have to throw some out.

It was lucky for Graham's family that his mother's southern roots had taught her to always stock a pantry well. She had always kept twenty-five pound sacks of pinto beans and rice in store. She shopped at Costco weekly and always prepared for emergencies. After having lived through the aftermath of several hurricanes, droughts, and other calamities while growing up in south Texas, she argued it just made sense to be prepared.

While the family quickly grew tired of beans and rice, they never grew hungry. Grabbing a second bowl for the boy, Graham considered him and asked something his mother had always asked his friends. It had always caused him great embarrassment as a kid.

"Are you allergic to anything?"

Bang just shrugged and made a face instead of answering. Not ever running across anyone allergic to rice and beans, Graham decided it was a safe bet Bang could have it. He knew now this parenting thing left him with a lot to consider.

Graham pulled out the little red plastic cup that had always been reserved for his niece. He filled it with cold tap water and handed it to Bang with the steaming bowl of food. The boy peered down at his bowl and for a second, Graham thought he might toss it on the floor, but hunger won out.

Seeing this, Graham felt a pang of guilt at how easy their family had had it compared to others; at least they had not gone hungry. He felt happy to be able to ease the boy's hunger even in this little way. Once he finished, Graham debated giving him seconds, but thought it might not be a good idea given how little Bang had probably eaten in recent weeks; he looked skinny. Instead, he offered more clean water; he did not want the boy to throw up what he'd eaten.

With their meal completed, Graham took the time to ask Bang a few questions. After all, he'd only known the kid a few hours and held full responsibility for his life now. As much information as he could get would help him decide their next step. Graham knew they would be leaving for the family cabin up near the Old Cascade Highway by the Skagit River tonight. The plans were already made. At least there, he hoped, they would be safe from the wild animals and the stench that had brought them to civilization. Even now he could hear the howls of the packs in the distance. Additionally, the fires that had started in Seattle continued to grow unabated. What started as a distant glow seemed to be spreading, rapaciously consuming the vast amounts of fuel on its way.

Waiting for his father to pass had felt like the only thing holding Graham back; his dad would never have considered being buried away from his mother. But now it was time to make a clean break.

"So, it's just you and me," he said to Bang, who sat on the counter with his small legs dangling down, resting his heels against the cupboard. Graham knew he needed to get some dialog going with the obstinate child. Remembering Hyun-Ok's letter, he asked, "So, how old are you, Bang?"

Instead of answering, Bang held up his hand and splayed five fingers. Graham tried again.

"Can you hunt?" he asked. The boy's face brightened a little and he nodded his response. "Well, I'll have to see you do that sometime," he said, trying to make the best of it, even if Bang did not want to talk back.

Graham thought he should probably make some things clear to his new ward before they got started. "Bang, we need to set a few rules to be safe," he said. Recalling his sister's voice to her own daughter, he said, "You need to always stay nearby. I need to know where you are, all the time. If you have any questions, you can ask me, all right?"

Bang just nodded.

"Do you have any questions?" Graham asked him, putting him on the spot.

Bang's face was blank, but then he asked, all of a sudden, "Do you have a truck?"

With a relieved smile Graham knew he'd made some kind of breakthrough with the boy. He also remembered being a boy of five himself and an aficionado of trucks.

"Yes, I have a blue truck. I thought we could use it today, but now I'm afraid we'll have to make different plans. We have to leave here tonight and go somewhere that's safer before the winter weather takes hold. We'll start packing now and leave after dark. We have a lot of work to do."

He helped Bang down from the counter, then pulled out several Ziploc gallon bags and showed Bang how to fill and seal them with the leftover dry rice remaining in the opened twenty-five pound bag.

Watching the child sift the little grains into the bags with a cup reminded Graham of memories, though very recent ones. His mother had been partial to the pinto bean—"as versatile as it is," she would say—but had not restricted the family to only one kind of rice. There were ten twenty-five pound bags of several different varieties— jasmine, Calrose, long grain, and basmati—stored in the garage. It kept things from getting too boring, at least.

Graham and his dad jokingly fought over which bag they would open next, finally settling on a system of rotation. Graham favored the jasmine, but Dad preferred the short, sticky grain Calrose. His father argued the benefits were that it "stuck to your ribs" and said, "Now that's rice that'll get you through men's work."

Here I go again, stirring up memories that will do nothing but hold me back today. Graham figured it was probably normal to go through memories after a loved one passed away, and he wondered if Bang was doing the same thing. He hoped that, since Bang was in new and different surroundings, there were not as many stimuli to provoke such memories. Graham hoped his own reminiscences would subside a little once they got to the cabin. He did not want them to go away completely, just enough to prevent him from going insane or living a life filled with grief.

After supervising Bang for a few minutes, he said, "I'm going to go right over there to the garage to work on a few things. I'll leave the door open, so if you need anything, yell." Bang just looked up at him, nodded, and then continued his work, but Graham noticed the boy glancing over to the couch where his mother had died. His memories were there too.

Leaving Bang to his task, Graham propped open the garage door with the petrified rock his dad kept there for that purpose. The first thing that came to him in the darkness was the scent of his father.

He flipped on the light and looked at the bikes, which neatly hung from ceiling hooks. He pulled down the one his dad often rode, as well as his niece's pink Barbie bike, which Graham's parents kept for their granddaughter's visits. He cringed at the pink sparkly tassels and pink basket. He would not have dared to be seen on one of these when he had been a boy of Bang's age, but these were not normal times, and the kid would just have to deal with it. Graham quickly pulled off the tassels and the basket, but that was the best he could do.

He brought the little bike over to his dad's workbench, where he could still sense the man now departed. He considered using the noisy air compressor to fill the tires, but it probably was not worth the risk of attracting attention, so he opted for the handheld pump they'd always taken with them on long rides.

Graham grew uneasy at the silence from the kitchen and went back to the door to check. The boy was still busy at the bottom of the big rice bag, and Graham said, "Come out to the garage when you're done."

He'd taken care of his niece a few times, but never held the sole responsibility of a child. He decided he both liked and disliked the duty. He could not quite pinpoint why the job came as a hindrance to him—perhaps because it made him feel vulnerable somehow. Graham had only been Bang's guardian for twenty-four hours, yet he knew he'd have to kill anyone who would try to harm the boy. This came as a shock; he'd never before adopted what he thought of as a macho-man attitude, but there it was.

Graham pressed his own weight down on the bike seat and handlebars, rolling it across the garage. He wanted to listen to see how much noise it made. After noticing the typical clickety-click of the chain, he heard something unexpected. He knelt and saw bunches of pine needles wrapped around the back wheel slot and bits of brush in the spokes. He picked them out and cleaned it up, then oiled the chain and spun the pedals to work the oil in. Satisfied that he'd made the bike as quiet as possible, barring the typical chain noise, he turned his attention to his own bike and did the same.

Next on the list was his mom's bike cargo trailer, which they'd often taken on picnics. It was a two-wheel configuration that attached with a hitch to the back wheel joint; its flat platform fit a heavy duty lidded blue storage container. Graham dusted it off, rolled it around to listen for any excess noise, and oiled its moving parts.

He attached the hitch to his bike and then noticed, out of the corner of his eye, Bang standing in the doorway with his finger in his mouth. "You can come in, buddy," he said in a cheerful tone, waving the boy in. Graham knew the little guy was not used to him yet and that he would have to build trust over time.

"Bang, do you know how to ride a bike?" Bang's face lit up like a sparkler.

"Yes, I can ride. I have a bike at home. My mom takes me lots of times. We even bike to school sometimes, and—." His little face fell to an expression that echoed the one Graham had seen in his mirror that morning: a happy memory turned, in a nanosecond, to devastation, the good thoughts replaced by the pain of their new reality.

"Well, that's great," Graham said, sidestepping the strong reel of emotion, clear as hell on the little kid's face. He hoped the pain would go away quicker if he didn't acknowledge it, if they didn't dwell on it. "Come on, then. Let's see if this will work for you." He motioned to Bang as he pulled the hideous pink bike out for him. Graham watched as the boy eyed the bike. With a look that could kill, the kid shut down.

"Look, I know it's pink, but it's all we have right now," Graham said. "If we come across something more suitable for a boy, we'll trade it then." He leaned the bike in Bang's direction and hoped the kid would take it, but he didn't move.

"Bang, I don't have time for this. If you ride this bike, as soon as we can, we'll find you a better one. I *promise*."

Then, in an abrupt about-face, Bang simply nodded his head and grabbed the handles.

"You'll have to ride around in here for now, and we'll see if we need to adjust anything," Graham said.

Bang looked eager to show off, so he hopped on the bike and began skillfully riding around in circles. Graham then realized Bang had no helmet. *Oh crap, there is no way that kid will go for that*, he thought, eyeing the pink Barbie helmet. *It probably won't fit him anyway; the kid has a big noggin.* Graham reached into the sports cabinet and pulled out his mom's helmet, which thankfully was olive green.

"Hey, Bang, stop for a minute. Let's see if this will fit you," he said. As the little bike skidded to a stop right in front of him, Graham realized that the kid really could ride, and loved to do so. After adjusting the helmet to fit snugly, he let Bang practice a few more times around the garage. He noticed that he even stood on the pedals, leaning on one side or the other when turning. *This boy has some skills,* he thought. *That'll come in handy—as long as he doesn't get reckless.*

After adjusting the seat, Graham went on to other matters. "Next, we need to start loading. We only have a little space, but we're going to load up as much as we can with food, sleeping bags, ammo, and a first aid kit."

Graham and Bang worked side by side, busily collecting and stuffing as many essentials as they could into the trailer tote, which seemed far too small for a trek like theirs. Using bungee cords, they strapped the sleeping bags to its top. Graham knew he should take several other things, but there just was not room.

He grabbed his dad's pocketknife, putting it into his jeans pocket. Then he noticed a smaller one—his own from childhood—which he handed to Bang. "Keep this in your pocket, buddy. It is for work, not play, do you understand?"

The boy met his gaze with a serious face, nodded his understanding, and put the knife in his jeans pocket. Graham hoped he could entrust Bang with such a thing, but he guessed that someday soon the boy, struck with a fit of boredom, would run his thumb along the blade, causing a thin red gash, as he himself had done as a child and as his father had done before him. By circumstance Graham was passing the gruesome rite of passage down to this boy.

Having just evoked yet another memory, Graham growled under his breath and retreated into the house. He went to collect a few pieces of silverware and some bar soap, as well as the first aid kit and the plastic shower curtain to use as a barrier against the constant drizzle. Most important, he went into his father's closet, with Bang close behind him. He opened up the gun safe and collected two of his dad's Garand rifles and his Ruger handgun. He put the rifles into cases and strapped his father's holster at his waist for the handgun. He felt awkward wearing it but, as with his own rifle, he'd soon get used to it.

They went back to the kitchen counter for the map that he and his dad had drawn up for the best route out of town. His great-great-grandfather had built the cabin as a trapping lodge in the 1920s. Over the years it came to serve as a winter hunting lodge and summer retreat for the whole family. They spent several weeks there each summer, and in the winter Graham and his father went there to hunt. Now, with everyone else gone, it belonged to Graham alone.

Almost every visit had brought improvements to the cabin. His grandfather had built on a bunkroom and the attached bathroom. Running water and electricity came next, and just the previous year an indoor composting toilet was added; it was a huge improvement over the old outhouse. Most recently they'd replaced the old woodstove with a larger and more efficient one his dad had found on Craigslist; hauling the heavy cast-iron thing had made them both ache and groan for days afterward, but it had been worth the effort.

The structure, built well in the beginning, had had many repairs and upgrades over the years. On one visit, as a teenager, Graham had helped rechink the grout and replace rotted boards. On another visit he and his dad had replaced the cedar roof shingles. He had always suspected his dad had arranged these chores to keep him out of trouble during the summer months.

He just could not escape the memories.

With their gear all packed, including their personal backpacks, Graham plotted his and Bang's possible route through town. Though he'd play it by ear, not committing them to any particular course, he'd adjust as needed for safety. Typically, they'd take the highway up near Seattle and then shoot northeast. But it was safer to snake up the less-traveled back roads.

Graham knew they would have to rough it on bikes until they bypassed the bad guy Campos. Since he had not ventured out lately, Graham really didn't know what conditions he would find, but he knew there were the feral animals to worry about. He also knew that the highways were cluttered with abandoned cars, and maybe they could secure one. The best idea was to adopt a wait-and-see approach. Once he could see where the bad guy hung out, then maybe he and the kid could slink through unnoticed.

Unfortunately there was no other way to get up to and across the overpass either by road or on foot. They would just have to go as quietly as possible under the highway and cross by the gas station.

Graham hoped to get past without drawing the guy's attention. According to Hyun-Ok's letter, this Campos character apparently stopped folks who were coming into town, not those trying to get out. If he had to confront him he would just reason with him or offer him food to pass through peacefully. But Graham would be armed, and he would have Bang ride on his left, providing a little cover for the kid in case things got hairy.

To get to the cabin on the outskirts of Cascade, along the Skagit River, they'd go hopefully by "borrowed" truck, up the road through Fall City and Carnation. Then, they'd go finally up to Monroe, but Graham doubted they could drive freely on Highway 2, so he opted for the less traveled back roads that would take them around the lake and then north to Granite Falls. From there, they'd take another back road through Darrington and then finally north to Cascade.

All these small towns were now deserted. If they ran into any trouble, they could always change their route. The last thing he wanted to do was end up hiking with a five-year-old, making it an epic trek through the wilderness.

Now that Graham had his plan mapped out, he also thought it might be wise to grab his dad's binoculars so that he could scout ahead.

Graham heard a grumbling noise coming from the little guy who was shadowing his every move; this signaled lunchtime. Again Graham resorted to rewarming the last of the leftover beans, forgoing the rice this time. There was just enough for the two of them.

"Okay, Bang," he said. "It's time we tidy up this place so if—*when*—we come back here someday it won't be a mess. We're going to ride our bikes out of here tonight, and I don't know when we'll get a chance to sleep. So, if you need to take a nap before we go, this is the time. What do you think?" he asked the boy.

Bang hastily shook his head, and with an offended glare, answered, "I don't take naps."

Note to self: Bang does not do naps. At least he was learning more about the boy.

Looking Bang over, he decided the boy needed more cold weather gear. Nightfall often brought cooler temperatures. Bike riding at night would be quite cold indeed until they could procure a decent vehicle to drive. He checked out the hall closet for extra gloves and jackets. He found pink gloves and mittens but did not even try to pass them off to the boy. Instead he opted for one of his own black knit hats and his mom's black knit gloves, which stretched to fit all sizes.

As he rifled through the closet Graham kept thinking about a potential confrontation with the Campos guy. He thought it might be wise to stash the boy and their bikes nearby while he confronted Campos on foot. He would wait to decide until he could get a visual of the situation. If it were true that Campos had already killed two people, as Hyun-Ok had claimed to witness, he'd likely killed more. "How crazy could this guy be?" he muttered. In a few hours the answer would be clear.

Graham looked through his mother's hall of portraits, about which he often chided her. He looked for one with a decent likeness of them all and small enough to carry around in his wallet. He rarely carried his wallet with him now, but in the impossible event the world did indeed come back, he wanted his identification and his family picture with him. Or, if he admitted it to himself, he just really felt like taking them along with him on this journey.

Never in a million years did he think he would trek by bike and an unknown truck to the family cabin, past bad guys and wild animals, with a kid named Bang, at the end of humankind. How life had changed in the course of just a few months. Graham had no idea what would become of them next year at this time. Staying alive was the plan right now.

The night started to descend, so Graham made the last of the rice for dinner with his mom's southern gravy recipe. He heated and then whisked together a little melted venison fat with the remaining flour and canned milk. He diluted it with water and sprinkled it liberally with salt and pepper. His dad would have been proud of the dinner. Graham offered a bowl to Bang and he wolfed it down in quick order.

After dinner, Bang and Graham walked out to his mother's garden. They gathered a few of his mom's remaining prized but faded roses and took them over to the six unmarked graves. He let Bang pick which one he wanted to place on Hyun-Ok's grave. They stood in silence, a solemn moment in the sunset haze, with no words needed between them.

Graham believed Bang was what he'd heard others talk about from time to time—a child possessed with an old soul. His silent actions today as they prepared their escape bore witness to this characteristic. Graham knew they'd get along well once Bang stopped resenting him.

After their impromptu memorial, Graham went around the inside of the house, making sure all the windows were locked, turned off the water heater, and then, after making one last ceremonial trip to the bathroom, he shut off the incoming main water valve. After he was satisfied that he had completed his checklist of the house, he securely locked the front door from the inside. It was all as if they were just going on vacation.

They donned their backpacks and headed to the garage. Along the way, he turned off the few lights. Grabbing his rifle, he slung it over his back to have it at the ready. He reached over to Bang, secured his helmet and retied his shoes while down at his level. He then remembered something: a few weeks back he'd seen his childhood bow and arrows in a quiver tucked in a corner of the garage. He grabbed the quiver and showed it to Bang.

"Would you like this?" Graham asked. Bang's face lit up, and Graham thought he detected the beginnings of a smile. Graham fastened the quiver to Bang with a strap that secured over his head and around his back. The small archery set seemed perfect for his size, but Graham doubted it would be good for defense. Nevertheless, if it made Bang feel more secure to wear the contraption, he did not have a problem with it.

After checking for any danger, be it from man or beast, Graham popped the garage door latch manually, making as little noise as possible. They pulled their gear out into the darkened driveway, securing the door behind them, and headed out, riding side by side. Graham's bike towed the little supply trailer with the rifle case sticking out awkwardly. With the unknown before them, they did not even think to look back.

Draped in darkness, the autumn hued trees didn't have their typical daytime appeal. To Bang they resembled the frightening and enormous goblins, Dokkaebi, from Korean folklore. Bang had always enjoyed his father telling him about these mythical mischief-makers, but sometimes he would have nightmares afterward. His mother would discourage his father from sharing the stories, but Bang just couldn't get enough of the tall tales.

The Dokkaebi were known to play tricks on unsuspecting mortals who traveled, as Bang and Graham were doing now. They would transform out of inanimate objects to challenge travelers in an impromptu wrestling match to guarantee their safe passage. Bang imagined this would be really scary about now; he did not want to find out what would happen if he failed, though—according to legend—winning such a match would often earn one a magical item. Bang moved in to ride a little closer to Graham, just in case the Dokkaebi appeared. He figured Graham could probably wrestle better than he could.

They quickly reached the neighborhood's main drive. From there they could see stationary vehicles all along the highway overpass, in both directions, leading up to where Campos's gas station was. A light could be seen in the distance, but at present no one was within sight. The ever-present fire glow to the west lit up the distant darkness. It seemed to grow a little each day.

Bang missed his mother. He didn't want to be there at night in the dark. He tried to honor his mother's wishes though; she had told him to obey Graham and to help him when he could. Bang tried to remember that, but his heart ached for her and he wanted to go home. At first he had hated Graham, but after he saw the man crying in the hallway he knew his heart ached too. *Maybe he isn't such a bad guy,* he thought. Graham had already saved Bang from the dogs, and because his mother wanted him to trust Graham, he decided to stay with him.

Events forced Marcy and Macy to learn how to drive. It had been weeks now, and they were tired of waiting for their dad to show up. They'd discovered their mom dead from the virus the night before last after they broke into her bathroom and found her on the floor. Their mom had locked herself away so as not to expose the girls, but even with the virus all around, in their house, in the air, neither one of them became ill. They moved her dead body to her bed. They each took one end, stopping several times; Mom weighed more than they had expected. Of course, they were both slight, though at fifteen the twins told each other they were really quite strong.

Afterward they washed Mom's face with a cool washcloth and pulled the covers over her. Not certain what else to do, they admitted the time had come to make their way to Dad's house. They took turns calling him, but he never answered. This was not new to them, so they kept at it.

"He has to answer at some time, right?" Marcy asked her sister.

So many were dead in their neighborhood, and with Mom gone now they were getting really scared. After crying themselves to sleep, they woke to a new reality. Dad lived at the apartments in Issaquah. To get there they would have to drive down the highway, a trip they had done many times before as passengers. So they pulled their mother's keys out of her purse. "She would want Dad to take care of us now," Macy said.

The Williamses, who had lived next door, were gone—or at least no one had answered when they knocked the day before. They did not hear anyone anywhere except for the dog packs. Not only that, but late the previous night they had been awakened by loud yelling from the street outside. The girls went downstairs and looked out the front windows, where they witnessed a man running down their road with several dogs chasing him. He screamed and screamed as he ran out of their view. More screaming came after that, and then silence. The girls clung to one another, too afraid to open the door. They were not sure what happened to the man. After the quiet had come finally, they cried themselves to sleep again, this time on the living room sofa.

Too scared even to go to the bathroom alone, the twins made the decision to head over to their dad's place by themselves. Considering the circumstances, they did not think he'd mind them trying to drive. "This constitutes an emergency," Marcy said, justifying their plan. And in an emergency, new rules are made."

They had seen Mom and Dad do this plenty of times, so how hard could it be? Since they'd probably stay at Dad's for a while, they both packed overnight bags. They'd both slept late, so they tried to hurry, because they wanted to make it to Dad's before nightfall.

Macy suggested that she should drive first, to which Marcy said, "You know how it works. We have to play rock-paper-scissors."

Macy rolled her eyes but started the ritual anyway. Their old ceremonial game seemed childish to her now, but it was how they had always resolved disputes. Having an identical twin had some drawbacks. Marcy was bossier, and Macy figured it was not worth the ensuing battle to point out that they were old enough now to make their own decisions.

Macy decided on rock, and Marcy, of course, paper. "You always win," Macy grumbled. Sometimes she thought Marcy could read her mind. Was it not enough that they mirrored each other, with blue eyes and blond, wavy hair? It just was not fair, but perhaps that's what had kept them alive and together. Macy felt ashamed of herself for being upset with her sister. It would indeed kill her, too, if Marcy died of the virus and left her all alone.

Marcy grabbed the keys out of Macy's hand and they walked out to the attached garage, making sure the car doors were closed before they let the garage door up. Adjusting the seat so that her feet could just touch the pedals, Marcy checked to see if she could see out the rearview mirror.

"Put your seatbelt on, Mace, this might be bumpy," she said.

Before Marcy could start the ignition, Macy advised, "You have to move that stick to *R*, like Mom does."

"I know, I watch her too—*watched* her, I mean," Marcy said, a small crack in her voice. She turned the key, hearing it complain far too loudly, and then removed her hand. "Oh, I think it's on now," she said. Then she moved the stick to *R*, but nothing happened. "Okay, what do we do to make it go?" she asked Macy.

"You have to use the pedals. I think the left one is the brake and the right one is the gas. Try putting your foot on the gas a little," Macy said.

Barely pressing the pedal on the right, she could hear the engine get louder, but the car didn't move, so she eased up on the pedal. Macy noticed the other handle next to the drive stick. "This is the parking brake, I think." She reached over and pushed the button to lower the lever. Then they started sliding backward down the sloped driveway. Marcy screamed, and Macy yelled, "Hit the brake!"

As Marcy stomped on the brake, both girls lurched forward, nearly hitting the dashboard. Shaking now, they looked out the window, having just barely reached the road. Macy noticed an audience of a single curious boxer dog, sitting on his haunches, panting. At first glance the dog looked like any of the once-beloved neighborhood pets. She'd seen this one on a leash walking with its owner many times before.

Then she noticed another dog and shouted, "Look, they're coming! Quick—close the garage door so they can't get in!"

The garage door closed just in time. A blood-stained Akita showed up, baring his teeth at the girls. The noise encouraged his entourage to do the same, and even the docile boxer joined in. "Time to go," Marcy said, lifting her foot off the brake. The car slid back as the dogs went from a low growl to ferocious barking that caused the girls to scream again. Then, remembering the brake pedal, Marcy pressed it again, but this time not so hard. Macy reached over and began to spin the steering wheel to move the car into the road, like their mom used to do.

With dogs trailing behind them and jumping up at the windows, Macy pushed the shifter from *R* to *D* and yelled at Marcy, who was too distracted by a German shepherd snarling at her window to press the gas pedal.

"Press the gas, Marcy!" she yelled, trying to get her attention again. Some part of Marcy heard her, and she stomped on the gas as Macy tried to steer from the passenger's seat. The dog pack chased them down the road, but soon gave up since more accessible prey was available.

"Slow down!" Macy yelled, and Marcy let off the gas halfway. Thankful that the road was clear of many obstacles, they soon approached a stop sign.

"Mom made this look so easy," Marcy said as she pressed the brakes again, stopping them fifteen feet before the sign. This time they only leaned forward a little when she applied the brakes.

"This just takes practice, Marce," Macy said. "Just move up a little more so we can turn onto the main road."

"Don't tell me what to do!" Marcy shouted. "You try to do this for the first time with wild dogs trying to get you. I just saved your life, Mace, so you should be grateful instead of giving me a hard time about it."

"I was not giving you a hard time, Marcy. I'm just trying to help!" Macy yelled back.

Approaching the stop sign, Marcy removed her foot from the gas pedal and stomped the brake again. They both flew forward sharply and then back again.

"Marcy! Not so hard."

"Sorry!" yelled Marcy, clearly frustrated about this driving thing.

With Marcy's foot easing off the brake pedal, the Grand Am glided slowly forward. This time Marcy employed her newly learned technique of softly applying pressure to the brake. Both girls leaned forward, turning their blond curls left and then right in unison, checking for oncoming cars; they'd seen their parents do this many times. Since there no cars, Marcy turned the wheel, not paying attention to the lines on the road. Her driving was simply an effort to stay on the road, and being in the middle just seemed like a good idea. The farther they got into town, the more cars they'd have to dodge anyway. If one did come the other way, she figured she would pull over then.

Macy checked behind. No more dogs followed them. Turning back to face front, she knew there were a few straight miles ahead of them before they got to the highway turnoff. She began to look around. Up ahead, the first stop light intersection came into view and there were cars stopped in one lane, even though the light had turned green.

Marcy slowed down as the lane divided, one for going straight, the other for turning. She came to a stop, trying to assess the situation. They waited behind a gray SUV at the green light. They had rehearsed this scenario many times in the past and both girls thought the car should have started moving by now, but it did not.

"Honk the horn," Macy suggested as the idea came to her.

Marcy studied the steering wheel, looking for the right thing to press. She finally noticed the horn icon and pressed it, allowing the intrusive sound to disturb the afternoon silence all around them. Birds flew up in haste along the street side.

Once the sound had dissipated into the late afternoon horizon, Macy put the drive stick back into *R*. Marcy then depressed the gas pedal and they rolled backward several car lengths. After applying gentle pressure to the brakes again, to keep herself and her sister from flopping around like ragdolls, Marcy came to a complete stop. Macy moved the drive stick to *D* again and Marcy rotated the steering wheel left and pressed the gas pedal a little to pass the parked car.

Slowing as they passed the SUV, Macy could see the driver slumped over the steering wheel. Though the girls could not see the face, they both knew what had happened; and now reality was settling in.

"I hope Dad's okay," Macy said, never having thought of the possibility that he, too, could have become a victim of the virus.

Driving through the intersection that led to the highway entrance ramp, the girls noticed several cars in the way. As Marcy snaked their car through, it scraped a Suburban; the horrible screeching continued as the Grand Am forced itself through the space between the other car and the guardrail.

Marcy continued to wind her way, having somewhat gotten the hang of this driving thing by now and squeezing between parked cars.

Macy sat high in her seat to help navigate ahead until the cars became so crowded that there was no longer much space between them.

Marcy, unsure of the next direction to take, killed the engine. After scouting around the area for dogs, Macy rolled down her window. She pulled herself through the narrow opening to stand on the windowsill, gaining a better view of what lay ahead. With wide eyes she returned to the passenger seat and rolled up her window.

"What? What's out there?" asked Marcy.

"The road's blocked, we can't get through this way. We're stuck, Marcy. We'll have to walk from here."

"No! What about the dogs?" Marcy asked. How could Macy have forgotten them so quickly?

"That's what I'm saying. We can't stay in the car. There are big concrete barriers up ahead with police cars on the other side with their lights on. We're not going to make it this way," Macy said.

Sitting in silence, both girls tried to solve the dilemma, knowing they did not want to leave the safety of the car.

"I think we should take our stuff, leave the car here, and walk to the barricade. Climb over and see if there is a car on the other side that we can take. The road is clear over there," Macy said.

Marcy's jaw dropped. "We can't steal a car. Are you crazy? You can go to jail for that. The police are over there. Maybe they can take us the rest of the way."

"Marce, things are different now. Look around you. We'll leave a note or something to let the owner know that we're borrowing it. This is an emergency and, like you said, we have to make new rules now. They'll understand. They're probably dead by now anyway. In fact, we haven't seen anyone alive since that guy ran from the dogs last night, remember? It'll be okay. Dad can explain it to them if the police come. Or if someone's alive in the car, we'll ask them to take us to Dad's, okay?"

Pausing in the silence to give it a little more thought, Marcy conceded. "Well, I can't think of anything else better, so let's get started. The sooner we get to Dad's, the better."

As the twins gathered their belongings, Marcy said, "We need something to fight with in case those dogs come at us again."

Looking around in the car for potential weapons, they came up with an ice scraper on the floor by the back seat and Macy's metal ruler. She'd been looking for it a while back; it must have dropped out of her backpack.

Then Macy lowered her window once again and scouted out the easiest path of escape through the cramped cars ahead. She saw a few places they'd likely have to climb over bumpers while they wound their way to the concrete barrier.

Climbing back into the car, she said, "Okay, it should not be too hard. Just follow me and we'll run as fast as we can. Stay close and don't make any noise. We don't want to attract the dogs' attention." She added a second thought. "You need to come out my side since you don't have any room over there. Don't slam the door, just push it in softly."

"Okay, that sounds like a good plan. How far is it?" Marcy asked, scared.

Macy had thought about this before she jumped back into the car. "From our front door to Mr. Sanchez's house," she said. Explaining the distance in this way was an old habit, one that Marcy would accept, and thus she would not be too afraid. Macy thought the distance was actually more like from their front door to the Christensons' house, which was quite a bit farther, but she did not want Marcy to know that or she might opt to stay in the car indefinitely.

Looking again to make sure there were no predators present, Macy opened her door and Marcy scooted over the center aisle controls to exit on that side. The area between their car and the one to their right was just barely enough for their petite frames to pass through. Marcy closed the door with just a click.

Macy led them in a crouch as they scurried along, armed with only the metal ruler and plastic ice scraper. With overnight bags flung over their shoulders, they made their way through the tiny passages left open between cars. They leaped up and over the hood of an Escort that had rammed against a 4Runner. Checking behind them for any threat, they occasionally stopped to listen carefully before resuming their escape to the concrete barrier.

Finally, when it was within sight, Marcy pulled Macy's sleeve. "I thought you said to Mr. Sanchez's," she protested breathlessly, "but this is *way* farther!"

"Come on, Marcy. It's not much longer—look!"

They were squatting behind the rear bumper of a dirty white Impala. Standing up slightly to get a better view, they were shocked to see several dead bodies. They looked like they'd been struck down in an attempt to confront whatever officers might lay beyond. There were dark blood smears where animals must have fed on them. Their scattered remains were all over the roadway.

"Oh God," Marcy said, and covered her mouth before she bent to heave.

Macy just stared beyond the carnage, forcing herself to plan a route. Patting Marcy on the shoulder she said, "I know it's bad, but look over this way. We can make our way over to the edge where there's a crack between the barrier and the railing. We can push back the barbed wire above it. I think we can squeeze through there to the other side."

Marcy began to sob in fearful desperation. "It really smells bad, and there are all these bodies. Let's get out of here before the dogs come back."

Macy realized this could be the beginning of one of Marcy's famous breakdowns and pulled her behind her at a crouch. "Come on, Marcy. We have to get through here," she said.

Macy knew she and her twin were always on the too-thin side, something they had often been teased about. But now this enabled a hasty escape, squeezing in between and under the coiled barbed wire traversing the top of the barrier. Holding their bags out to her side, Macy went through first. She pulled her bag through and then reached for Marcy's. She looked around at the scene before her on the police's side. After Marcy had come through, they both stayed hunkered in their corner before coming up with the next plan of action.

At least the bodies were behind them now, though the twins could still smell their stench. Before them were four police cars, arrowed inward on each side, with blue strobe lights working on one of them.

Waiting and listening, they remained in their spot to assess the situation. Finally, Macy said, "I don't think there's anyone here. We should go over there to the last car on our side and see if we can find the keys. Then we can back it up and take off from there."

"You can't steal a police car, Macy."

Ignoring her sister, Macy took off, scurrying to the end of the first car. Rather than be left behind, Marcy quickly followed.

Seeing no live souls nor roaming dogs in the vicinity, the twins inched their way past the first car. They squatted down next to the one beyond it on the passenger side. Then, they slowly stood and noticed a decaying form, lying back on the reclined driver's seat; Macy declared this guy "*way* dead." With the driver's door left open he looked like he must have passed right there, on duty, days before.

Macy bent low and around the back of the car, where they came abruptly face to face with a panting German shepherd who scared the hell out of them both. Panicked, Macy jumped backward into Marcy, causing the two of them to scream out and land in a heap.

The dog had spotted them long before they'd crossed the barrier. He had not seen humans without the smell of sickness in a long time, so he had come over to check them out, leaving his guard post.

To Macy's astonishment, the dog simply sat there, head cocked to one side, regarding them as if they were an oddity. Then, he stood slowly and padded over to them, sniffing them, but without seeming to threaten in any way. Still, Macy remembered the weapon in her right hand and thrust her ruler out at the dog. He sat again on his haunches, panting and tilting his head.

"Get back!" Macy yelled.

Looking confused, the dog lowered his head down to the pavement, as if to show he meant no harm. Then he huffed and lay still, though he never took his gaze from them.

"Stay!" Macy yelled. She'd heard other people order their dogs to do that and, to her surprise, the dog stayed. She pushed herself up and off her sister as she stood. Her ruler shook with the adrenaline rush.

The dog rolled over to his side.

Totally bewildered by this reaction, Macy reached behind her to help Marcy up to her feet.

"I think it's okay, Marcy," she said, "He's not trying to eat us."

"Don't trust him, Macy. He could just be playing and then turn on us," Marcy warned.

As if she just remembered her ice scraper, she looked around where they'd fallen to find it. Seeing it several feet away, she watched the dog cautiously while she reached for it. He did not move a muscle, only watched her movements with his eyes.

Macy, seeing this, decided to take a chance and reached over with her left hand to let him smell her. Her dad taught her to do it this way when approaching animals she didn't know.

"Don't do it, Mace," said Marcy.

The German shepherd merely studied her hand. He sniffed her, and then licked her. Macy began to pet his head and found that he had a black collar around his neck with a sheriff's badge hanging down to his chest.

"Look, he's a police dog," she said, holding up the badge for Marcy to see, then continued to pet the dog.

"Maybe that's why he has not turned mean," Marcy answered.

Macy noticed he had bite marks on his haunches, and as she ran her hand over chest, his ribs stood out. "No wonder he's panting a lot, he's thirsty. Let's see if we can find him some water."

"Come on, Sheriff, do you have water in the car?" she asked him as she got up. He rose from the pavement, trotted over to the open door of the car, and whined a little before the dead officer.

"Oh, sorry, Sheriff, is he your owner?" Macy asked.

The dog just sat down on his haunches. "He wants us to help him," Marcy said.

"Oh, so sorry, Sheriff, he's gone. We can't help him now," said Macy. She looked into the backseat window and noticed a gray blanket on the seat. Slowly reaching in, she pulled it out, unfolded it and showed Sheriff as she draped the blanket over the decomposing body of his former owner. Then Sheriff lay down on the pavement in front of the doorway and rested his head on his paws again. Macy stroked his fur; she knew his sadness and felt sorry for him.

Turning to Marcy, she said, "I think we should try to see if that car is available instead. If not, we'll have to move this guy, and I don't think Sheriff would like that very much. What do you think?"

Macy nodded. It was stupid to take the chance of aggravating the dog. They walked over to the other car across the road. There were no occupants, alive or otherwise, and the keys were on the passenger seat. Macy offered the keys to Marcy, who said, "Your turn. You'll find out it's not so easy."

By this time the sun was going down. "It's going to be dark soon," Marcy said, "so we really need to hurry up."

They opened the doors and the trunk to see if there was any water. Luckily, in the trunk they discovered a half carton of bottled water. Macy took two bottles out and walked over to the dog, opening one of them and offered Sheriff water in the palm of her hand. It tickled her terribly as his rough tongue slurped the water down easily. She repeated this process many times, pouring water into her hand, until Sheriff had drunk the contents of both bottles.

Macy walked back to the opened car to close it up, but Sheriff jumped into the backseat, surprising both of them. "Um, he wants to go with us?" Marcy asked.

"Well, it's up to him I guess. I'm not going to tell a police dog what he can and cannot do, are you?"

Shutting the trunk and doors and seeing no protest from Sheriff, Macy started the ignition. Having had the benefit of watching her twin, she smoothly guided the car into reverse. She then applied the brakes carefully and stopped to adjust the seat to the closest position possible so that she would not compromise her vision. She began again and swung the car around, heading toward Issaquah. Now that the road was wide open, they should be there in no time.

Horacio Campos had just finished pounding the last sign into the persistently damp earth surrounding his domain. It read NO TRESPASSING in big letters above VIOLATORS WILL BE SHOT, followed by SEE MAYOR CAMPOS FOR SUPPLIES.

Now that he'd posted it, everyone would know he owned this town, complete with all the homes and buildings, including their contents. No excuses would be accepted from any trespassers who ignored the rules and failed to pay the toll he established. "No more free rides, like those two bozos who thought they could just walk right through here without paying a fee," he grumbled aloud. There'd been rules even before he'd posted the signs. There must always be rules.

Just because most folks were dead didn't mean the few that lived could run off with everything else. After all, he kept the wild animals out—including the wild dog packs. He also kept the electricity on and the water running. If they paid, he'd even sell them gasoline. He had homes ready, complete with cars for those few he thought would be good citizens. They just had to pay in either work or trade. If they wanted supplies or a way through his town, they needed to prove they could pay.

Campos, having grown up here, where his father was the town's electrician, knew that people often took advantage if you let them. He didn't let them. Before Daddy's time, Granddaddy owned this land, including a gas station where he worked.

The government stole it from their family after Granddaddy refused their first offer. Back in the 1970s they claimed the tract of land, which they held was required for "urban renewal" or some such nonsense. What really happened—after they offered only half of the land value and Granddaddy refused—was that they stole it through eminent domain. That caused Granddaddy to get so upset, after spending his entire life farming here, that he up and died of a heart attack from the stress of it all. That had left Daddy fatherless at the age of fifteen.

With bitter resentment, Daddy had told of holding Granddaddy, dying in his arms, and watching Grandmama cry her eyes out. But not for long; soon after, she went whoring around, leaving her son, Campos's father, alone to fend for himself. Campos remembered Daddy swearing that he'd get the land back someday.

Daddy had gone into the navy. He learned to become an electrician and then came back to his childhood home. He resented providing service for those men who had once worked for his own daddy on the dairy farm. So when this virus struck and everyone began dying off, including his own father, Campos decided the time had come for payback. This land belonged to his family once again, and he wasn't going to let anyone take it away. If only he'd survived the virus to see what his son had done for him, Daddy would be so proud of him. He wouldn't get mad at him anymore.

Night and day Campos cleaned the place up. It took several days to round up all the dead bodies and burn them. He also killed family pets to keep them from becoming feral like the rest; he burned them right along with their owners. Since he owned this place now, he wanted it to look nice. He wanted it to look like it was back in the old days, just as his daddy remembered it.

From sunup to sundown he worked to put things back in order. He'd even gone through all the homes and stripped the beds, washing sheets and blankets, vacuuming mattresses and flipping them before making them up again. In the same manner, he went from room to room tossing belongings, cleaning and renewing each home so they could accommodate new citizens once he approved of them.

His daddy hadn't been one for charity, so Campos wasn't either—especially not for those last two who'd roamed into town. He offered them work, but he wouldn't put up with lazy asses. He knew his daddy would not approve of them.

One thing was troubling Campos since the virus had struck and the groceries had begun to run out: so too had his medicine. He broke into the pharmacy lockup, but couldn't find any Trilafon—the name on his bottle. The good thing about not having the meds meant that his face didn't twitch so much. So maybe he didn't need them after all.

But when things were real quiet and he wasn't so busy, he could hear the voices of those coming for him again. That's why he kept really busy all the time, from morning to night; mowing the lawns, cleaning the houses, power-washing dried blood off the sidewalks: the endless work meant he could keep the voices away.

His daddy would be real mad that he wasn't taking his medicine, but if he could see how nice the town was now he might not mind. Just in case Daddy was keeping an eye on him from the beyond, Campos stayed busy as hell. He really hoped Daddy wasn't one of the voices; that thought scared the hell out of him, more than anything else. "Please, no," he whimpered, because even the very idea made him shake. *I'll have to search some more to find them pills*, he thought. He'd checked all the houses already because surely someone else took the same drugs.

He'd have to check out the apartment building across the way. He hadn't made his way over there yet, and contemplated burning the whole thing down to the ground because of what had happened there once.

One day, he'd found a live one there. He heard her screaming as she ran from a feral dog. He'd run over there and shot the damn thing, and then she invited him into her apartment to thank him. He thought at first that she would make a nice citizen, but as he got to know her he soon realized she wouldn't. Daddy would call her sort the whoring kind, just like his own mama. She wore those short skirts and tank tops, not nice lady dresses like Mrs. Walker who had lived next door. Too bad she passed away.

He tried to tell the woman in the apartment that she could not stay for free, but she called him names—and no one could do that anymore. He told her she had to leave at once, but that only made her turn ugly. Then she called him a psycho and a crazy-ass bastard. After that, he remembered grabbing her by the arm, intent on walking her out of there like a gentleman, but she started screaming and hitting him on the chest. Then she took him by surprise and grabbed his manhood through his denim jeans, squeezing, instantly hardening him. He pushed her against the wall, but then he remembered Daddy said never to let anyone touch him there. So he grabbed her around the throat. And then he blacked out a little.

The next thing he knew, she sat leaning against the blood-splattered wall with her head off, neatly hacked from her neck. Then he found his bloody hatchet in his own left hand with her blood dripping from his clasped knuckles, staining the white carpet below.

He cried then, not for the girl but for himself. Now he knew for sure the voices were back. He hadn't planned to kill her. In fact, he didn't even remember doing it. He'd never murdered anyone before. He tossed her body in the burning Dumpster, like all the others. He went back to his own little house, still with the effects of her touch on him, to wash off the dried blood clinging to his skin. Daddy would be furious at him. He had really wanted to pull her to him, but Daddy's voice grew stronger and he knew he watched him then. It scared him still.

Today Campos would work on pulling all the spoiled produce, meat, and dairy products out of the little grocery store down the street. He wished he'd gotten to it earlier, knowing by now how rank it had gotten in there. The maggots were gaining ground, and he hated maggots. That's why he always made quick work of burning bodies. Burying them all would be impossible, so burning became his method of choice to stunt the maggot infiltration.

"Whew!" he said, and began to gag involuntarily after he'd open the door; he pulled his bandanna up over his nose and mouth to help block the stench. Having donned his work gloves, he grabbed a cart from the line and pushed it past the magazine racks to start with the produce. He would work his way around to the meat department in the back, and then to the dairy aisle.

He'd already taken the time to stoke the fire in the city's Dumpster that he'd made into a portable incinerator by attaching a hitch and tow line to his father's small backhoe. Day after day he towed it slowly to where he needed to work; this way he didn't have to go far to dump the things he didn't want to keep.

There was one loudmouth guy who'd called him Campos a nut job; he threw him in the Dumpster still alive after he shot him in the stomach. The screams lasted for longer than Campos had thought they would, but it served the vagrant right to try to pull one over on Campos. "Free gas is not possible here," he'd told him.

He had a difficult time touching anything with his bare hands, but with long work gloves on he fearlessly plunged his hands deep into the slimy maggot-covered territory. After he had dropped the bundles of rotting produce into the cart, he strolled out the door and onto the asphalt parking lot holding the blazing fire. From there he tossed the bundles into the fire, letting sparks fly upward toward the darkening sky; it was a sight that brought him pleasure. Then he went back into the little market for another load.

The store, being so low on supplies since the pandemic hit, luckily still contained enough for him and maybe five more people through the winter. Then, come spring, he planned a large garden and would need workers to help him keep it going. There was more than enough work for more than one man to do here, and Campos hoped a few decent folks would show up soon so that he could get his plans underway.

As he pedaled slowly, navigating through the stranded cars, Graham felt the hairs on his neck start to rise. He spoke in a hushed tone to Bang, telling him to stay quiet and to move over to Graham's left side. Underneath the overpass, they could hear what sounded like a distant dogfight. Graham worried that Bang might become alarmed and yell out, exposing them.

Now that they were pedaling their way through the cars, Graham remembered the clump of bushes and evergreen trees on the left side of the shoulder; this would be the best place to stash the boy and their gear, and then he could get a better visual of the situation at the gas station. They descended the short decline and walked through the brush and trees to find the best cover.

Graham got out his binoculars and crawled on his belly in the damp grass on the adjacent incline. He peered down the road to the gas station across the intersection, but with so many cars parked on the roadway it made it nearly impossible to get a clear line of sight. Judging from the odor emanating from the cars, Graham guessed that some cars still contained their original owners. He reluctantly crawled back to where Bang sat guarding their belongings.

"You need to stay right here. I'll only be gone a second so I can see which way we'll go. Watch our stuff."

Bang leaned against a tree that provided him some shelter and Graham assured him once again that he would return soon. The boy didn't look happy with the arrangement, but he nodded and crouched down with his bow and arrow out before him.

Graham walked a bit, then stopped directly across the street from the gas station. He crossed the off-ramp along the way, and he ducked behind a truck, using it to conceal his position. He spied no madman, or anyone else, in the general vicinity. He resolved that since the Dumpster fire burned brightly in a parking lot down the road, the madman couldn't be far away.

Pulling up his binoculars, Graham watched the entrance, but heard the man before he saw him. Hyun-Ok had described him well:

this guy sounded like he was short a few marbles. As Graham followed the voice—or voices, because there seemed to be more than one—he saw a man pushing a squeaky-wheeled shopping cart, often stopping, shouting as he made his way toward a blazing fire.

Graham tried to make out the conversation the man was having with himself. The guy talked mildly under his breath, then abruptly turned his head, completely changing his persona and the timbre of his voice, and roared, "I knew you were a fucking wasted sperm! I was right, you little bastard. Admit it!" Then another, in a feminine tone, shrilled, "Stop picking on him, you ass! He's working, can't you see that?"

Watching the scene sent chills up Graham's spine, and he started scouting around with the binoculars for an alternate route to safety. He needed to get himself and Bang through this place and far away from Campos.

Graham thought himself a fool now for having thought he might be able to talk reasonably with this guy. What the hell had he been thinking? This guy was dangerous as hell. His dad had told him he'd have to make new rules for himself, and this one came easy: stay away from the crazies. There was no doubt that Campos presented a physical risk; he was heavily armed. He also had a gnarly looking hatchet dangling from his back belt loop. Clearly this guy wasn't to be reasoned with.

Unfortunately, the road ran straight past the store where the man was currently working; the first left turn off that led around and back to the main road. If they went that way, he would still have a clear line of vision if he heard the man coming. If they crossed the street toward the gas station, they could take the first right and then go several blocks around the grocery store. Then they could meet up with the main road farther down the way. In either case they would have to take the chance of being seen, but the second path posed less risk than the first.

Graham thought it would be best to observe Campos a few more minutes to see how long it took the man to go inside the store before he ventured out to unload his cargo again, realizing that the man's mental state made him unpredictable. Dusk had come and gone, leaving them with the light of a full moon. He had hoped the man would just give up and head in for the night so that he and the kid could slip through undetected. A fleeting thought crossed his mind, making the hair stand up on his arms: what might happen to the boy if Campos got his hands on him? Then Graham remembered his promise to Hyun-Ok. Whatever it took, he would get the boy through this unscathed.

As Campos once again entered the store, presumably to reload, Graham lowered his binoculars and fell back. Then he sucked in his breath as he noticed a figure standing right beside him. Having never heard Bang approaching, he wondered how long he'd been standing there. With adrenaline racing through his veins, Graham covered his chest to calm his pounding heart. "Jesus, Bang! Don't do that!" he whispered.

Bang ignored the admonishment and pointed with his little finger down the ramp behind them. Then Graham heard the noise, too, and it was getting closer to their position. He pulled Bang behind him, lifted his rifle, and peered around the bumper to see the culprit.

"It's girls," Bang whispered into Graham's ear from behind.

"How many are there?" he whispered back.

"Just two, but they're the same kind," Bang said.

Graham made a quizzical face at that comment, though Bang couldn't see it. He looked through his binoculars at the pair now walking openly up the off-ramp in their direction; a dog followed close behind them. They didn't seem to be afraid of the dog, though, so Graham guessed it wasn't one of the feral ones. The girls looked to be teenagers; both wore jeans and T-shirts, they were skinny, and they carried backpacks. With shoulder-length light, wavy hair bobbing, they traversed the vehicle-packed road. They looked to be twins, so Bang's comment made sense now. But the fact that they were singing did not.

Graham knew that in another minute the girls would pass right by his current hideout. Knowing they might possibly walk right into a death trap if the madman spotted them, he didn't know what to do, but he did know he didn't want any more responsibility. Still, he had to warn them off this path. He reasoned they might turn right at the intersection and go over the highway, and that would be fine, but if they went left they were in for some trouble. There was no telling what would happen to them with this guy Campos around.

What do I do? I can't let them just walk right to their own deaths, but I also don't want to take on two more. "Shit," he said under his breath, then hoped Bang hadn't heard the expletive.

Gauging the girls' advance, he lifted the binoculars once again to check the madman's position. He hoped the guy would be too preoccupied to hear the voices of the singing girls as they approached.

Macy enjoyed driving. Maybe because she got the hang of it before Marcy had. In any event, she thought she would like to do it more often in the future, but from the looks of the traffic jam up ahead, her short experience behind the wheel would soon end. "There's no way through that mess." Macy nodded toward the tangle ahead. "You know what that means. We're almost there, but we walk from here."

"Well, just get as close as you can. Go up the off-ramp there," Marcy said, pointing.

Macy noticed that Sheriff sat up in the backseat as she slowed the vehicle. The dog looked out the window at the unfamiliar surroundings.

They could see smoke and flames flicker through the evergreen barrier up ahead, but it didn't seem like the big spreading fires they could see far off to the west. This one looked more like a burn pile, the kind their grandpa had when he burned brush out on his property. That made her think about her grandparents and hope they were all right.

As Macy came to a complete stop on the inclining ramp, she kept her foot on the brake and turned off the engine. But when she lifted her foot off the brake pedal, the car started sliding backward, so she depressed the brake again, a little too hard this time. It caused all three of them to dive sharply forward. Hearing a scramble behind her, she said, "Sorry, Sheriff, I guess I don't quite have the hang of this yet." Macy was sure the dog had seen better drivers in his day.

"Not so easy, is it?" Marcy said.

Macy sat there wondering which lever she needed to push or pull. There were other cars parked like this in the same position uphill, so it was possible to do, but so far, she couldn't figure it out.

"I think you have to move it off of *D*, to start with," Marcy offered.

Macy moved the stick to *P*, and then lifted her foot off the brake. The car still slid a little, but then it stopped. "Okay, I guess that's it," she said.

Sheriff poked his head forward, between them, as they looked around at their new surroundings, each searching for danger in the discernable darkness. "I really don't want to go out there," Marcy said.

"It's okay, Marce," answered Macy. We're only a few blocks from Dad's now. It's just up to the intersection, two blocks up and two blocks over. We have a guard dog with us now, so don't worry."

She tried to make light of the situation, but Macy knew the dog packs were likely out there, and she was scared too. Knowing it was her sister's favorite, Macy started to hum the pop song "Breakfast at Tiffany's" to calm her.

They exited the car as quietly as any two teens with a German shepherd could. At first Sheriff just sat in the backseat when Macy opened the back door. He didn't seem to want to leave, so she patted her thigh and whispered, "Come on, boy."

Seeing the invitation, he jumped down and immediately started sniffing the burning smell in the air. With his ears twitching, Sheriff tried to take in the sounds. Keeping pace slightly ahead of the girls, he ventured forward cautiously. The girls quietly picked up their tune again, bobbing along behind him.

There were many intermingling smells, and the girls watched as Sheriff's nose worked overtime. They smelled a strange barbecue odor from the fire beyond the trees. But their biggest threat would be any wild dogs. As if sensing it, Sheriff quickened his pace, then after a few minutes, as they rushed to keep up, he stopped suddenly in front of them. He growled in a low menacing tone, warning of something ahead.

The girls both stopped singing at the same time, and crouched behind the German shepherd. "I told you we should have stayed in the car!" Marcy hissed.

Macy grabbed hold of Sheriff's collar and tugged him over to the side of the road that met the tree line. "What is it, boy?" she asked.

Sheriff kept his low growl up while Macy petted him. He whined a little, then repaid Macy for the attention with a lick to the face, but went right back to growling in the direction ahead. "There's something up there, said Macy. "He's warning us."

"I don't care. I'm going up to Dad's," Marcy said loudly.

"Shut up!"

After a few moments of panic Marcy said, "We've got to go up there. It's the only way through."

Graham hesitated. His intention was only to get Bang and himself through this stretch of town. He didn't want to intervene where the girls were concerned. They would only slow him down. But he didn't want to see them fall into the hands of the madman, either.

After debating his options he decided to wait and see where the girls were headed. He watched them as they stopped because of the dog. *Smart dog*, he thought. Graham knew the dog could probably smell him and Bang.

But at least they were hidden by other vehicles on all sides where they hid behind the truck. The girls could pass them by and never see them. After much internal struggle, Graham fell to his third option of just waiting to see if the girls veered left or right as they proceeded up the road. That would probably tell him which way they intended to go and would buy him some time to decide whether—or how—to intervene.

Just twenty feet away from them now, the girls started to veer left. "Damn," Graham said, because now he knew they were headed for trouble. They suddenly stopped singing when the dog halted their progress. The German shepherd started growling, and the girls bent down behind him. They seemed more cautious now, and that was probably a good thing.

Wanting to make sure of the madman's position, Graham turned his head to bring up his binoculars, but before he even got them to his eyes he noticed an armed silhouette coming their way against the light of the burning fire beyond. The singing had probably alerted the man. Graham and Bang were concealed, but the same couldn't be said for the unsuspecting girls.

Options flashed before him. He couldn't startle the girls into running, which would cause Campos to fire out into the darkness, likely killing at least one of them. If he fired his own weapon to warn them, he'd give away his own position and jeopardize the boy whom he'd sworn to protect. *What the hell do I do now?*

Graham knew what his father would do. He'd take Campos out, here and now. He had a clear shot, after all, and the man posed a threat to the living. Graham's father would do what he thought was best, and for the greater good he would get rid of Campos. Graham lifted his rifle but just couldn't do it. *Maybe it'll be all right*, he thought. As Campos came closer, approaching the intersection, Graham ran out of options.

He made a sign to Bang to stay quiet and motioned for him to crawl under the truck. He crawled in behind Bang, over the pavement gravel, and pulled his rifle in along with them. He would be of no help to Bang dead. He needed to see what would happen, hoping Campos would see that they were just teen girls and probably run them off. That's all Graham had now—hope: he had wasted all other options in those few precious moments of indecision. He felt ashamed as, from under the truck, he saw Campos's boots getting closer.

From underneath the vehicle Graham could really only see things down low, and he wanted to make sure Bang was out of sight. He slid the little boy's body quietly against his side. He could hear Campos's booted footsteps approaching faster, and then quieter, obviously now positive that someone was coming. Graham hoped the dog's warning had sent the girls running off into the woods, but he couldn't see what they were doing, though he could still hear the dog, which was now growling louder.

He then heard one of the girls say, "He really doesn't like something up ahead. Something's not right, so we should stop."

The other one answered, "I don't care what that dog thinks. We're so close to Dad's now. I'm going up."

Then, just as Graham feared, Campos's footsteps stopped directly under the car parked in front of their truck. Straining from his cramped spot, he could see in the firelight that the man wore black leather work boots; then he saw the barrel end of a rifle. Graham was filled with both fear and regret. *Fuck! What the hell have I just done?*"

"Can't you hear that, you dumbass?" said a voice to Campos. Standing quiet and still, he listened, and off in the distance he heard something. Actually, he heard singing, though he couldn't make out the words. Grabbing his rifle, which leaned against the doorjamb of the market, Campos headed in the direction of the sound. He could hear better without the crackle of the fire in the background. The closer he got, the more he heard, and the little tune came in clearer.

"Who would be singing out here at night?" he asked.

"Someone about as crazy as you, I bet," the voice said.

Campos had learned long ago not to argue with the voices he heard, even when their remarks upset him. Usually, one of the other voices would stand up for him.

As he got closer he noticed that the sounds dissipated. Campos thought perhaps he'd only heard an animal, or two, or—more likely—whining or something. Or maybe it was his mind playing tricks on him again, which wasn't unusual. Then he heard a low growl. Something or someone was definitely out there. He saw movement in the dark. He heard footsteps. He stopped beside a parked car, weapon lifted. There was danger ahead.

Peering toward the approaching footsteps, he made out the silhouette of a young lady coming his way in the moonlight. Squatting, he planned to trail her for a few minutes to see where she headed and if anyone else tagged her.

As she got closer, he saw only a slight young lady looking worn out and a bit frightened by the darkness. She wore a light pink T-shirt and had a matching pink drawstring backpack on her back. She held what looked like an ice scraper in her right hand. She moved it back and forth as she swung her arms in her effort to climb the ramp.

At first sight Campos supposed this young lady would be a good addition to his town. She looked determined, and clean cut. Old enough to work, although right now she looked a bit cold as the breeze picked up her golden locks, highlighted by the firelight.

"Hi, miss," Campos said as he abruptly stepped out from his hiding spot.

She screamed. It startled Campos. He jumped back as much as she did. He brought his rifle before him, but before he could ask her to quiet down, a voice yelled at him, "Shut up!" Then he reached out with his unarmed hand and grabbed the girl by her long hair, dragging her toward the fire bin.

She kicked and screamed, so he let go of her, but only for a second so he could get enough leverage to backhand her. He sent her sprawling down to the hard asphalt, where her head bounced with a sickening thud. A dog barked in the darkness, and Campos knew he should get the girl inside in case the wild animals were coming. He slung the gun over his shoulder and reached down to lift the girl's light frame. He carried her to safety within his home in the blue-framed house next to the gas station.

He didn't know why she'd screamed like that. Campos knew young girls were often afraid of their own shadows. It was lucky that she had happened upon him; he could keep her safe from the wild beasts, and it sounded like at least one had been headed their way.

He brought the girl into his tidy living room and placed her carefully on the corduroy sofa. He noticed a stream of blood coming from her lip and trickling down to her chin. He thought it must have happened when she fainted.

He went to the kitchen to wet a clean towel and then gently mopped up the blood. He then applied pressure to her lip gently to stop the bleeding. He felt her icy cold hands, so he pulled a soft afghan down from the back of the couch and began to cover her when he noticed she still wore the backpack. He lifted her head and gently removed the bag to place it next to her. He studied the girl as he tucked her in, her lovely innocence unmarred in the wake of this world. *She's just a child*, he thought, feeling the weight of her life there with him.

Graham could only watch and listen as Campos startled the girl. He wasn't surprised when he heard the man's voice change, but it creeped him out. He began to slide out of his hiding place to intervene, but Bang grabbed him around the leg and buried his face in Graham's side, trembling. Then he heard a loud smack and watched in horror as the girl's head bounced on the pavement in front of him. Bang jerked, moving even closer to Graham's side.

Feeling absolutely at fault for not helping the girl to begin with, Graham cursed his stupid indecision. From underneath the truck he could see the girl's body in a heap on the ground. As Campos reached down, Graham feared he and Bang might be discovered. He truly felt like a coward and not at all worthy as his father's son.

Once the dog started barking, he feared the other sister would come forward and engage the madman, too, but then he heard the dog and girl run off to the safety of the woods. He needed to find her. He could have made a difference in their survival, but he'd chosen to remain silent. Now one of them was in grave danger, and the other needed him more than ever. Surely she was scared out of her mind with her sister attacked and taken like that. Shame enveloped Graham as he pulled himself and Bang out from under the truck.

He looked again through the binoculars and watched Campos walk away, carrying the girl through the door of his house. At least he knew where she was. Quietly he backed away with Bang and crept down the grassy slope to where the other girl hid, hoping to find her.

Not trusting his back on the man, Graham took cover at the beginning of the tree line and watched as Campos closed the door. He would find the girl who'd run off, and then wait until morning to rescue her twin.

All of this meant he would need to find shelter here for the night. Bang pulled on Graham's shirt, and Graham bent down to his level to hear him more closely. He noticed the kid had his fingers in his mouth again. "What is it, buddy?"

"I'm scared. Can we go now?" Bang whispered.

"I know you're scared," Graham said, rubbing the boy's shoulders. Then he took him into his arms and held him, hoping to dissipate some of the fear. "I promised I'd take care of you, and I will, okay? But one of those girls we saw earlier is hiding in the forest here and she's very, very scared and she's all alone now. I think we should find her. We might have to stay here overnight though, okay? What do you think—should we go help her?" Graham held Bang away from his body to see his reaction.

"Sure. Are we going to save the other one from the bad man?" Bang asked.

"I don't know yet. We'll have to figure that out after we find the girl in the woods. I think she went that way. I want you to stay close. The dog went with her, and he might not be in a very good mood, but we can't just leave her like this," Graham said.

As he walked with Bang close behind him, Graham really felt the pressure of his own indecision. Holding his rifle out in front of him, he wasn't surprised to see Bang swallow his own fear and pull his bow and arrow out for defense.

"Be careful with that thing," Graham said. Bang nodded but continued to look into the dark forest beyond.

Their progress slowed through the brush. Graham tried to still their movements whenever they caused a rustle. They often stopped to listen for any clues in the distant sounds to see if they might be from a distraught young girl or wild predators.

Fifteen feet above, darkness cloaked the canopy of tree branches, permitting only narrow moonbeams to filter through, like a celestial mirage, casting sparse rays of blue light within. It would be almost impassible if it weren't for the mercy of the moonlight, though even that made it difficult to see as the silver castings seemed to deepen the shadows.

Stopping every few steps, Graham raised his rifle and made sure Bang was close by. They'd begun to anticipate one another's movements in a rhythm of guarded devotion. One, two, three, four. Stillness, silence, scanning. One, two, three, four . . . And so the two of them went through the forest.

Macy sat huddled against a damp fallen log with her arms wrapped tightly around her knees. With her new companion lying alert across her feet, she thought of the events that had landed her in this current situation. Had it not been for this dog, she too would be in the angry grasp of the stranger.

Macy felt alone. She could only see puffs of steam coming from the German shepherd as he panted and sniffed the air on occasion. "Oh, Marcy, I'm so sorry!" Her sobbing distracted Sheriff from his vigilance; trying to comfort her, he stretched around to lick the back of her hand. Macy tried to suppress her tears and the fear. Gripping the dog, she buried her wet face into his course bronze fur, taking what comfort it provided.

Moments later, a little calmer, she peeked out into the night. Every now and then she heard the crunch of twigs, swooshing of leaves, or distant hooting of owls. She trusted Sheriff's proven senses, so she continued to crouch in her spot and lamented the events that had led her here.

The day before, her mother had died. She was afraid her father was dead, too; Macy could feel it, even if Marcy didn't want to believe it. And now her twin sister, whom she'd never been parted from, could also be dead for all Macy knew.

She vowed that when the morning dawned, she would sneak around to her father's apartment. She hoped her fear of his being dead was wrong and she could get his help to rescue Marcy. At the very least, she knew he had a hunting rifle hidden deep inside his walk-in closet. He'd showed her and Marcy how to use it last winter at her grandfather's place. She wasn't certain she'd be able to pull the trigger to kill someone, but she thought she could if it meant saving Marcy's life. She would never leave Marcy here alone with that man. Then, exhausted by the trauma of the past two days, Macy fell asleep deep in the fur of the haven that Sheriff provided.

Making sure the girl still slept, Campos quietly left the house to shut down the town for the night. "Time to close up shop," he said only to himself.

He'd made good progress today after clearing out most of the contaminated food from the market. "One more day will do it," he told himself. "With the girl's help, it might go even faster—if she works hard enough."

Smiling to himself, Campos felt happy to have someone to take care of as long as she pulled her weight. *No slackers here*, he thought. She wasn't as strong, not like the workforce of men he'd rather have, but at least he'd have someone to talk to about the events that happened on any given day. Truth be told, he felt kind of lonely these days; even though his father had never been a nice sort, Campos missed him. And Ben, the postmaster, could be counted on to greet him every time he came into the post office, handing over the mail and stopping to chat a bit. But Campos had recently found old Ben slumped over the breakfast table at his home, and he had buried him and his wife in their backyard.

"I'll have to come up with some chores for the girl. Jobs she can do to keep her busy," Campos said to himself.

"I don't like the little bitch," replied another voice.

"She's a darling girl, and she needs a home," the she-voice insisted.

Getting angry now, Campos said under his breath, "You leave her alone; only *I* talk to her. I'm warning you all." Campos stopped midstride on his way to the fire pit, hoping he had made himself clear to the others. He rarely even acknowledged the voices within, but he knew they could be a problem for the girl.

There were things he couldn't even remember, and he feared that those were times one of the others took over. He would find himself in a different place, with parts of the day missing; that's what had happened with the whore woman and the beggar man. He knew he'd have to find his medication soon; the girl's safety depended on it.

Some of the others were fine—friendly, even—but one in particular scared him.

Pulling on the makeshift barbed wire fence he'd rigged up along the open road, he closed up the front entrance. It wasn't a surefire locking system, but at least it kept the wild animals from wandering into town. When he'd walked outside a few days ago early in the morning, he'd found, out of his peripheral vision, a wolf standing sure as you please on the corner of the bank plaza. The wolf watched his every move, and then walked with those big pads of his off to the side. He finally disappeared between the buildings and into the brush.

From that point on had Campos decided to at least put up a few fences to dissuade the wild animals from freely roaming into town at night. Each morning he opened them up again for anyone of the two-legged variety who wanted the option of staying or trading.

Walking to the other end of town for the back entrance, Campos stopped at the market parking lot. There he found that the fire in the bin had died down from lack of fuel. He pushed the shopping cart back into the line of carts, turned off the lights, and closed the door he'd propped open earlier. Then, listening to the nightly insect chattering and the rhythm of his own boot steps, he walked to the darker back entrance and secured up his town for the night.

With a bit more pep in his step than in previous days, Campos thought about how the events of the day had finally taken a turn for the better. He looked forward to tomorrow. He'd feed the girl some breakfast and then find her a better home to live in. Not too far away from him, though, in case she needed him. Perhaps the one next door where Mrs. Walker had lived with her daughter, who had not been much older than this girl. Maybe there were clothes about the same size for her there too. It'd be nice if he found her a mother and father as well. "Girls need their moms and dads more than boys do," he said to himself.

Knowing the day was finally done and his nightly chores were finished, Campos stopped at the gas station to lock up the doors in case someone tried to steal his fuel. As on any other recent night, he stopped and looked up at the bright moon just above the tree line of the forest.

He listened intently as the quiet begged for even the slightest sound to say he wasn't alone. He heard nothing out of place, nothing out of the ordinary that would cause him alarm. Only the crickets chirping; an owl, known to make his calls every night, echoed in the dark with a lonely hoot. On most nights Campos felt himself a certain kindred spirit to the lonely bird.

Feeling secure, he accepted the yawn and soreness the day's work now brought. He ambled quietly over to his home and stepped inside. The girl lay unmoved from her last position. He felt her head for any fever, avoiding the lump that had risen on the side of her head. He watched her breathing and decided she just needed to sleep. Tucking one end of the loose cover in, he removed her shoes, placed them beside the couch, and went off to his room to close the day behind him while looking forward to the next.

Sheriff sniffed. He knew there were people there, not far from his young one in the night. He could not see them yet, but he could sense they were coming. He had lost one of them already and he was not going to let anything happen to this one. It was his job to keep her safe now, but he was not sure what to do. Those approaching did not smell the same as the bad one who had taken the other girl, but they smelled familiar.

Sheriff moved his head in the direction of the approaching people. He started a menacing growl, trying to warn them off. His young one still slept, and he didn't want to wake her but needed to ward off these intruders.

The closer the humans got through the darkness, the better Sheriff could make them out. A man and boy approached out of the night and into one of the beams of moonlight. The man lowered himself to his knees and the boy beside him did the same.

Sheriff warned them not to come any closer. Occasionally he stopped his threatening growl to take in their scent as best he could without leaving his girl's side.

The man stayed on his knees in the light; the boy was now hugging his side in fear. In a hushed voice, the man said, "It's okay. I'm not here to hurt you or her. It's good you're keeping her safe. I'm not going to hurt her."

Taking the man for his word, Sheriff stopped growling and simply lowered his head to his paws but kept the man and boy within his line of vision. He wasn't sure why he trusted the man, but he did.

Graham followed the low-pitched growl. He hoped like hell that the sound was coming from the dog he'd seen with the girl and not a wild one. His body was shaking, warning him that to trace the path of the growl might be foolish. Graham's stomach was telling him to get the hell out of there, but his heart was telling him this was the way to the girl.

Dragging a reluctant and scared boy behind him, Graham could finally see the dog and the girl asleep behind him. Bang took in a sharp breath and pointed at the dog beyond the brush. Slowly the two walked through the remaining brush; Graham squatted because that seemed the thing to do; this dog clearly was in no mood for intruders.

Graham tried to calm the dog's fears by speaking quietly. He leaned against a tree trunk and pulled Bang up against him. He tried to warm the frightened boy, who kept his bow and arrow aimed at the threat twelve feet away. Knowing the probability of separating the sleeping girl from her protector wasn't the best course of action, or at least not tonight, Graham decided they would camp right there.

At least the bedding remained dry under the tall pines and though the temperature was cold, it wasn't freezing. Graham used his hand to lower Bang's bow gently, urging the boy to put it away. As he did, Graham pulled the boy's hood over his head and settled him into the crook of his arm. He pushed loose pine needles up the boy's exposed side for extra warmth. All the while, the dog kept a close watch on his every move. The dog was not really afraid of him or he would have already attacked, Graham reasoned; he seemed, at least, to be tolerating their presence, and that was a good sign.

"Go to sleep, Bang," he whispered. "We'll try to make friends with the guard dog in the morning. For now he seems not to mind our presence. I'll stay awake and keep watch for a while. We'll figure things out in the morning, okay?"

Bang nodded and lowered his eyelids, cuddling into Graham's side, welcoming his warmth. Graham looked over at the dog staring at him and noticed the similarity in the way they were both protecting the ones they were with. Graham silently nodded to the dog, who blinked once and then resumed scanning the depths of the forest, as if somehow knowing they were now in this together.

Marcy woke at dawn's light. At first, her subconscious thought the prior days had all been a terrible dream. Then the smell of her mother's coffee wafted through to her, and she knew deep down that couldn't be right. Her mother had run out of coffee and her mother had . . .

Marcy struggled to regain full consciousness. Her head pounded, and then she remembered the events of the night before. Her fear came back in a rush, and she gasped as she fully woke to her new reality. She sat straight up, too fast, which caused the pounding in her head to increase.

"How are you feeling this morning? Hungry?" Campos asked.

She just stared at him, ready to scream again, shaking with fear.

"We have lots to do today," he said.

The man terrified her. Marcy began to inch away, pushing herself farther from him. She looked around at the unfamiliar surroundings and noticed that her backpack and shoes were neatly placed beside the sofa. She looked up at the man. "I have to go," she said, not certain what to expect. She threw off the blanket, grabbed her shoes and backpack, and ran for the door.

It took little effort for Campos to close the distance as he set his coffee down on the kitchen counter. "Hey now, you bumped your head pretty hard last night when you fell," he said. She stopped short just three feet from him and stared at the door.

She knew that even if she struggled, he could easily overpower her. She backed away a few steps and remembered how his outburst the previous night had terrified her. Yet today, he seemed different, somehow—nicer. The events of the night before were coming back to her now, and she remembered leaving her sister out there.

She had to get away from him, and to do that she knew she'd have to play it cool. She felt like running, but chances were she'd never make it. Making up her mind, she looked up at the man and said, "Yeah, it kind of hurts. Do you anything for a headache?"

Campos sensed her urge to flee. He gently guided her by the arm to the kitchen. "Yes, I think I do. Here, you sit down and I'll get you something. In fact, you should have some breakfast. I'm all out of eggs and bacon, but I still have cereal and instant milk. It's not as good as the real stuff, but it works in cereal. How's that sound?" he asked as he turned around with the found bottle of painkillers.

She held her head, trying to stop the pounding, and reached up to feel her split lip; more memories came back to her. Obviously, he had hurt her, but something told her to act as if she didn't remember. He watched as she touched her scabbed lip. "Can you tell me what happened last night?" he asked.

"I don't really remember," she said.

Looking at the girl, Campos turned to fill her glass with water as he said, "I saw you coming up the road last night. You must have been worn out by the time you got to the top of the road. You collapsed right in front of me. Then I heard a dog barking, so I thought that maybe you were running from him. It's lucky you found me. I brought you here and stopped your bleeding lip. Let's start with names. I'm Campos. Who might you be?" He handed her the water and pills, then went to the cupboard and returned with a bowl and spoon while he waited for her to answer.

Marcy kept doubting herself. This just couldn't be the same man from the night before. She knew she'd let the question linger too long unanswered. "My dad lives in an apartment complex near here. I wanted to see if he's still there. I haven't been able to get hold of him. Mom died, you see."

"I see. I'm sorry for your loss. Well, I can take you over there later but I'm sorry to say I haven't come across anyone alive in that direction, other than a lady who died of an accident shortly afterward. Where did you come from?" Campos asked.

Marcy was glad he'd let the name question go for now. She had always been taught that you never tell strangers your name and personal information. This conversation broke so many rules, but then again, she knew she had to survive. "I walked from near Lake Sammamish," she said.

"Did you see anyone else along the way?" he asked.

"No, no one. Is everyone gone here?" she asked, trying to divert attention from herself.

"Looks that way. I've seen a few, but no one worthy of staying here. Except maybe you." He nodded in her direction.

"Excuse me?" Marcy asked, not knowing what he meant.

"Well, I've been cleaning up this town, you see, and since your dad lived here, you can stay here too, as long as you're willing to work. We'll set you up in your dad's place if you like, or another house closer to me if you don't feel safe there. I must warn you, though, he's probably not alive at this point. You may not want to live there if he's been shut up all this time. It might not smell good, if you know what I mean."

Marcy sniffed and tried to stem the flow of tears. Even though she knew it was probably true, she felt more scared and alone now with the certainty of which Campos spoke. He wasn't unkind in his revelation, and this confused her more than ever. Suddenly the tears broke through to stream down her cheeks. Marcy sobbed and sniffed hard.

"It's all right. I didn't mean to make you cry," Campos said. He handed her a paper towel. "Wipe your eyes and blow your nose. Things like this are a commodity quickly running out, so try not to waste paper. You've been through a lot, you poor girl, but you're safe now."

Marcy looked at the man. She wanted to believe his sincerity, and he seemed genuinely kind, but she knew something wasn't right with him. It was all so confusing, because she definitely remembered the harsh way he'd spoken to her the previous night, and how he had hit her. He had not seemed like the same man who knelt before her now. She was not sure why he was being so nice to her. She decided she'd have to get away from him as soon as possible; he just couldn't be trusted.

"When do you think we could go check out Dad's place?" she asked.

"Well, I have a few things to get started this morning and then we can go over there. If you'd like to finish up eating, you can then use the restroom to clean up down the hall and meet me over at the gas station next door. Do you know where you are?" he asked her.

"Yes. So the gas station is right next door?" she asked, glad to have a reference, finally, to where she was.

"Yep, right that way. Take your time. Um, just one thing. Make sure you clean your dishes and put the milk back in the fridge. I like to keep things nice and clean. I really don't like bugs running around."

The way he said, "bugs" kind of made Marcy's skin tingle: he means he *really* does not like bugs. She nodded, and Campos headed for the door, adding, "I'm glad you're here. It's nice to have someone else to talk to. What did you say your name was?"

She smiled and knew she couldn't get out of it this time. "My name's Marcy. Thank you for having me," she said, smiling at his retreating form and pretending to go back to her cereal, which wasn't worth eating with the pain the split lip caused her.

Once the door closed, Marcy looked into her bowl as if the answers might be in there among the floating flakes. She wavered. *He doesn't seem so mean today. Maybe I should have told him about Macy so he'd help me find her. She's probably scared to death about now.*

Getting up from the table, Marcy went quickly over to the window. Unfortunately, the house was situated on the other side of the gas station, blocking her view of where she knew Macy must be hiding. *She must have gone through the woods to Dad's. Maybe she'll be there.*

Quickly she emptied the bowl down the drain and cleaned up her breakfast, as Campos had said to do. She didn't want to provoke the temper she feared lurked inside the man. Afterward, she walked, feeling a little dizzy, to the restroom. She felt quite guilty that, more than likely, Macy had slept outside, probably freezing.

One look in the mirror brought reality sharply into focus. Her reflection stunned her and left no doubt in her mind what had taken place. Not only was her lip swollen and crusted over with a scab, but her eye was black and blue with hints of green. She also displayed a painfully sore lump on her forehead. No wonder she was woozy.

Seeing the results of what she was sure she remembered from her meeting with Campos conflicted with this morning's events. Tears flooded her eyes as she accepted that the man was, without a doubt, crazy and dangerous. She could not trust him, and she had to find Macy. She needed to get away before his temper flared again.

The mistake she'd made by telling him where her Dad lived could be a problem if Macy were hiding there. She did not want to put her twin sister in danger too. She'd just have to play it cool and hopefully tonight she could escape and find her.

Running her hands through her hair to straighten it as much as possible, Marcy splashed a little water on her face. It stung. She dried off, patting gently and, after one last look, she broke herself away from the horrible reflection.

Marcy headed out of the little house, scanning the woods beyond and trying to subdue her worried thoughts. She knew Campos could see her approaching. She found him pulling back a crude fence from across the main road where she had come in the night before.

"Hi there, Miss Marcy, you're looking better," Campos said.

"Thank you, Mr. Campos. What can I help you with?" she asked him.

Graham woke in the night with Bang murmuring and flailing in his sleep. Graham pulled the boy up into his lap and tucked his head under his chin, cuddling him into his warm jacket to keep him warm. "Shhh . . . it's okay, Bang," he whispered, and the boy settled down against him. Looking over to his fellow guardian he noticed the dog shutting his eyes again after the brief disturbance and continuing his light but vigilant rest.

Graham listened to the quiet night for a few moments, lulled by the rhythmic breathing of the boy he held. God, how he wished it was his Nelly or their child that he held. Knowing there was no room for those thoughts now, Graham forced them from his mind and allowed himself to fall asleep once again.

The next thing he knew, a wet sniffle in his ear disrupted his sleep. He pulled away slowly and opened his right eye to see if the animal was friend or foe. Indeed, the guard dog had come up close and personal.

Bang held very still in his arms, but started to move his hands toward his bow and arrow, which lay beside them. Graham used one arm to lower the boy's. The dog sniffed the boy, then turned to look at the girl, who was staring at them.

Graham watched as the dog walked around the boy and licked his face. Bang quickly wiped off the goo, saying, "Ugh." Then he giggled.

Graham smiled at the scene, and then he noticed the girl, expectantly awaiting his attention. Sitting across from him, holding out her ruler and looking none too happy, she asked in a hushed tone, "Who are you?"

Holding up his hand in a peace gesture, he said, "Hi, my name is Graham and . . ."

"Like the cracker?" she asked.

"Uh, yeah, like the cracker. And this is Bang," he said in a reassuring tone, pointing at the boy.

"We saw what happened last night to your sister. I'm sorry I didn't stop the man before that," Graham said.

"Wait! You know him?" she asked, getting angry, or scared, or both.

"No, I don't know him. I was warned about him, and I was watching him, trying to figure a way around him last night when you and your sister walked up," Graham said, lowering his head. "I should have shot him when I had the chance, or stopped you girls before you got too close. I'm sorry."

She merely looked at him. "He must have heard you coming," Graham went on. "So afterward he hit your sister and carried her away. I followed you in here to make sure you were safe. When I finally found you, your guard dog here was taking good care of you after all. Are you doing okay?" he asked.

"No, I'm *not* doing okay!" she snapped, "Do you know where he took my sister?"

"Yes. Into that little house next to the gas station," he said.

She jumped up. "Right. I'm going to go get her."

"No," Graham said. "Trust me. He's really crazy. You can't just storm in there and get her yourself."

"I don't even know you," she said angrily, "so why should I trust you? That guy hit my sister last night and took her. I don't know who to trust."

"I know," Graham said. "All I can tell you is that I'm really sorry that I didn't intervene. I already have Bang here to take care of." He glanced over at the boy becoming fast friends with the German shepherd, who'd lain on his side so the boy could give him a belly rub.

"I'm trying to get through town so I can get to my cabin up near Cascade. Where were you two trying to go?"

"My dad's place, over at the apartments a few blocks down through town."

"All right. What's your name?" he asked.

She stared at him, her expression filled with doubts and questions. "Macy. My sister's name is Marcy, and this is Sheriff," she said, pointing to the dog.

"Oh jeez, so we have a Bang and a Sheriff?" he said.

She turned her head and watched Bang brush his hand along the dog's side. "Yeah and they seem to like each other. We found him yesterday with his dead owner. He's a police dog."

"I thought so after I saw his collar. Luckily, he doesn't seem to be reverting like the others." Graham drew a deep breath and let it out in a long, resigned sigh. "All right, Macy, I think we should get ourselves together and figure out how to get your sister away from that guy. Then I'll take you over to your dad's and we can see what to do from there. Sound good?" he asked.

"Yes." Her lips trembled. "Do you think he hurt her?"

Fearing that this was likely the case, Graham said, "I just don't know. I couldn't really see much last night. When I watched him yesterday, he changed his voice a lot, so I'm not sure. He seemed normal sometimes and then he sounded like someone else entirely, as if he's arguing with several people. He's certainly dangerous. Hopefully, he's been nice to her because she's a kid and not a threat to him, but I just don't know. I think the longer she's with him, the more danger she's in. We need to watch them and then try to snatch her when he's not looking."

Graham noticed she was still holding her ruler toward him unconsciously, only now it was not shaking. "I see you're pretty good with that ruler you're holding, but I don't think that's going to do it, Macy. I feel really awful I did not warn you two, so I'll help you get your sister back. Then you can do what you want, but I don't think you should stay around here."

Macy was thinking the same thing. "Listen," she said as a screeching, metal-on-metal sound came through the trees. "Did you hear that?"

"Yeah, sounds like he's up. Let's be really quiet now," Graham said. He got up, dusting the forest debris off his jeans.

Macy noticed Graham's gun lying nearby, and this made her more comfortable. She hoped she would see her sister again soon. Leaving the boy behind, Sheriff ambled his way over to her and licked her hand. She looked at Sheriff and said, whispering loud enough for Graham to overhear, "Good morning, handsome. Thanks for keeping me warm last night. I think you must trust his guy or he wouldn't be here right now." She scratched him under the collar to show her appreciation.

"He's a great guard dog," Graham said. "There's no way I was getting anywhere near you. You're lucky to have him." He reached down to let Sheriff smell his hand.

Another metallic screeching sound came and the dog suddenly went on the alert, ears perked up. A low growl came from his throat. Graham started to reach for Sheriff's collar, but Macy shoved his hand away. She squatted by the dog, one arm around his neck. "Hey, boy, no barking. Let's keep it quiet," she whispered, hoping the dog would listen to her commands.

"Macy, you take Sheriff and Bang farther that way," Graham said, pointing away from their direction of the ominous noise. "I'm going to sneak closer and look with my binoculars to see what's going on down there. I don't want him to hear you guys. I'll come back and find you after I know what's happened. Do you understand?"

"I'm coming with you," Bang said, holding his bow and arrow and pulling on Graham's jacket.

"I need you to keep Macy safe, Bang," said Graham, looking the boy in the eyes. "I will come back for you. Girls need looking after." Macy shot Graham a look, but didn't contradict him. "You and Sheriff will keep her safe, okay?" Graham continued. "Stay together. I won't be long." Without waiting for the boy's reply he headed off toward the tree line, holding his rifle ahead of him.

If I can get a clear shot, I should take it and get this all over with. Graham nearly felt sick at the idea. He'd never been the kind of man to harm another, but he knew he should have taken care of this problem the night before. He just hoped he had the guts to pull the trigger when the time came.

As he backtracked his way through the forest, Graham recognized the path he and Bang must have taken. He was very careful not to make much noise, and he could quite clearly make out two voices as he got closer to the gas station.

Pulling up his binoculars, Graham hid behind a pine tree, large enough to conceal his presence. He could see the man talking to the girl who mirrored Macy as she stood about five feet from him. Graham could see that she had quite the shiner and seemed a little nervous, but she didn't appear to be too afraid of the man she was talking to. The guy pointed up toward the market, telling her what it appeared he wanted her to do.

So far he hadn't touched her. She seemed to be there of her own free will, except that she kept scanning the tree line where Graham was hiding. She was probably looking for her sister. He hoped she wasn't beginning to trust the dangerous man; it could mean big trouble if she told him about Macy.

At least she looked healthy. Graham knew it would be a matter of time before the nutcase changed his demeanor again, and he watched as the pair walked toward the blue trash bin. The closer she got, the more nervous Graham became.

Campos was glad to have the girl here. It meant he would have someone to share the day-to-day workload with. But he worried that the others wouldn't like her and would try to scare her off. He had to find his meds. If he didn't, the others might harm the girl.

He opened the fence barrier and noticed her coming out with her backpack and shoes on, ready for the day. She looked a little worried, but he supposed that was to be expected. He would just do his best to make her feel welcome, and maybe she'd want to stay.

Greeting her, Campos showed her the fences that he'd made to keep the wild animals at bay during the night. "It's not foolproof, but at least it deters them from coming right into town," he explained. "Let's walk down this way and I'll show you the market where I've been clearing things out. We have about two more days of work there before we need to move on to the other stores," he said, pointing farther away.

"I've been cleaning everything up so that when nice folks come into town, they'll have a place to stay. I'm hoping we can have enough people to start a big garden come spring. We really need to plan for seed starting this winter. Things are pretty picked over. We have enough to get through the winter, but spring is going to be a problem."

As they got closer to the garbage bin attached to the four wheeler, Campos explained how he pulled the incinerator on wheels wherever he went to make the cleanup job easier. "Be careful, because it's hot. Don't touch the sides. Give me that gas can over there," he said.

Marcy did as he asked. He poured some gasoline into the bin, walking from side to side to spread the fuel around. He put the can down by the building door and walked back to remove matches from his back pocket. He tore several out at once, struck them, and tossed them in. The flames went up in a big *whoosh*, and Marcy jumped back with a scream.

"Oh, man, that scared me," she said. She noticed Campos's head twitch in an involuntary tic. She didn't think anything of it until he turned to face her with a twisted smile that didn't seem like his own.

"Oh, yeah, little darling. You want to get in?" he asked, smiling sadistically.

Marcy started walking backward from his suddenly evil-looking profile, highlighted by the roaring flames behind him. This wasn't him. *This is the man from last night.* She knew it now. It happened right before her eyes; he changed. There was something really wrong with this guy, and she knew for sure that she was in danger. He started laughing at her retreating form.

"Where do you think you're going, sweetheart?" he asked her.

Marcy continued to try to put distance between her and this crazed man as she stepped backward. "I think I should g-g-go to my—my dad's now," she stuttered, panicked. She turned and ran.

"No you don't, you little bitch!" this new persona yelled. He reached behind him to retrieve the hatchet he kept there, hidden from Campos. He aimed for the girl and threw it, overhanded, through the air.

Seeing the girl run, Graham knew he would not make it. It'd take him too much time to get there, considering the distance between them. Then he yelled "No!" as Campos reached behind him and threw the hatchet toward the girl with deadly skill. The girl whirled to look in his direction. He ran toward her, but she'd already fallen. Campos reached for his rifle. Graham stopped in his tracks. He aimed and fired before Campos even wrapped his hand around the barrel of his own weapon.

Campos fell as the shot struck home. Graham rushed to the fallen girl. She lay on the asphalt, blood running from her leg. "Marcy?" he asked, hoping she'd respond. Her blond locks were now tinged pink with blood. A quick glance back at Campos showed him down, and still; Graham could disregard him for now.

Graham pulled Marcy's hair back and saw that she was bleeding from a head wound, a result of hitting the rough pavement, but the worst damage was from the hatchet still embedded squarely in the back of her upper thigh. Blood spread in a radius around the gash.

"Oh, Jesus," Graham said. "I have to stop the bleeding." He pulled out the hatchet and pushed on the wound with the palm of his bare hand, trying to stem the flow. "This is really bad," he said, looking around for something he could use as a compress. Not seeing anything, he took off his jacket and removed his T-shirt, balling it up and pressing it into the red flowing wound. "She's going to bleed to death right here, dammit. I've got to do something!"

Looking over at the grocery store in front of him, he snatched Marcy up and carried her inside, searching for towels or anything he could use to help the girl.

He carefully positioned her on one of the register counters, trying to be careful of her head, and rolled her onto her side so he could see her wound. Grabbing the edges of the blood-soaked denim, he ripped the jeans open to get a better look. Blood seeped out of the wound, but not as much as before.

In the darkened store, a medium-size market by any real standard, Graham read the aisle signs for supplies that might help in treating the girl. He could not really see much, but he did notice a display rack of paper towels; he grabbed several rolls, ripped off their plastic wrapping, and wound a thick bundle of paper around his arm. He jammed the wad of towels onto Marcy's wound and applied pressure. With one hand holding that, he directed his attention to her head. She was knocked out cold from the impact. The previous day's injuries didn't look too good, either, but this new bump swelled up quickly.

"I need ice," he said, again out loud, looking toward the front of the store where it was usually kept. He wished Bang were here to help him. Noticing the blood seeping through the top of the paper towels already, he took hold of the entire remaining roll and pressed it down on top of the first wad. He slid Marcy onto her belly with her head facing away from him so that he could see the side of her face where most of the recent wounds were.

Looking around, Graham saw nothing that would help hold the pressure on Marcy's leg so that he would be free to get ice for her head. Giving up, he quickly took off pressure and ran over to the ice cooler and took out a bag, then raced back to her. He applied pressure again on the injury, causing some of the blood to cascade down her leg in streams. It slicked the floor, and he nearly slipped in it.

With the ice in his left hand, he punched his finger into the plastic, ripped it open, and then grabbed a plastic grocery sack off the dispenser at the end of the checkout counter. The counter was now a bloody, smeared mess, and Graham tried not to notice how much of the blood was covering his arms and bare torso. His stomach turned at the iron-like smell. He'd never seen so much blood before; the girl was soaked in it.

After reapplying pressure with his right hand, he used his left to open the bag enough to transfer handfuls of blood-covered ice into the grocery bag. He grabbed the loose ends and swirled the bag around to twist its opening closed. Then he laid the bag, dripping with bloody ice water, gently onto Marcy's head wound.

He wasn't sure how long it had been since he had left the others in the woods. Ten minutes? An hour? Everything had happened so fast. Surely by now they were getting concerned that he'd been gone so long.

He glanced again at Campos's body. Though he could not see if he still breathed, he certainly did not feel the need to help the man and hoped he was dead; *really* dead.

Next he knew he needed to figure out how to close the girl's hatchet wound. She was unconscious, and he could take advantage of that to sew up the wound, but he knew next to nothing about first aid. Other than having watched a very competent ER doctor sew up his sliced-open finger a year ago, he'd rarely visited hospitals. He'd watched then as the nurse irrigated his cut with saline solution; the young doc sewed it up, leaving the nurse to apply antibiotic ointment and a bandage. This was followed by a tetanus shot on his way out, along with a prescription for oral antibiotics.

Graham thought there was probably saline solution in the contact lens aisle. Maybe not exactly the same thing, but it should work. He would also need gauze, and maybe a sewing kit could be found somewhere. God, he was not looking forward to that.

He tried to remember the process as he watched the doctor stitch up his finger. He'd nearly fainted, and he was ashamed to admit it. Thinking of the details, he'd also need a cigarette lighter to sterilize a needle. The whole idea made his stomach roll, but he had to do it. He'd failed this girl twice now, and the weight of it was hard to bear.

Graham had liked coming in this store back when things were normal. There were not usually many people in line, and the butcher always smiled and asked what you were in the mood for that day. Too bad he was not here now. Graham knew the guy could probably stitch this girl right up without a second thought.

He had remembered filling a prescription here once and recalled the pharmacy toward the back of the store. Hopefully, the child would not wake up while he gathered the supplies in the dark. Making a mental list of the things he would need and where they were likely found, he checked the wound by lifting his hand. Seeing no increase in flow, Graham carefully left the paper towel roll in place and removed the ice, setting it to the side. He watched the rise and fall of Marcy's back as she breathed. Then he ran toward the pharmacy department.

He grabbed several boxes of gauze pads, regardless of their sizes, as well as adhesive tape and several very large Band-Aids. There was Bactine, but he knew he needed something to irrigate the cut as well. He turned around in frustration and finally spied the contact saline solution below the pharmacy window. He grabbed a few bottles, complaining, "This stuff is never where you think it should be." He went a little farther down, found the painkillers, and then had a stupid thought: How old was she? He tried to see the age requirements on the box in the dark. There was a slight bit of ambient light coming from the back door exit sign, but it made little difference.

Graham heard a snap and buzz of electricity and then the lights flickered on, blinding him for a second. He reached for his rifle, only to remember that he'd left it beside the girl. By the time he got to the end of the aisle, he was staring right at the madman, the one he knew as Campos,

"Get away from her!" Graham yelled, rushing at Campos before he had a chance to move. "*You* did this to her!" He grabbed the man by his blood-stained shirt and pushed him toward the open doorway. Campos did not put up much of a fight; he was struggling with what Graham said.

"I would never hurt her," Campos meekly pleaded. "She's just a girl. I was going to let her stay here," he said, and began to cry.

Graham began to doubt himself, but held the man in place. He watched as Campos swung his head back and forth, either out of confusion or pain or both. Graham did not know or care. Only one thing was certain: he'd seen the same man hurt her the night before and had seen him throw the hatchet this morning. Now, faced to face with him, he was convinced the guy was crazy, yet the look in Campos's pleading eyes showed he cared for the girl. The sentiment appeared genuine.

Then, before he knew it, Campos looked at Graham's blood-covered chest and smiled the most chilling smile Graham had ever seen. The hairs on Graham's arms and neck stood on end and he pushed Campos out through the doorway.

Campos jerked him toward the blue firebox, and at once Graham knew his intent. Campos released his arm briefly and slugged him across the jaw, stunning him, but not quite enough; he saw the nut job reach down and grab his own rifle. Graham had just enough time to grab the barrel in an attempt to wrench it from him, but Campos, though shorter, was much stronger. Campos, with his long sinewy muscles developed through hard labor, could easily overwhelm him.

Graham knew fear. He wanted to run away from this crazed man, but he tightened his hold on the rifle now in a tug of war. He knew that if he lost his grip, not only would he die but so would all the children. In a rush of adrenaline, he found what he had always believed he lacked, a capacity he had seen deep within his own father. This nameless thing, more than words could convey, enveloped him.

He can't win, Graham thought. *He cannot be permitted to take the lives of the few who remained living.* Graham was not the three children's father, but their safety, their preservation was a burden he'd accepted. He would see it through to the end and not fail them.

Campos laughed as he pulled Graham sharply toward him. It was as if he relished this fight, exulted in the chance to prove himself superior. He wrapped his left leg behind Graham's right, so when Graham pulled back with all his might, Campos began to fall and released his grip on the rifle. Graham grabbed him by the shirt collar instead, twisted to the left, and took the bastard down with him.

Having landed on his side, Graham rolled over quickly on top of Campos and struggled once again with the rifle between them as Campos wrestled the business end up toward him. Graham knew the danger, but he pulled strength from somewhere inside himself and pushed the rifle upward, sliding it along Campos's rib cage as he shifted his position to rest high on the man's chest so Campos could not buck him off.

Graham pushed the rifle upward, shaking now against the opposing force. Campos kicked and writhed; he tried all his tricks and then, finally, fear appeared in his insane eyes—or perhaps it was resignation.

Graham had not planned it this way. In fact, he had not planned it at all. Now the realization of what must happen fought within him. He knew there was no other way. Graham pushed on, past Campos's arm strength, past even his own strength. Instead of pushing the weapon away, Campos pulled it downward, desperately knowing where it was headed.

Once Graham had the rifle into the recess between Campos's chin and collar bone, he pushed onward, trying to make quick work of it, but still the insane man struggled, his face going from beet red to purple as he fought for oxygen. Then, suddenly, the madness seemed to go, leaving only the bewildered eyes of a man who knew he was about to die. Though he saw the madness fade, Graham knew he could not stop and maintained the force, all the while fighting the guilt that tried to overtake him. He pushed even harder when his victim stilled his movements, staring at him with glossy purple resignation. With the choking mostly over now, Graham heard movement beyond the door.

Quickly, he chanced a look up to see Marcy staggering toward him. "Stay back!" he yelled, but she continued.

Marcy held her head with one hand, steadying herself against the metallic doorjamb. With her right hand Marcy pulled around, dragging Graham's rifle toward him. Graham wanted her to stay away, not for her own safety but because he wanted to kill the man without bearing the guilt of having a witness.

Marcy dragged the weapon even closer and put her hand on Graham's shoulder. She collapsed by his side, not really knowing Graham but recognizing his sense of duty toward her.

Graham felt Campos's life lift away. The madness within him could now no longer menace and torture other beings, and death had surely come as a mercy for the kindly portion of him.

Graham pulled the weapon away and checked Campos's pulse to make sure this time. He wrapped his aching arms around the sobbing girl and lifted her slight weight up, staggered backward. He carried her several steps, and stood still, not willing to take his eyes off the dead man. Marcy's shudders interrupted him. She needed caring for now.

"I'm sorry," he said hoarsely, "It's okay now. You're safe." He tried to convince himself to some degree. Marcy just sobbed.

Trying to distract her, he said, "I know your sister, Macy. She's back there in the woods." He pointed in that direction, then turned away for a second, still not trusting what his eyes were seeing: Bang and Macy, and their dog companion Sheriff, coming down the hill toward them from their forest haven.

"They're coming now, you'll see her soon. It's all right, he can't hurt you again," Graham said, trying to convince himself again along with the girl of the madman's demise by his own hands.

As if she detected in his voice his own shock that the task was done, even at the innocent's cost, she patted him with one hand on his chest, as she herself shuddered at the wretched nightmare they'd both endured.

He could hear Bang and Macy's footsteps on the damp asphalt now, thumping nearer. Graham felt Marcy shift in his arms and noticed the dampness against his hand. Her wound was bleeding freely again.

Macy arrived and clung to her twin's side, unable to say more than, "Marcy, Marcy, Marcy," a ragged chant filled with anguish.

Bang sidled up, seeking Graham's attention; he wrapped his arm around Graham's long leg and leaned into him. Nothing more needed to be said. Bang and Macy had watched from afar, and they knew that Graham had done what needed to be done.

Silently, they stood for a moment more and watched as Sheriff sniffed over the body. Graham stepped forward, knowing he needed to pass the man to take Marcy inside to care for her wounds.

"No, don't go near him!" Marcy cried, too scared of what might happen and grabbed at Graham.

"He's dead, Marcy."

"Still, I'm afraid."

Without another word Graham lowered the girl to the ground and motioned for Macy to hold her up.

Sheriff stood over the man. Graham lowered Campos's lids over his bulging eyes, and then started to drag him away toward the side of the store.

Marcy broke her silence and yelled, "No, don't! He does not like bugs. Burn him. He would want that, I think." Graham understood she meant it for the good man, not the mad one.

"Turn around, all of you," Graham said, not wanting an image of what he was to do next to be etched into their young minds. They did, and his only witness was Sheriff; to Graham, a police dog seemed a fitting accomplice. He hoisted Campos's body into the Dumpster. He retrieved the gas can, poured in the remaining fuel, and reignited the fire.

"It's done," he said as he walked over to retrieve the girl. Macy and Bang collected the rifles along the way and they all walked back into the market together.

The store looked very different with the lights on. Now Graham could see how few items remained on the shelves and how lucky they'd been to discover the ones he had. He chose another checkout counter to set Marcy down on, since the first was a bloody mess. He covered her shaking body with his jacket. Macy clung by her sister's side as Sheriff stood guard at the open doorway.

Graham went over to the first counter and used the uncontaminated ice to clean the blood and sweaty death off as best he could. With the last several minutes replaying in his mind, the stinging cold of the ice water snapped him out of his own shock. He grabbed a fresh bag of ice and several more rolls of paper towels to clean Marcy, having Macy apply pressure to her twin sister's leg wound. After Graham had retrieved his rifle, he and Bang gathered the supplies he'd dropped earlier. "Look for anything you think we might need, Bang," he said, and then searched the store for a sewing kit as Bang trailed close behind him. Graham wasn't looking forward to treating Marcy's wounds.

Bang noticed on a low shelf a half dozen juice boxes with happy smiling green apples staring up at him. The boy stopped to pick them up while balancing Campos's rifle. He managed well enough and then caught up with Graham, who turned and realized he'd left a five-year-old in charge of the heavy weapon. Graham took it from him and silently chastised himself for the oversight.

He would never again be without his own firearm. If he'd had it earlier, he could have simply shot the man again. He would carry the cost of his mistake now and forever.

After retrieving a bottle of alcohol and antibiotic ointment, he went to the housewares aisle. Along with bleach, he looked for the sewing kit, something always present when not needed. He found one on a plastic hook, then decided they might need more in the future and took the other three as well. After looking at the dinky thread in the kit, he looked around for something sturdier and found a spool of black upholstery thread. He took that too.

"Okay, Bang, now we need a lighter," he said; he remembered they were usually up by the checkout counters near the cigarettes.

Back at the counter, Macy was still holding pressure on Marcy's leg wound as she stroked her sister's hair away from her bruised forehead.

"Is everything all right, Macy?" Graham asked

"Yeah, we're fine," she said.

He put down the items and noticed both girls quietly watching him with four blue eyes. It began to rain outside, which he welcomed because it would help clean away what had taken place earlier.

Marcy was shaking now, either from shock or the cold, he didn't know which, but he asked Bang to close the open door.

"Macy, go look for jackets or blankets; something to wrap her up in," he asked.

"Sure," she said, and wandered off to plunder the aisles.

"Marcy, I'm Graham. I met your sister and Sheriff early this morning. I tried to help you earlier before . . ." He chose not to continue the thought. He looked up at her that her teeth were now chattering too. "It's okay. We're going to get you warmed up and fix your leg. Then we are all going to get out of here," he said as Macy ran up holding an armload of XXL-size heather gray sweatshirts. She'd found them somewhere in the store. They were huge and bore the logo of the town's name across the chest.

"These are all I could find," she said as she rushed over.

"They're perfect," Graham said, and sat Marcy up to pull one over her. Then he balled up another one and put it under her head as a pillow. He laid the others, layer after layer, over the girl. He overlapped them and tucked them under her sides as if folding a burrito. "We'll get you warmed up in no time," he said, then added, "We need to get something warm into her too." He was afraid Marcy might be going into shock. He looked around for an answer and then remembered that there was a microwave to warm fast food next to the deli.

"Macy, you and Bang go see if you can find clean cups, bottled water and teabags or hot chocolate. Use the microwave by the deli to make her something warm to drink, but make sure the water's clean," he said as he sterilized several sewing needles with the flame of a cigarette lighter. He sat them on a clean paper towel to cool, and then decided that the larger thread would be the best way to go since it was sturdier and had less lint than the other. Luckily, one of the needles had a fairly large eye he hoped the wider thread would fit through.

He checked under the compression and saw that the hatchet cut had stopped bleeding but the swelling had increased. Graham knew it needed to be cleaned and dressed as soon as possible.

Bang and Macy must have found something appropriate because he and Marcy could hear the microwave humming. "Looks like they've got something for you," he said to her. She smiled a little, but her teeth continued to chatter.

"I need to rip your pants leg open more," he said to her, and she nodded. He grabbed each side and ripped the edges all the way down as cleanly as possible. When he got to the hem, he gave a little more effort and then just slipped it over her shoe. After he had moved the blood-stained excess out of the way, he wetted several paper towels and gently tried to clean off the dried blood from her calf.

Macy and Bang showed up smiling and bearing a steaming cup of cocoa. Bang carried the remnants of their excursion: a few unopened bottles of water, paper cups, plastic spoons, and an opened package of Swiss Miss. Where they had found water was a mystery to Graham.

"Perfect," Graham said as he helped Marcy sit up. They all watched her, so she grinned weakly and a little sheepishly, but she drank it all down.

"Feel a little better?" Graham asked. At least she'd stopped shaking so much. He took a deep breath and said to the girls, "I've got to get this cleaned out and closed. I'm sorry, Marcy, it's going to hurt." Both girls looked ready to cry. "It has to be done. The sooner we finish it, the faster we can get out of here," he said, trying to help them understand.

Macy reached over to help her sister roll to her side. "Just hold on to me, Marce," she said.

Bang appeared silently on the other side of the counter, pulling the makeshift sweater blanket over the girl to help cover her back. Graham nodded at him and the boy reached over and opened the various items they needed for the job, getting them ready for Graham.

Graham opened one of the water bottles and dampened several more paper towels. He cleaned up around the wound. Bang struggled to open the heavily sealed saline bottle while Graham used the alcohol to clean his own hands. Watching Bang wrestle with the bottle would have been funny in any other situation, but not now.

After smelling the alcohol in the air, Marcy started to whimper a little. "That smells like the doctor's office," she said. Macy held onto her sister, trying to soothe her. Graham would almost rather kill another man than do this—but only *almost*.

When Bang handed him the opened bottle triumphantly, Graham grinned at him, showing his appreciation.

"Okay, Marcy, the first thing we have to do is clean this out. It's going to be cold and it's going to sting. Just hold onto Macy and breathe. Don't hold your breath. I'll go as fast as I can," he said.

Marcy didn't look up or acknowledge him. She only held onto Macy and buried her head into her sister's neck. Graham began to spread the wound open, as gently as he could with his left hand. She made no sounds of discomfort yet. He popped open the bottle top and squirted a test stream, arching it across the floor. "Okay, Bang, I need you to come over here and hold onto her leg to help keep it still."

Macy tightened her hold on her sister as a warning of what was to come. Graham started the stream at the higher end, working as deeply as he could and flushed more blood out of the wound. Marcy moaned and her leg shook involuntarily. "I'm sorry, Marcy," Graham said to her, hoping she knew it was true.

He picked up the pace to get it over with quicker. The girl moaned louder and Macy tightened her grip. Big tears streamed down Macy's face as she repeatedly said, "It's okay. It's okay."

Graham focused completely on the task at hand. He used up the entire bottle of saline and then took most of Bang's pile of gauze, pushing on the wound in hopes of stemming the new flow of bright red blood. Graham held the pressure on Marcy's leg, and her moans subsided a little. He noticed she gulped air now and then, and held her breath. "Don't do that, Marcy. Breathe normally, or you'll make it worse. I'm sorry, but we're halfway there now. You're a brave girl."

The rain outside got heavier and made plunking sounds against the pavement so loud it could be heard inside. Occasionally Sheriff was distracted by it when he wasn't fixated on the people doing what must be done. Once he whined, when he knew the girl was hurting, but stood where he was, alternating between watching his companions and guarding the door of the store.

Graham wiped dry the injury and then the area around Marcy on the counter. He put several more paper towels under her leg, getting it ready to sew up. He reapplied alcohol to his hands, hoping this would help keep infection down, then wiped carefully around the wound and let it dry. He threaded the needle, knotting one end, and glanced at Bang, who gave him a sympathetic smile.

Graham had no idea what he was doing. He'd only seen it done once before, and he hoped that was enough direction to get him started. The gash was about four inches long, with the worst part about an inch and a half deep. He thought it would be best to just start at the right end and pull the sides together as he went along. He would try to space the stitches evenly and use enough of them to close the wound. He wanted to do it right the first time.

"All right, Marcy," he said, "We're almost done. This last part is going to hurt again but then we'll be done and we can get out of this place. Are you ready?"

"Yes, just do it," she cried from under her coverings. Macy nodded at him.

"Good girl," he said.

Graham first held the two ends together and pushed a clean ice cube against the skin to help deaden the nerve cells, then started sewing in the middle. As he pushed the needle through the skin, he worked his way down and then tied it off. He continued from the middle up, again using ice cubes to help numb the pain as much as he could. Marcy began to scream. By the time he pulled the last one through, he was shaking and his eyes were tearing up. He wiped the site clean and applied antibiotic ointment. Bang looked sheet white as he handed Graham a large bandage to cover it up.

He pulled Marcy into his arms and held her, whispering, "I'm so sorry I had to hurt you, but it's over now." He let her go, and on his way to the pharmacy area wiped away his own tears. He thought he would have to break into the pharmacy, but as it was, the door was already open. Graham tried to remember what he'd been prescribed for the finger incident, but he could only remember it started with a *D*.

There were rows of white shelves behind the main counter with large bottles in alphabetical order. He found the *D*'s: Demerol, Depakote, Depo-Provera . . . dopamine, doxazosin, doxycycline. "That's it, doxycycline!" he said, and then thought to himself, *God, this could be dangerous; how much do I give her?* He looked around for some kind of guide and saw a stack of rather thick books on the counter; one was titled *Merrill's Drug Encyclopedia*. He turned quickly to doxycycline and it read:

> *Doxycycline is a tetracycline antibiotic. It kills certain bacteria or stops their growth. It is used to treat many kinds of infections, such as dental, skin, respiratory, and urinary tract infections. It also treats acne, Lyme disease, malaria, and certain sexually transmitted diseases.*

"Bingo!" he said, but then realized it didn't tell him how much to give her. He remembered taking one twice a day, and thought he'd just go with that for her as well.

The nonsensical thought of dispensing a few into one of those honey-colored pill bottles occurred to him. *But things are different now. I need to think like it*, Graham said to himself. Their lives depended on him thinking in this new world, not the old one.

He grabbed the entire bottle and looked around for ibuprofen too. Then he looked at the book in his hands, and decided it needed to go with him as well. He searched around for something to carry all of this in and found a bright red empty cooler lying against the wall. He laid the jumbo bottle of antibiotics in along with the pharmaceutical encyclopedia. The thought crossed his mind just to take all the drugs on the shelf, but he knew there would be pharmacies along the way.

What mattered now was just to get everyone out of here. He grabbed a bottle of Tylenol with codeine, knowing that it could come in handy.

Graham stopped in the first aid aisle once again and picked up more tubes of Neosporin and their generics and as much gauze and bandages as he could see. Keeping Marcy's cut clean would be a real problem.

As he approached the kids he noticed that they looked a little stunned after the morning's events. "Hey, Bang, let's all have one of those juice boxes! Here, Marcy, I want you to take one of these. You'll need to have one twice a day. And one of these painkillers"—he handed her the bottles—"every six hours."

"I think I need to eat something before I do," she said.

"That's probably a good idea. Macy, see if you can find her some crackers or something to eat. In fact, you and Bang take carts and load up as much on edible food items as you can find. I need to find a truck we can use to load this stuff up. We'll go to your dad's apartment first and then make plans from there. I don't want to stay here tonight and I'm sure you guys don't want to either." They all nodded in agreement.

"Graham, I . . . uh . . . need a bathroom," Macy said as she pulled one of the oversize sweatshirts on. It fell nearly to her knees.

"Please hurry and don't go far," Graham answered.

He needed a bathroom too. He picked up his own jacket lying on the table and put it on. "You guys stay right here. I'll be right back. Sheriff, you stay here and watch these guys."

The dog looked up at Graham as if he knew exactly what he meant.

Graham stepped out into the dampness of the empty parking lot. It was past noon, and he was thinking about lunch but, noticing the smoke rising out of the blue garbage bin, he did not have much of an appetite even though he'd not eaten since the day before.

Graham stood still, one hand on his rifle, scanning the horizon for usable vehicles. He headed across the street where several residences lined the streets and apartment complexes lay beyond. Graham saw a few cars in driveways and along the street, but he saw no trucks. He knew he'd need something with four-wheel drive where he was going. To the right, he noticed a reddish Toyota SUV, but he had no idea if there were keys in it.

He set off in that direction when he heard a rustling. Farther down the road, he noticed three deer pulling at the green lawn of a yard. It was yet another reminder of encroaching wildlife and the need to get somewhere safe from their predators. Camping out in a festering grocery store held no appeal for him, knowing the smells would bring in more than just the deer looking for tender grass.

Graham approached the truck and tried the door, but it was locked. He took in a deep breath, knowing he'd have to go inside the home to see if he could find the keys.

With a peaked roof and matching doorway, the little white house was edged in green. "It must have been built in the forties or fifties," he said under his breath. These little postwar houses had been put up quickly to accommodate the troops coming home after the Second World War.

Whoever lived here took pretty good care of the place. Even the concrete walkway had recently been power-washed. He did not bother knocking, but simply tried the door and found it unlocked.

The darkness of the interior seemed daunting. He opened the door farther, but slowly, as if someone might come to meet him, which Graham knew was not likely. The only smells he encountered were mild, musty and moldy but not of death or decay. It was just like some grandmother's closet or basement filled with mothballed coats.

He had looked first by the door before he stepped in, hoping there would be a set of keys on a nearby table or on the wall. He looked around the small living room as the light shone in and revealed a brown moleskin sofa facing the blackened screen of a TV no longer needed. The back of the sofa created a hallway that extended beyond to what Graham figured must be the kitchen.

Graham stepped onto the chestnut parquet flooring. "The real stuff, not the fake kind. Must be the original," he said absentmindedly.

Still with his hand on the door, he said, "Anybody home?" When no one answered he left the door open, looking back across the street, feeling tethered to the kids. It was as if they were his own, or at least like he needed them to feel like his own. *Who else's would they be?* he thought. He released the doorknob and began walking through the strange home and into the kitchen. He hoped the kitchen would be the next likely place someone would leave their keys, possibly on the counter or on a hook by the garage door.

Graham peered around the well-lit kitchen, which was clean and tidy right down to a candle placed in the center of a small island. *This is a redone kitchen for sure*, he thought. *No way this cabinetry is original.* They'd been redone with raised panel oak, and the countertops themselves were a light peach laminate, obviously not up to date but definitely not harking back to the 1940s, either. The place was oddly neat as a pin. Had someone been home when they died, their stuff, in the haste of disorderly living, would be everywhere. He looked around the countertops and a small oak square kitchen table beyond for keys, but with no luck.

"Maybe the bedroom," he said aloud and looked to the short hallway he'd already passed that must lead there. Graham held his jacket up to his nose and mouth. He expected the worst as he turned the doorknob. He opened the door an inch, then two, but what he saw was only a neatly made chenille-covered bed.

"Nobody's home," he said to no one in particular. Just behind him was the door leading to the garage, possibly the last hiding place for the keys.

He opened the unlocked metal door, thinking it was surely a replacement and not the original to the old house. He then peered inside the darkness of the one-car garage, reached for the likely light switch, and flipped it up. By accident, in the process of his search, he dislodged what sounded like keys, sending them jangling to the floor.

As his eyes adjusted to the new light, Graham was surprised to see an older but well-maintained gold and white International Harvester Scout, probably a 1975. It had two rows of seats and a decent cargo area in the back for supplies. He could probably load the bikes up on the top, tying them to the rack. He located the keys he'd dropped and examined them. The ring only contained the keys for the Scout, not the Toyota out front. He hoped this thing was a four-by-four. Graham hit the garage door opener and heard a familiar racket as the door lifted.

He walked over to the driver's side and opened the locked door. He inspected it for the necessary conversion to switch over to four-wheel drive for rough terrain, which to his surprise it had. He started the vehicle up and laid his rifle in the passenger's seat area. It smelled clean and there was no litter lying around. He was happy to see it registered a full tank of fuel.

It dawned on Graham that this must have been Campos's doing: he must have gone house to house, getting them ready for the new residents he expected. He truly wished he hadn't had to kill the man; part of Graham would always feel guilty about it, because the truth was that part of Campos had been good—the part of him that wanted to make this town clean again and the part that had cared for Marcy. Graham knew that part of him, too, because he'd seen it just before he died in the look he gave Marcy. But the other parts of Campos just couldn't have been allowed to remain. Graham knew all lives were especially precious in this new world, and that made his guilt even more so. He laid his forehead onto the steering wheel for a minute while he let the engine run and idle down.

~ ~ ~

It was only late afternoon, but already Graham felt spent. *It's time to get the kids out of here*, he thought before backing out of the skinny driveway and onto the main road. He left the vehicle running and parked right outside the market to warm up the inside. The kids already had two carts full of boxed food ready to load. Graham walked over to Marcy.

"How are you feeling?" he asked her.

"I'm okay," she said, "but my head really hurts."

A little concerned, Graham looked her over again. He didn't see anything unexpected, considering her injuries.

"Let's put some ice on your head to keep the swelling down. You just took the painkillers, too, right?" he asked her.

"Yeah, I took two just like it said on the bottle," Marcy said.

"How old are you girls?" he asked.

"We're fifteen, but I'm older than Macy by five minutes," she said.

He smiled at the girls, amused that she had said something normal in this abnormal world. "Well, you keep taking those pills every six hours then," he said.

"All right, let's get you in the backseat and warmed up. Then we'll load up the rest of this stuff," he said.

Graham lifted the girl, making sure he didn't disturb her wound, and carried her out into the misty cold. He opened the door to the backseat and slid her in onto the warmth of its vinyl.

"You couldn't find anything newer?" she asked.

"No; we were actually lucky to find this one," he said.

"At least it's warm," she conceded.

He shut the door gently and then looked over at the dog, who watched his every move. Graham moved over to the back, opened the top window and then lowered the tailgate.

"Come," Graham said to Sheriff, who just looked up at him, not knowing what he wanted. Then Graham said, "Hmmm, what's your language, big guy?"

Macy pushed one of the carts through the door, coming around to the back of the vehicle. "Do you know what kind of commands to use for him?" he asked her.

"I have no idea. He just jumped into the backseat of the last car we were in. I haven't tried to tell him anything."

"Well, let's try this, then," he said as he patted the back of the tailgate of the truck. Sheriff did a running turn and jumped right up and in. "Good boy!" Graham said and scratched Sheriff behind the ears. "Bet you're getting hungry too."

"Bang found some dog food," Macy said. "They're fast friends, those two," she added, while handing Graham the food supplies from the cart.

Graham loaded quickly, tossed everything lightly into the back. Sheriff walked up to Marcy and sniffed at her head rising over the headrest. She reached up and patted the dog, who sat on his haunches and let her continue the affection.

"Wish I had listened to you, boy," she said lightly.

"Don't do that to yourself, Marcy. Don't regret; it does you no good, believe me," Graham said, speaking loud enough for all of them to hear.

"Look, we all have to be more careful now. There are wild animals everywhere, and a few people who are willing to hurt you, for whatever reason. These are the new rules now. No one goes *anywhere* without telling me, and you must always have someone with you at all times. I'll carry my weapon with me wherever we go and you three need to learn to do the same. A ruler and an ice scraper aren't bad, but they're not good enough to defend yourself with."

The girls looked at one another.

"I know we haven't really talked about this, but it's your choice. You two should decide together. After we load up, we'll go get the bikes that Bang and I hid last night, then go over to your dad's place. Girls, I'm pretty sure you know he's not with the living, but we'll go there and make sure at least. Then it's up to you two if you want to come with Bang and me up to my cabin in Cascade. It's safer there. I know the hunting and fishing grounds, and not that many people know the area. Those fires over there"—he pointed toward Seattle—"are inching their way over here and I don't want to be anywhere close to them when they get here. Besides that, this place welcomes people and you don't know what kind you're dealing with. I'm not saying it's bad to stay here, just that *I'm* not. It's up to you to come with me or stay by yourselves. There are a lot of houses that are livable if you want to stay."

The girls looked at one another again and Macy spoke first. "We're going with you—at least I am. I don't want to stay here. Do you, Marcy?"

"No way, not after this," Marcy said and gestured openly with her hand. "I can still feel him here," she said, with goose bumps rising and shuddering from a chill.

"All right, then, I just wanted to make sure you realized it was your decision," Graham said, and continued loading what little food they'd managed to find. It wasn't a lot, but it might get them through a couple of weeks.

Graham walked back to the market and scanned the inside, retrieving the red ice chest he'd packed earlier, and looked around for anything he thought they should also grab. He noticed a few fire starter logs and took them, as well as several lighters and a snow shovel leaning near the entrance door. He carried the goods out with Bang's help and locked up the back end of the truck while Macy and Bang climbed in the backseat next to Marcy. Before Graham got in, he noticed the sickly sweet burning smell again, coming from the damp, smoking blue trash bin, and his stomach clenched. "Sorry, Campos," he said under his breath. He meant it, but he wouldn't regret what he'd done.

Graham got into the running vehicle and headed over to where he'd stashed their bikes the night before. For him it was returning to where Campos had struck Marcy the first time and, more important, where Graham had failed. Hopefully the lesson he'd learned would stick with him.

Shutting off the truck, Graham said, "All right, Bang, let's go get the bikes and stuff. Girls, this shouldn't take long," he added, shutting the doors to keep in the warmth. Graham looked around to make sure there were no predators; he could not be too careful these days.

Graham and Bang walked between the cars and over to the brush where they'd hidden their bikes and trailer, only to find that something had tried to get into the plastic storage bin containing their food. The shower curtain was ripped to shreds and scattered about. The rifles had been tipped onto the ground but, thankfully, they were still there.

The first aid kit was smashed and scattered all over the ground, but to Graham's amazement, the storage bin itself was intact and unmolested.

They unhitched the trailer and left it where it was. "I wish we could take it," Graham said, "but there's not enough room." He picked up the gun cases and the storage bin and balanced them on the seat of his bike. Meanwhile, Bang retrieved his bike and then they both made their way back to the truck, winding through the scattered maze of cars. Graham took a second to look down the highway and noticed several dogs milling about below the overpass. One looked up at him. "Hurry up, Bang," Graham warned. "If they come up here, just drop the bike and run for the truck," he said.

They both picked up their pace as one of the dogs lifted its head at their scent and barked, alerting the rest of the pack. Graham heard growling and turned around just in time to see the boy let a little arrow fly into a coyote's side as it snuck up behind them. The coyote let out a yelp and took off in the opposite direction.

"Okay, that's enough for me, leave the bike," Graham said, and awkwardly grabbed the tote with the guns balanced on top in his right arm and reached down and pulled Bang up in the other. He ran the rest of the distance to the truck, with more of the pack in pursuit behind them.

Graham opened the front passenger door, pushed Bang in roughly, and then stuffed the bin in right behind him. He then jumped in himself and quickly closed the door.

As they looked out the windows they saw a large coyote come to the rise, followed by a Rottweiler barking insanely. Sheriff growled in their direction, the fur on his back standing on end. Somehow, domestic dogs had gone so far as to join with the wild packs. The girls were shouting and crying and Graham turned around to them, waving his hand up and down, trying to calm them.

"It's all right, we made it back," he said. "Whew, that was too close!" He climbed over the bin, and lifted Bang back to the passenger side. "You're pretty good with that bow and arrow, buddy!" he said.

"Those are bad dogs," Bang said, pointing. "They're coming over here," he cautioned.

The girls' cries started to increase as they remembered their drive the day before. Graham started the engine and circled around, even though the dogs were many now and they were jumping and snarling at the truck.

He sped down the main street and turned left toward the apartment complex beyond. The dogs gave up the chase before long. "Okay, girls, can you give me some directions here? Which building is it?" Graham asked.

Marcy pointed to a gray building with white trim and looked up through the back window at the second floor pointing north. "That's it, number B204," she said.

The building itself was fairly new, built within the last two years or so; behind it there were several more, still under stalled construction. Graham stopped the truck and let it idle right in front of the breezeway that led to the stairs of the building; he looked out the back windows and didn't see any vicious canine brigades. He turned off the engine and then turned back to the girls. "I think I should go up there first. Do you have a key?"

Macy pulled at a lanyard around her neck that held a key hidden within her shirt. She took it off and handed it over. "It's the first door on the left there," she said, pointing to the second floor.

"Don't forget the rifle. It's in his closet," Marcy added. She paused, then said, "His name is Brian."

Graham nodded to them, not sure what else to say; he looked deep into Marcy's eyes, and then Macy's. He took the lanyard and said, "Keep the doors closed, and if there are any issues, honk the horn. I'll just be a minute."

All three nodded in unison. Graham looked at the dog and said, "You're in charge, Sheriff," and the shepherd returned the look with smiling eyes. Graham saw Bang grin back at the dog, then switch his gaze to the girls' faces. The kid sobered quickly. After one quick survey of the world outside, Graham stepped out and silently closed the door, taking his rifle with him.

When he approached the building, Graham noticed debris scattered around the concrete breezeway. What looked to be cheese crackers and cereal were strewn all over.

The door to the apartment wasn't locked or even fully closed, and Graham had a bad feeling about what lay inside. He pushed the door open a little and looked around, holding his rifle up as he entered. The smell hit him right away, pushing him back out the door. He looked down at the truck below and then pulled his jacket back up over his nose and mouth. He entered again and pushed the door against something lightly blocking it. He looked around the door itself and found a large unopened bag of sugar, just lying there wedged against the wall as if someone dropped it on his way out. The place was a mess, and the smell was terrible. Someone was dead in there somewhere. Though Graham couldn't see the body, he had no doubt that the girls' father had perished.

The lights to the kitchen on his right were blinding. He kept his rifle out and peered around the counter, scattered with cans of corn, a box of gelatin, and another of pancake mix, opened and spilled of its contents.

Nobody's in here, he thought. Then he looked over at the couch in the little living area, covered in tossed clothing. On the wall above the sofa he recognized two photos of the smiling girls, Macy and Marcy. One was a gold-framed picture of the girls and their father on what looked like a family fishing trip; each proudly held up a fish.

Graham made his way over to the bedroom and pushed the door, which was slightly ajar. He opened it farther with the end of his rifle.

What he saw wasn't a victim of the pandemic but a bloody massacre. Two decomposing bodies were sprawled on the bed. The odor even seemed to latch onto his eyeballs. He dry-heaved, then pulled the coat closer to barricade his senses further if it could. There was a man, or what looked like one, with a gunshot wound to the face and blood spray covering the wall behind him. A naked woman lay across his middle, face down; she appeared to have taken a shot to the back of the head.

Graham looked around quickly for any rifle within the closet and around the room, but it was clear the place had been ransacked, and a rifle would have been among the first things taken. He quickly made an about-face and ran toward the living room. He picked up the two pictures he'd seen on the wall and left, closing the door behind him as best he could. He looked down at the truck below and dreaded what he had to do now.

Checking below the stairs for any predators, Graham walked around to the driver's side and entered the truck. He was glad to have fresh air to breathe into his lungs, even if it was cold and damp. "Here, I thought you might want these," he said, and handed the pictures over to the girls who had wide, questioning eyes. "He's not alive; I'm sorry," he said.

Marcy said, "I want to see." She looked beyond Graham, staring out the windshield.

"Let me tell you something, Marcy. You don't want to see that. I'm telling you," he said, shaking his head.

Macy cried now, and tears ran down Marcy's face too. "I don't know if I can believe you if I don't see him," Marcy said.

Taking a deep breath and fully understanding her statement, Graham said, "I know, but, Marcy, I don't think he died of the virus. I think he was killed for supplies." Then he added, "There's food all over, like someone tried to cart it all off at once. I think he was shot in his sleep. He didn't suffer. I'm sure your dad wouldn't want you to see this." Marcy let the tears roll, sobbing and holding her sister. Now they knew for sure, but the truth held no hope, and they were alone in the world together.

Graham let them be and turned his attention to the road; he needed to make some distance between this place and the place he would be taking them. He headed back out to the main road and scoffed at his own habit of putting on the loud turn signal, flipped it off, and turned left. They all looked at the parking lot in front of the market, the blue trash bin still smoking in front of it, as they headed out and they saw a black crow nibbling at bits on the pavement. No one said a word as they headed to the other end of town, where the final makeshift gate remained, blocking their freedom.

Graham put the truck in park and looked around before heading out to move the barrier. He didn't feel the need to reclose it now, and when he got back into the cab, they drove on without looking back.

What should have taken them five hours to drive had culminated into a full day, a rescue, a murder, surgery, and a discovery that would remain with Graham forever. He looked back in his rearview mirror at the girls, and farther to the dog looking out the back window, then over to the boy looking up at him, and realized how much his life had changed in forty-eight hours with the death of his original family and the accumulation of this new one in such short order.

His Nelly would have loved each of them, and he was sorry she wasn't here now, especially knowing she would instinctively know how to comfort the girls grieving in the backseat.

"Bang, why don't you open the bin and get the map out for us," Graham said to the boy. He did, and Graham saw how the boy smiled up at him whenever he asked for his help.

The trip north was a winding one, through forests, over hills, and into valleys. In most ways it seemed like any drive through the countryside in the fall—until Graham noticed that the brown cows who usually grazed in open fields were eating the tender green blades along the roadside and sometimes lounging on the warm blacktop road.

It had only been a day since Graham and Bang had left his home, but it felt like a week or more; Graham could feel the soreness in his shoulders from so much exertion earlier in the day. Pushing the memories of the awful day from his mind, he looked in the rearview mirror at Macy and Marcy, each gazing out her own window, but each also holding the other's hand at the center of the backseat. He knew he'd have to stop in an hour or so to change Marcy's bandage and find something in the back to eat.

When they got to the cabin they would have to take an inventory of their food and then look in town for more. He remembered there was a little store, though he was sure it was mostly open only during the summer months. He hoped they still had some supplies in there.

It had only been an hour since they'd left, and everyone was caught up in quiet thought. *Too quiet*, Graham thought. He reached over and turned on the radio, which emitted static at first. There were no search buttons on this thing. He turned the tuning knob slowly and tried to find some sign of life.

Macy said out of boredom, or curiosity, "What are you doing?"

"I'm checking to see if there are any news broadcasts or anything out there. Did you girls listen to the news after all this happened?" he asked.

"Yeah, but we were waiting for Dad . . ." Macy said; then she looked over at Marcy.

"We thought we should stay where we were so he could find us," said Marcy. "Then, when he did not call back, we thought we should go find him."

"The first broadcast said to go to the high school near where we lived, but then the next day it said not to. So we didn't really know what to do," Macy added.

"Yeah, I think everything happened so fast that there was a lot of confusion. And then it ended," Graham said, raising his eyebrows as if to say he had no other answers and then pausing with a catch in his throat. "Anyway, here we are now."

They were silent once again except for the sound of the static Graham made with the radio knob and the noise of the engine propelling them farther north on the wet highway.

Marcy began to nod off, and Graham saw Macy made her sister more comfortable so that she could fall asleep. He felt again he'd done the right thing; these twins needed each other, and he had saved them. Finally he found a beeping sound that was not static and tried to fine tune the station further. A woman's dour voice began repeating an announcement he'd heard parts of before.

"This is a public service message. This pandemic was a weaponized attack starting in China. Due to faulty security measures, it quickly grew out of China's control and spread globally. There is no one left to blame now. Fewer than 2 percent worldwide show immunity to this virus; some will try to hide from its effects, but those who are survivors most certainly are carriers."

Then came the part he had not heard earlier but had suspected would turn out to be true.

"This means," the sober voice continued, "if you are a prepper and successfully hid from the virus, you are still in jeopardy and should remain separated from any immune survivors or you will succumb to the pandemic after all.

"Additionally, The Charters of Freedom, including the US Constitution, the Declaration of Independence, and the Bill of Rights, have been automatically secured in a high-security vault, located beneath the Archives building on Constitution Avenue in Washington, DC. They should remain so until all borders are secure and the population has succeeded in creating a republic once again. Until that time it is best to leave them where they remain.

"This is a difficult world you live in now. Food and shelter should not be a survival issue in the short term, but you should educate yourselves and the younger generations on growing crops, hunting, fishing, and basic medical care.

"Due to the lack of public services, your biggest enemy now is Mother Nature, including wildlife, weather, fires, and even humankind. Gather and take care of the young, because they will need your guidance. Above all, live peacefully.

"This concludes this public service message."

Graham looked forward through the rain-streaked windshield, down the long winding road as they made their way through Falls City. There was the familiar alert beeping, and then the message began again. Graham reached over and turned the radio off. He did not need to hear it again; he was still trying to comprehend what he'd heard the first time. He looked over at Bang, who was now fast asleep with his head lolling onto the side armrest.

Graham looked into the rearview mirror and saw Marcy asleep, her head on Macy's lap. Macy looked directly at him with a worried expression in her vivid blue eyes. Sheriff must have been asleep too, because Graham had not seen even the tops of his ears over the seat for some time now.

Macy still stared at him. "Do you have any questions, Macy?" he asked, not knowing what she was thinking but seeing that she looked terrified.

"Does this mean it's all gone? Everything?" she asked, as if trying to comprehend the incomprehensible.

Graham swallowed, "Macy, it means we have to take care of each other now. There are no schools, no police, and no hospitals anymore. No grocery stores or farmers, for that matter. It means we have to do all of those things for ourselves now. At some point the fires or weather will hit the power stations and there won't be power any longer or gas for vehicles. No iPhones, computers, or video games. It means we have to think differently and make new rules that make sense to us in these times.

"We left the city because of the animals coming in after the smells and because people can no longer keep them at bay with everyday noises. Not to mention the fires that will soon come in and consume all the buildings and houses; there's no fire department to put them out. That's why I decided to head out to the cabin, because I know the area and I've hunted and fished there every year since I was a kid. It's where my great-great-grandfather who was a logger lived, way back when. There's an old apple orchard a few miles away too, so I know we can grow things there. It's been done before," he said.

Graham looked back at Macy again and thought she looked a little more hopeful and a little less terrified. *I'd better keep pushing these guys to think ahead and not look behind them or we won't get through this*, he thought.

"We're going to try to stop up here in Carnation and get some gas," Graham said. "I'll change Marcy's bandage and give her some more medicine. We can get something to eat and hopefully find a bathroom. Sound good?"

"Yeah, especially the bathroom part," Macy said with a faint smile. "Graham?" she said. Her tone led him to believe she wanted to ask more questions.

"Yeah?"

"Thank you for saving Marcy. You could have left us there. I just wanted to thank you for helping us."

Graham just looked Macy in the eyes through the reflection in the rearview mirror and nodded solemnly.

~ ~ ~

Macy hoped Graham knew how grateful she really was. So she would not cry, she looked out the window as the gray rainy day gave way to a few patches of blue sky in the late afternoon, set against the autumn hues of the landscape that rushed by.

She was caught in a vicious cycle. She kept feeling as if she and Marcy were on a normal road trip with Mom or Dad, but then she would look up and see a stranger named Graham driving, a forcible reminder of why she was there. Then she would remember all that had happened that day, and the weeks before, as it replayed in her mind.

Macy looked back out the window to get away from it all until she felt like she was on a road trip, once again.

Graham slowed as he approached the little town of Carnation on Highway 203. There was an apparent attempt at a roadblock as he went into town, with a few vehicles parked in the road. Graham just drove around them on the soft shoulder. There were no signs up or any other warnings, so he just assumed it was an early attempt by the residents to keep traffic out of their town. He drove a little more slowly, dodging a parked semi truck just before the Tolt River bridge.

They passed a baseball field, and Graham felt a pang of sorrow as he remembered the little league team he'd helped coach last spring at the insistence of his brother-in-law. He had not heard from that side of the family at all; he'd tried to call them when Nelly passed away, but no one ever answered. He shook it off and continued looking straight ahead.

Carnation was a typical little northwest farming community. The main street led past a pizzeria, an Ace Hardware store on the left and a Mexican restaurant on the right. He noticed a little nondescript gas station and pulled up to one of the pumps. Not certain if they would work, Graham got out quickly and slid his credit card through. To his surprise, his card was accepted as if all was right with the world. He filled his tank while he looked around and noticed a few dogs lingering in front of the Mexican restaurant, but they did not seem to be paying him any attention. He finished, hopped back in the truck, and continued driving down the street.

Two raccoons scrambled across the road ahead of him, which caused the loitering dogs to take chase, and Graham let up on the gas to slow the truck as they ran in front of him and across the street. Once they were out of sight he continued on, not wanting to stop anywhere close to the animals while he looked for a decent bathroom.

Toward the end of town on the right was the Carnation Elementary School. Nothing but farm fields were farther down the street. He assumed the school doors were locked but pulled into the circular parking lot and got as close as possible to the front doors, providing for an easy getaway if they needed it. Part of him felt he was being paranoid, thinking of every contingency, but after the events of the past two days he just could not be too safe.

Graham put the truck in park, and Bang woke up and looked around, stretching. "Is this a school?" he asked as Macy woke her sister and even Sheriff popped his head up in the back cargo area.

"Yep, but don't worry, we're just here to use the restrooms," Graham said. "If we can, that is." He looked around for any dangers that might lurk before he grabbed his rifle and opened the door. "You guys stay right here until I call you, and keep the doors closed."

They all looked around through their windows for any signs of life as Graham approached the double glass doors. He was certain they'd be locked, but when he reached to try the right-hand door, it opened freely. *Thank God, I don't have to shoot my way in*, he thought, and turned back to the kids, who watched him expectantly. He held up his hand to tell them to stay until he checked the inside of the school.

He walked in onto the blue rubber flooring. Hardly making a noise, he peered around the foyer, beyond what must be the office window, for the closest possible bathroom. The hall was a cheery place, with lots of natural light coming in the windows and had probably been remodeled recently. It smelled like crayons and disinfectant, like any elementary school. Graham knew the schools were shut down early in an effort to prevent the spread of the virus, but could not figure out why the doors had been left open. He listened intently and looked up and down the halls but did not leave the sight of the kids beyond the doorway. He noticed boys' and girls' bathrooms signs near the office, along the wall next to a water fountain, and walked back out to the truck after surveying the landscape for any possible dangers.

The coast appeared to be clear, so Graham opened Macy's door and motioned to Bang to follow. "Close it lightly, and be quiet. We don't want to attract any attention," he said. Macy grabbed the first aid supplies for Marcy, as well as the empty water bottles. Bang took his bow and arrow, as always. Graham reached in, picked up Marcy, and called Sheriff out over the seat. Again, the dog did not respond and just looked up at him confused.

Macy patted her side and said, "Come, Sheriff." He jumped quickly out of the back and onto the pavement.

Graham shook his head, confounded as to why the police dog didn't know common commands. "Bang, lead him into the building," he said.

The dog happily trailed the boy, sniffing at the new surroundings as Macy followed along.

"The bathrooms are right over there. Let's get in and out and be quiet about it," Graham said.

He could tell from their expressions that the kids felt as out of place as he did, sensed a wrongness. The need to be cautious in such a pleasant room, untouched by their new circumstances, went against the grain; it just did not seem right, juxtaposed as it was to the happy, colored balloons and the laminated cutouts of brown squirrels that were stapled to the walls. Marcy huffed a little, but no one said anything about it.

Sheriff sniffed the hallway from side to side but stayed close by the others. Graham took Marcy into the girls' bathroom. He opened the swinging door and peered inside. There were two white wall-mounted sinks to the left and three stalls behind them; all appeared safe. He put Marcy down on her good leg and helped her over to the first stall. Macy came in right behind him. "When you're done, let me know and I'll come back in and change the dressing by the sink," he said, letting the door close behind him. He and Bang went into the boys' bathroom and did their business, leaving Sheriff out in the hallway. After they had washed up, Graham went over to the girls' door and knocked lightly. "Are you ready?"

"Yeah, you can come in," said Macy.

She was getting the first aid supplies out of the bag as Graham pushed a rubber doorstop under the door to prop it open. "Macy, you and Bang refill those water bottles while I do this," he said.

He took a deep breath and walked over to Marcy, who hopped on one leg over to the sink. "How's it feeling?" Graham asked.

"The cut throbs some, but not as bad as before," she said.

"Well, face the wall. I'll try to be as gentle as I can," he said as he washed and dried his hands. He started to peel away the soaked dressing.

She cringed a bit, so he stopped. "It's okay, Graham, just go ahead and do it," Marcy said.

Graham exposed the raw looking flesh. He gently dabbed at it with sterile gauze and washed it with more sterile saline. Then he dried it by patting lightly. He applied new ointment and recovered it with a clean bandage.

"I think we should just use the gauze to cover it after we get to the cabin to let more air get to it. Now, let's get more meds into you and get going," he said. Graham repacked their supplies and threw the bloody dressing in the nearby gray trashcan. *At this point, that will probably stay there for eternity*, he thought. Then he looped one arm around Marcy's waist while toting his rifle with the other.

"Graham!" Macy called from the hallway, a little alarmed.

"What?" he said as he turned into the hall.

"Sheriff's growling at something down the hall." Sheriff was crouched in front of them in the middle of the hallway, warning them of something beyond, down past the cheerful squirrel cutouts.

"It's probably a dog, so come on, it's time to go," Graham said as he ushered them all to the doorway. Looking to make sure the coast was clear, he opened the door and shepherded them all back to the truck. He held Marcy up with one arm as she hopped on one leg.

"Come on, Sheriff!" he yelled. The dog dropped his warning growl and ran out, but instead of getting back into the truck right away, he ran over to the left of the door and lifted his leg at the nearest bush, all the while looking around for enemies.

Graham shook his head, but got the kids into their seats quickly and then called the dog over. Sheriff jumped into the back as before. Graham held up his rifle and scanned the outside of the building while he edged closer to his own car door.

As they drove away Graham noticed movement in his rearview mirror; someone was running across the street behind them. He stopped, rolled down his window, and yelled, "Hey!"

The young man stopped. Sheriff started barking and the girls panicked. "No, Graham, keep going, please keep going!" they yelled.

"Shhh, he's just a kid," he said back to them.

The six-foot figure turned out to be a teen—Graham guessed about eighteen or so. He wore a blue plaid flannel shirt over ratty denim jeans and boots. The boy stared at him through suspicious eyes and dark brown, unkempt hair. Graham started to back up the truck, but the boy ran again. Graham put on the brakes. "Wait!"

The kid stopped once more, but Graham could tell he was ready to bolt at any time.

"I'm not going to hurt you," Graham said. "Are you okay?"

"I don't need your help." The kid looked distraught.

"Okay, that's good," Graham responded, then after a few moments of silence with just the sound of the truck's engine running he added, "We're going up to Cascade. Do you know where that is?"

The boy paused in thought, then nodded that he did.

"If you want to, you can come up there when you're ready. Leave me a note at the Cascade post office and I'll check it when I come into town, once a week or so. Do you understand?" Graham asked him.

"Yeah, but I don't want to leave them just yet." For the first time, Graham noticed the boy was armed as he pointed toward his home with a pistol that he'd had hidden behind his back.

"It's all right, I understand. When you're ready, you're welcome. Leave me a note, and stay somewhere safe in town. I'll check for it." He did not know why, but he trusted the kid.

He watched the teenager's eyes light up with momentary interest and turned to see Macy staring out at him from the backseat window. Again, the youth hesitated, looking undecided. "Okay, I'll probably come, but not yet," he said, jogging away down a side street.

"Whew!" Macy said.

Graham rolled up his window and moved on down the road. "That was weird," said Marcy.

"He's all right," Graham said. "He's just scared. Maybe he'll meet up with us after a while."

"He had a gun," Bang pointed out.

"He sure did. I think we'll see a lot of that now, people carrying guns." Graham stepped on the gas and the truck moved on. He reminded the kids to find something to eat in the back, and Macy pulled out a package of cheese and peanut butter sandwich crackers and began passing them around. They each had their own refilled water bottle, and Graham reminded Macy to give her sister more medicine. Soon they were silent again, having finished off their light meal and drifting off to their own thoughts without having much to say to one another. The drive made things seem too normal, but at least it gave them time to consider things as they were now.

Night was descending as Graham pulled up to the narrow dirt road turnoff that led to the cabin. He was a little saddened and surprised that he'd gotten this far and only run into the one young man and no other living souls. He felt a little less optimistic about the future.

Graham came to a complete stop and turned on the overhead light to see just how to put this unfamiliar truck into four-wheel drive. This caused the sleeping occupants to stir.

"Where are we?" asked Bang.

"We're almost there. I have to get this thing in four-wheel drive. The road is always a bit muddy up there. I hope there are no downed trees in the way. If there are, we'll have to get out and walk," Graham said. He turned off the obtrusive light and drove slowly on the single-lane dirt path leading up to the family cabin; the truck bounced up and down over unseen dips in the road.

The long day had been difficult. Graham held back the memory of killing a man and having to perform crude surgery to save a life. He never thought he was capable of doing either, nor did he ever want to again have the responsibility of such actions any time soon. His father had been that man, not him. Graham was a math professor—or had been. His father was the brave one, a soldier who'd fought in Vietnam and Korea. Reluctantly, he realized that he was his father's son after all, and it was a good thing he knew it now because their lives depended on it.

Graham peered through the light beams and saw a few brown deer that stared back at him before leaping away through the ferns and pines. He looked up ahead, noticed a faint light, and had a sinking feeling. He killed the truck's headlights and, by memory, drove closer. Soon it became apparent that someone was already in the cabin; there was flickering light gleaming through the windows.

He pulled up slowly into the clearing and saw a little red Ford Escort under the brush on the left side of the cabin. "Damn, someone's here," he said as he turned off the engine. "I'm going to check it out,"

Graham said as he pulled out his rifle. "You guys lock the doors. Macy, can you drive?" he asked.

"Sorta," she said.

"Good enough. Anything happens to me, you get the hell out of here and go back to that boy we saw today, all right?" Once again he couldn't explain his trust in the boy.

Sounding confused and scared by his tone, Macy answered, "Okay."

Graham quietly pushed the door closed and Macy climbed over into the driver's seat while Bang reached around and locked all the doors manually.

Graham moved around to the side window to peek inside. Through the wavy, dirty glass he could see that someone had started a fire in the woodstove that he and his dad had installed not so long ago. Flames could be seen behind the stove's glass and ceramic door. No one was walking around in the main room, so he assumed the trespassers were asleep. Quietly and slowly Graham went up the wooden steps so as to not alert whoever might be inside. He tried the front door and found that the lock had been busted, so he pushed it in gently.

Once inside he saw what he couldn't have seen from out in the yard: the firelight danced on a woman who lay on the couch, sweating and shivering at the same time. She looked to be at least part American Indian and was obviously suffering from the virus—or something similar.

Graham stepped halfway into the cabin, then stopped abruptly at the sound of a rifle bolt clicking back to his right.

"Hold it right there, buddy," a gravelly voice commanded. Graham remained frozen in place; he couldn't believe he'd been through this horrible day, only to be murdered at the very end of it in his family's own cabin.

"Who the hell are you?" the stranger said, coming into view. An ancient man stood before Graham, probably the oldest man he'd ever laid eyes on. His sparse white hair was a striking contrast to his black skin. Graham pulled his right hand up, then lowered his own rifle with his left hand but didn't drop it entirely.

"It's all right," he said calmly as he tried to reassure the old man. "My name's Graham Morgan, and this is my cabin. My family's cabin, that is."

"So you say," the old man retorted.

"Really, it is. I've been coming up here every summer, my whole life. Now please lower that gun, before you hurt someone."

The old man complied, then Graham asked, pointing to the woman, "Does she have the virus?"

"Hell, I don't know. Don't think so. She kidnapped me and took me here," he said, complaining.

Graham walked over to the woman. Beads of sweat covered her exposed face, and he pulled back the covers a little and saw that she was armed with a handy pistol at her stomach. She was unconscious, so Graham removed the pistol just so there weren't any accidents and placed it on the floor under the couch.

Listening to her breathing, Graham said, "Something's not right. Her breathing is too clear for this to be the virus. It's some other infection," he said.

"I could've told you that, dummy," the old man said.

Graham looked at the old man, irritated. "Do you know her name?" he asked.

"No. Dumb girl said I had to come with her, is all. I don't know her. She said I had to come on account I wasn't dying. I told her I couldn't help it and she dragged me out here anyway." The old man opened his arms wide, still holding onto the rifle.

"Put that gun down now," Graham said and realized the old man was short a cell or two and couldn't be trusted with a weapon.

"It's not loaded," the woman said quietly.

Graham looked back at her, surprised by her soft voice.

"Hi, I'm Graham. I can see you're sick. Is it the virus?" he asked.

She swallowed and looked at him, "No, I had a miscarriage yesterday, and I think there's some kind of infection," she said, tears flooding her eyes.

This news hit Graham in the gut. "I'm really sorry to hear that" was all he could think to say. "Do you have any water?" he asked.

"There's some in my car. I just couldn't make it back out there after getting him in here," she said.

"All right, I'll get you some. Listen," he said to both of them, "This is my family's cabin. It's fine if you stay here, but I want you to know I've got kids out in my truck and I need to bring them in here." Then he added, "I'll be right back."

Before he reached the door, though, he strode over to the old man and grabbed the gun, pointing it at him. "You behave, mister," he said, guiding the cranky geriatric to a nearby chair.

Back at the truck Graham informed the kids of the situation in the cabin. "Don't be offended by the old man. He's just cranky," he said to them. "The lady's really sick so we need to give her some of our antibiotics," he said.

When the children finally stepped out into the cool night air, they carried what they could and walked through the tall, dewy grass to the cabin. Macy helped her sister, and Sheriff walked along with Graham and Bang, nose twitching in response to the new smells along the way. The girls stopped at the porch, and Graham handed what he carried to Bang and lifted Marcy into his arms to climb the steps.

By the time they entered, the lady was asleep again. The old man silently beheld the new intruders.

"Them's just children," the old man said, a little disgusted, and pointed at them as if Graham promised him something else.

"That's right, they're children. And you be nice to them," Graham warned.

"They can't fight," he said.

"Fight what?" Graham asked him.

"This war!" the old man said indignantly.

Macy and Bang stopped behind Graham and stared, astonished.

"There's no war right now," Graham said.

"Dat's what *you* think," the old man said, rising on his old bowed legs and making his way slowly to the bunkroom at the back of the cabin.

The kids clearly didn't know what to make of all this and looked at Graham for an answer. He just shook his head with a little smile.

"Man, this has been the longest day ever," Graham said, realizing he still had Marcy in his arms. He put her down in the chair the old man just vacated.

Sheriff walked over to the sleeping woman, sniffed at her, and looked up at Graham. "I know, buddy, she's sick," Graham said. "Marcy, let's get your leg taken care of first. There's a bathroom over here to the right." Graham quickly redressed her wound, which didn't look any different from that afternoon.

Back in the kitchen, he asked them if they were hungry, but all three said they simply wanted to know where they could sleep. Graham walked them into the back room, where four hefty double-decker bunk beds stood like sentinels on guard. The old man appeared as a lump on the farthest one back on the right. They quietly tiptoed over to the other side, and Macy pulled back the covers on the bottom at the front end of the row, nearest the doorway, and motioned for Marcy to lie down. Graham helped Marcy onto the mattress, and Macy covered her up with a soft blanket he handed her from the stack that he pulled from a big, cedar chest at the end of the room.

Bang climbed the ladder at the end of Marcy's bed and settled down above her. Macy stood on the edge of Marcy's bunk for a moment and covered up the boy. "Goodnight, Bang," she said, and he smiled at her. Graham could tell Macy was the mothering type.

She tucked her sister in again and brushed back her hair, "Goodnight, Marcy," she said.

"Goodnight, sis," Marcy murmured sleepily.

Macy got into a lower bunk near her sister, nearest the doorway on the left, and waved goodnight to Graham, who watched all of this from the doorway, wondering how they could perform such a normal ritual after such a hellacious day. They'd lost so much, and yet life went on. Graham walked away, amazed, and into the living area, where another life lay in harm's way.

As Graham entered the main room he saw Sheriff waiting by the front door. "You got to go out, boy?" he asked. He opened the door, adding, "Don't go far, Sheriff." He shut it lightly, walked over to the fire, and added a log, which cast an ambient glow on the woman behind him.

He heard the dog pad up the wooden porch steps and walked over to open the door. Sheriff trotted right past him and into the bunkroom like he knew where he was going, so Graham shut the door and reached up to lower the original locking lever, which the others had neglected to notice before, guarding against any nighttime intruders.

Graham felt the woman's forehead, and noticed her fever was dangerously high at this point. He removed her covers and saw that she visibly shook. "We've got to get you cooled off," he said, not knowing if she could hear him.

She wore a lacy white button-up blouse that was soaked through with sweat, along with denim jeans and cowboy boots. *She must have had a difficult time getting herself and that cranky old man into the locked cabin*, Graham thought.

He grabbed water and a washcloth from the bathroom and wiped the woman's forehead, face, and neck to cool her off. She woke and stared wildly at him with deep brown eyes. "I'm so cold," she said.

"Here, drink this," Graham said, holding a glass of water up to her chapped lips and supporting her damp head. He gave her a doxycycline pill and two Ibuprofen to lower her temperature.

"I know you're cold, but we need to get you cooled off more. Your fever's too high," he said.

She nodded her head, but he wasn't sure if she recognized him from earlier or if she might be hallucinating now. Graham began removing her boots and socks. "I've got to take off your pants. Are you okay with that?" he asked.

She was shaking, but she looked up at him, nodding. He unfastened the zipper on her denim jeans, reached behind her, and tugged them down. She tried to lift her body to help him but was clearly too weak to offer any real assistance.

In the process, Graham tugged her pale pink panties down partially, exposing a bloody pad and a foul smell. He reached over and pulled them back into place. "Sorry," he said, but he wasn't sure if she was even aware of what had happened.

Once he got the jeans down to her knees, she curled up her long creamy legs and rolled to her side, trying to warm herself. Through chattering teeth, she said, trying to smile, "You've done that before, I think."

Graham looked at her, a little embarrassed. "I'm married. I mean, I *was* married. She's gone now," he said.

"Me too," she said.

"You said you miscarried. How far along were you?"

"About six weeks," she said, and a tear ran down her face. He wiped it away and tried to comfort this stranger who was in such private pain.

"My wife was pregnant too," he said. He didn't need to say any more than that; she understood "I'm so sorry," she said.

"What's your name?"

"Tala."

"Tala," he repeated. "Doesn't that mean wolf?"

Surprised, she looked at him. "Yes, it does," she said. "You obviously know a little about Native American culture."

"Yep," he said, covering her lower half lightly with the blanket and seeing that her shaking had subsided a little.

"So tell me how you made it here?" he asked.

"Well, I came from around Sedro-Woolley. There were a few looters going house to house. It just became too dangerous for me to stay. So, I got into my car and went to check on my nana at the home and found *him*, instead." She smirked. "I just couldn't leave him there in the stench. I had driven as far as my tank would allow, before the gas light came on, and then I found the dirt driveway, so I followed it and made it here. I hope you don't mind. Maybe we can find another place to stay in the morning," she said.

"I'm not going to kick out a sick lady and an old man, Tala. We'll see how things work out. For now, let's just get you better. I'm not sure about the grouchy old man, but we'll give it some time," Graham said.

He felt her forehead and it seemed to be a little less searing than before. "I'll be right back," he said, heading to the bunkroom, where he picked up two extra pillows and a few blankets.

He lifted up her head so that he could put a clean pillow under it and made himself a pallet next to her on the floor by the fire.

She began to protest, "You should go sleep on a bed in there."

"Shhh, Tala, get some sleep. I'll be fine, and I need to keep the fire going anyway. We'll talk more in the morning," he said, justifying his intentions.

Tala allowed herself to slip off to sleep, and Graham checked her fever once more to make sure it was continuing to subside before he finally closed his eyes on this day.

In Graham's dream, *Campos* was the one pushing the rifle down on *his* neck, squeezing the life out of him. Campos was sneering and shaking above him with a reddened mad expression, and then Graham could hear Marcy's screams from beyond, but this time he could not help her.

He woke on the hardwood floor and sat up with a start as the old man kicked his boot again and pointed to the bunkroom.

"She's having a damn nightmare. You going to do something? She scarin' me in there."

Graham scrambled up, threw his blanket off, and grabbed his rifle. He ran to the bunkroom.

"Marcy, it's okay. You're fine," Macy said to her sister as Graham rounded the corner. Bang sat atop his mattress and leaned down from above, trying to see Marcy. Sheriff stood on top of Macy's bunk, whining, not knowing what to do about the girl's crying.

Macy held her sister, sobbing.

"Marcy?" Graham called from the doorway and his voice seemed to get through to her where her sister's hadn't. She stopped shrieking. "Marcy," he said again.

Marcy drew in several ragged breaths and finally focused. "S-s-sorry," she said, out of breath.

Graham squatted beside her. "Don't be sorry. It was just a nightmare." He patted her golden locks and felt her for a fever, but there was none. One side of her forehead was black and blue now. He knew it would turn many shades in days to come. Hopefully, her scars inside would heal soon too. "This is hard for all of us, but at least we can stay here for a while." He didn't know what else he could say to comfort her.

"Thanks, Graham," Marcy said.

"Hi there, Bang, you sleep well?" he said to change the subject.

He laid the rifle up against the bed and reached to pick the boy up. Then he took Bang and the rifle back into the main room to give the girls some privacy. Sheriff followed along.

"She woke me up with that racket," the old man said to Graham.

"Be nice, Ennis," said Tala, who sat with the blanket wrapped around her.

Graham watched Tala. She looked better, but she was not out of the woods yet. Her long glossy hair had come loose from the ribbon she'd had it tied in and hung loosely in waves well past her shoulders, giving her a wild look. Graham walked over to her and put Bang down beside her.

"This is Bang. Bang, this is Tala." Tala put her hand on the boy's head.

"Hi, Tala," Bang said, and Sheriff nosed his head between them to sniff her out.

"Be a gentleman, Sheriff," Graham said.

"Sheriff?" the old man asked.

Bang pulled Sheriff's collar around and showed Ennis the star. "He's a police dog, see?" Bang said.

"He's a cop dog. Takes one to know one," Ennis said and walked over to pet the dog.

"You were a policeman?" asked Graham.

"Yep. I'm retired now," Ennis said.

Graham chuckled to himself, and Tala caught on and tried to suppress her own laugh.

"Do police dogs have special commands?" Graham asked. "He doesn't answer to 'come.'"

"Police canines are often taught in languages other than English. The ones we had were taught commands in *Hebrew*, believe it or not." Ennis tried out several words to see if the dog reacted to any of them, but no luck.

"Tell me again. How'd you find him?" Graham asked Tala.

"I went to check on my nana at the nursing home, but she'd passed away. They were all gone. It was terrible. Then I noticed several were covered in white sheets. Except *him*," she said, pointing at Ennis. "He was the one who covered them up after they'd died— even the nurses," she said.

Graham looked at the man for some explanation. "You can't just leave them like that, starin' at you. It ain't right," Ennis said.

Graham felt Tala's forehead again and said, "You still have a fever, but it's not as bad as last night. Let's get some breakfast into you, and you and Marcy both need to take more meds."

"Is that one of the girls?" she asked.

"Yeah, Macy and Marcy. We ran into some trouble yesterday and Marcy got hurt," he said. "She's fine, but she has a deep cut and we're trying to keep it clean," he added.

"They're twins?" she asked, surprised. She realized now she'd not really gotten a look at them the night before.

"Yeah, Bang and I found them walking up the highway with Sheriff here," Graham said.

"He was keeping them girls safe," Ennis speculated as he peered into the dog's soulful eyes.

"Yeah, well, it's a long story," Graham said. He didn't want to go into it. He walked over to peer out the front window, and after being sure that everything was safe, he opened the front door for Sheriff to trot out and relieve himself.

The cool morning air spilled into the cabin, releasing the stuffy sour smells trapped inside. Graham scanned the area for any signs of life. The cabin was circled by tall old-growth evergreens. They had been here even back when his second great-grandfather had bought the three hundred acres it was more or less centered on.

Graham saw the familiar dark trail leading from the west side, meandering down to the lake below where they could fish for their dinner later today. He descended the porch steps and walked over to their newly acquired truck to bring in the supplies they'd brought.

Bang showed up beside him, so he handed the boy as much as he thought he could carry into their new home. With six people, this meant that Graham would need to spread their food plan thinner and get busy hunting. It also meant he'd have to change out the composting toilet at least once a month. Although Graham had resented the extra work it took away from his fishing the previous summer, the facilities upgrade was worth it—no more walking outside in the weather to use the john.

Graham heard a rustling in the brush behind him and went to bring his rifle up when he saw Sheriff dart out after a hapless brown squirrel. "Well, at least you hunt for yourself," he said to the dog.

Graham packed up as much as he could carry into the cabin, and as he entered the front room, all eyes were on him as if to ask a question. "What?" he asked.

"How do you use the bathroom?" Macy asked.

"Oh!" He sat the supplies down on the rustic dining table and addressed them all. "It's a composting toilet, designed so the liquids are filtered up front and the solids go toward the back," he said tactfully. "Then, there's a canister next to the toilet and you scoop a layer of sawdust over it. There's no flushing, it just drops down into a tank that I have to change out once a month or so. It's pretty simple, really, and the venting system keeps the air smelling fresh."

"Mystery solved," Macy said as she guided Marcy toward the bathroom.

Graham and Bang separated the food supplies on the dining table to take inventory. With six people, this wouldn't last them more than a few weeks. In addition to hunting, he knew he'd have to make a trip into town to scout out more supplies.

"How many days do you think we have?" Tala asked. Graham thought she must have read the concern in his expression.

"About a week, I'd say, if we cut down to two meals a day," he said, "for adults anyway. The kids can have a snack in between."

Then he heard the girls come out of the bathroom.

"We need to have a group meeting after breakfast," Graham said.

Tala started to get up, wrapping the blanket around her waist in modesty, but Graham noticed she tried to steady herself with one arm on the couch.

"Wait a second, there," he said, walking over to her side.

"I just need to use the facilities," she said.

"I'll walk you over. You still have a fever, so take it easy," he said, grabbing her jeans before he led her there.

Tala felt weak and defenseless, which scared her in this situation. Graham opened the door for her and she leaned against the bathroom sink as he reached in and laid her jeans on the counter. "I'll be close by," he said softly. "So just shout if you need anything."

Tala swallowed hard. "Thank you. And . . . thank you for taking care of me last night too," she said. She shut the door and took stock of herself in the little wall mirror. Her hair was a tangled mess, and her eyes looked dull and puffy and were marked by dark circles. Above all, she noted how gaunt her face looked. She was much paler than her typical pallor, but her appearance in comparison to the twin she knew as Marcy made her heart ache. The poor young girl must have gone through a rough experience to receive those kinds of injuries.

Tala had always been the strong one in her family. After her mother had died, Tala had helped raised her two younger brothers and made sure they attended college as her mother would have wanted.

Her father worked for the railroad and became quiet and distant after her mother's death. He was the first in her family to succumb to the virus, followed by her two brothers and then Nathan, Tala's husband, who worked for the postal service. They had only been married a year and Tala felt they'd finally turned the corner when they found out she was pregnant and told her father she was expecting. He was overjoyed at the prospect of having his first grandchild.

Tala looked down from her reflection. It was never meant to be, and in the end she'd even lost her baby. At the thought of her loss, tears came to her eyes once again.

She turned the tap on to a trickle and splashed cold water on her face, shocking the intrusive emotions out of her consciousness. This was a new day, and at least she didn't have to take care of the old man by herself anymore. He'd been tough to handle on her own. She counted herself fortunate to have stumbled onto Graham's cabin last night, not having any idea what she was going to do. It was a godsend that he wasn't dangerous, as far as she could tell, because she had been completely defenseless the night before.

Tala used the toilet then took care to clean herself, wrapping her refuse in paper. She followed Graham's directions to shovel a scoop of the sawdust and hoped it covered the foul smell of the stale blood her miscarriage had caused. She felt dirty, and wondered if she could take a shower. She wasn't sure if there would be hot water. She poked her head out the door and asked Graham, "Is it possible to use the shower?"

He looked over at her and said, "Sorry, I don't have it set up yet. I'll get it going so we can have warm water later tonight. There are washcloths under the sink though, so you can at least rinse off."

"That's great. Thanks, Graham, I feel really lucky even to have a bathroom these days."

"I'm the thankful one," he said. "I think I'll need all the help I can get, especially with two girls." Tala smiled and closed the door.

~ ~ ~

Ennis walked into the kitchen, eyeing Graham. "Where's breakfast?" he demanded.

Graham picked up a Snickers bar and thumped it against the old man's chest. "Here you go."

"I can't eat that," Ennis said. "Don't you know how to make bacon and eggs? I don't know what I'm doin' here."

"I don't see any pigs or chickens around here—do you?" Graham was getting a little irritated with the old man.

"Boy, you are underprepared," Ennis declared with a chuckle.

"Look, right now we'll have to make do with what we have; after breakfast, let's have a meeting to discuss our situation. If you have any constructive suggestions, I'm all ears," Graham said.

The old man looked at him and shook his head. "This is a fine mess for sure," he said.

"You got that right,' said Graham. "Listen, Ennis, I know you're playing the cranky old man bit, but you're more with it than you let on. So cut the crap. I need your help. You have any suggestions, then make them. You might have gotten away with that in a nursing home, but not here."

He heard a scratch at the door, so he opened it for Sheriff, who was waiting to come in. The dog sat on the porch with two dead squirrels at his paws and looked up at Graham with a silly grin. Graham reached down and petted the dog's head. "Thanks, boy," he said. He bent down, picked up the offerings and brought them into the kitchen.

"Well, I'll be," Ennis said, "that dog is something."

Graham retrieved a knife and took the squirrels outside to the gutting log, where he and his dad had cleaned fish and game in the past. He made quick work of the two squirrels.

He knew the girls would probably be too squeamish at the prospect of eating squirrel, but Graham would just cut it up and pan fry it, making gravy with the drippings and the canned milk they had; he'd serve it over the box of instant grits he'd brought in earlier. He hoped they wouldn't ask about the mystery meat, because they needed all the protein they could get right now. Satisfied with the idea, Graham set to work. He wasn't a great cook, but his mom had taught him the basics, at least.

Tala had finished getting herself presentable, and as she emerged, passing Graham on his way to the kitchen, he thought she looked better, but still worn out. Ennis had nodded off in a chair, snoring loudly with the dog by his feet, and from the bunkroom came the voices of the three children.

"Sit down, Tala," Graham said, noticing how frail she looked as she leaned against the dining table.

"I wish I could do something," she said. "I should be cooking breakfast."

"Another time; I've got it under control." Graham filled a glass of water and took her some meds as well as a few crackers.

"Macy," Tala said as the girl came into the kitchen area of the big room, "would you happen to have a hairband I could borrow?"

"Sure," Macy said. She hurried away and returned with one, sweeping her gaze over Tala. "You look kind of weak. Want me to braid your hair for you?"

"Oh yes, that would be so nice. You're a sweet girl to offer." Tala's relief and gratitude sounded genuine. She must be even in worse shape than he'd imagined, Graham thought, if even the effort of braiding her own hair was too great a task. He'd have to make sure she rested; he did not want her to get any sicker.

While Graham prepared breakfast he watched Macy separate Tala's raven black tresses and begin the familiar ritual. He saw Tala close her eyes, obviously taking comfort and maybe even pleasure in the process. Macy tied the long braid off with a pink band she'd brought and said, "There you go. I love your hair."

"Thank you, Macy." Tala fingered the thick braid. "You did a nice job. How's your sister doing?"

"She's okay, it was just a nightmare. Our mom and dad both died." Maybe saying it out loud would somehow make it real to her.

Tala reached out and held Macy's hand. "I know, dear. All of my family died too. You're lucky to have your sister, you know?"

Graham saw Macy's chin tremble and quickly spoke. "Thankfully, we all have one another here," he said, hoping to bring a bit of optimism into the room.

Tala pulled Macy close, hugging her. "Graham's right. Just the smell of what he's cooking makes me feel thankful." The aroma from Graham's creation brought the other children out of the bunkroom, and it seemed to wake Ennis.

"Macy, can you help me dish this up?" he asked, tapping the cupboard where the bowls and plates were kept. With his other hand, he reached into a drawer for cutlery.

They all dove into the hearty breakfast, commenting on how good it tasted, never asking what the mystery meat was, but when Tala gave Graham a little wink from across the table, he knew she'd guessed.

"All right, gang, before we clean up, let's talk about a few things," Graham said. "Tala, what was your job before the pandemic hit?"

"I taught first grade. Not a skill that will help us here, I'm afraid."

"And Ennis, you were a policeman?"

"Yeah, but that was over twenty years ago, in Seattle," Ennis said.

"Can you still shoot?" Graham asked him.

"Maybe," Ennis answered doubtfully.

Tala spoke up. "I can shoot. My dad made sure we all knew how." She issued a sad sigh.

Bang walked away from the table while the conversation continued and returned shortly after with his bow and arrow for all to see.

"Boy, can you shoot that little thing?" Ennis asked him.

Bang was a bit afraid of the old man and nodded, then looked down.

"He's pretty good at it," said Graham. "He got a coyote that tried to sneak up on us. The girls here were armed with a ruler and an ice scraper when we first met them," he added, poking a little fun at them.

"We didn't have anything else," Marcy said tersely.

"Well, that's the problem I'm getting to," Graham said. "Rule number one: No one leaves the cabin unless they're armed or accompanied by someone who is. Understood? Right now, we have five rifles and two pistols between us. Later, we'll try to find more. Tala, you know how to fire your piece?"

"Yes, my husband bought it for me and we practiced at least one weekend every month," she answered.

Graham nodded, and then looked over to Ennis. "Do you think you can handle her rifle?" he asked. "I mean, when it's loaded?"

Tala spoke up. "I have shells for it. It was my husband's rifle." She sounded a little embarrassed.

Graham looked over at the old man and repeated his earlier question, "Can you handle a rifle?" he asked.

"I can handle it." Ennis spoke a little gruffly, making the girls jump.

"All right, then, I'll get it ready for you. We can't afford any accidents," Graham said. "That leaves one pistol and three rifles." He looked at the girls.

"I want the pistol," Macy said.

"I don't think you can handle the Garand, Marcy, so that leaves Campos's rifle. Do you think you can work it? I'll show you how."

"I don't want it. It was *his*," Marcy said, remembering.

"Marcy, look at me," Graham said. "It's ours now, and you need to learn how to use it.

"I'm not touching it." Her tone offered no possibility that she'd be persuaded otherwise.

"I'll learn how, Graham, if you show me. Then she can have mine," Macy said.

"No," Marcy said to her sister.

"You have to learn how," Graham said.

Tala reached over and placed her hand on Graham's arm, quieting his next comment. "Marcy, how would you like it if I taught you how to use my pistol? It's lighter. I'll take the other rifle," she said.

"That's a good idea," Ennis said, trying to put in his two cents.

Graham thought it was kind of Tala to offer and could see now she would be a great asset with the girls. They were fifteen, and though they'd gotten along fine so far, he knew Marcy's attitude could be a problem.

The next subject he brought up was cabin security and daily routines, and who would be responsible for which daily chores to keep things livable. Someone would always remain behind in the cabin to guard their supplies. They also decided, as a group, that any thoughts or concerns would be discussed at the evening meal. When they both felt better, Tala and Marcy would be in charge of meal preparation and food rationing. The rest would go on daily hunts and scavenging trips. Graham expressed his concern for the need to get enough supplies in before the coming winter snow took hold. It could be a long and lean winter, he warned them all.

"What do we do if we see other people, and what about the boy we saw?" Macy asked.

"We shoot 'em," Ennis said.

"No, listen," Graham said with a quick shake of his head at Ennis. "That's a good question, Macy, and it brings up another topic we should discuss. I heard a public service announcement on the radio on our way here last night. It seems there are possibly preppers who managed to stay away from the public and haven't been exposed to the virus yet. If they are exposed to us, they will catch the virus and die. I don't want to be responsible for that. So, I suggest if you come across anyone, you keep your distance—not only for their sake but also for your own. They might not be friendly. You just don't know. Hide out, and let one of us know as soon as you can. Do not approach them. Is that understood?" Graham emulated his own father's voice to get his point across, though he knew Marcy didn't need to be told this.

"As for the teen we saw"—Graham explained to Tala and Ennis their encounter with the boy—"we never got that close to him, so I don't know if he was part of a prepper group or not, but if I had to guess, he's a carrier, like the rest of us. If he shows up, we will deal with it when the time comes."

"Now, first things first. Medical care, and after that, you girls stock the pantry and Tala, lie down and rest. Ennis, Bang, and I will go down to the lake and see what the fishing is like. Hopefully we will catch a few for dinner. Then we need to get some target practice in," Graham said.

"We also need to make a list of meals that we can create out of our supplies." Tala said. "Graham, I think you and Ennis and I can do with two meals a day for now. Growing ones need a little more—or at least at more frequent intervals."

"We can do with two a day," Macy said. "Can't we, Marce?"

"Sure."

"You're both underweight," Tala objected.

Graham backed her up. "You two and Bang get three meals until we see how things go. Fine. Now, Tala, back to the couch. I'll get you a paper and pencil and the girls can call out to you what supplies we have so you can start planning meals. We can do this if we work together."

The twins looked eager to help out. "Make sure she doesn't do too much and get that fever up again," Graham added. "If you get too tired, take a nap, Tala. We're going to need you healthy and well."

They all got up from the old table and went about their plans for the day. None of them needed to be told that their days would be filled with work to survive—child or adult. Graham checked the woodpile on his way out to the shed for the fishing poles and realized he had a daily chore ahead of him each evening.

Graham decided that in a few days they'd try to go into town and scavenge for more winter clothing, food, and any other supplies they could find. Right now they all needed a break, including himself. Having them all walking around in a daze of exhaustion could only be dangerous. They needed a little time to get over the shock of the way things were now. But somehow Graham wasn't sure he ever would.

He so very much wished his father were here to tell him what to do and alert him to dangers he could not foresee. He knew there were many, and he felt ill prepared for so much responsibility resting on his shoulders.

The ax fell again with another thud onto the pine log. Graham noticed a bead of sweat now dripped off the end of his nose. He removed his shirt to keep the laundry down. The afternoon had been warm for this time of year, but Graham preferred it to the chilly autumn winds that were the norm.

He took advantage of it from dawn to dusk to get as much outside work done as possible. He felt like he was in a race. Just as the squirrels were collecting nuts, Graham too was trying to outrun the coming winter.

They had fished for several days now, with a decent haul. They'd even shot a brown-eyed buck with chestnut fur. The ladies proved very efficient in breaking down the meat. Tala taught the girls everything from domestic affairs to proper handgun safety, and they were willing students.

She had drawn up a design for a smokehouse like the one her father had, and the men had made quick work out of the wood scraps to put it together. The meat that did not fit the tiny freezer made its way into the smoker.

Macy turned out to be quite a good shot with the pistol, and Ennis devised a harness out of the seatbelts in Tala's Escort to fit the girl's small frame, so she and Tala were armed wherever they went.

In fact, Ennis turned out to have quite a few useful skills. He could fish with the patience of a saint, when he finally made his way down the long narrow trail between the pines to the lake below, and often took Bang along to teach him all his tricks. Ennis carried a pocketknife and showed the boy how to whittle more arrows from soft pine branches and he made him a quiver to hold them all, since Graham's childhood quiver was pretty beat up and wouldn't last long. Bang used his newly acquired knife and watched the old man intently. In the evenings, Ennis was often observed sitting by the woodstove in what was now "his" chair, working on what Graham thought must be a larger bow for the boy.

Tala's fever subsided, and her strength grew a little every day. She knew the children needed her, and she had found a new purpose in them. One day she told Graham quietly that if it had not been for them, she would not have made the effort. Marcy had told Tala about the events that took place with Campos, and though Tala was thankful nothing more happened to the girl, she understood why the child was so upset by the incident. Smiling, she explained to Graham that while the twins were physically identical, their expressions and natures revealed quite separate identities. Where Marcy was obstinate and bossy at times, Macy was obedient and brave. They each carried themselves differently, and because of that, they were easy to tell apart.

Bang, on the other hand, was very quiet and quite shy of Tala. Graham told her about how he came to be with the boy. "He feels closer to you, and for good reason," she said during that conversation. "I might also remind him too much of his mother. Poor little guy. He's lucky to have you."

"I'm lucky to have him."

"Even when you're so exhausted you can hardly move?" Tala asked him. "You still feel like that when he nudges you to take the time to play with him?"

"Yeah." Graham smiled. "Even then. Maybe *especially* then. It's good to be reminded that kids haven't changed their basic natures and their needs remain the same."

No one ever made conditions on the bunkroom. They just naturally separated into the boys' section on the right and the girls' on the left. A similar tacit understanding came regarding the rest of the household chores; if something needed to be done, one of them would just pitch in without being asked.

Graham often wished Bang could grow up a few years, all of a sudden. Being the only able-bodied male around, he found life difficult as the days went by. He finally decided that Macy would have to give up domestic life and help him chop wood.

Tonight he thought he would bring it up, along with their scavenging trip into town. He could hear old Ennis and the boy coming up the trail with Sheriff. Ennis was toting a string of what looked like perch and bass and, not surprisingly, Bang came running up holding a rabbit by the ears. Dinner would be good again tonight. It was nice that the old man could do the fishing right now, because come colder weather, Graham didn't think Ennis would be able to stray far from the cabin's warmth to hunt. And Ennis going fishing gave Graham more time to get things done around the cabin before the first snowfall.

"Looks like a nice haul, guys," Graham said as he wiped the sweat from his face with his shirt. Bang beamed at the praise.

"He done it all. That boy's a natural huntsman!" Ennis said.

"I only caught one of the fish," Bang corrected.

Ennis stared at Graham. "You got to get some help with that," he said, pointing at the woodpile. "You can't do it all by yourself, you'll kill yourself doin' that. What good you be then?"

"I know, Ennis, I was just thinking the same thing," Graham said, raising a sweaty hand to stop Ennis's lecture. "We'll talk about it at dinner." Then he split the block of wood into two pieces and tossed them onto the pile behind him.

After Ennis and the boy had gone to clean their catch, Macy emerged from the doorway and brought a glass of water to Graham. "Tala said you need to drink this."

"Thanks, Macy. What are you doing in there?"

"Tala and Marcy are doing the laundry and I just finished packing the last of the smoked deer meat, like you showed me."

"That's great, kiddo. Do you think you could work outside with me for a while?"

She looked at the woodpile. "Working inside all day drives me crazy. I'd *love* to help you."

"Great. Help me stack this wood and I'll even teach you how to handle the ax," He pulled up several blocks he'd cut from a downed tree with a chainsaw from the shed. Graham showed her how to alternate the stacks, and though they didn't have any gloves that would fit her small hands, she didn't complain at the splinters she got.

As Macy tossed another chunk onto the pile, Graham heard the single loud shot from behind the cabin. He grabbed his weapon, Macy pulled hers, and they ran.

By the time they had arrived, they saw a cougar lying partly on the boy. Had Ennis hesitated, Bang would surely be dead now. The big cat had sprung on the boy and pinned him face forward to the ground. Ennis simply raised the rifle and shot it in the chest, dropping it instantly.

"Oh, shit!" Graham said, reaching down to pull Bang, who struggled from the weight of the cat, to climb out from beneath it.

"Damned cat. I hate cats," said Ennis, spitting.

By that time the ladies in the house had come around the corner. Their eyes went wide as they saw for themselves what had taken place. Bang had several deep scratches on his back and skull, though nothing serious; he was scared more than anything. Graham pulled him up and the boy buried his head into Graham's neck, trying not to cry. "It's okay, Bang. You're all right," Graham said as he held him tightly, trying to convince himself as well. He and the boy had come a long way together.

Tala came up and patted him. "Let's get you cleaned up, Bang." Graham handed him over to her. Tala held the boy's hand and took him inside to tend to his wounds—both inside and out.

The others stared down at the massive cat and Macy broke the silence first. "Can we eat it?" she asked.

Graham, who was holding his hand over his heart trying to calm its beating, burst into laughter at the practical question and, after a moment, so did the old man and girls.

"God, that was lucky, Ennis. Good shot. Thank you," Graham said. He felt awful for not being there when it happened.

"It was so fast, I didn't even think. I guess I still got what it takes," Ennis said, looking up at Graham. They all laughed again at their near miss and good fortune.

"You girls go ahead and pull that cat over here," Graham directed. "Macy, I'm real proud of you for whipping out your pistol like that," he said, patting her on the head. "That was good. Now you girls can see why it's so important to be cautious. Someone's life could depend on it," he added.

Marcy nodded solemnly and picked up one of the cat's big paws, avoiding its claws, still warm from life. She helped Macy attempt to drag the heavy animal over to Graham's ready butcher knife. Together they could barely budge it. Graham let them struggle with it a while and then jumped in to help them. This was real life now, and they needed to adjust to it.

Meanwhile, Tala washed the boy's wounds with soap and water; though they weren't too deep, she knew cat wounds could easily become infected. He was silent, but she talked to him anyway and tried to soothe his fears. She asked him about the medallion he wore around his neck. He didn't answer her when she asked if it had been his mother's.

After an awkward silence he finally asked her, "Did you have children before?"

She stopped her ministrations and looked at the boy. "No, but I was a teacher and I miss those children very much." She patted the scratches dry and added antibiotic ointment to each one, all the while thinking how very lucky the boy had been. She looked at the torn green flannel shirt that he'd worn night and day since this all began and said, "We need to find you a new shirt."

"I have another one in my backpack," he said. She helped him down off the counter and he disappeared around the corner to the bunkroom.

Tala was glad to have made a little headway with him, and now that the ice was broken, she hoped they could talk more freely. She went back into the kitchen and began stirring the deer meat chili she was preparing for their dinner.

Soon Graham and the others brought in the cougar meat, ready to be processed.

"You know that predator animals have to be treated differently, right?" she asked Graham. By the look on his face, she didn't think he knew what she was talking about. "They carry the trichinosis parasites, so we have to cook it thoroughly, with no pink center. We can slice it into steaks and freeze it for now," she said loudly. Her intention was to educate them all about the danger.

It had been several days now since they had found themselves together at the cabin and they had already settled into an easy and predictable routine with one another. Without saying much, they each paired off and began slicing up the freshly cleaned cougar meat into piles as Ennis helped Bang put them into bags and wrap them tightly into bundles.

Once they were done, Graham guessed there were about sixty pounds of meat there. The small freezer was already full, so they made room in the little refrigerator that was mostly empty, turning down the temperature to accommodate the new load. Bang closed the door on the fridge. "It was going to eat me. Now, we're going to eat it!"

Tala ruffled his straight, shiny hair. "Yes. Confusing, isn't it? But that's the way things are, Bang. I'd rather we eat the cougar than have to think about it eating you."

Bang managed a wobbly smile at Tala's words and sidled closer to Graham.

"Tomorrow," Graham said, "we're going on our first scavenger hunt. We need a deep freezer, if we can get our hands on one; ammo and winter clothing too."

They cleaned up the mess they'd made, and then Tala served the chili. Since it was later than usual, and with the unexpected work on the cougar, they were hungrier than they normally would be. They continued to discuss the things they'd like to find the next day, creating a wish list. They agreed that Ennis and Sheriff would stay behind to keep an eye on the cabin since, Ennis was an old man and slow to get around. Ennis pretended to be offended, but he understood.

~ ~ ~

That night Graham tucked Bang into bed and hugged the boy. Graham's guilt rose up again. He vowed once more to guard this little boy who'd been placed in his care.

As he snuggled Bang down and stroked his hair, Graham heard a soft sob come from the other end of the bunkroom and saw that Macy was sniffling. He said goodnight to Bang and walked over to the girls. "What's going on?" he asked.

"It's just . . . we're being . . . too *normal*," Macy said with tears running down her cheeks. A little confused by her statement, Graham looked over at her sister for an explanation.

Shaking her head, Marcy said, "She misses Mom and Dad, and this feels too much like summer camp to her. She sort of feels like maybe tomorrow we'll go home."

Graham sat on the edge of Macy's bed and almost banged his head on the bunk above. He reached over, smoothed his hand over her back, and said, "I feel the same way, kid. We all do." Both girls looked up at him. "I think any minute my dad is going to walk through the front door there with his red plaid shirt on, carrying in the trout he just plucked out of the lake, and ask if I want to have a beer with him out on the porch. We did that a lot when we were here. I miss him terribly."

"Our mom and dad were divorced, but they talked about getting back together," Marcy said. Graham remembered the grisly scene he had discovered in their dad's apartment, and the woman who had perished with him. He doubted the girls' hopes had been destined to come true, but he wasn't about to say anything. Instead, he asked, "Did your dad ever take you girls fishing?"

"No, but Grandpa did," Macy said. She was calm now, and Graham thought that perhaps they needed to remember those they'd lost. Maybe, after all, it was best to talk about them and remember their lives. Keeping it all bottled up was causing them more pain and suffering.

"You know what I think we should do?" Graham asked. The twin pairs of blue eyes were on him, questioning. "I think we should have a night after dinner around the woodstove once a week where we remember them all. Talk about what they did, stories we remember about them," he said.

"I don't even know what day of the week it is," Marcy said. Graham agreed that that was a problem, and they vowed to add to their wish list a calendar when they went scavenging the next day. That way they could keep track of birthdays and holidays, too—especially in case Graham's calendar watch quit working.

"Is there anything else I can do for you girls, besides making it all go away? I would if I could, you know that, but I can't."

"No, Graham, you've done so much for us already. Thank you for making me feel better," Macy said.

Graham patted her shoulder and then Marcy's. "Anytime, kiddos." He turned to Marcy. "How's your leg doing?"

"It's much better. Tala's been taking care of it and I'm still taking the antibiotic," she said.

"Well, your face sure looks better now that you're past the green phase, Graham teased. "In a few more days, no one will be able to tell the difference between you two and you'll start playing tricks on us all."

Marcy smiled, and Graham thought it was perhaps the first time he'd really seen her do it. Where smiling came easily to Macy, it did not to Marcy.

When Graham emerged from the bunkroom, Tala was drying the last dish from dinner. "Are all your children tucked in?" Tala asked him.

"Well, they're yours too. I thought this was a group effort," he said.

"Of course, I'm happy to help. You're a kind man, Graham. I heard what you said to the girls, and I think it's a good idea, what you suggested. You'd have made a wonderful father, just as you make a good leader for our little pack." Tala smiled. "We're lucky to have you."

He saw her throat choke up as she swallowed. "I miss my husband terribly, and know if he'd survived, you two would have been great friends."

Graham went to put another log into the woodstove. Tala finished cleaning up the kitchen and went into the living room to join him. She curled up on the couch with a cup of hot chamomile tea and watched Graham staring into the flames.

"You know, I was talking to the girls today, and we are going to need to find some feminine hygiene products, quickly," she said in a whisper.

"Aw, man, that's all we need," Graham said. "That's your department, by the way." He leaned back against the couch and moved stiffly with his sore, overworked muscles. Tala put down her mug and asked him if she could massage his shoulders.

"Yeah, but only in the we-are-just-friends-in-a-postapocalyptic-world way," he said.

Tala smiled at his joke and began kneading Graham's sore muscles. "I miss him so much," she confided.

"Your husband?"

"Yes, of course," she said. "I would do this for him after dinner and he would moan and carry on—very silly. I miss that man."

"I can see why he did," Graham said, feeling her fingers work his tired muscles. "I'm stifling the moans." After a few minutes, he couldn't help it anymore. "God, that feels good," he finally said. And then Nelly sprung into his mind. "I met Nelly in college. She was a teacher too," he added.

"Oh, where did she attend?" she asked.

"Pacific Lutheran in Tacoma," he said.

"I went there too and did my student teaching at Carver Elementary," she said, and added, "I don't remember a Nelly, though."

"Actually, her name is—*was*—was Nelson," Graham said, having a difficult time with the past tense.

Tala stopped massaging. "Did she have shoulder-length red hair?"

"Yes!" Graham twisted around and looked at her.

"Oh, my God! I knew her. We were in a few classes together. She was a year ahead of me."

The amazement of sharing a link like this brought pain to Graham's eyes, pain he saw reflected in hers.

"She was pregnant too, Tala," he said, lowering his head to his knees, shutting his eyes, trying to erase his terrible last image of her—dying—from his mind. He replaced it with the one he cherished of her smiling, on one of the rare days in Seattle where the sun beamed and the evergreens gleamed an emerald shade. They had taken advantage of it, strolling to the park that day, her round tummy already disturbing her balance. Graham had spread a blanket down and they lay down reading and dozing all afternoon. He tried to keep that memory in the forefront.

"Tell me what you remember of her, please," he said.

"Nelson was a wonderful person. I remember her infectious laugh so well. You always knew it was her if you heard it from a distance, and she loved the kids. Some people become teachers for all the time off. Everyone knew she did it for her love of the children. She was just that kind of person. Even the most difficult ones seemed to melt in her presence. She just had a way of getting through to them. I'm so sorry that you and the world lost her, Graham."

The door creaked open and Ennis and Sheriff entered, letting some of the cool air seep into the room.

"Getting colder out there," Ennis said as he carried his rifle and the bow he currently worked on.

"You making headway on that one?" Graham asked him.

"Yep, it's for one of those girls in there," Ennis said.

"I'm sure they'll like it. Where did you learn to do that?" Tala asked.

"I didn't. I just took that boy's little bow and used it to model this one. Just made it bigger, that's all," Ennis said. "I've been carving, whittling something, mostly figurines, since my pa gave me a knife. He taught me how once, years ago," Ennis added.

"You should teach Bang and the girls too," Tala said.

"This boy already knows. He makes his own arrows now," Ennis said.

"Yeah, we need to teach them everything we can," Graham said. Who knows what will happen to them? I was thinking about that this afternoon before the cougar attack. Hell, we need to learn things ourselves, but this is an entirely new world for these kids."

"Not only that, we all need to learn how to start growing a garden. I don't think we'll find too many vegetables through this winter that we got coming."

Ennis was right. "That's for sure. Maybe we'll at least come across some canned vegetables tomorrow." Graham added that to his mental wish list as Sheriff came over and sat next to him on the floor. "How you doing, boy?" he asked as he scratched the dog under the collar.

"That dog's got it together more than we do," Ennis said.

Tala nodded. "He sure started growling before Marcy and I ever heard the gunshot this afternoon."

"He's a keeper," Ennis said. "Goodnight, kids, this old man gots to get some sleep."

"I'm right behind you, Ennis," said Graham.

The next morning Ennis waved good-bye as the group left him and Sheriff behind. Sheriff moaned a little at their departure, clearly wanting to go along. "What's the matter with you—I'm not good company?" Ennis asked the dog.

Sheriff stomped his front paws, agitated that he wasn't invited on the ride.

"It's all right, we'll go get us some fish," Ennis said, and they wandered off down the trail with Sheriff casting a look back to where the others had gone, clearly worried.

Ennis had already pulled in two trout when he saw the canoe. Like any old man who'd made it this far, even without an apocalypse to contend with his eyes weren't very good. So he figured it'd been there for a while before he'd even noticed the thing, breaking its way across the far end of the lake. There were two men paddling. Both appeared bearded, which wasn't unusual these days, but they also looked fat, and that was quite unusual. Not only that, but something about them triggered Ennis's long-buried cop intuition. That was a bad thing.

Sheriff came up beside him and stared out into the distance as he tried to smell them. As if he sensed Ennis's apprehension, the dog's hackles rose and he growled low and ominously.

Sheriff looked up questioningly at Ennis, and Ennis knew he wanted an answer. "Those some bad guys." As if they'd heard his conversation with the dog, one of the two occupants of the canoe raised his hand in recognition, like one would do in the old days. Ennis did not raise his hand back, hoping they'd get the message that they were unwelcome. He was uneasy about them, but couldn't say just why. They continued on their route to the other end of the lake, but Ennis thought it wasn't good, those guys knowing he and the rest were there. Still, he continued to bait his line and cast it out from his spot on the shore, tossing a too-small trout back into the water while Sheriff waded out to watch it squiggle under the water until it faded into the murky depths.

~ ~ ~

Graham stopped the Scout outside the post office and checked for predators before he got out. The door jingled from a bell attached to the handle, now a bygone symbol, alerting those no longer in the back to customers waiting for service. It sounded strangely out of place here in this time. Somehow, he still expected to hear a disembodied voice call out, "I'll be right there."

His boots made a foreign sound now on the tiled flooring. He looked at the wall of tiny brass mailbox doors and knew all the previous owners were gone now. He stood still and listened for a minute but heard nothing and smelled only a musty odor. He looked around for any sign of the boy from Carnation but found none. The main door to the postmaster's counter was locked, and Graham didn't see any reason to break it open. He could see through the glass, and what lay beyond held no use for them.

He walked out, having forgotten to check before he opened the door and saw Tala frantically pointing out the window, trying to get his attention. Before he turned his head, he heard what they were concerned about.

Graham could only later describe the sound like a "gruffling" for the loss of any better word. The sight was much more horrific than the sound though, which froze Graham in his spot. Hoping the bear was as unaware of him as he'd been of it, he moved slowly to his truck door, opened it quietly, and jumped in.

Tala had made Bang and the girls get down on the truck's floorboards to stay out of sight. Graham caught her gaze and shared with her the horror of watching the carnage as the bear gnawed at a long dead human, pawing at the old corpse and spreading its spoiled entrails around the sidewalk. It apparently had dragged the individual out of what was once the corner market.

"Can we go?" Marcy asked in a small but clearly agitated voice. Graham suspected she'd looked, despite Tala's attempt at protecting the kids.

"You bet," he said, and made sure his door was locked before he started the engine, quickly putting it into reverse and moving on.

The bear never looked in their direction, being too invested in his current prize.

Somehow, a week of the relative safety of the cabin had made them forget just how bad it was in the real world. They certainly had their own dangers there, like the prowling cougar, but having not encountered a dead body in more than a week, Graham had allowed himself to relax into a false sense of security on the issue of dead flesh and the creatures that desired it.

It didn't take them long to get to the first house they were going to scavenge for useful things. Their earlier, jovial mood had been sunk by the bear incident, so now they were each a little on edge, but Graham had a feeling that it should be that way, anyway; too much complacency and they would slip up and lose someone through carelessness.

Cascade was a tiny town with only a market and a post office, surrounded by the downtrodden remnants of a long-gone logging industry. Its glory days had been way back during the gold rush and even then, due to the rough terrain, the town didn't get much traffic. The last decade had brought in a little more wealth in terms of campers and nature seekers, but it remained nothing more than an insignificant town—*town* being the loosest of terms.

Graham had planned to take a look at the first house next to the post office and work his way around, but in light of this recent event he adjusted his tactic. Instead, they drove to the farthest point away from the bear and started at what was once the check-in office of the campground. They hoped to get hold of some first aid supplies, especially bandages, as theirs were dwindling.

The campground office door was clearly knocked off its hinges and hanging partway into the shabby building. Graham remembered attending summer camp here, swimming in the lake, and once or twice he'd come into this building as a boy with a scraped knee or some other ailment. He looked around for signs of danger, and then stepped out of the truck and over to the entrance. The smell hit him first, causing him to wince. Someone had been inside this place. That's when he noticed the bloody handprints dried on the walls, as if someone had been clinging to the doorframe as he or she was dragged out by the feet. The hairs on the back of Graham's neck stood on end. Someone had met a violent end here, and it gave the whole place a very creepy feeling.

He scouted around outside the small building and didn't see a dead body anywhere, so he wondered where the horrid stench was coming from. He went back in and pushed the flimsy door in midway; it teetered at an odd angle, attached by only one hinge.

The place had already been ransacked. Papers and useless material cluttered the floor and counter. Then he heard a loud buzzing. Flies; a huge abundance of them. Though the weather had grown cooler, they'd certainly found a haven in here. He peeked in farther and saw what was left of a body. He couldn't tell if it was male or female, but the thing he did know was that this was a recent kill. This person had been alive in the past week and had not likely died from the virus. It was obvious that animals had taken their share. If Graham hadn't had already been unnerved, he certainly was now. He wheeled around and vomited at the side of the building and as quickly as possible went back to the truck.

The kids looked even more scared now, and Tala looked at him inquiringly. "There's a dead body in there. It smells pretty bad and the place has already been ransacked," Graham said.

"Do you think there's someone else here?" Tala asked.

"If there is, I don't want to meet him," he said.

"There's more, but I don't think I should say. We'll talk about it later," he said, gesturing to the back. "I think we should make our way back and start closer to home."

Tala nodded; the prior enthusiasm in the truck had already been diminished by the bear, and even more so with this incident.

Graham knew what his gut was telling him, but he wasn't prepared for another Campos; that is what he feared most beyond wild animals.

They all kept a look out for anything unusual that lurked about, but everything about Cascade seemed much like the desolate towns they had driven through on their way here. Cascade had the dreaded bonus of bear activity, however.

They drove through the loop of the small town and looked at the houses along the way for signs of break-ins. A few stood with opened front doors that they hadn't noticed before. They wouldn't bother to check those, but drove farther out to the road by the turn-off, the way they'd come in.

Graham rolled down his window to listen as they slowly rolled up to a home on the outskirts of town. They drove along the graveled drive and parked behind a maroon Chevy truck. "If we can find the keys, it might be a useful truck to take back," Graham said to Tala.

"Yeah, the open bed could come in handy to haul more. We have limited space in this thing," she said.

Graham looked around for predators; this was becoming a much stronger habit now. The large house, set back at the end of the long driveway, was more secluded than most. The lime green exterior with white trim harked back a couple of decades or more, as did the split-level design. The place appeared to be well kept. The green front lawns and numerous trees, including a monkey tree located as a hallmark in the center of the front lawn, showed signs of someone who really enjoyed yard maintenance. He could see part of a swing set in the backyard, nicely maintained, with pea gravel bedding and railroad ties bordering the play area.

"Great—kids," he said under his breath, and caught Tala's look of sympathy.

"All right, guys, this is what we're going to do. Tala, you cover me. I'll go up to the door and try to peek in to see if everything looks okay, and then I'll motion for you to come in," Graham said. "Make sure you bring your weapons with you." He thought for a second how ironic it was that, in such a short time, he'd begun urging children to use guns.

"Tala will walk you guys in. Bring the bags and boxes with you. If you see any people, hide and let me handle things. If you see any animals, yell. Understood?"

They all said that they did, and Graham looked around once more and wondered if this was such a good idea after all. Maybe they would just make do with what they had, because this wasn't worth losing someone. He decided this would be the only house they checked out today because a suspicion that there were other people in town continued to prey on his nerves.

So far, this morning had carried a blanket of mist, which the lazy sun was just now beginning to burn off. There was a faint odor of what might be spoiled food inside the home and he guessed it would be stronger once the door was opened. He walked past the truck and tried the door handle just in case it was unlocked. It wasn't.

Graham moved slowly up the stairs and knocked, feeling foolish, but in case someone was home he didn't want to get shot at. No one answered, so he tried the door and found that it was locked too. He peered into the side window by the door and could see through the sheer drapes into the living area. From what he could see, it looked tidy enough. Across the room he spotted a sliding glass door through the dining area. He descended the steps and went around back, up a long wooden staircase, and onto the back porch. He looked inside the tidy and well-kept home and saw no living thing apparent. He tried the slider and it moved open a few inches, so he listened for any reaction and heard none as he continued to open it.

Graham walked onto the rug of the dining room and saw that not only was the kitchen sparkling clean, without a dish in the sink, but a dining table before him was laid out with dishes on placemats and cloth napkins artistically looped through rings. He closed the door and wiped his feet on the doormat, then thought himself foolish for being so polite as he stepped on the vinyl flooring.

With his rifle ready, Graham quietly looked around the wall that led to the living area, and then followed the hallway that led to the laundry and bathroom combo, where he found the keys to the truck and house neatly displayed on wooden pegs. Then he went out to the two-car garage. A man hung there, dangling from a rope tied to a rafter. There was a pool of liquid that had spread under the overturned stepladder the poor soul had kicked aside. He saw a note pinned to the fellow's shirt. Holding his breath, he approached closer, pulled the note off the body, and took it back out with him into the light of the bathroom.

To whoever finds me:

My wife Camille, son Jacob, and daughter Emily died of the China Pandemic. I find I cannot live without them. Whoever finds me, please bury me with my family in the back. I already dug the hole, so just drop me in there. In exchange, please take whatever you need. May God be with you.

Marvin Chandler

Graham wondered how many other people had done the same. He himself had considered suicide after Nelly died, but his dad had made him promise. Now Graham thought that might have been too much to ask of a man, and he could see this fellow must have thought the same.

He closed the curtains on the sliding glass doors to block the view of the backyard, then walked over to the front door and left it open, letting the others know everything checked out. He motioned for them to come in and, after looking around for predators or other dangers, they closed the doors of the truck silently and moved toward the house.

"I have to do something in the garage and yard first, but you guys go ahead and start packing. Don't come out there, though, and leave the curtains closed; we don't want to attract any attention—from bears or anyone else. It'll probably take me about twenty minutes, and then we need to get out of here."

Tala didn't question him and closed the door behind the kids. He headed out back to the garage and saw a big orange wheelbarrow loaded with a shovel, hacksaw, and gray tarp situated by the door leading to the backyard, all at the ready.

"Made it as easy as he could," Graham muttered underneath his breath. He felt an obligation to honor the man's wishes, and at least now it didn't feel like he was stealing the man's belongings.

He moved the wheelbarrow over to the body and righted the ladder, then unfolded the tarp under the body and grabbed the hacksaw. As best he could, he positioned the wheelbarrow beneath the hanging man and cut the rope; the corpse fell into the sturdy wheelbarrow in a heap. The stench of rotting flesh became overpowering and Graham rushed to the back door to let in some fresh air. He vomited again, then tried to take some of the unspoiled damp air into his lungs. As he was bent over he heard a meowing, and saw a thin and dirty white cat with blue eyes staring up at him.

Graham decided it must have belonged to the family. He scratched the cat behind the ears, but it continued to meow at him, clearly hungry. He left the door open to air the garage out and walked over to the stairs leading to the back porch to open the slider. The cat followed him and ran inside the house.

"Awww . . ." Marcy said and stopped taking cans out of the pantry to come over to the cat.

"We can't keep it, so don't even ask," Graham said.

"Sheriff would eat it," said Bang.

"Maybe not," Marcy interjected.

"Look, see if there's any cat food around. It must have been the owner's. Feed it and let it back out. It's a miracle it's survived this long anyhow," he said. Graham then whispered to Tala, "I have to bury someone out back. Keep the kids from looking if you can."

"Sure, no problem. Can we start loading up the truck while you're busy?" she asked.

"No, just start putting stuff inside the front door. I want to make sure the coast is clear," he said.

Before he could go back to the garage to finish his task, Macy spoke up and said, "Check it out, Graham, I found a calendar!" She displayed it with a wave not unlike like Vanna White's on *Wheel of Fortune*. He smiled and returned to his grim business.

Graham had his gun slung around his back as usual, and he wheeled the corpse out to where the open grave waited. He looked into the hole; other than rainwater and a few fallen leaves, it was clear. He really didn't have time to make it a more noble procedure, and he didn't think the guy expected that anyway. It wasn't difficult. He tipped the corpse, tarp and all, into the grave and began shoveling the mound of dirt over the man.

Afterward he was sweaty, so Graham rubbed his shirtsleeve across his face. Somehow, the smell still lingered. He wondered when this would come to an end, this staring at graves.

He put the shovel back into the wheelbarrow and walked it back into the garage. He went inside, washed his soil-covered hands, and saw the water turn gray and then clear again.

As Graham went back into the garage he noticed a small white Kenmore freezer next to the door to the kitchen and was surprised he'd missed it, since he'd walked right by it when he first came in.

Bang, with big eyes, came out to the garage and wrinkled his nose at the smell, but all he said was, "There are lots of guns on the bed upstairs, with bullets too."

Graham smiled at him and nodded. "That's great. Good find, buddy. I'll take a look at them, but there's a freezer here I need to get loaded into the new truck. Tell Macy to come give me a hand."

Tala came out to the garage to help Graham instead. Even though Graham had left the back door open, the smell caught her off guard and her eyes started to water.

They pulled the spoiled meat from inside the freezer. The power was currently on, but it must have gone off for a time because the food inside looked like it had thawed and refrozen. Ice cream had melted onto the bottom and mixed with crystallized meat blood. They began dumping the cargo into one of the empty trashcans in the garage. Once the freezer was empty, Graham pulled the loaded trashcan outside and farther away from the house into the trees. They cleaned out the bottom with shop rags and then Tala used bleach and hot water from the laundry room sink to melt the refrozen liquids coating the bottom of the freezer and to sanitize it.

"This will be great for the cougar we have in the fridge," she said.

Graham began to laugh. "Did you ever think you'd hear yourself using that phrase?" Tala caught the absurdity of it, and they both laughed again.

They opened the garage door manually and manhandled the freezer, pushing and pulling it into the truck bed of the Chevy, then went back to shut and lock the garage doors.

Apparently, the now dead homeowners had been avid Costco shoppers, as were many who lived this far from a major city. There were several cases of canned green beans, corn, peaches, pears, and chili. They also found unopened twenty-five pound bags of flour, sugar, and cornmeal. This would keep them baking through the winter months, at least.

Upstairs it seemed the homeowner had thought ahead. He'd neatly laid out his two pistols and three hunting rifles onto the beige striped bedspread, along with boxes of ammunition. The walk-in closet held winter wear for both Tala and Graham. They left the pretty dresses and high heels, but took all that Tala and the girls could use, as well as all the men's clothing and winter boots. In all, it was a great find, but it cast a dark pall on their mission. They had spoken openly downstairs, but upstairs they could only formulate whispers.

In one of the children's rooms they found little girl's clothes, though too small for the twins, in a room painted a soft pink hue, but took the hairbrush sitting on the dresser. None of them wanted to disturb the stuffed animals displayed atop the white canopy bed, but they did because the blankets and pillows suited their needs, then replaced the stuffed animals carefully.

In the boy's blue room, they found several jackets, pairs of jeans, and shirts, as well as snow boots that both the twins and Bang could wear. There was a skateboard leaning against the wall, and a baseball bat and glove in the corner. They took the baseball bat—it might come in handy as a weapon—but as they had with the girl's room, they left the other things as something of a memorial.

Tala and the girls also gathered all the razors, soap, shampoo, and feminine hygiene products they could find. These last items were in great need; they could bide some time before Tala would have to help prepare the girls for a more organic way of dealing with their periods.

"It's too bad this place is too close to town, or we could just move here," Tala said.

"Yeah, but it is just not defendable, being so much in the open. At least with the cabin we have some warning if someone tries to get to us."

"We could hear them coming up the long drive," said Macy. "Our tires crunched on the gravel. I bet footsteps would, too."

"That's good thinking, Macy," Tala said, looking as impressed by the girl's statement as Graham appeared to be. "Because, really, that's what it's going to take for us all to survive here now. Thinking ahead and being cautious."

"Hurry up, now," Graham said. "Let's just take what we have and we'll come back another time to get more if we need it. It looks like it's going to rain, so let's spread a tarp over the truck bed." Graham went back into the garage, once again wincing at its powerful odor, in search of another sturdy tarp.

He found not only a tarp but also several tools he knew he'd need someday. He picked up the hacksaw he used earlier, as well as an ax, a sledgehammer, and a box of nails. Several bungee cords lay in a tangle on the work bench, and he took those too. He bypassed all the electrical tools but noticed a small metal fishing boat hanging on the wall. *That'll have to wait till later*, he thought, and hoped the locked doors would protect it until they could make it back here.

He loaded the tools and fixed the tarp over the bed of the truck and then went back into the house and let the cat out. He locked all the doors and took the house keys with him.

By the time they were finished loading, a slight drizzle grew to a steadier rain. Graham drove the Chevy with Bang as passenger, and Tala drove the Scout with the girls.

When they pulled up to the cabin Graham let Tala drive in first so as not to scare Ennis with an unfamiliar vehicle. On their approach, Ennis waited on the porch chair, with Sheriff and his rifle beside him. Smoke rose from the chimney, and Graham thought it looked like a scene from a distant past: an old man and a dog on the front porch of a cabin in the woods.

"Got a new truck, I see," Ennis said as Graham stepped out.

"Yep, everything okay here?" Graham asked.

"Mostly," Ennis said slowly, which caused Graham to raise his eyebrows.

"It can wait till later," Ennis said.

Graham knew this wasn't good news or Ennis would have spilled it right there.

They unloaded both vehicles, and Graham set up the freezer in the bunkroom, by the only other outlet in the cabin besides the one in the kitchen. He ran an extension cord under Tala's bunk to plug it in.

His grandfather had run power to the cabin back in the 1950s when Graham's dad was a boy, so the kitchen had power outlets for the refrigerator. In the past few years, his father had retrofitted the cabin with solar panels to augment the electricity and top up a large bank of storage batteries kept in a shed out back. Graham hoped the load of both appliances wouldn't drain the reserve batteries too quickly. He still planned to drag the larger freezer outside during the winter.

Tala said that the inside of the freezer was cooling nicely, so she shut the lid to let it get down to a freezing temperature before they transferred the cougar meat.

With that settled, they filled every nook and cranny with the bounty they'd brought. The items of clothing were parceled out to those they most suited, with each person storing it under his or her bed. The extra coats went into a small hall closet, and the boots were lined up by the front door, largest to smallest.

These things really didn't belong to any individual; rather, they went on an as-needed basis, and that is how things would continue to be from this time forward with the exception of a few personal mementos.

Graham could see the family photos he'd taken from the apartment for the twins nailed up between their beds. Bang kept his diary under his pillow. He'd seen the boy open it, looking intently at his mother's reflection, touching her face with the pad of his small index finger. He wore his mother's medallion around his neck at all times.

Graham kept the photos from his father's house in a tote under his bed. He hadn't looked at them yet. He just couldn't bear to, though he wasn't sure why.

Tala had a locket at the end of a leather cord around her neck with a picture of her husband on one side and her father on the other. As far as Graham knew, Ennis didn't have any talisman from his past other than his pocketknife—and a handy tool it had turned out to be.

Graham could hear and smell venison strips being fried in the kitchen by Tala. The twins talked and clanked dishes as they set the table while Sheriff and Bang enjoyed a scuffle over a sock.

Anyone who looked in on this scene would believe this was a normal family drama played out daily in normal times. But these were not normal times, and they'd fallen into this routine much too easily. It worried Graham; his subconscious warned him of hidden dangers. *We're becoming too complacent. It's a trap we must not fall into, because there is nothing normal about our situation.*

"Mr. Graham," Ennis called him from the front door.

"Mr. Ennis?" Graham answered back, amused at the formal tone.

"Get out here. I need to talk to you."

Ennis's tone was more serious than Graham first anticipated, and he knew something grim was about to be discussed.

Graham stepped through the doorway and leaned his rifle against the jamb, then stretched his arms toward for the blue sky above, glad the rain had ceased. Ennis sat in the old rocker he'd found in the house and had dragged outside so he could keep an eye on the world—for what that world was worth now.

"Close the door," Ennis said, and Graham complied.

In addition to the chair, an old bench for taking off dirty boots leaned against the cabin wall. Graham planted his tired carcass upon it and leaned back.

"Something happened out by the lake while you were gone," Ennis said.

"What?"

"There's trouble across the lake."

"What do you mean?"

"Saw two no-gooders earlier," Ennis said.

Graham sat straighter, automatically checking the position of his gun. "Where'd you come across them?"

"At the lake. They went by in a canoe. Saw me, too, and waved like they were sayin', 'We know you're there.'"

Graham leaned forward and rested his elbows on his knees. "Well, did you wave back?"

"No! I ain't no fool, you know!" Ennis glared at Graham.

Graham held up his hands. "I know, Ennis, I know. But tell me more. These two guys in a canoe paddled by and waved—to *you*, right?"

"Yep."

"But you didn't wave back because . . . ?"

"Because I figure they did it as a kind of warning. They mean trouble. I'm sure of it. Like sayin', 'Hey, we know you're there, and we'll be back,'"

"Could you tell where they were going?" Graham asked.

"They was coming from this side and going to the other, about midway in the lake, when I saw 'em."

"Could have shot you from that distance?"

"Yeah, they could've," Ennis said.

"But they just waved?" Graham asked a second time because it didn't make sense to him.

"I already tol' you that!" Ennis said, sounding more than a little annoyed. "After you been a cop for as long as I have, you learn to read folks. These guys, they's up to no good."

"I know, Ennis, I'm just trying to figure it out," Graham said. "You think we're going to see more of them, then?"

"We got things they would want, ya know? We got food, cars, fuel—and women, too," Ennis said, looking more worried about the women than anything else.

The thought made Graham run his hands down his tired face. He scratched at his beard and said thoughtfully, "Inside earlier, I listened to the rest making a commotion getting dinner ready. It sounds like a real family in there. It worries me. We've adjusted well, but maybe not in the right way."

"I know. We got a mom and dad with three kids, a pops, and a dog, too, though none of us is related except them twins." Ennis let go a faintly amused smile, then added, "It could get us all killed, being too relaxed in these times, you know."

Graham nodded. "That's what I've been thinking. We need to start keeping watch. It's probably good training for these kids anyway, to keep them a little on edge and more vigilant."

"If it was me," Ennis said, "I would put an adult with one of them kids on watch in rotation night and day. One at each entrance to this place, by the lake trail, and hidden down by the drive."

Graham agreed. "It gets damn cold at night now. We should build a deer stand, hidden at each site to be safer from roaming predators, and come up with some warning calls."

"We have any radios?" Ennis asked.

"No, and the last time I checked my cell phone, there was no signal so the towers must all be out by now." Graham met Ennis's gaze, and continued. "Something else happened when we were out. I didn't tell the rest, but when we stopped at the campground building, the door had been kicked in. There were bloody handprints, like someone was dragged out of there. There was a dead body, too, but I don't think it had been there very long."

Ennis raised his shaggy white eyebrows at Graham. "That don't sound too good. Hope these two things aren't related."

"No, it doesn't sound good at all. As we drove away there were several more homes in succession that also had their doors kicked in."

"Sure hope it ain't them guys I saw." Ennis's brows drew together in a frown.

"Well, in any case, we are not alone here, that's for sure," Graham said. "So we need to take better precautions and stop treating this like a damn family vacation or we'll get ourselves killed in our sleep."

"Those children in there need a chance to grow up. We have to make it so they can," Ennis said, and Graham was glad they agreed on the important things.

Bang opened the door and told the two men that dinner was ready. "I'll keep watch," Ennis said to Graham. "You already put in a hard day's work, scavengin' and unloadin'."

Graham nodded. "I'll eat quickly, relay the news to the others, and then come relieve you."

"Sounds good to me." Ennis pulled up his rifle and laid it across his knees. After seeing the cougar, Graham pitied anyone crossing Ennis's barrel end.

Graham walked in and unconsciously stomped his boots off even though he'd not gotten them dirty. He smelled the aroma of chicken-fried venison strips, instant mashed potatoes with gravy, canned green beans, and biscuits. His stomach complained, as if to tell him to hurry the hell up to the table.

Macy passed him the biscuits, and even though they didn't have butter they were good to dredge through the white pan gravy Tala had made. Graham had almost devoured one and reached for another when Macy asked, "Where's Ennis?"

"He's keeping watch. I'll eat now and then he'll come in after," Graham said, "So let's save him a plate and several of the biscuits too. He'll like them. They're really good."

"Tala made them even though she didn't have a recipe," Macy said.

"Thank you, Graham, glad you like them." Tala turned to Macy and added, "They're not hard to make. I'll show you how to do it. So we're keeping watch now?" Tala asked, returning her gaze to Graham.

"Yes. Ennis saw two men cross the lake in a canoe today, and we don't know if they are good or bad. Not only that, but we ourselves saw several doors kicked in back in town. We need to be more vigilant. We have food, cars, and fuel that other people might want to take from us by force, so we really need to start being more careful around here. And that means each of us is going to start keeping watch, night and day."

They all stopped eating and stared at Graham with worried expressions.

"This is the way things are now. Two people will keep watch, in teams. One young person and one adult. We are going to build stands at the front and lake entrances. Understand?" he asked.

"All night, too?" Bang asked.

"Yes, even at night. Those who do the night watch will sleep during the day," Graham said.

Marcy bit her bottom lip. "What if we see something?"

"Ennis and I are trying to come up with some kind of alert system. We don't have cell phone use anymore, and so far we haven't come across any two-way radios," Graham said.

"There were some in that house, in the kitchen, above the fridge," Macy said.

"There were? Why didn't you say so?" Graham asked.

"I didn't know we needed them."

"These days those are a necessity. We'll go back for them tomorrow." Graham finished his hearty dinner so that he could switch off with Ennis before the old man's food got too cold.

Graham rose from the table and grabbed another biscuit, stuffing it into his mouth. "You"—he pointed to Tala—"must make these every day now," he said with a smile. He grabbed another, along with his rifle, and headed back to the porch.

Tala's pleased laughter followed him. "Happy to provide some enjoyment."

"You're relieved, Ennis," Graham said, opening the door.

The old man rose the way that old men rise—slowly, with soreness in their aged bones and muscles. Graham noticed the chill in the air and knew Ennis couldn't handle the colder temperatures, and it wasn't even winter yet.

He knew he'd have to take on the brunt of the night watches, but even the daytime watches would soon get unbearable for Ennis. He wished Bang were a bit older, then reminded himself he needed to stop thinking of the girls as useless when it came to outside work. Macy could be tough, and she'd proven to be a really good shot.

Graham settled down into the rocker and listened to the quiet around him. He could hear faint conversations at the dinner table. The deciduous trees scattered among the evergreens were turning brilliant shades of yellow, orange, and red. The wild grasses, having expended their chlorophyll for the season, now turned dry and brittle underfoot, paving the way for winter's arrival. Soon the snow would cover this hidden oasis—or so Graham hoped.

Tomorrow he would take Macy with him back to the supply house and retrieve the radios. With them he hoped they'd be able to practice better vigilance.

That night, Graham and Macy took their first watch after Ennis and Bang took a shorter four-hour watch because he just didn't think either could handle more than that. He positioned the girl behind the bushes, bundled her up in two coats. If she heard or saw anything alarming, she would sneak around to the cabin and alert the others. Graham positioned himself likewise and climbed up a scrawny tree to get a better view, and found watching to be boring and mundane at best but at least it gave him time to think.

~ ~ ~

In the morning, Graham watched as Macy high-fived Marcy before dragging her own tired butt up to the cabin door. He knew he wasn't the only one exhausted. Ennis and Bang were still asleep, snoring softly as Graham and Macy made their way to their own beds, pulling the covers over their heads because the dawn was beginning to show already through the windows.

When Graham awoke a few hours later, he saw Macy still sleeping, so he slipped off to the shower. When he was done he woke her so they could get their errand underway. He wanted to get the platforms built before the day was over and the night watch began.

While Macy was in the shower, Graham wandered into the dining room, where Tala handed him a cup of steaming black coffee.

"This is going to be an adjustment for all of us," she said.

"You don't look so perky yourself," he said.

"Well, Marcy scared me to death last night. I'm surprised you didn't wake up. I heard her call out, and I ran over there to find her trying to climb up a madrone tree; a raccoon had scared her." Graham choked a bit on his coffee at the thought.

They were both chuckling as Macy came out of the bathroom. "What's so funny?" she asked.

"Oh, nothing much, but ask your sister about raccoons when you see her," Graham said, then turned his attention back to Tala. "Who's where right now?"

"Marcy is taking her turn fishing with Bang on watch there, and Ennis is by the entrance," she said.

"Okay, that's good." Tala had made more biscuits, and Graham went to grab one. She wrapped several in a cloth napkin and handed it to him as Graham went out onto the porch to enjoy his breakfast, waiting for Macy to be ready.

The morning mist gave way to blue skies, just like the day before. They took the new truck and drove slowly with the windows down, listening and watching for anything to move as the dirt road gave way to pavement. At one point Macy held up her hand to alert Graham to stop as a parade of four turkeys crossed in front of them without any sense of haste, puffing their black and white feathers out and displaying their bright red neck waddles as they crossed to the other side and disappeared into the brush.

"Should we go after them?" Macy asked.

"Not today, but we will soon. A couple of turkeys could feed us for a week. My mother used to save the turkey carcasses after Thanksgiving and then boil them to make broth. We just have to be careful not to take too many of them at once."

As he pulled up the long gravel driveway, Graham half expected the paperboy to pedal by and toss a bundle at his feet. That's how normal everything felt here now, and he had to find a way to reconcile this vision with their current circumstances.

He listened for any potential danger, and then waved for Macy to join him. They unlocked the door and he had Macy keep watch at the window while he went into the kitchen to retrieve the two-way radios. It was quiet in there—too quiet, unlike the other day when they'd all been busy scavenging.

Graham opened the cupboard and saw the radios right away. These weren't the cheap toy models either. Probably a Costco find. There were three units, perfect for their current needs. He also grabbed the charger base just as he heard Macy scream, "Graham!"

He dropped everything, pulled up his rifle, and ran for her. He found her staring out the corner of the window, trying to be inconspicuous, "Come here," she waved frantically.

He looked out the window and saw an old camo-painted army jeep parked in the street at the end of the long driveway. One man dressed in a dark blue hazmat suit with a respirator got out of the driver's seat and stood guard, while the passenger, also in a hazmat suit and respirator, exited and moved to the back gate of the vehicle.

"What the hell?"

As they watched through the window, the man in the back struggled with something. Macy turned the deadbolt, as if that would help against an intrusion. The driver could clearly see Graham and Macy, but made no motion to do anything but guard the jeep as the other man emerged from the back of it carrying a body, zip-tied at the hands and feet and with a black sack tied over its head. The captive person struggled.

"Shit!" Graham said.

"What are they doing?" Macy asked.

"I don't know, honey," he said.

The man carried the uncooperative body with some difficulty. He walked partway up the grassy yard and laid the body on its side while the driver aimed his weapon in their direction. The other man pulled out what looked like a note and held it up for Graham to see, then dropped it on the body and walked away. They sped off quickly. By the time Graham got down the long drive, there was no sign of them.

He knelt by the body and untied the black bag over the head, pulling it off, revealing a blond teenage boy struggling against the gag still in his mouth. When Graham tried to help him, the youth jerked away as much as the ties would let him. Fear flared in his brown eyes.

"I'm not going to hurt you," Graham said.

The boy shook his head violently from side to side and pulled back again, tears forming in his eyes.

Graham pulled out his pocketknife and grabbed the back of the boy's head, shoving it forward to release the gag.

With bruising on his cheeks and bloodshot eyes, the young man had clearly been beaten.

"Are you a prepper?" he asked Graham as soon as he was able. His lips were cracked and bleeding, making it difficult for him to be understood. His mouth was probably dry as a bone, too.

"What? A prepper? No," Graham said, reaching for the note when he heard Macy approaching.

"Stay back, Macy," he said. "Just wait there."

He opened the note and read it aloud:

We took this boy after accidently killing the man he was with. He's a carrier, like you all. We cannot keep him with us, and are making a goodwill gesture by turning him over to you. In return, we expect you to adhere to the boundaries on the attached map marking our territories. One encounter will kill us all. We have voted to let you live, but one act of defiance and we will exterminate all of you.

D. H., President, Cascade Prepper Assoc.

Graham folded the note, put it into his jacket pocket, and reached for the boy's hand with the pocketknife. When he flinched away again, Graham said, "Now look, I'm trying to untie you, all right?"

After the boy's arms had been freed, Graham helped him bring them around to the front. He knew the boy's muscles must ache from struggling against the restraints. He cut the ankle bindings.

"Can you stand?" he asked him.

"I don't know. My legs are really weak."

"What's your name?"

"What's *yours*?" the boy shot back.

Macy came around before Graham could answer and said, "Look, kid, he's trying to help you. Don't be such a loser."

"It's okay, Macy," Graham said to her.

"Mark. My name's Mark."

"How old are you, Mark?"

"Sixteen."

Graham touched his cheek. "Did those guys hurt you?"

"No, not really. I tried to untie myself and fell face first on the floor of the shack they had me in."

"Did they feed you?" Graham asked while he and Macy helped Mark to the truck.

"Once a day they gave me an MRE. They said it was all they could spare," Mark said.

"How'd they come across you?" Graham asked.

Mark lowered his head, breathing hard, and Graham saw that he was trying not to cry.

"Macy, go in the house and get those radios and the charger that goes with them," Graham said.

When she'd run back up the drive, Graham gave the boy's shoulder a comforting squeeze. Tears filled the kid's eyes.

"Mr. Bishop was the only one left here, so I stayed with him after my folks died. We saw these guys coming door to door one night from across the street and they were wearing blue hazmat suits. Mr. Bishop, he shot at one of them but missed. I told him not to, but he didn't listen. The one guy shot him. He was standing right beside me!"

Graham watched with sympathy as Mark turned white at the recollection of the terrifying ordeal. Mark turned his face away.

"Was he the man I found dead in the campground office?" Graham asked.

"Yeah, that's where I dragged him and he died there on me. There was blood everywhere. I tried to stop it with my hands, but I couldn't. Then I heard the guys arguing, and they broke the door open and dragged me out of there. They blindfolded me, and the next thing I knew, was tied to a chair in a wood shack somewhere. That was at least two weeks ago. Two different people came in every day in those suits, blindfolded me, took me somewhere to do my business, and then took me back into the shack. They gave me water in a bag with a straw and an MRE thing. They made me eat all of it quick, tied me back up, put me on a cot, and left me till the next day. I heard one of them say I was a carrier and too dangerous to keep around," Mark said.

It looked to Graham as if the boy's statement drained everything out of him. It would be a while before Mark was healthy again, but he could see that he possessed an inner strength and was sure he'd be all right. He heard Macy coming up behind him. After she had put the equipment into the truck, she helped Graham walk Mark over to the cab. He practically lifted the emaciated boy into the seat and Macy stayed with him while Graham locked up the house again.

When he got back to the truck, Macy held the boy up; he was shaking from the cold. "Why'd they do this to him?" she nearly yelled.

"We are carriers of the virus, and some are still susceptible to it," Graham explained.

"They almost killed me. I could hear them arguing about doing it," Mark said through chattering teeth.

"That is the million-dollar question. Why didn't they? You were a great threat to them," Graham said as he put the truck in gear and headed back to the cabin.

~ ~ ~

They pulled up to the cabin and took the boy inside. Graham watched anger flare in Tala's dark, expressive eyes as she treated the bloody marks on Mark's wrists and ankles and expressed anger over his poor treatment. She gave him a glass of water, told him to sip it slowly. When it stayed down, she made him a cup of hot tea. A few minutes later she broke up a couple of leftover biscuits, moistened them, and fed them to him slowly. They sat him by the woodstove and piled extra blankets around him

Bang went up to him shyly and showed him his bow and arrow. Mark held it, felt the smooth wood, and smiled at the boy. He told him it was good and asked him to show him how to use it sometime.

Ennis called Graham outside to discuss the situation.

"What the hell happened to the new stray?" Ennis asked.

Graham explained in detail about the boy's delivery and showed Ennis the note with the territory map.

Both men were breathing hard and angry. The old man had his hands on his hips and scuffed the ground with his boot. "This ain't right," he said after a bit.

"They should've killed him, and us too. Why didn't they?" he asked Graham.

"I don't know. They sure as hell have the equipment, and reason enough to do it. Why'd they keep the boy and go to the trouble to seek us out to keep him alive? We carry the virus that with one contact could wipe them out completely."

"Do we know where their camp is?"

"I can only assume it's somewhere in their territory." Graham ran a finger around the edge of the map, "They kept the boy blindfolded, so he doesn't know where their base is."

"You think he's the one that left the bloody handprints at the campground office?" Ennis asked.

"Yeah, the kid told me, the guy he was with, shot at one of them and then they returned fire and killed him. They took him and kept him in a shed all this time, with these low temperatures at night. It's a wonder he survived without even a blanket."

"It just don't make sense," Ennis said.

"I know. For now, I say let's just get that kid past the hypothermia stage and fatten him up a little. It's going to snow soon, and getting through the winter might prove to be a bigger enemy than the preppers at this point."

Graham started to walk toward the cabin when Ennis called out, "We only have room for this one Graham. No more strays."

Graham nodded, then thought to ask, "Who's on watch?"

"Me and Marcy." Ennis shuffled off to his hideout at the entrance in the woods, while Graham pulled out the radios and connected the battery packs, testing them to see if they worked properly.

~ ~ ~

Tala kept pouring warm tea into Mark, worrying about dehydration. A bit later she gave him some of the dried venison and told him to eat it slowly. He tried to pull a chunk off with his teeth, winced, then tore it with his fingers into small pieces and chewed it with an expression on his face that made it clear he savored every bit of its sweet taste.

"When you want to, Mark, the bathroom is this way," Tala pointed. "I've set out some clothing on the counter in there for you. You can take a warm shower if you like."

The young man looked at Tala. "Thank you," he said in a way that showed he truly meant it.

She could see the pain in his young eyes. Like the other survivors, Mark had suffered deeply, been through and witnessed too many things for a person of his age. For a person of *any* age, she thought. She stroked his head and, at first reluctant to receive caring of any sort, he pulled away. She murmured softly to him until he relaxed against her, allowing her to hug him. He was sixteen, still just a boy, as her brothers had been.

"You're going to be fine here," Tala said. "We all get along pretty well. You haven't met Marcy yet. She's Macy's twin sister. She's on watch right now, but she'll be back here soon.

Graham came in the front door and the boy started to get up on shaky legs. Graham helped him to the bathroom and, smiling, the boy told him that he could handle it from there.

"Well, that's a darn good thing," said Graham, grinning at Mark.

"He's been through a lot," Tala remarked after the door was closed.

"Yeah, haven't we all." Graham then called to Macy. "Yes?" she answered from the bunkroom, zipping her jacket.

"We're up, kiddo," he said.

He gave her one of the radios and they first walked out to Ennis's spot together to try them out. Macy used long strides to keep pace with Graham, crunching the autumn leaves and dry needles underfoot with her brown suede work boots.

He gave her one of the radios, having left one in the kitchen with Tala, who listened to their conversation from there. Ennis walked up to them and talked about police radio codes; he told them that 10-12 meant people were present and that 10-34 meant trouble at this station, but terms rather than numbered codes came to him more readily when Graham asked about them. Ennis couldn't remember the code for "all clear," so they decided that the phrase itself would suffice.

Marcy greeted her twin happily, admired the radio, quickly learned the code system, and then raced back to the cabin, ravenous for more of Tala's cooking.

Inside she warmed her hands by the fire and removed the pistol from the holster Ennis had made for her, placing both on the table by the door. She then removed her coat and hung it on a peg and pulled off her boots and lined them up in their spot within the range of biggest to smallest.

She turned around to warm her backside in front of the stove. Tala smiled at her from the kitchen. "Is it getting cold out there?" she asked.

"Yeah, especially when you're sitting up in a tree for hours freezing your buns off." Marcy walked into the kitchen to wash her hands. "Do you want me to set the table?"

"Sure. We're seven now, so add an extra place," Tala said.

"What? Why do we have an extra?" Marcy asked as she pulled the right number of plates out of the cupboard.

"Didn't Macy tell you?" Tala asked.

"No, who is it?" Marcy asked.

Mark opened the bathroom door, and warm mist spilled out. Dressed in gray sweatpants and a white T-shirt, he said hi to Marcy, then asked Tala, "Where do I put these?" He was holding a bundle of dirty clothes in one arm and the doorjamb with the other as he swayed, a bit unsteady.

Marcy put down the dishes and hurried over to help him. Mark acted kind of embarrassed to have her support, but he accepted it. She took the dirty clothes from under his arm, walked him over to a chair at the table, and shot Tala a questioning look.

"Marcy, meet Mark. Mark, this is Macy's twin."

He stared at her. "Wow! You and your sister . . ."

"Yeah. I know," she said. "I'll take these and put them with the others," Marcy said.

"You might want to burn those," Mark said.

"Dinner's almost ready, Mark. Are you hungry?" Tala asked.

"Yes, thank you."

Marcy returned to the stack of plates and began laying them out. Mark reached for one to put on his side of the table, trying to help her. Marcy could smell his shampooed hair, still wet from the shower. He looked pale against his bruised cheek, which had shades of deep purple spreading out to green.

As if her glances made him uncomfortable, he refused to meet Marcy's eyes. "Tala," he asked, "is there something I can do to help?"

"No, you need to rest and get better so that you can help us in lots of other ways later on. There is certainly plenty to do."

Tonight they were having pinto beans and rice, like Graham's mom always made. It was a nice break from all the strange types of meat they'd been eating. Tala managed to make a peach cobbler out of canned peaches as a surprise for after dinner, and though they now ate in shifts, there would be plenty for everyone. With two good meals a day, they were gaining back the weight they'd lost during the chaos. They were also gaining muscle as their work schedule demanded a lot of physical labor that none of them were used to.

Tala called Ennis and Bang to the old table and the five of them got to know one another over dinner. Marcy watched Mark's eyelids drooping, and was glad when Tala saw it too and suggested that Ennis help him into one of the bunks.

"But . . ." Marcy whispered after peeking in, "Ennis is putting him in Graham's bed."

"Probably because Mark's too weak to climb the ladder, just like you were at first," Tala answered.

"Yeah. I guess."

"I'll check on him before I go to bed," Tala said, "and make sure he's okay. He'll probably need a couple of extra blankets—tonight, at least."

~ ~ ~

The next morning Marcy smiled as she awoke, hearing Mark tell Tala he wasn't really sure where he was or if he was dreaming and the nightmare might come back. Marcy could relate to that.

When the carriers—at first just a woman and an old man—showed up and broke into a cabin near the lake, Dalton was about to initiate the original plan of action, which was to suit up, go in, and take them out. But while they were on their way through the forest, Graham arrived with the kids and a dog, leaving Dalton's group with a hard decision to make. They aborted that mission and, though it took some planning and stealth, managed to infiltrate Graham's camp that night and hid several motion-activated cameras among the trees to keep an eye on them. The cameras were linked via radio signals to a monitor back at the preppers' camp; this would mean regular maintenance trips to refresh the cameras' batteries, but it would be worth the effort.

Some thought they should follow the guidelines originally set in place and argued for taking out the whole crew of carriers because they were too close to the base camp. All it would take was one encounter to introduce the virus into their secure area, and the preppers would die, yet the thought of killing anyone in cold blood just seemed wrong and Dalton said so. Rick asked if there was any benefit to keeping carriers so close, and the only thing Dalton could come up with was that they posed no hostile threat and might act as a warning system for other intruders to the area.

They'd prepared for this scenario, and in theory the right thing to do was make every attempt to terminate the virus for the good of all, but Dalton couldn't go through with it. For one thing, he recognized Graham, the guy who'd moved into the cabin. They'd gone to summer camp together when they were kids, even visited each other's cabins, and had fished together and done the things twelve-year-old boys do. They'd only run into each other a few times as adults when Graham visited in town. They exchanged numbers once, and told each other they would get together with their wives to visit, but neither one ever did call. Something always came up, and now Dalton really regretted it because he'd always thought Graham was a great guy.

It was one thing to kill in defense of one's family, but a managed risk with the carriers, with proper parameters, was another. They were not a threat to the prepper camp unless they got near.

The preppers knew Graham had weapons, but essentially, he was one man with one woman taking care of an old man and several children. Dalton had to respect him for taking them in.

Then one day he and Rick, while checking out the town, had spotted a man and a boy. The man had shot at them, and Dalton took him out before he recognized the boy as Mark, his own aunt's youngest son, and shoved the barrel of Rick's rifle aside so he wouldn't kill the kid.

That night Rick argued, "Dalton, you know this goes against everything we've trained for. That kid could kill us all."

"I know. But he's my *cousin*, Rick." We can't kill him, and we can't just leave him out there on his own. There's no one left to help him.

"All right. It's your call," Rick said in a tone of disdain.

Dalton sometimes regretted not taking the action, but he also regretted not convincing the rest of his family to join the prepper group he'd founded just five years ago. Too much had happened in the world, and he'd seen firsthand, with five tours in Iraq and Afghanistan, what crazy crap people were capable of. He'd had his money on trouble coming from terrorist groups, not the Chinese. But that's where the disease had come from and, while not exactly a planned attack, it had worked just as well as if it had been, leaving most of the world dead— even in China.

Dalton's family chalked his prepper activity up to PTSD and kept quiet about it. He practiced every other weekend and prepared for the worst. Now he, his wife, and their two small sons were holed up in their hideout along with thirty other adults and their children.

Things had gone to plan after he initiated the alert to converge on the hidden location. They'd quarantined everyone who wanted in, and more than a few didn't pass. It was too bad, but they'd incinerated the remains of those who died from the virus in quarantine. The name of the game was survival, and if they had to be ruthless and sometimes inhumane, they all knew it was necessary.

It shocked Dalton that the boy had made it. He'd assumed that his entire extended family had perished. Rick reluctantly agreed to risk capturing Mark, taking him back to camp and isolating him, but the kid's residence there took a toll on Dalton's conscience because the shelter they had to keep his young cousin in wasn't sufficient for his survival through the winter. Not only that, but the boy continued trying to escape. It was only a matter of time before he would, and the possibility that he might expose one of them was just too much of a risk.

Finally Dalton made the decision to take Mark to Graham's place. When the surveillance team radioed that Graham and just one girl were on the move toward town, he and Rick hauled Mark there, instead of the cabin, where the risk of exposure would be greater to them.

Now that the transfer was complete, they burned the shack they'd kept the boy in and sterilized their suits as well as the jeep compartment they'd used to transport him.

All in all, Dalton felt good about the situation but was still worried, so they doubled up on their surveillance to keep track of Graham's group's whereabouts at all times. As far as he knew, the kid didn't know who had saved his ass, nor had Graham recognized him in the suit.

Dalton had thought about revealing himself, but if he did and had to exterminate Graham later it would be harder, so he thought he'd just keep his name secret for now.

It was a lucky thing they were monitoring them, too, because as they watched the old man by the lake, the surveillance team spotted the strange men in the canoe and realized there were more across the lake, though they didn't seem to be associated with one another, nor had the old man waved back. That bothered Dalton.

If the canoe guys were hostiles, they would surely go after Graham's people first, and that would give the preppers some warning.

Only after the men in the canoe had made themselves known had Graham's little group begun to keep watch on their own camp.

They really were vulnerable to anyone who came in, because they lacked a military mindset.

Dalton's team accepted this, and besides surveillance, they decided as a group they'd only step in to help if there were no risk to themselves in doing so. Now he just hoped Graham and his team, including his own young cousin, would follow the rules and not cause them to regret their mercy.

The next morning Mark was awakened by a rough tongue licking his face. He shouted when he realized it was a dog. Marcy came running around the corner, thinking Mark was having a bad dream, but then started laughing when she saw him cowering at the head of his bed. "It's just Sheriff," she said. "He won't hurt you, he's a police dog. He found Macy and me. He hasn't turned wild like the others, and he even brings us food sometimes," she said, reached for the dog and scratching just under his ears.

Mark reached out his hand, shaking with fear, and Sheriff smelled it, then walked out of the room to go about his own business for the day.

Later that day, because he was still so weak, Mark helped where he could. Bang took him outside to practice with the bow and arrow, and with each shot he took Mark got better at it. He was a little embarrassed to have a five-year-old teach him how to shoot straight but, like Graham said, "Might as well learn from the master." Mark was surprised to learn that the girls had also learned from the little boy.

"That's funny that your name is Bang and the dog's name is Sheriff," Mark said that night at the dinner table, but it seemed like no one else thought it was funny.

"Yeah, we know," Macy said, breaking the awkward silence. "I guess it doesn't really mean much anymore."

The next day Mark got bored and asked Graham if he could take his turn on look out.

"I don't know, son," Graham said. "You're still pretty badly bruised, and you look washed out. We can't have you falling asleep on watch or not being able to react fast enough if there's a problem. But I'll tell you what. Why don't you stack that wood over there and split five more blocks with the ax? If you do that for the rest of the week, it will help build up your strength.

So Mark set to work, and the first day he did split five logs and stacked all the wood, and the second day he split six. Each day he ramped up his efforts, and every night his muscles ached from the unaccustomed exercise, but he felt good about contributing, and he was getting stronger every day.

By the end of the week Ennis noticed the boy stretching before he got to work with the ax and said, "You gonna be Paul Bunyan before this is through."

"Who's Paul Bunyan?" Mark asked.

Ennis shook his head, muttering something about the state of the school system, then walked away with his fishing pole over his shoulder and Sheriff trotting along beside him.

After dinner that night, while Tala and Graham were on watch, Ennis called all the children into the living area and told them stories about Paul Bunyan and Babe the Blue Ox.

When she learned of his lessons, Tala scoffed and told them there was a lot more they all needed to learn than American folklore. Ennis just scoffed, and Mark was glad. He liked the old man and his tales. Later, out of earshot, Mark explained to a wide-eyed Bang that folklore meant a made-up story. He didn't want the little guy scared witless of a giant man with an ax and a blue ox showing up when they were out in the woods working. Bang had already told them all about Korean folklore and how the Dokkaebi scared him, so Mark figured he'd also worry about this tall tale.

~ ~ ~

When he thought the boy was strong enough, Graham put Mark on his first night shift, and was damn glad he had. At Sheriff's sharp bark, in response to the radio in the kitchen coming alive, he tumbled out of bed and asked Tala what was up.

Mark had reported seeing a canoe coming their way at two in the morning. He called in a 10-34, trouble at this station, and bypassed the 10-12, visitors present, because this late at night he figured these guys were up to no good anyway.

Graham thought the boy was maybe just seeing things or pulling a fast one, but he didn't take Mark for a prankster and wouldn't take chances either. He hurried and put on his coat and boots, grabbed his rifle, and exited the cabin to find Tala running in his direction. Together they went down the trail quietly until they heard unfamiliar voices.

As Tala had told him to, Mark stayed hidden in the tree stand. Graham's heart nearly pounded out of his chest as the three men pulled up their canoe and silently moored it in the brush, out of sight but easy to get to. He and Tala crouched down and Mark could see the intruders were heavily armed and headed toward their camp. Graham heard the men coming up the trail, so he put his arm around Tala's waist and pulled her deeper into the woods out of sight. He held up one of his fingers to his mouth to tell her to be quiet. He held her closer to his chest and could feel her pulse quicken to match his own. He didn't hear Mark's voice, so Graham figured he hadn't been discovered. It was too risky to use the radios now; Graham didn't dare make a noise that would expose Mark's position with the strangers so close.

He aimed his weapon toward the men as they walked past on the trail, letting them think they were undetected. He wanted to stop them before they got too close to the cabin, but far enough from the lakeside in case they had reinforcements. One clumsy step in the brush at this distance would alert the intruders to their presence. After they'd passed, Tala reached up to whisper in Graham's ear, "I don't think they're preppers."

With the intruders safely out of earshot, Graham told Tala to go find Mark and to stay hidden unless he called her. Then he tightened his arm around her in a quick hug before releasing her, confused by why he felt the need to do that.

She touched his hand. "Stay safe," she whispered, and walked through the woods quietly to find Mark.

Graham picked his way through the trees, keeping an eye through the forest for the two strange men. He stopped at the woods' edge as the two got closer to the end of the trail.

"This was longer than I thought. Let's just grab one of the girls and get the hell out of here," one of the strangers said.

Knowing their intent now made Graham's heart beat even faster, and rage led to an adrenaline surge. Just as Graham lined the nearest one up in his sights, he heard Sheriff growl. One of the guys aimed his rifle at the dog and Graham changed his aim quickly and shot the man. He dropped, but the other two now knew his approximate location and began shooting into the woods blindly.

Suddenly Ennis appeared and began shooting at the two remaining men, who made a hasty retreat back toward their canoe, continued to shoot behind them as they ran. Sheriff was hot on their heels. Graham ran through the woods, worried that Tala and Mark might be in the crossfire. The two strangers were long gone when they heard another shot coming from Ennis's location. Graham startled Tala and Mark from behind, making Mark yell out, but no one heard him.

They watched the men paddle away toward the other end of the lake, silhouetted between dark water and a dim light from a sickle of waning moon. Sheriff barked his deep-throated warning from the shore. Graham walked Mark and Tala through the woods back to Ennis's location, where they saw him standing over the twice-shot intruder. Sheriff sniffed the dead body. "You two, go inside. I'll be there in a minute," Graham said; he wanted to have a word with Ennis alone.

At least now, they knew where the enemy was coming from.

"He's really dead now," Graham said.

"He was still breathin', but not no more," Ennis shot back.

"I heard them talking. They were coming for one of the girls," Graham said; he tried to register disgust in his voice.

"*That's* not going to happen," Ennis growled through clenched teeth. He looked as furious as Graham felt. "You shouldn't have let them get so far in," he said.

"I had Tala in front of me, and they were too close," Graham said in defense.

"We have to come up with a better plan, Graham. They'll be back for revenge now that we got one of theirs. I know how dangerous some of these guys can be. I was a cop, after all."

"What the hell do we do with the body?" Graham asked, looking over the dead man. He bent to retrieve the man's rifle and noticed that he showed no signs of starvation but smelled pretty bad.

Ennis kicked the body. "I say we chop off his . . ."

Graham stopped where this was going. "No, we're not like them. Help me load him into the truck. I'll dump him in the woods, far away from camp, later."

Once they'd loaded the intruder's body into the truck, Graham and Sheriff went into the cabin, but Ennis stood guard outside. With all the commotion, Graham found everyone awake. Marcy was softly whimpering, scared to death, while Macy tried to reassure her.

"Good job, Mark," Graham said when he came in. He patted the young man on his shoulder. "That was exactly the right thing to do."

"I should have shot them when I saw them coming," Mark said, his frustration clear in his voice.

"There were three of them and one of you. They would have killed you and then Tala before we had a chance to get into position. You did exactly the right thing here."

Graham knew the remaining intruders would be back. He was angrier for the fact that they'd been watching them and they'd had the audacity to try to take one of the girls by force.

"Listen up, everyone. We got lucky just now. That was a close call. They'll be back, though. Let's get one thing straight right away. I made a mistake once before in not shooting a dangerous man and it cost us"—he nodded at Marcy—"a lot more headaches later. If you have to shoot someone, shoot to kill. I should have already made that clear a long time ago.

"We've been too complacent, and this proves it. Those men have been watching us. Hopefully now they realize we aren't easy to tangle with, but I have no doubt they will be back. We have something they want, and now they're angry because they didn't get it and they lost one of their men. We need to keep watching and change our locations so that they can't detect us. For now, go back to bed and get some sleep, Tala, you too. I'll handle the watch for the rest of tonight. I just want everyone inside, behind locked doors."

~ ~ ~

Sitting in a chair in the living area, Graham looked out the window and saw the first snowflakes drifting down as rays of morning sunshine slid over the horizon, lighting the area in a dusky blue. Several deer munched on frozen greenery, which the snow was quickly covering.

Nothing further had happened in the last few days, but Graham was pretty sure those men encamped across the lake hadn't given up. Ennis was on watch from the blind by the water, and Marcy in the one near the road. Graham knew he should be sleeping, having just come in from his own shift, but rest eluded him. He felt he had to stay here near the door, just in case.

Having the skittish deer there helped ease his fear that the intruders weren't in the area at the moment. It gave him time to think, not only about recent events but also about his reaction to Tala while they had hidden in the dark a few nights earlier.

Graham felt utterly ill-equipped to protect these people he'd somehow become responsible for, and his attraction to Tala was making things worse. He still loved his departed wife, and he couldn't fathom these feelings for Tala. He hung his head with the weight of his thoughts.

Graham never heard Tala coming unless she wanted to be heard. She was talented like that. Now he smelled her before he felt her hands wrap around his tired shoulders and began to massage his tight muscles. Tala bent down and whispered, "I'll take over now. You go to bed."

He stopped the massage with his one free hand and gripped her, pulling her in front of him. He sat her on his lap and hugged her, burying his head into her thigh. She held him. He just needed to hold onto someone and told himself that it didn't have to be Tala, that it could be any one of them—except, maybe, for Ennis. At least, that's what he tried to convince himself. He missed his wife, who'd only died a few months earlier, and he was ashamed of his reaction to Tala. It made him question the love he'd had for Nelly, and that scared him, along with everything else these days.

"It's all right, Graham. You're just tired," she said. In the morning light, just peeking into the windows through the snow, she stroked his back and drew her hand through his thick hair, from the bottom of his neck up, making him sleepy. He wanted nothing more to than to stay like this for a long time.

Graham lifted his head and avoided her gaze. "I'm okay," he said. "Thanks."

Tala got up and walked over to retrieve her weapon. He walked past her into the bunkroom to rest while the others started a new day. She smiled at him as they passed and suddenly he knew she shared his feelings. He didn't know if that made him feel better or worse.

~ ~ ~

Graham wasn't sure what the smell from the kitchen was, but it was good and his stomach growled to let him know it felt neglected. He climbed down from his bunk.

Graham went through his clothes and decide he needed to switch these out. Unlike the old days, they changed clothing only once or twice a week. Tala had had a long conversation with the twins on the necessity of conserving water; getting teenage girls to wear dirty clothes and shower less was a challenge. Graham and Tala had the opposite conversation with Bang and Ennis, trying to coerce them into taking a shower once a week because they both became ripe quite quickly. Graham smelled his underarm and made a face to himself, deciding it was time for him to get cleaned up. He gathered his change of clothes and headed to the bathroom, only to find it occupied.

He wandered into the open dining area, where whatever Tala was frying proved to be the source of the tempting aroma. "What is that you're cooking?" he asked. "It smells great, and woke me out of a deep sleep."

"It's fried mystery meat," she said with a quick, concerned look.

"What?" he asked.

"It's the cougar meat. I think Bang will have a problem eating it," she whispered.

"We should just be honest with him, Graham said. "If he doesn't want it, he doesn't have to eat it, but we don't waste food—ever."

"That's probably for the best," Tala agreed.

Graham saw that she had her hair hanging loosely in long glossy waves without the braid she usually wore. He wondered what it would be like to run his fingers through the soft strands. Tala noticed Graham's intent gaze and went back to tending the skillet. She wore the white peasant blouse, tied with thin straps at her back. He had seen her in that on the night he first discovered her.

Crimson flushed her cheeks. At first Graham thought the heat from the cooking caused it, but then he realized he'd been staring too long, probably making her uncomfortable.

"Who's on watch?" he asked, trying to ease Tala's discomfort while he waited for the bathroom.

"Marcy and Mark at the lake, and Macy and Bang at the entrance," she answered.

"Well, that explains who's in the bathroom, and why it's taking so long." After thinking about it, Graham asked, "Are you sure it's okay to have those two on watch together? Mark and Marcy, I mean?"

"They're fifteen and sixteen, Graham. They're good kids."

"You taught second grade, right?" he asked, doubting her logic.

"Yeah, what's your point?"

"I've been a sixteen-year-old boy. I think I'll have a talk with Mark, just in case," he said.

"That's probably a good idea. It can't hurt," she said with a smile.

The bathroom door opened and out wafted a foul stench, along with Ennis. Graham grumbled at the old man, waved his arm up and down, and made a show of holding his breath as he puffed his cheeks out. "What did you do in there?" Graham asked him.

"None of your business. Wait till *you* get old," Ennis said, frowning. "Then you'll understand."

Graham looked at Tala and made a big show of holding his breath again before entering the bathroom, causing her to laugh, which he liked the sound of. He turned on the hot water to help disguise the stink he was trapped in.

"Are you feeling all right, Ennis?" Tala asked in all seriousness.

"Yeah, I'm a tough old bird." Ennis pulled out his whittling knife and picked up his current project, taking it into the living room to work on, dropping the shavings into a bucket. They'd later be put to good use.

Tala watched him from the kitchen. She knew the cold was getting to the old man, and instead of working on the porch where he had more light, she's noticed him hanging around the woodstove more often. She would have to mention something to Graham about relieving Ennis from watch duty; it wouldn't be good for him to get pneumonia from being outdoors. He was clearly into his late seventies or early eighties. She wasn't sure which, but knew he couldn't regulate his temperature like the rest of them. She hoped he would make it through the winter, but noting how he moved through the room, in pain from arthritis, she knew the freezing temperatures would not help.

Graham emerged from the shower with business on his mind. He'd decided, he'd announce, that it was really too risky to have the girls on watch by the lake. He and the boys would have to take turns there. He'd also stored extra ammo down there in case there was ever an instance when they'd need to engage intruders for an extended period.

Tala watched him tug on his boots after he piled his dirty clothes in the area she'd designated for that. In answer to the question she hadn't asked, he said, "Going to make a patrol of the perimeter, then along the road a bit, looking for tracks in the snow. I'll take the Scout."

"Are you going to scavenge while you're out?" she asked.

"I wasn't planning on it. I don't want to leave camp for long. Why, do you need anything?" he asked her.

"I was just thinking we really need to find vegetable seeds at some point. We're going to need to start some come February," she said.

"That *is* a good idea. Let's write a list and make a plan, but today I want to stick close to home. I'm taking Bang with me on my way out," Graham said.

~ ~ ~

Graham and Bang drove down the icy drive, and the Scout slid briefly as they turned onto the main road. Graham put the truck into four-wheel drive.

Farther down the street he pulled off to the side of the road where a few homes were. This was near where he'd pulled the dead guy out of the back of the bed by sliding him along on the top of the tarp. Bang had been with him then, too. Graham had been careful to explain to Bang what had taken place and what they were doing with the body then.

Now with the Scout pulled over near that spot, more to check and see if animals had continued the disposal than for any other reason, Bang looked a little apprehensive. Maybe it was because the child's nerves were on edge, but suddenly he snapped his bow into place and was about to loose an arrow when Graham stopped him. Bang was about to shoot a real chicken—a hen, to be exact. After a stealthy search, they found several more chickens taking refuge on the forest floor, pecking for grubs and grains. They captured five of them, stuffing them into the cab of the truck. It was an interesting drive back home with five unruly chickens squawking for their lives, and it proved to be great entertainment for the boy.

Once they got back, Tala was delighted at the prospect of future eggs, and she sat the guys down for dinner. As the chicken-fried cougar meat was passed to Bang, he looked at it suspiciously. Graham looked at the boy and, though he was tempted to lie, he told him what it was but added that he didn't have to eat it, though it would be good for him if he did. To Graham's surprise, the boy stabbed the piece of meat with his fork, dragged it through his instant mashed potatoes, and bit into it. He chewed a few times, pronounced it good, and asked for seconds. Since there were none left, Graham gave him his last piece, knowing the boy deserved it.

~ ~ ~

When Graham and Tala resumed watch, Ennis and the others devised a chicken coop out of the old shed that sat upon concrete bricks which served no real purpose after his father had built a new one. The old shed used to house various kinds of tools useful in digging ditches and chopping trees. Graham's dad once said it owed its existence as a compromise between his grandfather and grandmother. His grandmother had argued that, even though they were in a cabin, it wasn't a barn and he couldn't leave his axes in the kitchen. His aunt had accidently backed into one, slicing her heel wide open on the blade. This incident resulted in a trip for several stitches into the next town, where there was a resident doctor, late one dark and windy night.

To make the chicken coop secure, Ennis had the boys prop it up and brace it on the side that leaned. They swept it out and wiped out the cobwebs surrounding the two small windows that let in light, then cut a hole in the door and made a little ramp that led to it. Then they installed three branches to use as perches, setting them at varying heights for the birds to roost on at night. At the far end they put wood shavings down for bedding, which they had plenty of thanks to Ennis's whittling. On the shelves and floor they put more, hoping the chickens would lay eggs there.

The lack of heat was an issue. Although there were two old weathered windows of ancient wavy glass on each side for plenty of sunshine to enter, they needed heat or the low temperatures would surely freeze the birds. They couldn't run electricity out to them, so keeping the hens warm became a topic of concern until Ennis came up with a solution.

As a boy, it had been his job each winter morning to bring the "chicken brick" out to the coop each night as he closed up the hens. It would become a daily and nightly chore here, since the weather was even colder. They would alternate two cinder blocks, heating them on the woodstove morning and night to take them out to the chicken coop to keep them from freezing.

Predators were the next issue. Although they were perfectly safe from them at night, during the day they needed to peck at the ground and forage, as chickens do. There was no way they could run loose or their five chickens would end up being three—or none—in no time.

Without chicken wire around, Graham and the boys went on a mission to find some elsewhere the next day. Mark knew of an older, run-down cabin about two miles east into the forest as the crow flies. He and his dad had sometimes ventured there when hunting.

The next afternoon, after letting Tala and Ennis know, Graham and the two boys left the others on watch and trudged through the woods to find the old cabin. On the way, Graham took the time to talk to Mark about getting too close to Marcy. Once Mark realized where Graham's lecture was going, he quickly became embarrassed and reassured Graham that he wasn't going to "do" anything to Marcy.

They found the small cabin, which was slowly becoming a part of the forest itself. A spindly pine tree that lost its battle reaching for the light had crashed over the back corner of the small shack. They marveled at the cabin's diminutive proportions. "It's just your size," Mark kidded Bang.

Graham wouldn't let the boys go inside because as he pushed hard on the corner of the building, the whole thing began to sway. So he went in, bent over so he wouldn't disturb the ceiling, and started to swipe at the leaf-covered floor. He revealed a few treasures forgotten to the past world: a rusty pie tin, a hole-riddled green wool army coat, an old wood carving of a whale, an ivory stoneware coffee mug monogrammed with an *S*, a thick piece of wood that looked like it had once been a butcher block, a pair of old rusty bear traps, and an old metal serving spoon. Graham collected the items and handed them to the boys through the tiny door. There were probably smaller things hidden under the brush, but Graham started feeling like spiders were making nests in his hair. Nothing more important for their needs was to be found today.

Outside, they nearly tripped over a small rusty fishing boat lying on the ground, top side up. Graham lifted it and all manner of creepy forest crawlers began to squirm around. Underneath, they discovered a roll of rusty chicken wire and an oar. Jubilant with their find, they piled the smaller things into the boat and headed back home, dragging it behind them.

With Graham pulling in the front and Mark and Bang pushing from the back, they began their trek toward home. It took them about an hour to get most of the way back, taking several breaks along the way. Being patient with the boys came easily to Graham; he drew on his own father's treatment of him over the years. He paid close attention to the boys, and made them stop right before he suspected they needed to take a rest.

During one break they stood silently in the forest and could hear many creatures. A brown rabbit scurried through the brush and stopped just in front of their little metal boat, startling them as much as they startled it. The rabbit froze for a moment and then jumped right over the boat, continuing its retreat. Bang giggled.

Then a light rustling snapped Graham's attention in the direction the rabbit had come from, sending shivers up his spine. It grew louder and Graham instinctively pulled his weapon, surprised to see the boys do the same with theirs. He saw it coming and just had enough time to aim and shoot as the two gleaming wolf eyes shone through the greenery. He knew at once he hadn't hit it. Options raced through his head like a mathematician going through known formulas, but nothing fit the equation. He believed the wolf was biding his time before attacking them. Should they run back to the abandoned cabin, or try to make it to their own? He couldn't risk the wolf tracking them back to their place and possibly try to pick off one of them.

Spotting a tree with low enough branches for climbing, he shoved both boys toward it. Mark lifted Bang up, then followed him, shoving the smaller child ahead, higher and higher. The whole time Graham kept track of the dangerous creature.

"Be careful, Graham," Mark said. With both boys up and out of danger, Graham crouched down and walked toward the foe, armed and ready. He wasn't about to take a chance with his boys. Indecision had caused him anguish in the past, and he wasn't going to let that happen again. Any present danger had to be dealt with immediately.

As Graham got closer the gray wolf turned his head, looking behind, then looked back at Graham and lifted his head to howl. The eerie call made every hair on Graham's head stand up. He took that moment of clear view, aimed, and shot the wolf, which slumped to the ground.

Graham took several more steps toward it on the ground and heard something coming out of the brush ahead. "Shit," was all

Graham could say as another, bigger wolf came growling out of the woods into view. He could hear the boys yelling behind him, and then everything happened in slow motion.

The wolf lunged at him, springing itself on its hind legs from a fallen log as Graham aimed and fired but missed again. Then out of his left peripheral vision, he saw Sheriff come flying to intercept the wolf, hitting him just as the wolf impacted Graham's chest, sending him tumbling backward to the ground.

The German shepherd took the wolf completely by surprise. It turned from attacking Graham to vent its fury on the dog instead. The fearsome sounds of the two animals, each one fighting for his life, chilled Graham's blood. He found himself lying on his back with his weapon knocked from his grasp. Not certain it was a good idea when he thought of it, he reached out and grabbed Sheriff by the flank and hauled him toward his chest to get a clear shot at the wolf. Graham aimed and fired but just grazed the wolf. But it was enough: the wolf ran off, but not before stopping at the edge of the brush to look back at them as if to get one last good impression. It then entered the dark forest and was out of sight. Graham, breathless from the struggle, looked up at Sheriff. "Thanks, buddy." Sheriff licked his face, then continued panting.

Both boys were still screaming, not sure if Graham had been injured in the melee. Mark was trying to convince Bang to stay up in the tree while he went to check. Graham stood and motioned for them to calm down and stay in the tree, not trusting yet if the coast was clear. He continued to check behind him as he carefully walked around the downed wolf as Sheriff sniffed the carcass.

He and the dog returned to the boys, and Graham saw Bang's snotty and tear-streaked face; he even caught a stray streak of moisture on Mark's face, which he pretended not to notice. He held his arms up so that Mark could lower Bang to him, and caught the little boy close in a comforting hug before putting him on his feet. Then Mark turned around and Graham caught his sneaker to help lower him down. He gave Mark a hug like a father would give to his teenage son. "I'm okay. It's all right," he said to them both. Bang grabbed Graham's leg, wiping his tears on his jeans. "It's okay, guys, we have to get through things like this," he said to them.

"Thank God for Sheriff," said Macy behind them, startling all three. Mark turned his head to wipe his eyes. "Did you trail him?" Graham asked her.

"Yeah, we heard a shot and Sheriff was acting funny and ran like a dart in this direction. I ran after him and heard the commotion. When he stopped, I stopped, and I heard the growling. He moved so fast that I couldn't keep up, then I heard it before I saw what was going on. The next thing I knew, Sheriff was attacking a wolf and you were on the ground. I yelled, but I don't think you heard me," she said.

"No, I didn't hear anything else. It was all in slow motion for me. All right, party's over," Graham said, clapping his hands. "Let's get this stuff back to camp and then we need to check out our hero there and make sure he doesn't have any injuries."

Macy kept her pistol ready; she and Sheriff guarded the party as they made their way back to camp.

Once there, they were greeted by a very concerned Tala and Ennis. They put the boat down, and Mark was welcomed by Marcy as she came up and hugged him, kissing him on the cheek. "I was so scared," she said.

Mark looked a bit embarrassed and said, "Graham put Bang and me up a tree. So, no heroics here."

Graham tried to ease the moment by saying, "Actually, if it hadn't been for Sheriff, I don't think we'd be talking right now."

"Sheriff jumped right at the wolf before it got Graham," Bang said, choking a little on the last word, motioning with his hands as he remembered the action occurring just minutes before. They were all a little surprised when the boy spoke up. Tala hugged Graham, and he pulled her close as Bang hugged his leg again. "I'm all right," he said, just for her, but let's see if Sheriff has any bites or scratches that we need to treat." He started running his hands through the dog's fur.

Sheriff was pumped up, thinking he was receiving much needed attention, and began licking Graham's hand in gratitude. Then he returned his attention toward the dangers of the forest, his ears twitching and turning for any indication of danger.

They were all getting a little cold standing out in the open in two inches of glistening snow. After they put the small boat away and removed the contents, Tala hurried those not on guard duty indoors, where they removed their boots and put them all along the wall. She made them hot tea and cocoa, and they all warmed up from the steaming cups—and more so from being together after coming so close to tragedy. Other than a few scratches around Sheriff's muzzle he seemed unharmed, and for that they were all grateful. Graham suspected he would encounter the wolf again and he would need the dog and any other help he could get next time.

Dalton got the surveillance report of action in Graham's camp. A commotion of some sort had happened, but it appeared that all the occupants were accounted for and none of them looked injured, including their pet dog.

When the previous report had come in about the three men in the canoe approaching Graham's camp at night, Dalton and several of the other preppers crowded into the small observation room. They held their breath while watching the video of Graham and Tala slinking into the woods just before the men came walking into the camp. They could just barely make out and piece together what happened next. Though there was no audio, it was clear one guy was down and the other two made their way back to the canoe in haste with the dog after them.

"This guy doesn't know what the hell he's doing," Dalton remembered Rick, their technology specialist, saying at the time. "He should have dropped all three already."

In Graham's defense, Dalton said "He's a math professor, not military—remember? He doesn't think like us, but you're right, he should never have let them get that far in. Now they've got a better layout of the camp." Dalton knew those guys would be back.

Since then he'd felt edgy and helpless. If something were to happen to Graham's crew, he knew he shouldn't act. It would be too dangerous, exposing himself and the others. But he couldn't stop his emotions; he owed Graham for caring for his young cousin, and he liked the man, for that matter.

What made things harder was the rest of the team becoming more attached to the carriers. Graham's camp became a sort of soap opera for them. Rick started it all one evening at dinner as a source of entertainment that he often recalled during their evening meal for the other members to enjoy. Rick suspected that Graham and Tala were getting "better acquainted," as he put it. He regaled the other preppers with the humorous chicken story: Bang pulling the birds out of the truck cab, and when one got away how the boy finally pinned it down with its wings flapping in his face. He told them about how Macy and

Marcy were very different twins. Macy often helped Graham and Mark with splitting wood and other outdoor chores, and Marcy aided Tala in all things domestic.

Theirs was a boring life, and these little entertainments of human activity kept the preppers looking forward to the next day. They'd been sheltered since the beginning in the safety of their haven. Occasional hunting groups allowed the men to venture out a little now. Planning for next year's vegetable gardens and the care and keeping of tools and equipment became mundane.

So the news from Graham's camp each evening provided something to look forward to and helped keep them from dwelling on their recent past and the losses all had endured. This practice wasn't unlike "television in the old days, after a hellacious day on the job," Rick said.

Concern about the safety of Graham's camp due to the invaders occupied Dalton and Rick's conversations lately. Rick had become enamored of Graham's camp because of his daily surveillance of them.

Rick wanted to talk to Dalton about reaching out to Graham to help him secure his camp more efficiently. He was sure Dalton wouldn't go for it, but since they were now all involved in their story, he might entertain the idea, even though he knew logically they shouldn't do it. If they didn't do something soon to help, Rick felt certain the invaders would attack Graham's camp and its residents would be wide open for slaughter. Of course, in doing so, they risked revealing to Graham that they were watching them.

The people in the small cabin had suffered much more than any of those in the prepper compound. Somehow these few had found one another after losing their entire families and realizing their immunity to the virus made them a much hated minority, endangered by the fact that they were known to carry the virus.

They could see Graham had somehow picked up foundlings whom he might have determined as being of no concern to him, but despite that he'd collected them and brought them to safety. They knew he'd just stumbled onto Tala and the old man, but even they had been accepted. Graham's kindness in taking in Dalton's young cousin without question had earned him a great deal of respect from all the preppers. They felt they owed him, in a way, and maybe that's why they'd all become emotionally involved and were cheering the carriers on. It was not just that Graham was Dalton's boyhood friend; he'd taken these others in without question, in these horrible times, and the preppers couldn't help but feel admiration for the man.

~ ~ ~

Dalton walked into the dining tent, where his wife Kim and another woman, Tammy, were making lunch for the children, who were watching the cartoon version of Pocahontas in the underground shelter.

They'd established a strict rule about what they could bring into the compound when an emergency hit, but one of the other dads had smuggled a DVD player into the shelter. When they found out, he argued it was necessary to keep the kids safe and occupied. They continued to argue about it until he revealed his collection of DVDs with all the Disney movies in addition to most of Clint Eastwood's films. After the rest of them saw that, they voted that it was actually a good idea and then started having a weekly movie night for both the children and adults, using a wide-screen computer monitor. All in all it became an escape for them from the reality and dangers the carriers posed.

"Whatcha ladies making today?" Dalton asked Kim, planting a kiss on the top of her head.

"Tuna sandwiches and dehydrated apple rings." Then she renamed them. "Otherwise known as tuna triangles and apple snacks," she said and laughed when Dalton tickled her neck with his kiss.

"Stop that, mister, we're working here," Tammy butted in, amused at the two's little love scene.

Dalton loved Kim's smile. Actually, he loved everything about her, from her strawberry blond hair to her slim figure to her perfect, unpainted toes. Dalton had been terrified when the chaos broke out; he couldn't get Kim and the boys to safety fast enough. Now the challenge was to keep them safe.

When everyone first gathered, they ate only MREs and stayed locked up in the underground shelter they'd built in secret over the years. Then, when things settled down—or, more precisely, when most of humanity had perished—they opened the doors, pulled out the military tents, and established new rules.

They began cooking with what supplies they had and the meat they'd hunted, saving the MREs for leaner times. Kim and Tammy also started baking bread, more out of a need for comfort than anything else. Tammy had always made their own bread at home, and now she was doing it on a larger scale for the rest of the group; it was something everyone appreciated. They were now able to make sandwiches out of peanut butter and jelly, or tuna, or even canned chicken. One night she caught Rick making one out of some cold roast venison and he swore it was the best thing he ever had. The only thing it was missing was the fresh tomato and lettuce.

They had yet to see the really cold snows of winter, but were already dreaming of tender green onions, crisp red radishes, heads of romaine, and peas tucked in their jade-green pods. This pastime, not unlike the drama of Graham's camp, came a close second in the evening conversations. So much so that they would begin salivating until someone would put a stop to it by asking for mercy. Spring could not come fast enough. Even though it was way too early, they'd already set up the tables and hung the grow lights in anticipation of next February.

Tammy had the most knowledge of this, having worked in a nursery. She even knew how to spot plants in the wild that were either medicinal or edible if it came down to it.

One of the first outdoor projects that Dalton and the other men got busy on, besides putting up the tents, was fencing in their immediate compound. They'd stored the metal fencing in a buried bunker, complete with chain link pullers, posthole diggers, sledgehammers, and bags of concrete, and they worked quickly and efficiently. Since they'd spent so many weekends working together, they had already worked out the kinks in their relationships. Where Rick was bossy, Sam was contemplative, but they all figured out a way to work together and, surprisingly, there were few arguments. They depended on one another, and this was crucial in their situation. Above all they respected Dalton's final word on any debate. He'd gotten them this far, and they owed him a lot.

With the perimeter up they were safer from wild animals and the occasional human who might stumble onto their camp, though that was unlikely these days. At first, after Graham's camp established itself, exposure became their major concern. Now they realized they needed to keep an eye on his camp to keep its residents out of danger.

After the women had kicked Dalton out of the kitchen, he wandered over to check out Sam's work on the deer hides. This man knew how to utilize every part of any catch. No one else had ever learned the art of tanning, but Sam had it down to a science. With the colder temperatures, there were fewer flies to contend with, even though he worked with a smoke fire nearby to keep the pests away.

"How's it going, Sam?" Dalton asked.

"Good, and you?"

Dalton watched as Sam never broke the rhythm of rubbing the fat off the flesh side of the deer pelt during their conversation. After that, he knew Sam would layer plain salt over every inch of it, flat out. Sam had explained once that it drew the moisture out and helped keep the fur from falling out or decomposing. Because of the moisture in the air there, he often kept smoky fires nearby the pelts in progress and covered them loosely at night with tarps. After this procedure, Sam would soak the stiff pelts in cold water for a few hours, making them soft before the tanning process, which involved boiling a concoction. When it cooled he added volatile battery acid to it.

Sam did not permit any observers nearby during this process, not because he wanted to hide a secret ingredient but because of the danger it imposed. Submerging and soaking the skins in the solution became the next step. Then the extensive rinsing process, and then hanging to let the pelt drain. Finally, he would add oil to the skin inside with a sponge and put it on a frame stretcher.

Sam always made a point to neutralize the barrel of tanning solution with baking soda, keeping everyone far away, including himself, due to the toxic gas it emitted. Afterward he poured it over the gravel drive; it was no longer toxic to humans, but it kept some of the weeds down.

He would check on the hides daily, and when they were dry in the center he'd take them down and rub them with a wire brush on the skin side, softening and fluffing it a bit so that it would be workable. Then he'd dry it even more. So far these tanned pelts occupied a small corner of the compound building in increasing quantities, waiting for their final use.

Dalton knew Sam had never spent time in the military, but the experience would have been lost on the man. Sam said he'd learned everything he knew by being raised by his grandfather deep in the Montana forest. Dalton stipulated in the initial rules that all members must have spent some time in the discipline of the US military to join their group. After seeing what Sam could do, however, they made an exception.

Tanning hides, hunting, tracking, snaring, fishing, knife fighting, bow making, and beer brewing were only a few of the man's many talents. Not only that, but Dalton liked the man because he didn't talk too much. They got along well and would often have a beer, sitting in lawn chairs at night, with little pressure to talk, and Dalton liked it that way.

Sam's sinewy frame, deeply tanned skin, and thick dark hair revealed him to be a true woodsman. Dalton guessed his height to be about five eleven. He'd never seen a man tread through the forest as quietly as Sam did, and he liked to go on hunts with him just to watch the way Sam manipulated various natural obstacles without a sound.

Often the group would debate different decisions they needed to make, since Dalton required everyone to have a voice. This became the only cultural difference in the group, as Sam would often just act on his own expertise without consulting the others. It was automatic for him. It always ended up being the right decision anyway, but Dalton explained to Sam that he needed to consult them first before acting on something that affected them all.

Sam didn't have a problem adjusting to this. He wanted to get along, so when the issue came up for building the outdoor bathroom facilities, Sam waited patiently for all in the committee to have their say, adding to the design.

Then he said, "You could put it there and do it that way if you want to breathe in the aroma right around supper time as the cool evening breeze floats this way. But I'd suggest you move it down the natural slope of the land *here*." He pointed his worn index finger to the corner at the back of the sketch. "Dig two fifteen-foot holes to put the outhouses over, keep plenty of ash and wood chips to spread after use. Also, I suggest each father teach his boys to piss out behind it through the fence into the brush to help keep the deer and their predators away. But that's what I'd do. Otherwise, you're going to have a line forming in the morning with this many people and we'll have to fill in the shit-Popsicle holes in the middle of winter when the ground is too frozen to dig new ones."

After Sam's rare monolog, he walked off to work. They were all silent, imagining what a year's worth of "shit Popsicles" would look like. Rick broke the silence by laughing, and then said, "Sounds good to me; let's do it his way." The others emphatically agreed right away without further comment and walked away to get two outhouses built in the newly designated location.

Sadly, when Sam had arrived at the camp, he revealed his wife had died three months earlier of breast cancer. He and his seven-year-old daughter had stayed in quarantine together, and never showed any sign of the virus. It was tragic for the two in quarantine to suffer such a personal loss as they were observed and tested. Dalton attributed much of Sam's quietness to mourning, though they never talked about it.

Anyone could see that Sam had once been a very happy man. His daughter Adelaide—Addy, for short—greeted him each evening by jumping into his strong outstretched arms, her dark ponytail swinging as he carried her to bed. She often fell asleep with him sitting at the edge of her bed. Dalton had seen Sam carry Addy to their quarters, walking in that same soundless way of his, many times.

Dalton left Sam to his work and went back to what occupied most of his time: planning for the safety of these people. Rick was where he'd left him, watching *The Days of Graham's Camp*, which was the soap opera name the preppers had given the surveillance videos. "Anything up?" he asked.

"Nope, nothing but watching mud dry here," Rick answered, leaning back in his office chair. "Something must have happened, though, to cause that dog to run off into the woods like that with Twin Number Two right behind him, her weapon at the ready," Rick speculated. "What do you think about putting up a few more cameras out there?"

"Is it integral to our safety, Rick?" Dalton asked, "or simply for our entertainment?"

"I know we have to draw the line at what makes sense for us, but let's say something happened to one of them out there and we couldn't see it and the person died as a result. Wouldn't you want to know how it happened, and if it could have been prevented?"

"We're not God, Rick. We can't save them every time. I agree we should try to prevent any danger that comes to them that could also jeopardize us, like the men that came in the other night. But if Graham gets taken down by some wild animal, the lady will just have to take over. She's capable. We can't step in for stuff like that," Dalton said, trying to convince himself in the process.

Rick sat up in his chair. "All right, look. If the little guy was running for his life from that cougar in our direction, you can't tell me you wouldn't throw on your hazmat suit, grab your gun, and go running if you knew Camp Graham wasn't aware of it. We are involved now, since that first night we let them live. If it weren't for the virus, we would have already brought them in. They're good people and mostly children."

"Deadly children, and that's why we monitor them. You were the first one to argue against picking up Mark when this all started, and rightly so. It's just because of boredom and you watching them that you've become so soft, Rick. If one of those kids comes wandering into our camp, no matter how innocent, we'll all die. Are you willing to risk Bethany for that?"

"No, of course not. I just think it can be managed."

"They need to learn about us so that doesn't happen. These kids are going to grow up. Theirs and ours. They need to know about the dangers." Rick pointed at the monitor. "We need to teach *them* how to live with *us*, apart and together, if that makes sense. We can help each other."

"Look, for now I don't see the real need to put cameras on the east side of their camp. We can debate the rest later with the council. Is the hunt group back yet?" Dalton was changing the subject.

"Naw, they'll be checking in soon though."

Dalton began looking over plans for the aquifer for the garden when he heard Rick say, "What the hell? Look, camera five!" he shouted.

Dalton came up behind Rick's chair and focused on display five as he watched the two previous men in the forest on the lakeside hiding behind brush watching as Tala and the girls were hanging clean sheets up to dry on the outside line. "Go to camera three. Can you turn it along the shoreline? See, *there*." He pointed to brush lying over their canoe, half concealing it. Going back to camera five, they watched as the men backtracked to their canoe. They quietly slipped away through the water without detection in the late afternoon.

"Dammit, if someone had been on watch south of there, they would have shot the bastards," Rick said. Then they saw Bang running from the forest line, as fast as his little legs would go, up to Tala.

There had been a witness after all.

"So they were watching the girls? Then what happened?" Graham asked, trying to remain calm. He held Bang out in front of him. The panic-stricken boy was breathing hard and trying to catch his breath. Mark had found him first and taken him to Graham right away.

Bang looked at Graham, and then up at Tala and shook his head, like he wasn't going to say more with her standing there. Graham picked up on it and asked, "Tala, can you leave us alone for a minute?"

"Sure," she said, leaving the men to decipher the issue at hand.

"All right, go on," Graham said.

Bang made a confused face. He knew it was bad, but didn't know why exactly or what it meant and then said, "Those bad guys said, 'They have too many women.' Then the other one said that the younger two wouldn't hold up, so it would be better to take the mom. They think Tala's our mom?"

Graham stood up and called, "Tala, where are the girls?"

"They're on watch," she said.

Both Graham and Mark raced out the door without saying a word. Each headed in the opposite direction to secure the girls as fast as possible, without having to mention who would go where. Graham came up on Macy's back, startling her from behind.

"What? Graham, you scared me!"

"Nothing, I just want you to come back to the cabin." Graham was pointing, and Macy noticed that his finger was shaking. Then, out of breath, he rubbed the side of his bearded face and neck.

"What's wrong with you? Do you always do that when you're nervous?" Macy asked. He only pointed, indicating that Macy get back to the cabin.

"Did I do something wrong?" she asked him as they walked, with Macy marching in front of Graham.

"No, Macy, you didn't do anything wrong." He stopped and hugged the girl into his side and looked behind him as he took her back to the cabin. Once they hit the clearing, he saw Mark dragging a disgruntled Marcy behind him.

"I can't believe this!" Marcy said, outraged.

"What?" Macy demanded "What's with you guys? Now there's nobody on watch."

"Get in the cabin," Graham nearly yelled at them. "We'll talk about it in there," he said in a slightly lower tone.

Graham held the door open for all of them to enter.

"Look, gang, we have a serious threat. I had hoped they'd given up after we took down one of them, but it looks like I was wrong. My first thought is that no females should do watch," Graham said.

"That's crazy. You can't keep watch with just you and the boys," Marcy said.

"I said it was my *first* thought, Marcy."

"What exactly happened?" Macy emphasized the word *exactly* with her hands out.

Graham looked her in the eye and said, "Basically, Bang saw the two men that escaped from here the other night spying on you ladies putting the laundry up on the line. They said something indicating that they wanted to take one of you. So, that makes it a threat—to *you*. Understand now?"

Macy looked a little white, because she understood exactly what he meant then.

"I knew those jokers were up to no good the moment I spied them," Ennis said.

"Yes, you did," Graham said.

Tala spoke up, "Marcy's right, though. You guys can't do the watch work all on your own. What are we going to do?"

"I think we should block the lake entrance," Mark said.

"That's not a bad idea," Ennis said. "But how?"

After a few seconds of silence, no one had an answer for the situation.

"Ennis, what do you think?" Graham asked.

"Well, we know they're coming by canoe from the southeast, across the lake. We've only seen the three men, but that doesn't mean they don't have more at their base. And they want to take one of ours by force, and they're planning to do it soon," Ennis said, his angry voice increasing in volume.

"What we don't know," Ennis continued, "is when they will act on this threat. But they *will* act on it, and we need to be ready for them."

"They'd have to drive a long way, and we'd hear them coming if they came down the driveway. So don't you think we can still keep watch there?" Tala asked.

"I don't want to chance it, Tala. They could just as easily go through the east side of the forest, grab you or one of the girls, and haul you back through to their canoe in the middle of the night and we'd never know it," Graham said, shaking his head as the image of Campos carrying off Marcy popped into his head.

"There are just not enough of us," Mark said, putting his arm around Marcy's shoulders. She dropped her gaze; obviously she was thinking about the scenario Graham had just presented.

"I agree," Graham said aloud. "We'll run ourselves ragged just on watch patrol and not get the things we need to get done daily. So, we only watch from the lakeside during the day, with two on, and at night we keep sentry up in here." Graham nodded. They'd already started doing that when it really became too cold to ask anyone to stay outside at night.

"When any of the ladies goes outside, we always have them under guard," Ennis said.

"We could set up a trap for them," Bang said. They all looked at him now, not having noticed him before because he was so quiet. But Bang had come up with something brilliant.

"Yeah, we could booby trap the shoreline with those bear traps we found. Too bad we only have two. Some hidden cameras would be nice," Mark said.

"That's not a bad idea, boy," Ennis agreed.

"We have to be careful one of us doesn't accidently fall into the traps, though, especially Sheriff. That's all we need—someone getting their leg clinched by a rusty bear trap," Tala said.

"No one goes near the shoreline then. We'll set it up. The trail leading down is off limits for now," Mark said, as if making up rules as they went along.

Then Graham remembered his days from camp and how they pranked one another. Those were the good old days. His mind switched back to planning exactly how they could maintain their perimeter with a few well-placed traps. Perhaps they didn't need greater numbers after all. Graham got to work, taking the boys with him and confining the girls to the cabin for now, just to be safe.

"Dammit, I wish we'd put cameras in the cabin now!" Dalton could hear Rick yell through to the mess tent.

He smiled to himself as he stirred his coffee. "What the hell are we going to do without nondairy creamer?" he muttered absentmindedly. These odd things continually went through everyone's minds. The "what happens when?" scenarios seemed like a game they played in the evenings now, right after *The Days of Graham's Camp* spiel.

As Dalton walked back into their tent, he knew his friend was running various scenarios through his well-trained military mind. He was the technology equipment expert and, frankly, Dalton could count on his right hand how many times Rick had saved his life with that blessed orb of his. Dalton came through the opening, ducking his head under the frame, and could see Rick as he'd expected to find him, leaning back in his swivel chair, fingers intertwined over his balding scalp, thumping them. It was Rick's thinking pose.

"Stop it," Dalton said.

"What? I'm just thinking it through," Rick said.

"I know, that's the problem," Dalton said, pulling up his chair. "Just hear me out."

Dalton wanted to tell him they couldn't get involved again, but he knew the man wouldn't stop until he had his say. Rick turned in his swivel chair and lifted his hands. He was a hand talker, and Dalton often wondered, if they were to literally tie Rick's hands behind his back, would he be able to say a word?

"Let's say these are really, really bad guys," Rick began. "We don't have audio, but we know they were spying on the girls. It's highly possible that they're up to something and plotting a dastardly deed as we speak. The boys and the old man are not enough to help Graham protect that camp.

"These bad guys want something, and they're going to take it if there are no obvious consequences. If they come in and kidnap Tala, or one of the kids, Graham will go after them and probably get himself killed in the process. Then what? The kids are left with an old man, who probably won't make it through the winter and then we"—he pointed around—"will have to intervene anyway. Those kids won't make it on their own. We all know that," he added, spreading his hands wide for emphasis.

"Let's just say we give them a few supplies," Rick continued. "Or better yet, we set the cameras up for them covertly and leave them a note."

Dalton shook his head. "Too risky. They're expecting the bad guys to invade, and *we* walk in? They'd probably shoot one of us. You have to remember that, in their minds, we're the bad guys too. They don't know we're watching them or looking out for their best interest. They just know that we dropped off a boy, tied up and suffering from starvation, dehydration, and hypothermia, and they had to nurse him back to health. Not only that, but we threatened to exterminate them if they didn't stay to their own areas.

"I'm pretty sure Graham would do anything he could to protect those kids and the others, and if he perceived us as a threat, he'd shoot. They're armed. Don't forget that. You're getting too wrapped up to see the real risk here." Dalton fell into thoughtful silence, frowning. And, because this had been Rick's plan all along, he waited with bated breath to see what Dalton had to say.

Finally Dalton spoke again. "But, you know, if we were to go in, two men, use the mist gas. Knock them all out and then put up the cameras with audio. Take them a few gifts so that they're not too pissed off when they wake up . . ."

Rick nodded, hiding his triumphant smile. He knew from experience that the lure had worked again.

"What do they need, and what can we spare?" Dalton asked.

Rick grinned, but not for long, because he knew better. Dalton recognized he'd been played, but it was a game of theirs initiated many times in the past. Rick called it the Make It Dalton's Idea Game and said it worked on his wife too, but she was harder to deceive than Dalton—if one could call it deception.

Rick pulled a prewritten list out of his pocket and began to read:

"A generator; motion detector lights; shots for Fido; tetanus and flu shots for the rest, and a pneumonia shot for the old man; a water pump, a can of garden seeds; multivitamins; a radio unit with our call sign in case Graham needs our help."

"You think you're pretty swift, don't you?" Dalton asked rhetorically, then rose from his chair, put on his hat, and said "Get it ready" as he left the tent.

Rick did a silent little happy dance in his chair and started making the arrangements. Secretly, most of it was already figured out. Since the Sterns family, unfortunately, hadn't made it through quarantine, several immunizations were going to go to waste anyway. Why not use them on the carriers?

~ ~ ~

Later that evening Dalton addressed the council, which consisted of one member of each family. In most cases that was the husband, but in a few it was a wife. After Dalton had stated the affairs of Graham's camp everyone agreed the best course of action would be to intervene now, knowing what the consequences would be if something were to happen to Graham. No one wanted to see the children suffer more, even if they were carriers.

It was decided that Rick and Steven would go since Rick was the tech specialist and Steven the paramedic and could perform the immunizations on the sleeping carriers.

"It should take them no more than ten minutes to pull this off," Dalton said.

"As long as there is no risk of exposure to us," Steven said.

"There's always a risk of exposure, and that's why they will both go directly into quarantine again on their way back. We can't take any chances. That's our protocol anyway. Questions?" Dalton asked.

Nancy raised her hand. "If Rick's in quarantine, who's going to monitor Graham's camp?" she asked.

A few snickers came from the group. Dalton rolled his eyes and said, smiling, "I will, in rotation with others. Look folks, I know they're our only form of entertainment these days, but let's keep in mind that one encounter with them in person could kill us all. It's that dangerous. We've gotten this far together; let's be smart about this. Rick's right about intervening at this point, but we can't keep doing it." Dalton hadn't forgotten, though, that he'd been the one to insist on bringing in his young cousin, then finding a home for him, so in a way, he was the one who'd started breaking the rules. Shoving that thought aside, he added, "Those people have to take care of themselves, just as we do."

Dalton always hated being the voice of reason, but he could see that if they kept down this road they might become too lax in their vigilance against the virus, and none of them could afford that.

In the dim evening light, Graham, Ennis, and the boys went down through the snow to the lake, the younger ones making use of their tactical maneuvers. Ennis walked with cautious steps. He wasn't complaining, but Graham knew he was in pain. As he watched the boys, armed with their bows and acting quite serious, he still only saw boys in pretend mode.

"For the end of the world it sure is getting crowded around here," Ennis said and Graham had to chuckle at the old man because he was right—cranky, but right.

For some damn reason, those that were left all headed for the woods. Graham wondered if there was something to human nature that embedded a survival instinct to do just that. Like the monarch butterfly, flying from Canada to Mexico every year of its life. Perhaps humans have a natural instinct telling them that when the world goes to hell, head for the trees.

Ennis had scrubbed the rusty bear traps and Mark helped test them to be sure they worked properly. After setting them, they had Sheriff watch, while Graham used a stick to set the traps off several times. The dog jumped back and learned the danger. They hoped that would be enough to keep him from injury. They found a few obvious places a man would have to step in trying to come up to the camp, and they placed the traps in these likely places, covering them lightly with shoreline debris to disguise them. This only worked if the intruder stepped in exactly the right spot and, of course, there was no reliable way to make that happen.

"More than likely we'll see a deer running like hell, with one of these caught on its hoof," Ennis said.

"Uh, I don't want that to happen," Bang said, because he was partial to the animals.

Ennis shook his head. "It can't be helped."

Graham found a black permanent marker in the glove box of Tala's car, took a piece of scrap plywood, and wrote TRESPASSERS WILL BE SHOT. He nailed it to a tree so it couldn't be missed on approach to their lake entry. It wasn't lost on him, the irony that Campos had also posted such signs. It disturbed him, but he didn't know what else to do.

Though it wasn't a perfect plan, he lacked supplies and better ideas. The men began to pull back strategic tree limbs that would flip loose at the slightest jolt and startle a person sneaking in at night up the trail. They also camouflaged boards with upturned nails in them along the meandering path.

After they were done, the four of them gazed down at their handiwork and Mark said, "Too bad they're not lasers."

The two older men chuckled at that. "Yeah. If they were, they'd have a hell of a time getting through in one piece," Ennis said.

"Well, I think that's good for now," said Graham "I'll stay up tonight. Ennis, you can take over around three," Graham said.

Graham held the cabin door open for the others to enter, and then whistled for Sheriff to come in. Soon the dog appeared at the edge of the forest and trotted in for the night. Graham took one last look at the bright, moonlit clearing, and then closed the cabin door to the outside dangers for the night. He smelled the wonderful barley and cougar stew Tala had created, along with the pinewood scent in the crisp air from the woodstove.

After Tala's wonderful dinner, Graham took his post as the rest wandered off to bed. Unlike the world of the past, there was seldom idle time. You woke with the light of dawn, and then crashed at night as soon as permitted, only to do it all over again the next day. Actually, he thought it was good for the kids. They all seemed to be doing well, considering what they'd been through, and for Graham, at least, that said something.

As for the adults—well, he missed his family and work. Tala had pretty much replaced one family for another in terms of caring for them. Sure, she missed her family terribly but you wouldn't know it, watching as she cared for this bunch. Old Ennis had been written off by relatives who felt he wasn't worth anything any longer. Boy, if they could see him now! Graham wasn't sure what he'd do without the old guy's advice and company, even as cranky as he was.

Graham kept watch with Sheriff by his side. This dog was another family member to him, really. Sheriff had saved his ass once and warned them of danger countless other times. In the past Graham had often said he preferred cats to dogs. What a ridiculous notion that seemed to him now; in this world a dog like Sheriff was essential, and now he understood the classic novels like *Old Yeller* more than ever before.

He sat in the quiet room draped in darkness, listening to the soft snores from the bunkroom. He wondered about Tala and knew something had begun to grow between them, but he wasn't ready to give it a name just yet. Something still held him back, even though he could smell her across the room at night. Their eyes often locked randomly during odd moments during the day, and that night when he'd held her close in the forest as the invaders came in, his instinctive protectiveness had surprised him in its intensity.

After that he'd noticed she did little things for him too. Even though she didn't drink coffee, she made the brew and presented it to him every morning just the way he liked it. Nelly had done that too. Though he appreciated Tala's effort, it was a painful reminder of the past, as if his gratitude toward Tala was somehow dishonoring Nelly. This had the effect of making him feel a bit jaded about the feelings he knew were developing. He thought it might be mutual, but he wasn't certain if she just enjoyed playing house or if she really sensed the same thing.

Graham looked out the window and up toward the bright moon. You could always tell when things were going to get chilly: when the moon was especially clear on a winter night, it was going to be extra frosty the next day. He got up and added another log to the fire, disturbing Sheriff in the process. The dog jerked and settled down again after watching to see what Graham was doing. Then his ears went on radar patrol again. It was funny to watch the dog do that. His eyes would slowly close and then his ears would continue to pivot like some sort of radar detection device put on autopilot when the dog slept. Graham ran a hand down his furry back. "Dude, you smell like bad Cheetos," he whispered.

Graham once again scanned the perimeter and noticed a doe walking into the snow-covered clearing, followed by two smaller deer munching on the dry, telescoping grass near the tree line. They knew he had his eyes on them, but seemed not to care enough to leave. Graham liked to watch them, especially during the silence of the night. He wanted to go wake Bang up to show him what they looked like in the early morning blueness, but he resisted the temptation.

Of all the kids, Bang seemed to be closest to him, perhaps because he was the first of the immune that Graham had encountered or maybe it was because the boy was completely dependent on him and had been entrusted to him by his brave mother. Whatever the reason, he could say with full honesty that he loved Bang as his own now. Graham knew that if something were to happen to the boy, he'd grieve as if he were his own flesh and blood—and maybe that had been Hyun-Ok's intention all along. He was honored now that she'd chosen him for the boy.

Graham could hear footsteps shuffling his way. The old man couldn't sleep past three in the morning anyway, so that seemed a good time to change watchman. "Hey, Ennis, sleep well?" Graham asked.

"As well as an old man can after the apocalypse," Ennis said, then asked, "anything happen?"

"Only intruders are those deer," Graham said, motioning to the window.

"It's too light with a bright moon for some fool to come to try something stupid," Ennis said.

"Sure is, but I'm off to sleep right now, Mr. Ennis," Graham said, and as he got up, Sheriff followed him into the bunkroom, climbing on Macy's bed as usual. It seemed to Graham that, even though Sheriff was a family dog, he was ultimately locked to Macy. If it came down to it, he'd abandon them all for her alone. He didn't blame the dog; she was a good girl.

Graham fell fast asleep thinking of this new family unit and the events that had brought them together, meeting here in his grandfather's cabin after the end of most of humanity. His next conscious memory that night sounded very far away, like a glass breaking and then a bark out of Sheriff, warning him. Sudden dread raced through him, but he could do nothing about it.

They worked without even hand signals. Though the light outside was bright for the dead of night, they were able to put up all the exterior cameras without a hitch. Many of them were disguised as natural evergreen items you'd find in any garden variety forest, so their detection was unlikely. With that done, they headed for the main event. It was a little risky, mostly because of the dog.

They had to plan it right. There was no better detector than a family police dog, so charming Sheriff was essential. Since that was impossible, the next best thing was to put the dog under as quickly as possible.

The first windowpane came out fairly quietly but the second one shattered in with the cold temperatures. It couldn't be helped, and with the noise there was no turning back now.

Rick already had the canister ready and simply pulled the fuse. Instead of tossing it in willy-nilly, he sprayed the stream directly at the dog first, which put him out fast, then tossed it into the cabin. At least they wouldn't have any accidents now, and knowing that relief, they were able to pull the old window open without incident. They'd already loosened one pane close to the old man by the front door, sending him to sleep right away.

Rick was a little concerned for the small boy. The amount of gas that he would inhale could result in a respiratory issue for him. But, as luck would have it, he slept in the farthest bunk and received less of the gas. Once they were in, Rick blew a sigh of relief when he realized Graham had his hand around the trigger of his shotgun and one foot off the bed. He wasn't sure if the man actually slept that way or if he'd had a chance to react. In any event, Rick quickly pulled out the prefilled needles for the man and popped the common flu shot into his right shoulder. The next, larger one, he slid under his right arm's back fat. That one was special and they all got it. He and Steven kept it a secret, and when Dalton found out, Rick hoped he wouldn't be too angry. Then Rick quickly gave Graham a tetanus shot.

Each man, contained in his hazmat gear, carefully and quickly went from person to person. Rick then wandered into the living area to get the old man by the door. He had four shots coming. "Poor sucker," Rick whispered, "got to get you through the winter, Pops." After he had finished administering the shots, he put up the tiny hidden cameras in several spots throughout the cabin living space, and on his way back to the bunkroom, he continued to plant a few more, adjusting their view as he went.

By the time Rick finished, Steven had completed the dog's inoculations too. Then Steven reached through the open window and pulled in the gifts, handing the contents to Rick one by one. Rick put them ceremoniously in the middle of the living area floor, so the residents of Graham's camp would know it was intentional, like Christmas morning. He laid a note from Dalton on the very top.

Having completed their tasks without incident, the two men exited the window once more and replaced the glass panes with ones they'd brought along for the occasion, quickly piping the sealant into place. They knew the mystery of how they entered the cabin would be revealed in time, but in their thinking, they were keeping the heat in on this family that they had come to care for during their evening entertainment.

With moonlight guiding their way back, they needed no artificial lighting. It seemed like the old days to them, and somehow they felt gleeful to be back in action again. When would they have the chance to do something like this again? Unfortunately, Rick and Steven now had to go into quarantine on their arrival back at their own camp, but the mission had gone off without a hitch and they felt good about it.

Joking while they ran through the night, Rick said, "I can't wait to see Graham's face in the morning," as a parent would say in anticipation of Christmas morning.

Steven looked at his comrade through his suit's clear safety casing and laughed aloud, but both became solemn when they heard Dalton's voice saying, "Cut the crap and get back to camp." Rick had a strong suspicion Dalton was smiling, too, as he stood watching them on his computer screen, though he didn't let it come through in his voice.

As the men got closer they scared a few unsuspecting deer away and the deer scared them back in turn when several the men hadn't detected rushed past them.

Knowing the procedure, they entered the wash chamber camouflaged outside the security area of the preppers' campgrounds in the forest. As they stood in their suits, chemicals sprayed them as they turned around. They danced the Hokey Pokey for the cameras, complete with singing. Both men were feeling a little goofy after all the seriousness they had been through. They'd started doing this Hokey Pokey business a while back, and now it was an established ritual to break up the gravity of the situation as they entered quarantine.

Both men finished their last twirl, and the next set of doors opened for them. They stood in place, removed the hazmat gear, and stepped into the new sterile environment. Then the doors behind them closed, and they were again misted. With closed eyes they twirled like airplanes in a tailspin, but there was no singing this time, as they had to hold their breath for too long. The final set of doors opened and then they entered another room set up with two cots beside monitors that they needed to hook up to one another. A small refrigerator with a microwave on top and a toilet behind a screen were positioned in the far corner.

A disembodied voice broke the silence: "We loaded a little surprise this time. Check the play list on your iPad, Rick."

Rick walked over to the digital read and saw that all the episodes of *Seinfeld* were listed. "*All right!* Thanks, guys!" he said.

Steven said, "Shit, seriously?" and picked up his own iPad to see what awaited him. "*House* and *The Walking Dead.* Very funny," he said to the voice known as Clarisse, the Quarantine Queen.

"Your families are waiting to hear from you, of course, but have already been notified of the mission's success. You've both been here before and know what to do. This is the first hour, so get started. We have to treat this just like the first time," Clarisse said.

Both men unzipped their disposable Tyvek suits at the same time, stepping out of them and tossing them into the chute that extended to the instant incinerator. They could hear the first chamber going through the incineration process on the front part of the building. In a kind of silent ballet both men, wearing standard issue boxer shorts and white T-shirts, walked over to their separate sides and inserted needles into the ports that were had been placed in their arms ahead of time for the continuous blood draws the quarantine procedures demanded. They withdrew their own blood with use of the ports, and put the samples in airlock chambers on each side that would be tested the first hour, second hour, sixth hour, twelfth hour, and so on and so forth, to make sure the probability of the virus detection maintained the predicted outcome.

This was not the fun part. If the virus was present, you were given the choice to use the red injection syringe which you could take with you to the incinerator portal to make things easier for the living. Simply inject it into the port, fall asleep, and never wake up. When no vital signs were detected after a certain amount of time, the portal would simply incinerate the remains and the virus along with it. Or, as some of the arrivals found, they could spend the last of their days in the comfortable bedroom chamber until nature took its course and then the whole room could be set to incineration to keep the virus from spreading.

This is what they'd had to do with the Carsons. Each and every member of the team watched as first the son and then the daughter, followed by the father and then finally the mother, all succumbed to the virus. The mother cared for each of them until she no longer could. A wonderful mother and wife to the very end, she saw them through. It tortured the preppers to watch it all, and it came as a relief to see the last vital sign finally go flat. Then, of course, they felt guilty for feeling the relief. Since then, all who had to go through quarantine tried to inject some humor as armor when entering the chamber. The reality of what might be required of them was too damn hard.

After the two guys had finished their blood withdrawals, they put on the vitals monitors, expertly attaching them where they needed to go, and then pulled back the covers to their cots. Once comfortable, they used the radio system to check in with their families. Both chatted with their loved ones only briefly because it was late; better coherence would come in the light of day. They were too punch-drunk to go to sleep just yet, so Steven got up and checked his little refrigerator, stocked with the things he favored. For now he pulled out a bottle of water and drank that down.

Rick asked because he wanted to know and because he knew they would always be listening: "Are the cameras up and ready? Camp still asleep?" he asked the disembodied voice.

Dalton answered, "Yes, Rick, they're still asleep. I'm zooming in on the boy right now. He's on his side, so I can't tell much other than his chest is rising and falling, but that's a good sign. Did Graham have any reaction time?" Dalton asked.

Rick lay in bed looking up at the wall with his arms crossed behind his head, tapping his fingers and making the wires jiggle in the process. "His trigger finger was happy, with one leg ready to go, but that was as far as he got," Rick said.

"I have something to tell you, Dalton," Rick said after a moment of silence, feeling guilty about his omission already. Dalton let it hang in the air a moment as he wrote down notes, observing the sleeping members of Graham's camp.

"Save it, Rick. I already know," Dalton said grouchily.

Rick winced.

"Wished I'd thought of it first," Dalton said, knowing Rick felt guilty about implanting the trackers without his permission.

"They're all going to be pretty pissed in the morning, including that dog," Rick said looking over at Steven, who just shrugged his shoulders. Somehow, this thought just now occurred to Rick.

"Don't worry, I told them it was all your idea in the note," Dalton said.

"Goodnight, jerkwad." Rick rolled over, taking his covers and wires with him.

"Goodnight, princess," Dalton said.

~ ~ ~

Dalton continued to monitor Graham's group from the cameras. Soft snoring sounds crept through the microphones and not-so-soft snoring sounds invaded the one in the living room. Everything seemed fine as Dalton paid close attention to the lakeside and front perimeter cameras at the same time. One risk was having the carriers off sentry duty, making them defenseless. Dalton risked the chances that the intruders wouldn't attack during such a bright moonlit night, and this had paved the way for the preppers' own shenanigans. They had to do this now to give the members of Graham's camp the things they needed to protect themselves better—and sooner, so they would be prepared for the next night attack.

It was quite something as he watched them get through the lake trail without falling victim to one of their primitive booby-traps. The ambient light of the moon cast down on them and the intricacy of the traps challenging as they maneuvered through the maze, often tripping, which caused the other men watching the monitors to hold their breaths.

At the second hour, both men in quarantine were prompted to get up and make the second blood withdrawal. After that, they could each sleep for four hours until prompted again. "So far so good," came Clarisse's soft voice.

"Goodnight, Clarisse," both men said in unison. It somehow was reminiscent of a bygone cartoon involving two chipmunks.

The voice laughed and said nicely to them, "Goodnight, boys."

The lights went off, and the two men drifted off finally as infrared lighting watched their every breath and pulse for the first of the ten-day observation.

It was Sam who first detected movement. It was pretty damn cold outside, so he'd come in for another cup of coffee to warm up between projects. He'd passed by Dalton, who was asleep with his head down on his arm in front of the monitors, drooling on himself.

Sam filled his mug, walked up behind Dalton's chair, and observed the screens. "Hey, Dalton," Sam said quietly, tapping him on the shoulder. "I think one of them is up."

Dalton lifted his head and tried to focus on the screen Sam pointed to. It was the little boy moving. Dalton watched and then refocused the hidden camera closer. He said a quick thank-you to Rick for instinctively knowing the exact spot to place the concealed cameras. On the top of the last bunk, he saw the boy's leg pull up; then the boy pushed up on his hands.

"Oh, thank God," Dalton said under his breath, releasing his fear as he emptied his lungs. Of all the carriers, the boy was the one at greatest risk of overdose by the sleeping vapor they had used. They had no way to calculate where he slept in the room, so this was the biggest hazard. The vapor gas was good, but had been known to have a 15 percent chance of death, especially in small children.

Dalton and Sam watched and were able to tell by the look on his face that the sleepy boy, looking around, was coming to the conclusion that something wasn't right. It was clearly daylight and everyone remained in their bunks. The two men watched as Bang climbed down the ladder, looking confused. He jumped the remaining two rungs without making much of a sound. The microphones were working well; Dalton could even hear the blankets as they moved about.

The boy walked up to Graham's sleeping form.

"Oh, here we go," Sam said.

Bang shook Graham's shoulder. No response.

"Graham, wake up," Bang said, whispering at first.

Graham showed no signs of life. Bang tried again with more force, using both of his hands and his weight as he pushed on Graham's chest.

"Graham, wake *up*," Bang said again, a little louder this time.

Getting no reaction, the boy started to look around. It appeared to Dalton that the boy was on the verge of panic.

"Calm down, buddy, they'll be fine," Dalton said out loud to himself and Sam, but wished he could reassure the boy himself.

Bang returned his attention to Graham and put his ear on Graham's chest, presumably to hear his heartbeat. He lifted his head, patted Graham twice lightly on his chest, and looked around at the others.

"Crap, poor kid," Sam said, making Dalton feel even more guilty.

Bang walked over to the girls' side of the room and slid his hand down Sheriff's furry side without getting a reaction. He laid his head down on the dog's side too, and must have heard the rhythm he needed to because he stood up again.

"Smart kid," Dalton said.

He pushed roughly on Macy's back, moving the whole mattress with both her and the dog, but neither stirred. Then, as if it just occurred to him, Bang ran around Macy's bunk to Tala's against the wall and saw that her long black hair fell over her face. He gently moved it away and then said, "Tala, wake up" as he shook her shoulder. He put his small hand up to her mouth and nose. Feeling for breath? Yes. Of course.

"Uh, this is hard to watch," Sam said.

"He'll be fine. At the back of the room, he was the least affected by the gas, so it's likely that either Mark or Graham will wake up next," Dalton speculated.

As if the boy read Dalton's mind, he ran from the girls' side and climbed the ladder over Graham to investigate Mark. This time, he climbed up right over Mark's legs and up to his chest, shoving the older boy hard and saying in a loud voice, "Mark, wake up."

"Stop it, kid!" Mark yelled, scaring Bang and causing him to jump back.

Sam sloshed his coffee in reaction to the surprised response. Dalton also jumped back.

"Whew!" Dalton said and grabbed his chest as he saw his young cousin alive and pissed off. Sam slapped Dalton on the back, knowing it was important to Dalton that the boy was cared for.

Bang leaned down and whispered to Mark, "Something's wrong. Everyone's still asleep."

Even though the boy whispered, all Dalton had to do was turn up the volume to hear the conversation. Sam was surprised and a bit concerned such technology existed.

"That's not right," Sam said, and took a sip of his cooling coffee.

"Yeah, well, I wish we'd had these in China before everything went to shit," Dalton said. He turned the volume back down to a normal level. Dalton started noting the time each boy woke up on the log he had in front of him. If there were problems with the others, they could at least read the data and try to gauge what the likely waking time should be based on location and weight.

They could see Mark struggle to come around. He put his hand blindly on Bang's shoulder and tried to reassure the younger boy. Even though it was fully bright in the bunkroom, Mark said, "It's okay, Bang, it's just too early yet. Go back to bed."

Bang nudged him again. "It's *daytime*, Mark. Even Sheriff won't wake up, or Graham or Marcy." It was as if his using Marcy's name triggered some automatic reflex; Mark elbowed himself up, squinted, blinked several times, and stared across the bunkroom at Marcy. "Crap, you're right," he said, rubbing his eyes. He sat up quickly, swayed, then asked, "What is going on? Ohh, the room's spinning."

He made his way down the ladder, then stumbled across the room. "Marcy? Marcy!" Mark yelled over to her, but there was no response. Dalton saw panic in his eyes, terror. Mark reached out to touch her, and winced. "Crap, my arm hurts," he complained, rubbing the sore area.

"Mine too," Bang said.

"Whiners," Dalton kidded as he observed the scene.

Bang shimmied down the ladder after Mark and tried to push on Graham a few more times.

"Graham!" Bang said again, a panicky pleading in his voice. "Wake up, please wake up!"

Bang wiggled Graham's bearded chin, causing his mouth to open slightly. Mark came and tried to help Bang. "Graham, wake up, something's wrong!" he yelled.

"Wake up, something's wrong, Graham. We need you!" the boys said again.

Dalton met Sam's eyes and saw a reflection of his own feelings of culpability as they watched this unfold. "It'll be okay," Sam said, but didn't sound so sure.

"Yeah," Dalton answered. He didn't feel all that certain, either.

~ ~ ~

Graham started moving reluctantly. He muttered, "Lea' me 'lone," and tried to roll back into the dream where Nelly and he lay on a blanket under the warm sun as he ran his hand over the life within her that they had created. Nelson for a boy, they'd decided, and Grace for a girl. The sunlight sparkled on her red hair and she laughed . . .

"Graham! Please! We need you!"

The boys? Yes. Both boys. Bang and Mark were shaking him, insisting something was wrong. Right, the boys needed him. He needed to help them. "Okay, I'm coming," Graham murmured.

His eyes were still closed as he moved his legs around. Mark moved the gun away until Graham awakened fully. "I'm coming," Graham repeated, but he dozed off again, so Mark tugged on his shoulder once more.

"I'm coming," Graham said again.

He opened his eyes a slit and saw both boys looking at him with concern. "Wake up, Graham. *Please!*" Bang's small voice trembled.

"I am," Graham said.

He blinked his eyes a few times and then shook his head, trying to break free of the sleep that held him down.

"What's going on?" he asked and felt a deep stab of pain in his right arm, like he'd been slugged, or maybe he'd pulled a muscle.

"We don't know yet," Mark said, and left his side to go over to look at Macy and Sheriff, who were in the same state as Graham, half awake, just beginning to stir. Mark climbed the ladder to Marcy and pushed her legs over. "Marcy," he called to her again.

She lay on her left side. As the boy shook her back and forth, she became annoyed at the motion and lamely swiped her hand at whoever was pestering her.

Graham watched the commotion as Bang trying to help him stand. Not seeing Sheriff in motion concerned him right away. He squinted at the dog and then looked beyond him to Tala. "She's still sleeping too," Bang said, and Graham looked up at Bang, not certain how he knew that Graham's concern was more for Tala than the others.

"Where's Ennis?" asked Graham as Mark jumped down from Marcy's bunk. Both boys looked at him like they didn't know.

Graham swung both feet to the floor, hoping the room would stop moving if he planted them there. He rubbed the sides of his face and looked blearily at the floor in front of him, then stumbled toward the living area to check on Ennis.

"What's all this?" Graham motioned with his opened hands to the pile of stuff lying on the floor of the living area.

"I don't know," Mark said. "We never left the bunkroom. We were too worried about you." Graham shook his groggy head. He willed his legs to work, and walked around the pile of stuff, not even trying to inventory it yet, even though there was a big generator sitting there. Then he returned to the bunkroom and made it to Macy's bunk first.

"Hey, Macy girl, wake up," Graham said, shaking her slight body. When she only peered at him, confused, he grabbed her chin and shook it sideways a few times to bring her out of her stupor. She started to stir on her own and then Graham walked around to Tala.

"Tala," he said. She lay on her side facing him. He completed what Bang had started and pushed the rest of Tala's black raven hair over one ear, out of her face, and then sat on her mattress. "Tala, wake up," he said again.

"What in the hell is going on in here with all this yellin'?" Ennis asked from where he stood in the doorway.

"Something's wrong with people," Bang said. "I don't feel good, and no one wants to get up."

Graham looked back down at Tala, who had opened her eyes at hearing Ennis gripe. "What's the matter?" she asked him. "What's Bang talking about?"

"Just try to wake up," Graham said, and found himself stroking her long silky hair.

Mark got Marcy to sit up and she tried her best to stay that way, but her eyes closed again. She fought to stay awake, but wanted nothing more than to slide back to her pillow.

Bang tried to wake Macy up, but she was having none of it.

All at once, the four males seemed to notice, during all the commotion, that Sheriff had not budged at all. Nor was his chest rising, as it had earlier. His ears were not rotating to the obvious noises.

"Oh, no," Graham said and pushed his weight over the edge of Tala's bed.

The dog's dead weight held Macy's legs down under the covers. She wasn't fully awake yet to comprehend what was really going on. She could only tell that everyone insisted she get up because she obviously had forgotten something important, though the group had not told her what that was yet, and she was annoyed by their demands.

Graham stroked the dog's fur and reached his head down to listen to the dog's heart. "He's alive. He's got a heartbeat. Let's just give him time," Graham said.

Then, looking from one to the other, he said "Does anyone know what happened?" He got nothing but negative head shaking. When he came back to Tala, she'd begun fading again, so he wrapped his arm around her waist and hauled her over to him. Ennis walked in and sat down behind Macy to help set her up with Bang's assistance.

"Maybe we're getting it," Bang said, and everyone knew what he meant but didn't want to acknowledge it.

"Bang, you go get some water for the girls," Ennis ordered.

Bang ran off, and Graham heard him shove a chair across the floor, then heard the water running.

Ennis felt Macy's forehead. "She's not feverish," he said.

"How are you feeling, Ennis?" Graham asked while he rubbed his hands up and down Tala's arms to help rouse her.

"Drugged up is the best way I can describe it," Ennis said.

"Nothing happened last night? You didn't see anything?" Graham asked him.

"No, I watched those deer in the yard and I don't 'member much after that. Musta fell asleep," he said.

Bang handed him a glass of water, and Ennis put the rim under Macy's lips. "Take a sip, girl."

She did, and then opened her eyes a little, but closed them just as quickly.

Macy was able to blink her eyes more now, so Mark reached down for the glass and Ennis handed it to him to do the same for Marcy.

Graham continued to rub Tala's arms to keep her awake, but she just leaned against his chest, eyes closed.

"Tala, look at me," Graham said, raising her chin. "You have to stay awake now, okay?" She nodded and tried to stand unsupported, but slumped. He grabbed her and thrust her toward the living area. "Walk," he said. "We all need to move around more. That'll help us, throw off the sleepiness we're all feeling."

"Ugh, what's wrong with me?" Tala asked, stumbling forward as Graham propelled her into motion.

"I don't know. We haven't figured it out yet." Graham guided her around the stuff on the floor. "Ennis, Mark—get those girls up and moving."

Graham took Tala into the kitchen and pulled out a chair for her to sit in. He then went back into the bunkroom and grabbed the note off the pile of stuff. Ennis had Macy mostly mobile, and Graham just picked her up and carried her into the kitchen. Tala pulled the chair out for Macy and when Graham put her down, she held the girl upright.

"Bang," Tala called. "Can you make some coffee, like I showed you?"

He nodded and began the work, carefully measuring coffee.

Mark and Ennis helped Marcy down the ladder, and they joined the others. Marcy sat in a chair beside Mark and put her head on the table, falling asleep again. Mark pulled her up and slid her over to lean upright against his chest.

The coffee aroma filled the small space, perking them all up, as Graham read the note to himself, then read it again and said, "Son of a bitch!" Hell, he hadn't meant to say it out loud, but it sure caught everyone's attention.

The letter shook in Graham's hands. "They drugged us. That's what this is. So they could break in here and give us this." He motioned to the items on the floor.

"Your arms are sore, right?" He turned to address the rest of them. "They gave us all flu and tetanus shots and Ennis, you also got a pneumonia shot," he added and shook his head in disbelief.

"That would explain why my arm stings," Ennis said.

"I don't know how to feel about this," Graham said with indignation.

"Who did it?" Mark asked.

"The preppers, the people who had you," Graham said.

Graham walked back into the bunkroom and looked at the stuff in the middle of the floor, then walked over to Sheriff and ran his concerned hand down the fur of the animal again. Sheriff felt warm and Graham could feel the dog's pulse. He scanned the room and looked for any sign of forced entrance.

"Is the front door locked, Ennis?" Graham asked.

"Yep, been locked," he said.

"The only other way in would be through the windows, then," Graham tried to open the one closest to Tala's bunk. The lock from the inside appeared in place. He opened it, letting in some of the cold air along with its moisture. Graham reclosed it and snapped the lock tight.

"How in the hell—?" he said under his breath as he strode back to the pile of items and knelt. Something about the window caught his eye again, and then he knew what he hadn't seen before. From this low view, he caught on right away. He got up quickly and examined the panes. Clearly they were replacements, because the two on the bottom were newer, not with the wavy flaws of old glass and with a new bead of off-white caulking, unlike the rest.

"Too simple," Graham said. Then he turned his back to the window and tried to see what the intruders would have seen in the same position.

"They got Sheriff first, and probably with the strongest hit. I'll bet that's why he's still knocked out. He damn well better be okay," Graham said with an ominous warning.

Still holding the letter, he watched as Ennis and Bang carefully handed out cups of coffee. Coming out of the sleepy stupor proved a challenge, especially for Macy, whom Tala kept jiggling, as much to snap herself out of it as to rouse Macy.

"I'm trying," Macy said, grumbling.

"I know, dear. Here, try this." Tala held a coffee mug to Macy's lips. She looked as worried about the girls as their own mother would have been.

Graham watched them recover, trying to make sense of the situation. "I think they meant well," he said with reluctance. "If they get exposed to us as carriers, they're dead. I guess I can understand, but jeez . . . So they broke two panes out of the window. Used something to put us all to sleep. Opened the window and climbed in. Gave us all immunizations and dropped off some supplies for us to combat the intruders," Graham said, trying to make sense of it all.

"The shot fairy and Santa Claus, all in one," Macy said, swaying back and forth with her eyes barely open. They all snickered a little and Graham put his hand on Macy's shoulder to steady her.

"Yeah, the prepper elves," Mark said. "What'd they bring?" he asked. "Can we trust them?"

Graham turned around. "Well, there's a generator," which was the first, most obvious thing to mention. He left Macy's side, knelt in front of the pile, and rummaged through it. "There's a water pump, what looks like a large can of something," he picked it up and almost dropped it, surprised by the lightness of it. He turned it over to read the label. "Vegetable seeds, so I guess we don't have to worry about that now," he said.

"Yay!" exclaimed Tala, suddenly more awake.

Graham picked up two large bottles. "Multivitamins for adults and children," he said. Then he noticed three large boxes. "Motion detector lights, surveillance kit with cameras, radio," Graham said, in a reluctant manner, "and a first aid kit." He moved the kit aside to find, last but not least, a large package of Oreos hidden beneath it; he took it over to the others. "And—Oreos," he said, prompting them all to cheer.

They tore open the package and shared the rare treat with one another, dipping them into their black coffee. The sugar rush helped exterminate the last fleeting grogginess left behind by the injections and sleep mist.

"Look, he's moving," Bang said with a mouthful of cookie. "Sheriff!"

They all turned around to look at the beloved dog. "Let's give him space to come out of it on his own," Graham said. "I think if we're hovering, he might get defensive," he added.

"What did the letter say exactly?" Tala asked.

"Oh, here." Graham handed Tala the letter while he stood Macy up. He wrapped one of her slender arms around his waist and held her close as he walked her around the living area, trying to help the girl to fully come to as Tala read the letter out loud.

To: Graham's Camp

We wanted to extend our hand of friendship in these dark times. We've observed your camp and know you recently encountered a potential threat. Please accept these gifts to help defend your camp and yourselves. We suggest you use these cameras and motion detectors to help provide surveillance. We've also inoculated all of you from the standard flu virus, tetanus, and the elderly gent from pneumonia as well as your pet against rabies. Sorry about the sleeping gas. Because you are all carriers of the virus, we had to take certain precautions to protect ourselves. We hope you can understand the risk our community is under and the necessity of these actions.

It's in our best interest to help, since we are neighbors of sorts and we would not want to see a camp of children on their own in this unforgiving environment. We commend you for taking them all on and are grateful you accepted the boy we brought to you.

Stay well,
Cascade Prepper Group

"They've been watching us," Tala said, though not in a surprised way.

Smiling up at him sweetly, Macy said to Graham, "I think I'm okay now, Graham, you can let me go."

"You're just saying that so you can curl up somewhere. I know you. You're sneaky," Graham teased.

He let her go anyway when Tala stood up to start their day.

"I call the bathroom," Graham announced, and the rest of them moaned. Living with three teenagers proved a challenge mostly with bathroom use. He'd learned this new maneuver from Mark, who had previously lived with two sisters. So after he observed this practice, as soon as the urge hit him, he started "calling it."

"Well, girls, we have more meat to dry and laundry to do today," Tala said, then added, "Ennis, can you run down to the store and pick up more detergent?"

Laughter ensued when he said in all seriousness, "Yessum, what brand? You kids want anything else?"

These little joking moments kept their lives sane, but they couldn't be used more than once without falling flat. It kept the kids from dwelling on the past and the pain. They had to move forward, and Graham and Tala, without ever having discussed it, tried in little ways to keep their focus on the kids, helping to shape them into the people they needed to be now to survive this world.

Before the laughter faded, Graham heard Sheriff's claws tapping on the wood floor. The dog trotted out into the middle of the living room, and then let out a big sneeze followed by three more.

Though this caused another gale of laughter, Graham saw relief in everyone's eyes. Like him, they'd been worried about their comrade too. He'd become more than a family pet to them. Once he finished sneezing, Sheriff leaned back and stretched his front paws, splaying his long claws out in front of him. It was his way of dealing with the lethargy that they all still fought. He walked closer to the door, and Bang opened it for him to go do his business.

Within the prepper camp, Dalton and Sam watched the awakening of the carriers. "Graham's going to be pissed off when he figures this out," Sam said, stating the obvious. Dalton had to agree; he would be angry too, in the same circumstances.

"Yeah, if I ever get to talk to him, I'm going to tell him it was all Rick's idea," he said, only half joking.

When everyone was awake and more or less functional, Dalton focused his worried gaze on the big German shepherd. "Dammit, come on, dog," he urged.

"You guys calculated the effects on the dog, right?" Sam asked.

"Yeah, but there's always a risk," Dalton said. "The girls and the dog got the brunt of the mist, so it's going to be harder for them to come out of it."

Dalton changed to a different camera feed and adjusted the audio so that he could hear and see what exactly was going on. Even now he wondered if it was right to have put snooping cameras inside their dwelling. It was necessary, he told himself. *Our own lives depend on knowing what's going on with this group.*

When the dog staggered out, huffed, sneezed, then went to the door to be released, Dalton felt released, too. He breathed a sigh of relief and switched to the outdoor feed. "Glad that's over."

"Yep." Sam got up to go back and finish his current project while Dalton stretched back in the swivel chair, stretching his hands toward the roof of the tent. He checked the time and figured the guys in quarantine were up for their next blood withdrawals, so he would go over there to give them the updates he knew they were waiting for, as soon as Reuben showed up to relieve him. Just as the thought crossed his mind, the man appeared with his coffee and toast in hand. Reuben had obviously stopped at the mess tent on his way over to relieve Dalton.

"Hey, man, how'd it go?" he asked in his deep voice.

"About as expected, really," Dalton said.

Reuben gave him a once-over. "You look spent, man,"

"Thanks."

"Everyone's upbeat and buzzed, waiting for the details."

"They'll just have to wait till Graham's Camp Hour," Dalton said, smiling.

"Okay, update *me*, then," Reuben said.

Dalton liked Reuben. He was a tall and imposing guy of few words. He'd always chitchat a little, and then get right down to business, as he had just now.

He'd served with the man in Afghanistan and had come to respect his quiet, deliberate ways. Reuben often noticed small details others missed, things that would help keep them all alive. Dalton and some of the others called him Spock behind his back. Truth was, he wrote passionate prose and other works, but he just didn't verbalize much.

Reuben's dark skin had saved their asses one night when they were trapped between two clusters of enemy forces and forced to hide in the not-so-abundant desert brush. The only way out was to set off a radio beacon, but their low altitude disallowed the connection. In the dead of night Rueben calculated the risks, and before anyone else could come up with a better solution, he removed his gear and his shirt. He climbed up onto the top of their enclosure with the enemy in plain sight. He was able to make contact, saving them by calling in an air strike. It worked and Dalton often wondered if someone as lily white as he was could have done the same. He would have lit up like a Christmas tree—in more ways than one.

Dalton started on his report, reading it to Reuben: "Carrier subjects woke within safety limit allotment without incident. Graham read the letter with the anticipated result. They're getting on with their day. No intruders spotted. So far, no sign of the China virus within our men."

"Sounds good, man, get some sleep," Reuben said.

"I will, after I go see the ladies." said Dalton, and Reuben knew that he meant Rick and Steven.

Dalton got up, ran both hands through his already disheveled hair, and took his time walking through the camp, waving at those just rising to meet the day. He saw anticipation in their eyes.

In the mess tent, Kim met him with a kiss and hug. She smelled of coffee and bacon already. Everyone knew not to ask what had happened. They would all find out that evening.

"You're sleepy," Kim said, "and you look both stressed and relieved, too." She held up her hands. "No, no. I'm not asking. I don't have to," she added with a grin. "I know your expressions, and I can see it all worked out. I'll wait like the others for details tonight. You get off to bed."

"I'll see you later. I'm going over to quarantine, and then I'll hit the sack," Dalton told her. He left her with a discreet tweak and grabbed the piece of buttered homemade toast that she handed him. He savored it as he walked. Years ago he had wondered why in the world they'd bought so much butter in the stores and stockpiled it in their freezers; it had seemed like an unnecessary luxury then, but Dalton certainly did appreciate it now. Once gone, it would be the powdered stuff or none at all.

The gravel crunched under his boots as Dalton walked out in the morning light. He saw Sam already hard at work, with beads of sweat dripping off his forehead even though it was chilly out. He knew the man worked hard every day. He didn't want to disturb him, so he just raised his hand and Sam nodded back without breaking his momentum.

Dalton continued on to the guarded entrance where someone was always in the sentry post. Even though they had the whole place monitored, a real eye gave them extra insurance, and it kept them in practice in terms of vigilance. Everyone took their turn, even the women and children. Kids over ten years of age were matched with an adult until they were fourteen and trained in all security protocols. So far, the plan had worked well for them.

The sentry for the day buzzed the gate open for Dalton and then re-engaged the magnetic lock behind him. Dalton waved at the guard and then continued on to the hidden quarantine bunker. Finished with his toast, he marched, swinging his arms smartly, an old habit from military training.

He heard an eagle call, looked up, and saw the majestic bird circling with obvious hunting intent. The birds of prey had ample feeding grounds, like most other wild carnivores. He imagined their numbers would also rise like those of the other natural predators. He definitely smelled something decaying in the area, but that wasn't unusual these days.

Snow lay in spots where the tree clearings allowed it to fall and its frozen crust crunched beneath his boots along with the fallen pinecones and needles. Dalton recalled when this path was muddied and slippery from frequent traffic, in the days when more people had to be quarantined. They finally had to resort to the use of galoshes they kept at the gate to reduce the mess. Now, the path was frozen hard and much less traveled. Those early days had been hard for everyone.

These days the quarantine building stood mostly as a grim reminder of what they'd gone through to get to where they were now. Many hadn't made it from this place, leaving it embedded with troubled emotions he thought he could feel it as he got nearer. Family after family had been admitted through the process, desperate to make it clear of the facility.

Most of those who developed the China virus accepted their fate, but one man that Dalton remembered did not. As soon as Clarisse whispered the news that only he was positive, both she and Dalton watched in horror as he calmly approached his wife and baby, who were sitting on the other end of the room, and shot them both dead. He decided to end it immediately for the three of them, not just himself. He smiled at them through the observation glass as if he'd won some prize, and then shot himself. The whole time Dalton and Clarisse were begging and screaming, but there was nothing they could do. That was the day Dalton had held Clarisse back from the entry door. Mostly because of that man, Dalton felt this angst whenever he approached the quarantine area.

Dalton shook the awful memory from his mind. It was time now to focus on his friends who, having taken the risk for the carriers, were locked inside—temporarily, he hoped—and he needed to be upbeat for them.

The guard greeted Dalton casually, having been alerted to his approach ahead of time. "Morning, sir," he said, smiling.

"Morning. Any news?" Dalton asked.

"No, they don't tell me anything," he said, joking.

"Clarisse inside?"

"Yes, of course. She never leaves this place." The guard typed the code into the door's keypad. Dalton ducked his head under the doorway of the domed building and walked down the darkened hallway toward the light that shone through from the observation room.

He found Clarisse looking at the slides on the miniature projector. She looked up at him through her dark framed glasses as he entered. Her chestnut hair was up in its tight bun, as always. As the camp scientist, Clarisse, took care of all quarantine procedures as well as medical care, both major and minor. She wasn't known to socialize much with the men because she didn't want to be responsible for gossip or fear among the wives. Everyone highly respected her opinion and willingness to work with dangerous subjects.

Dalton's only concern for Clarisse was that she didn't have anyone in her personal life and he wasn't sure how she coped through all the stress without the relief valve of a personal connection. When the families were going through the quarantine process, she'd held steadfast through it all, often sleeping on her cot right in the observation room to help provide them and herself with a sense of security. She reran positive tests multiple times, fully knowing what their outcomes would be but wanting to be sure nonetheless.

"Good morning, Clarisse. How are the boys?" Dalton asked.

"I'll tell you in just a second. They just finished the third draw and so far, as of now, they're negative." She peered into the microscope without looking up at Dalton, and then dropped the slide securely into the trash receptacle.

"That's good news, so far. Are they still awake?" Dalton asked.

"Yeah, they were just giving me a hard time for not including Twinkies in their rations," she said, rolling her eyes.

"Those bastards!" His mock indignation brought a bit of a smile to her face.

"Now they're in for the twelve, so I imagine they'll go back to sleep in a while. If you want to talk to them, go right ahead. I have their com off in protest of the Twinkie remarks, but you can turn it back on," she said.

Clarisse had a gorgeous smile, and Dalton thought she would make any man blissfully happy. He never asked her why she kept to herself. It just wasn't his business, being a married man.

He looked at the pair on the monitor. It was like observing an old married couple arguing with one another. Rick motioned with his hands as always, and from the looks of things, the argument was getting heated.

"God, they're already fighting, and it's only the first day," Dalton said. He flipped the audio on, but kept silent until he could figure out what the two were debating.

Clarisse came over behind him to see what was going on in case it appeared to be something medical. After a second of observance, she shrugged. "Just chalk it up to their flawed personalities, Dalton." She returned to work on her logs.

Rick's arms were going up and down now in parallel motion as Steven shook his head back and forth. Each was on his own side of the room.

"You know I'm right, you asshole, you just won't admit it. Batman has the Batmobile, the guns and, for crying out loud, he owns his own company. What the hell does Spider-Man have? All he does is shoot silly string, and he's a goddamn reporter!" Rick spewed with mock venom.

"All right, ladies," Dalton said, cutting off Steven's retort.

"Morning, boss." Rick's furious expression changed in an instant, as if the heated argument had never taken place.

"Hey, Dalton," Steven said.

Dalton secretly got a kick out of the two guys' antics. They could appear about ready to strangle one another but were the best of friends. This was just their way of dealing with stress.

"Any afterthoughts?" Dalton asked them.

"No. Yes, is the dog okay?" Rick said. "I had to blast him first. He might have gotten a little too much."

Dalton figured the dog would be the one they were most worried about. "He's fine. They all are, in fact. That's why I came by. I just wanted you to know, they all woke up. They were pissed, as we predicted, until they settled down and saw the gifts. The Oreos went over really well, too. That was a nice touch, putting them on the bottom."

"How's the little kid?" Steven asked. "I was more concerned about him getting too much."

"He's fine. First one up, in fact. Good job," Dalton said, then added, "He freaked out a little bit trying to wake the others, but then Mark was up soon after. Oh, and Graham has already figured out how you guys got in."

"Figures. Smart fella," Rick said with admiration.

"He's a good guy. All this time we've been watching them, but now, after this, they're more real to me. Those kids really do need him," Steven said.

Changing the subject, Dalton said, "Well, it looks like so far you two are clear, but we all know the rules. Try not to kill each other. It's only the first day."

Both men started wrestling, just for Dalton. They pretended to punch each other and fell over on the beds in slow motion.

"See what I have to contend with?" Clarisse said behind Dalton as she motioned toward the two beyond the glass window.

"Good luck," he told her, walking toward the exit, "I've got a date with my pillow."

"Sleep well, Dalton. See you later."

Turning her attention back to Rick and Steven, she said, "All right, you two, you've got five and a half now." Looking at the log clock and before she turned off the microphone, she added,

"Catwoman could kick both their asses." She hung up before they could react.

The guys looked at each other.

"She's right," Steven said.

Rick had to agree.

"Oh, man," Mark said, having gone outside. He saw the young doe struggling, having caught her hoof on one of the nail boards, and was caught between two trees. He could see the cuts in her hide, and blood seeping out. Now that she saw him, she scampered, trying to free herself, but only managed to twist her limbs even more.

He and Bang approached her from two different sides. Bang held her attention while Mark snuck around behind the doe, trying to free her from the trap, and at the same time, trying to stay clear of her other hooves as they flailed about.

"This was a bad idea," Bang said.

Mark wrenched the nail that tethered her, setting her free. He strategically left his hand around her ankle, a few seconds longer, until Bang cleared her path. She stood still for a few hushed seconds, watching them, until Bang raised his arms, shooing her to freedom. She was off like a flash through the greenery.

With that done they began pulling up every last hidden trap so that wouldn't happen again. They had the security cameras now.

Graham climbed the makeshift ladder and secured the last camera at the front entrance with Ennis's help. As the sharp bitter wind seeped into his own jacket, Graham knew the old man couldn't handle much more, even with gloves on.

"That's it," he said. "Let's get back inside."

He helped Ennis walk, though the old man protested. "What are we going to do if you break a hip?" Graham asked him.

"You'll have one less mouth to hunt for," Ennis said.

"We need you, Ennis. Even if you don't realize it." Graham searched for the boys as they headed up to the cabin. "Here, you get inside. This wind's picking up. I'll get the boys. It looks like a storm is coming on."

Gone were the days of TV and radio station weather reports, gone the cheerful reports of "cloudy with a chance of sprinkles" or "duck and cover, a category five is headed your way." It was back to primal instincts only, and Graham could tell from the sky that something big was on the way. It looked blizzard time.

He picked up his pace on the cleared trail to find the boys. He'd seen them earlier, working their way through collecting the nailed boards that they'd all deemed a bad idea. He called to them.

"Over here!" Mark's voice rose over the wind. They were both kneeling down, looking at something in the rocky shoreline.

"What's up?" Graham asked.

"The bear traps are missing," Mark said.

"And there are more footprints," Bang added.

"Graham, the sign is gone too," Mark said, pointing behind him.

"All right, let's get to the cabin. There's a storm coming," Graham said.

The previous light mood had turned dark. The boys were worried now. Graham thought at first that any animal could have come along and maybe moved the traps but with the sign clearly torn free, it was undeniable that the intruders were sending a message. This was not good.

He looked around at the waves lapping at the shore under tumultuous layers of clouds above, warring in the sky. It sent a chill through to his spine. He looked toward the intruders' general vicinity and couldn't imagine why they'd want to bother with Graham and his newfound family. Why would any human fathom committing a crime like this? Hadn't they all been through enough? He knew he had to be even more vigilant now. He wouldn't let it happen again. He'd shoot them on sight, one at a time if he had to. Ennis was right; all along, the old man had echoed Graham's dad's attitude. So now, they had been warned. If he saw them once more, he would shoot to kill them all.

Turning his back to the lake, Graham had to pull up the collar of his coat as the wind started pelting his back with sleet, a prelude to the snow he'd predicted.

Once in the clearing he could see Tala standing on the porch waiting for him. He thought she looked lovely in an old gray sweater she'd pulled tightly around her waist, watching his approach through the swirling snow, some of which stuck to her long raven hair. She was beautiful, he could see that—and he could feel it too.

Her kind eyes watched him. Covered in snow, he started up the stairs to the porch, and stopping right in front of her without losing stride, he pulled her to him. She looked up into his eyes. That was all he needed to bring his lips down onto hers, kissing her. She opened her dark eyes, questioning, and he said in a low, husky voice, "There's a storm coming."

Tala nodded, uncertain what to say. Graham turned her around and opened the cabin door. "Everyone in the cabin?" he asked.

"All except Sheriff."

Graham opened the door again and whistled. Seconds later the dog appeared with his brown fur turned white from the snow.

"Get in here, pal," Graham said.

Tala grabbed a spare towel and wiped down the dog before he started to stink up the place. Still a bit groggy, Sheriff lay down by the fire and quickly fell into a deep slumber.

Graham could hear the kids gathered in the bunkroom talking among themselves, and Ennis was asleep in his chair already. He took it all in, and wished there was a separate room built off the living area; he really wanted to have some private time with Tala. *No, stop thinking that way.* It was confusing. He felt deeply for Tala, more than he'd cared to admit so soon after the death of his wife. Something about being cooped up at the world's end made one feel the urge to mate, and that is why the thought of one of those men getting their hands on Tala or one of the twins made Graham crazy.

He reached over to the door and locked it tight to the outside world as Tala looked up at him from the kitchen with a little smile on her face.

He took off his boots and put them by the wall, then hung up his coat so that it wouldn't drip on the floor. With his rifle slung over his shoulder he walked into the kitchen where no one could see them and put his hand on Tala's waist.

"Tala, are you okay?" he whispered.

"Yes, are you?" she asked and turned to face him full on. "Regrets?"

He answered her by brushing his lips across hers lightly. He reached his hand up to the back of her slender neck, feeling her silky hair and tangling his fingers in it. He felt her warm breath on his face and watched as she closed her eyes.

A soft snoring sound came from the living area and the children's voices in the bunkroom sounded like they'd opted for a game of Monopoly. This was all the privacy the two shared, standing in the kitchen. Graham briefly thought of pulling her into the bathroom and then felt ashamed at the idea.

Tala parted her lips, and then he couldn't help it. Graham pulled her by the hips closer to him, wrapping his arms around her slender waist and ran his hand up her side, feeling the length of her, the shape of her before he kissed her. He felt a shudder of pleasure run through her muscles. It sent shock waves down to his toes.

Moments later, he heard Bang speak his name.

He pulled back from Tala's embrace. "Yeah, buddy, whatcha need?" He thought he must look guilty as hell, acting as if he'd not just been making out with Tala in the kitchen.

The boy looked confused but then said, "Do you want to play Monopoly with us?" Though it was about the last thing he wanted to do right about then, Graham said, "Sure, give me a minute."

After Bang had gone back into the other room, feeling like a heel, Graham sank onto a kitchen chair and lowered his head.

Tala massaged his shoulders. "It's all right, he doesn't know what he saw," she whispered.

"I promised his mother I'd take care of him. I just hope I'm not screwing up already," Graham said.

"Graham, she could not have chosen a better guardian than you."

He stood, turned, and faced her. "We'll talk about this another time," he said, pressing a quick kiss on her forehead. He told himself it was right that he spent a little time with the kids anyway. As Marcy dealt him the phony money, he could hear Tala working in the kitchen and knew they'd soon be breathing in the good aromas of her cooking.

At least this storm gave them all a chance to be together, and he didn't have to worry about one of the girls being snatched.

Checking each monitor and writing in the events logs, Reuben did a double take when he saw Graham and Tala in the kitchen. "Oh, Lord," he said under his breath, then turned away out of some sense of respect. All he wrote in the log was, AIW: "All is well." *It is, isn't it?* he reasoned.

Then the quarantine line flashed, indicating an incoming call. Reuben picked up, and Clarisse said, "We've got a temp."

Reuben's heart jumped. "Who?"

"Steven."

"What is it?"

"Hundred and four point three."

"Is it . . . ?" he asked.

"I don't know yet. Rick's in there, too, and he's fine right now. It's just Steven," she said.

"Maybe it's something else, Clarisse."

"Yeah, Reuben, let's hope so."

"I'll let Dalton know."

"Okay, I'll give an update in twenty minutes, when my scan's over," she said, sounding nervous.

"Deal."

Reuben buzzed Dalton. "Sorry to wake you, man, but we have a probable positive."

"What is it?" Dalton asked, waking up out of a light sleep.

"It's Steven, he's showing an elevated temperature."

"What does Clarisse say?"

"Twenty minutes and she'll know more."

"And Rick?"

"Fine, so far."

"I'm coming in," Dalton said, and he hung up.

Reuben liked Steven. The man was quiet but amicable, and he was the only one who could put up with Rick's constant bullshit and then simply sit quietly, like Sam did, without the need for conversation.

Looking up at the screen again, he noticed the little boy had caught the pair making out in the kitchen. "Oh, man," he murmured, "better you than me." Then he thought of why he'd been able to capture that little scene. "I sure hope this scheme didn't cost us."

~ ~ ~

Dalton went directly to quarantine through the blizzard. In his mind, if this were the virus, it would all be his fault; he'd never forgive himself. He brushed off the accumulated snow and stomped is boots as he entered the building.

"What do you have, Clarisse?" he asked, barging in without the usual pleasantries.

"Give me five more minutes," she answered.

He walked over to the observation window. Steven lay back against his pile of crisp, white, sterile pillows, watching Rick's *Seinfeld* reruns, occasionally laughing. When he saw Dalton standing in the window, Steven waved an arm wide in a dismissive gesture. "I'm fine, it's just a little fever."

Rick lowered his comic book and gave an "I don't know" face.

Dalton knew they were aware of the risks. This was their way of dealing with the danger. He looked at the screen monitoring Rick's vitals and they appeared fine. Steven's temperature was now 104.4. The man looked a little glassy-eyed, but other than that he seemed fine.

"Diarrhea? Anything like that?" Dalton asked Clarisse.

"Not so far. It's just a fever," she said.

The buzzer went off, breaking the trance.

She read the data.

"I don't think that's it," she said after reading the printout. "It's not viral. It's some kind of bacterial infection!" She almost shouted for joy.

"I don't know without examining him, but it isn't viral," she said again. She went over to the microphone. "Steven, the results are in. It's not viral. It's an infection. Do you have any pain, anywhere? Cuts, a toothache, a stomachache?"

Steven sat up. "I don't think so. I feel kind of crummy all over though," he said.

"Rick, get up off your ass," Clarisse demanded. "I'm going to need your help. I know you're not trained, but I need you to examine him."

"Does this involve touching him?" He waved his hands. "Ooooh, ick!"

"Yes. Now knock it off," Clarisse said in all seriousness. "Go wash your hands. With soap and hot water."

Rick washed his hands in the steaming hot water singing "Happy Birthday to Me," aloud, twice, just as his wife had taught their kids to do. Apparently, two runs through the song was a sufficient allotment of time to kill germs while washing.

"Okay, boss, now what?" he said, holding up his clean, hairy hands.

"Strip, Steven," Clarisse said.

"Really!" Steven said, acting happy.

"Yes, and do it now. No more bullshit, you guys. Get serious, because this *is* serious."

"Ah, Jesus," Steven said, and began pulling off his T-shirt and boxers.

Steven stood there in the nude and Dalton took note as Clarisse lowered her gaze, trying to provide the man's privacy but needing to do her job.

"All right, Rick, start with his head," she said.

They both looked at her, not willing to let it go.

"You know what I mean, goddammit," she admonished.

Steven bent down to let Rick go through his hair, touching his scalp.

"Rick, you're looking for any kind of sore or inflammation. Does he have any bumps anywhere?" she asked as he ran his hands through Steven's light hair.

"I don't see or feel anything," Rick said.

"Okay, check behind his ears, and then look down his back," she said.

"Sorry, dude, turn around," Rick said to him.

"I do have a headache," Steven complained.

"Okay, but that's not enough to go on," Clarisse said.

"Steven, now raise your arms. Rick, look carefully," she said.

Steven did so with reluctance, but when he raised his left arm, it took only a second for Rick to say, "There it is. It's a tick." He pointed at it.

Steven tried to see what the hell Rick was pointing at, but it was out of his range of view. "What the hell?" he asked Clarisse, turning to face the window at the same time as he tried to probe his armpit.

"It's behind your armpit, at the base of your shoulder blade; you can't see it, dude," Rick said.

"Oh, thank God; tick fever." Clarisse couldn't have sounded happier.

"It's red and swollen, with a damn tick right in the center. Could have been there for days," Rick said.

"Come over to the lab table, Steven," Clarisse said.

He started to walk that way, but then doubled back to put his boxers back on. Clarisse stopped him.

"Um, you could have more ticks. Rick, check out the rest of his backside, the areas he can't see."

Rick gave Steven a quick but thorough once-over, then proclaimed, "All clear! Just that one."

"Steven, can you do the rest of the examination yourself?" Clarisse asked.

"Yep."

She gave him a minute to perform the procedure. Meanwhile, Rick washed his hands again, with added drama and louder birthday greetings to himself. When Steven was through with his self-examination he put on his briefs on and moved to the examination area.

"I love you, dude, but not in that way," Rick said, steam rising over the sink.

Steven lay down on the partitioned lab table. Clarisse put her hands through the gloves in the wall and prepared the instruments she needed to extract the entire parasite.

"Okay, lift your arm a bit, let's see it," she said, stepping closer so she could examine it. Clarisse quickly removed the parasite, cleaned the wound and gave him a fast acting antibiotic injection and a few oral anti-inflammatories for swelling and his headache.

The four of them blew huge sighs of relief, knowing in these days what a fever could mean and the catastrophic consequences it could bring.

Steven went back to his cot and soon later drifted off to sleep.

Four days passed with little to do other than watch the snow fall, layer upon layer as it drifted downward, magnificent in its scope. When it stopped, the sun rose high, making the ice crystals sparkle brightly. Deer, moose, rabbit, and wolf had left their tracks everywhere. The evergreen boughs bent low under their frozen loads, highlighting their beauty. Both treacherous and elegant, quiet tranquility abounded for those who ventured out bundled from head to toe.

Graham shoveled off the porch once again. He didn't need anyone slipping—especially not Ennis. The kids were busily rolling enormous snowballs to conjure up a man as round as he would be tall. Graham delighted in their activity, with Sheriff jumping up and down, running alongside them. That sight itself evoked both sadness and joy; it wasn't that he wanted them depressed, but Graham felt they had no real reason to be happy. Yet they were, in spite of it all.

Tala walked out with a cup of piping hot cocoa and handed it to Graham. There remained tension between them, with neither of them certain of where things between them might go. Graham identified his own emotions as guilt laced with grief and a touch of madness. They held him back, though at night he couldn't help but look at Tala's sleeping form, wishing her body lay next to his.

He realized that Ennis had sensed this all, maybe before they knew it themselves. He often said to Graham, "Why don't you two take a walk. I'll watch the kids," as if he were the grandfather of their large brood. But Graham always ignored the offer and went about his day. He didn't think she would oblige him anyway, other than the occasional touch or hand-holding throughout their days. They were held captive in the cabin, so Graham tried to ignore these insistent feelings.

"County roads plowed yet?" Ennis asked. He took great amusement making these kinds of jokes.

"Naw, you know it takes them forever to get to these backcountry lanes," Graham said, playing along.

"It's too cold for an old man out here," Ennis said, watching the children playing in the snow.

"Go inside. I'll make you some cocoa," Tala said, putting her arm around Ennis.

"Stop bossing me around, woman," he griped playfully.

Truly, the old man had become a treasure to them all. Even when he was cranky he was adorable.

As far as supplies were concerned they were doing fine; they had stored enough to feed themselves two meals a day, with a bit extra for the growing young minds and bodies that needed more. With Tala's vigilance in the pantry, they wouldn't starve; she kept precise records. The only things they really yearned for were butter, potatoes, and fresh milk.

Unfortunately, it wasn't likely for them to come across a cow during the winter, but dry and canned milk seemed to be getting them by. They'd even adjusted to drinking the powdered stuff now without too much complaint. Graham vowed to find a dairy cow as soon as possible come spring, even if it killed him.

The multivitamins the preppers had provided helped a lot as well. As a result of the immunizations, they had felt groggy and sore for a few days but fortunately, the snowstorm gave them time to rest and recover.

Ennis went back inside, and Tala followed him in to check on dinner. The days were short this time of year, and Graham could already see the light fading from the bitterly cold sky. One by one, the kids came in, having succeeded in making their snowman. They climbed the steps with rosy cheeks and drenched with melting snow. They knew the drill at the door by now, and Tala didn't have to mention it to them again: boots in a row and all.

Having finally run off pent-up energy, they welcomed the warm minestrone soup Tala put together along with her now famous warm biscuits. She even made soft molasses cookies, surprising them all after dinner. Though the chickens did not produce many eggs this time of year, they managed to get two before they ceased laying for the winter. Tala decided to use eggs in baking so they could all enjoy them together.

"Bang, let's you and I go feed the chickens and make sure they're put up tight for the night," Graham said.

They rounded up the chickens and took them their warmed brick. They also fed them what few scraps and biscuits Tala saved for them. They kept fresh water and bedding for the birds, and hoped eggs would be plentiful in the spring with higher temperatures and more daylight.

~ ~ ~

The next day brought a surprise warming trend, and the snow turned to a soupy melting mess outside. Tala threatened to have everyone start lining their boots up outside now, since she was constantly wiping up the melting snow in the cabin.

For the lack of anything better to do and a good case of cabin fever, Graham and the boys began shoveling a trail through the melting mess to both the lakeside and driveway entrances, so that when the slush refroze, they would at least have access to each.

The snowman that the kids had built leaned at an angle now. They all gazed at it sadly, knowing its hours were numbered. After a while, the sun beamed down on them, warming their shoulders through heavy jackets. They began to sweat with the work, feeling invigorated with each heft of the shovel.

The girls watched them from the porch. Since the guys were finished with the driveway side, Tala and the twins decided to take a walk. They waved to the guys as they made their way up the lane. Graham watched them and thought the only thing abnormal about the bucolic scene was seeing that all three were armed.

He'd warned them about the wolves, and they promised to return in twenty minutes, timing it to ten minutes up the road and ten back. He relented and let them go, knowing they must be bored having stayed inside too long. He would have gone with them, but really wanted to help the boys finish the almost complete task of trail clearing.

Trudging through the melting snow helped the women work their leg muscles. It was a joy to breathe the fresh air and get away from the cabin for a short while.

~ ~ ~

Graham heard the engine and the shots at the same time. A chill ran up his spine before he even heard the screams. He grabbed his rifle and ran through the forest to where he thought Tala and the girls might be, jumping over fallen logs carelessly as fast as his might would carry him.

Only eight minutes out, the dread fell over him. The intruders were coming for them by land, not lake. The girls ran as fast as they could, but with sinister intentions and stronger bodies, the intruders would win. Marcy raced for the tree line with Tala and Macy right behind. They might have made it had Macy not tripped over a chunk of ice. One of the intruders grabbed her easily. Then Tala turned and pulled on the girl, clenching Macy as the intruder yanked Macy's pistol from her chest harness and aimed it at Macy's temple.

"Let her go!" Tala screamed.

"We just want one of you, darlin'," he said, making her skin crawl.

He had his thick fat fingers entwined in Macy's hair.

"She's a child. Take *me*," Tala said, lowering her rifle.

"No, Tala!" Macy screamed.

The man pushed the girl down hard into the road in time to grab Tala harshly before she could fight back. Tala dropped her weapon to Macy's side as he dragged her to their jeep. The intruders planned a quick getaway. Having already heard a vehicle breaking the silence, they made their escape.

Their mission was simple: to pick up one of the three and get back to camp without any trouble. They didn't care which, but the woman would be better than one of those scrawny girls. They needed someone to cook and clean for them and to take care of their "other needs," as they had put it between themselves.

"No!" Macy screamed again.

"Run, Macy!" Tala cried out before her captor covered her mouth with one hand and pulled her onto him in the passenger's seat of their jeep, which then sped away.

Macy did run. She grabbed the extra rifle and took off following the jeep as far as she could when she heard Graham behind her, yelling, with Marcy following him.

He knew he'd failed. He wanted to shoot at the vehicle speeding away in the distance but couldn't risk hitting Tala. The next thing he knew, Mark pulled up, driving the truck from the opposite direction, "Get in," Mark yelled when he pulled up to Graham and the girls.

"No, *you* get *out*," Graham said. The boy began to protest, and Graham reached in and yanked him out of the driver's seat.

"I need you here," Graham said, throwing the truck into gear and taking off after Tala.

"Come on, he's right. Let's get back," Mark said. Both girls were crying, and he embraced them, hurrying them back to the cabin.

Reuben switched from one camera to another. One minute all was well, the next it was not. The women went for a walk and the guys were working outside, maintaining trails. Ennis did what old men do on cold winter days; he napped. The scene was like something out of *Little Women*, which Reuben had read to his daughters.

After he had seen the girls leave on the north camera, he watched as they faded into the distance. He was happy for them to get some fresh air for a change. The south side camera showed the guys working and joking together.

Then he heard the shots on the audio and looked at the screens frantically to find where it had come from. The boys stood momentarily frozen, but Graham had already sped off toward the sound.

"Something's up," Reuben said.

He started switching through cameras and found Mark running into the cabin and retrieving keys.

Reuben radioed Dalton, "The girls and Graham are off camera to the north. It looks like Mark's going for a drive, speeding north in the truck."

"Coming in," Dalton said.

Reuben turned up the volume when Bang and Sheriff stormed into the cabin and Bang called for Ennis.

"What's up, lad?" Ennis asked.

"Someone's shooting. Tala and the twins went for a walk. Graham ran after them, and then Mark drove the truck. I don't know where Graham is," Bang said, clearly scared.

Ennis patted the boy, knowing he and Graham had a special bond. To reassure him, he said, "Graham will be all right. I'm sure whatever it is, he'll be right back."

Bang's lower lip trembled. "You come warm up by the fire, boy," Ennis said. You're too cold."

"No! We need to help them!" Bang urged.

"Sounds like Mark has it all under control. I think we should stay here. If everyone goes off, no one will be watching the cabin and I know Graham would want you to keep an eye on it. I can't do it all by myself anymore," Ennis said, hoping that would keep the boy from worrying.

They heard footsteps running through the snow and coming to the door, so Ennis grabbed his shotgun and peered out the window before he opened the door. He saw the twins with Mark, so he let them in.

"What's going on, son?" Ennis asked Mark.

"The intruders from the lake took Tala!"

The girls were sniffling, and now that Bang knew he blubbered too. "Where's Graham?"

"He went after them. He wouldn't let me go with him. He said he needed me here." Ennis could see that the teenager felt like he'd somehow failed Graham.

Ennis was at a loss in a situation like this. He knew there was nothing he could do to help Graham. The only thing he could think of was to try to keep the children calm and stop them from doing something stupid.

"Graham's right," he said to Mark, "you need to be here. I can't take care of them on my own. I'm an old man. Graham can take care of himself. He'll get Tala and come back, don't you all worry. You girls come dry off by the fire. Warm up your hands. You're shivering."

The girls were still sniffling. Ennis could see that Mark's internal wheels were spinning, and he tried to comfort him. "Son, there's nothing you can do but wait. Have faith in Graham; he's a smart man."

"Are they going to hurt Tala?" Bang asked.

Macy was the first to snap out of it. Kneeling, she hugged the little guy. "I don't know. Hopefully Graham will get her back. She saved me," Macy said, and instead of comforting Bang, she burst into tears again.

He hugged her back and said, "Don't cry, Macy. Graham won't let them hurt Tala. He loves her. He kisses her."

Ennis looked at the back of Macy's bent head as she wept on the little boy's shoulder. Blood dripped down her back and stained her long blond hair. Ennis pointed, and Mark jumped forward.

"Macy, you're hurt," he said, reaching for her.

She stood up too fast and swayed, her knees buckling, tilting her dangerously toward the woodstove. Mark pulled her away from the fire, and half carried her to the kitchen table, where he propped her up on a chair. Marcy took off her coat to search for the source of the blood. They found a handful of hair falling away as they searched her head. A part of her scalp was ripped up, with rivulets of blood pooling into a stream down to the floor.

"Ennis! What should we do?" Marcy cried as she snatched a clean dish towel and placed it against her sister's head. Ennis helped lay Macy across Mark's knees, then cut away the hair still hanging on the tab of torn scalp. "Those sons of bitches! Press down on that bleeding spot again," he instructed Marcy.

Bang pulled off Macy's wet boots. Marcy wiped away the blood and pressed on the wound again, holding it still.

Macy tried to sit up. "What is it?" she asked. "What's happening?"

"You have a cut on your head," Marcy said. "We're just trying to stop the bleeding. Then we'll put some ointment on it and give you something for the pain."

Hearing this as he returned with the new first aid kit from the preppers, Ennis thought she sounded a lot like Tala would have in the same circumstances. "He has to get that woman back safe," he muttered, and Mark nodded.

The men must be real brutes to have pulled Macy so hard by the hair that they had yanked out a fistful of her lovely curls and hurt her so badly. It only made Ennis more worried for Tala's safety.

"I want to kill them." Mark's low comment sounded like a growl. "How could anyone hurt a girl like that?"

"There are plenty of bad people in the world, still, I guess," Ennis said as he handed Marcy a tube of antibiotic cream. When she'd applied that, he passed her a sterile dressing and some short strips of tape. His police first aid training was coming back, but his hands weren't steady enough for this kind of work.

"It's okay, Macy, I'm sure Graham will get Tala back and make those guys pay," Mark said as he and Ennis helped Macy up and steadied her. They walked her to the front room and Bang took her a cup of cocoa, as Tala would have done.

"The only thing we can do now is sit and wait," Ennis said, dragging his chair closer to the door with his rifle ready, just in case.

Mark checked the monitors, but he knew the intruders were long gone by now. "Ennis, what if I were to take the other truck and go see if I can help Graham?" Mark whispered.

Ennis didn't want to tell the young man what to do. He just said, "If you did and something was to happen to you, what would become of these guys?" Ennis said as he pointed to the three. "Graham wanted you to stay here for a reason, Mark."

"You're right, I know. I just want to do something. I hate not knowing," Mark said in frustration.

"You are doing something. You're keeping them safe. He needs you to do that," Ennis said, then added, "I'm an old man. I can't chase bad guys. I can only watch the door."

Mark paced in front of the woodstove with his hands braced behind his head.

Bang sat down by Sheriff on the floor and picked up one of the many sticks he was carving into arrows after Ennis showed him how it was done.

"That's a good idea, Bang," Mark said, and continued to work on his own since they might need them.

"What the hell happened?" Dalton asked Reuben.

"The girls went for a walk up the drive. Said they'd be back in twenty minutes. They were armed. They went off camera to the north. Everything was fine. The guys were shoveling the south trails and the old man was in the cabin. Shots were fired, and Graham took off through the west forest toward the north drive and off camera. Mark ran in the cabin and grabbed the truck keys and drove—I presume toward the shots. Then the next thing I saw was the twins and Mark return on foot," Reuben said, taking a breath.

"In the cabin, they said something about the lake men taking Tala. I figure Graham must have taken the truck from Mark and gone after her. Macy's injured, but she seems okay," Reuben said.

"She get shot?" Dalton asked.

"No, it looks like the intruders manhandled her a bit, nothing too serious," Reuben said.

"So the rest are in the cabin but, as we predicted, the intruders took Tala and now Graham's in pursuit?" Dalton asked.

"That's right. It's just what we predicted and tried to prevent," Reuben said.

"All right, dammit, what can we do?" Dalton was asking himself the question more than Reuben.

"Logically, we shouldn't do anything," Reuben said, then they both looked at the cabin screen, seeing the old man and four anxious kids waiting for news.

"Did you pull up the tracker?" Dalton asked.

"Not yet, I thought I'd wait for you. Plus, this is Rick's department; I'm not fluent in human tracking devices."

"Shit, he has three more days in the box," Dalton said, and then added, "Patch in Clarisse."

One moment later, Clarisse rigged in a patch for Rick to walk them through activating the trackers on Tala and Graham. Rick hadn't a chance to activate them yet, thinking he'd have time once he was sprung from quarantine.

Three minutes after Rick told them how to activate the tracking, they could track the series of numbers on the screen indicating Tala being sped away, presumably to the intruders' base camp, while Graham's icon followed more slowly. Dalton knew Graham would follow the tracks to locate them. At least there would be a trail. But the night was descending fast, and it would hinder his progress.

"Dammit," Dalton said.

"What? What's going on?" Rick demanded to know. His disembodied voice resounded through the tent. "God dammit, what's happening?" he yelled again when no one responded.

As news got out about the situation, several of the preppers now hung in the background watching the situation unfold. For once, Rick wasn't the one in the know, and it drove him crazy.

"They got Tala, and Graham's in pursuit," Dalton said.

"Kids all right?" Rick asked.

"Yeah," Dalton answered.

"You got to go help him, Dalton. They won't make it. You know that."

"The risk of exposure is way too high at this point," Reuben interjected.

"You look at those kids and tell me that," Rick shouted back to Reuben.

"I *am* looking at them, and I'm looking at *mine* too, Rick. You know the rules, man," Reuben said.

"Let me out, I'll go," Rick said after a pause.

"No. Dammit, Rick. No way!" Dalton said.

"Well, someone's got to go. What'd we do all this for? You're wasting time!" Rick yelled.

"I'll go." A determined voice spoke from the back and when Dalton looked behind him, he saw Sam already heading for the door.

Two minutes later, Dalton and Sam were suited up with Reuben's help. They would intercept Graham and converge on the enemy camp, retrieve Tala, and be on their way. It was that simple— or so they hoped.

Tala fought the man holding her. They hadn't slowed since they'd left and drove at breakneck speed along the slushy road in a small jeep. She was terrified, but thought that perhaps if they did crash it might be a better fate than what she knew awaited her.

Already the man holding her, grabbed her through her jeans and sweater. When she resisted him, he'd punched her from the left so hard that her lip bled freely down her chin. Tala tried to wriggle free from the beefy monster. "Please don't," she pleaded, but it was no use.

"Don't let her freeze. Remember, I'm first," the driver yelled at the bigger man. Tala shivered and cried, but he wouldn't stop.

"I think we're good. No one's following us," the driver said and reached one hand under her sweater.

She knew what was coming and could only take solace in knowing she'd saved Macy from these horrible beasts. Somehow she had to start calculating how she could escape—or kill these bastards. Tala closed her eyes and tried to detach herself from her body, thinking instead of the eagles she loved to watch, soaring over land and sea.

Graham raced, stopping every now and then to make sure he was on the right path. Thank God the icy snow tracks left an undeniable trail. With so few vehicles these days, he knew this was the right trail to follow and they did indeed go in the direction of the other side of the lake.

It was pitch dark now, and even though he had to stop occasionally to check to make sure he was still on course, he made progress, but too slowly. He pushed away his despair, and the anger over what he knew they'd do to Tala.

Just as he began to pick up speed, bright headlights dawned in his rearview mirror, flashing at him. They must have had their headlights off and only then flashed him, creeping up in the distance. It was too late for Graham to make a defensive move as the vehicle pulled around him, cutting him off. Graham grabbed his rifle, ready to shoot, when he realized it was the preppers, suited up, driving a Humvee. Dalton put up his hand in what he hoped Graham would take as a sign of peace.

"Get out of my way!" Graham yelled.

"We're trying to help you!" the prepper in the passenger seat yelled back. Though the voice came distorted through the suit, Graham thought he recognized it. "Dalton?" he said, confused.

"Yes, it's me. Get in the back. Hurry, there's little time."

Graham grabbed his rifle and ran over to the other vehicle. Some of the pieces of the mysterious prepper community were falling into place, but he didn't have time to reflect on it now. He jumped into the backseat of the Humvee and they sped off into the distance without their lights on.

"I think I saw their taillights up ahead. You know they have Tala, right?" Graham asked.

"Yes. We're tracking her now, so try to stay calm. We'll get Tala back, but you need to let us help you. This is Sam, and—well, you know me," Dalton said.

"Yes, I do, and later we will talk about why you didn't say it was you in the first place," Graham said, clearly upset. "Those fuckers grabbed one of the twins first. Tala traded herself," he added, continuing to curse the situation.

"We'll do what we can. You have to keep in mind, we're still susceptible to the virus you carry so if something happens to either of our suits, do not approach us, all right?" Dalton said.

"All right."

"Are there just the two men?" Sam asked.

"As far as I know. I don't know if there are any more in their camp. Three came by canoe from across the lake one night, but we took one out. It seems you already know that though. *Son of a bitch!* This is my fault. I should have wasted all of them that night," Graham said.

"Stop it, Graham. We've watched it all. This isn't your fault," Dalton said.

Graham went on torturing himself. "I should have kept them in the damn cabin!"

Sam spoke up then. "Look, Graham, can you see this screen?" He tapped a gloved finger on a glowing device on the front seat.

"Yeah?" Graham said as he watched two little sets of numbers moving forward, one gaining on the other.

"This one is Tala," Sam said, indicating the farthest one out.

"And the other one is me? You shits!" Graham said incredulously. "You can't just fucking tag someone just because you can," he added.

"The point is, this one is Tala," Sam said, and Graham was relieved to see some connection to her there.

"Here's the plan," Dalton said.

"Stop fighting me, bitch," the big one said, as he tried to shove his hand down the front of Tala's pants. Clearly frustrated, he yelled to the driver, "Hurry up, man."

"I told you, she's mine first," the driver said, and shoved him to make his point, knocking Tala along with him. She leaned forward, grabbing the dashboard, trying to get away from the shoving match as the driver swerved and then overcorrected as they slid in the snow, causing the jeep to tip sideways as it careened off the road. It flipped over twice before coming to a complete stop, throwing all three occupants free. When it landed it caught fire.

~ ~ ~

Graham and the preppers saw the fire from a distance and sped faster over the snowy road, almost to the point of recklessness, saying nothing to one another. They didn't know what to make of the scene before them, lit by the jeep fire when the three exited the Humvee. Tala lay face down in the center of the road, not moving. Her left leg was at an odd angle, definitely broken in the crash. Graham rushed toward her as Sam yelled, "Wait!"

They scanned the area and detected no movement. One man lay half under the burning jeep. On further inspection, he clearly proved to have died on impact, with his head gashed open and his brains exposed. There was no sign of the other. Dalton nodded for Graham to go to Tala's aid, and Graham checked her pulse and found that she was breathing, but she had obviously been knocked unconscious from the accident. Graham was afraid to move her.

It was pitch dark in the perimeter around the burning jeep and headlights of the Humvee, so Sam stood guard. Dalton checked Tala out and decided it just couldn't be helped. They needed to just lift her, despite the badly broken leg, and get her into the Humvee before she died right there.

Graham put his arm under her, and Dalton helped flip her over so that Graham could pick her up. She had a bad gash on her forehead that was bleeding copiously.

They started for the Humvee when the hair on the back of Sam's neck started to rise. He turned around quickly and saw the second intruder pulling himself up, aiming at Dalton and Graham. Sam fired but not before the man also fired off a round, aiming at the last second for Sam.

"Sam!" Dalton yelled as he watched the man recoil from the hit. Graham saw the intruder aim yet again, but at Dalton this time. Graham dropped to one knee, with Tala to his left, and pulled his rifle up. He shot the other man squarely between the eyes, leaving no question of his death.

"I think I'm okay," Sam said. Dalton looked at his side; the shot had clearly shredded his hazmat suit but hadn't come into contact with Sam himself. "That's a fucking miracle," Dalton said, feeling pretty damn lucky. But before he got back into the truck, Dalton got the emergency tape to patch up the suit to decrease Sam's risk of contamination.

Dalton drove quickly back to the preppers' camp. They needed to assess Tala's injuries and at least set her leg in a cast before they took her and Graham back to Graham's camp.

"We have a decision to make," Dalton said, looking at Graham in the rearview mirror. "We don't take carriers into our camp because it's too risky. I hope you can understand that."

Graham just looked at the man through the rearview mirror. Cradling Tala in his lap, he'd managed to straighten up her clothes as best he could, anger curdling in his veins as he did. The swelling in her leg remained a problem, and she clearly had a concussion.

"Look, she's hurt really bad. She might even have internal injuries. Is there someone you have who can look at her?" Graham asked.

Dalton looked at Sam. "Call Clarisse, Sam. Maybe she's got a suggestion."

"Hi, Dalton, what is it?" Clarisse asked urgently, knowing that if he summoned her it was a medical emergency.

"We're going to need another quarantine room. Sam's suit was compromised, but we don't think he was exposed. It's taped now, and the female has several injuries. She has a leg fracture, concussion, and possible internal injuries from a car accident," Dalton said.

"Dalton," she said in a soothing voice, feeling his desperation through the line. "You know we made rules against bringing them here. I'm not against it, but you know you're risking direct exposure to us all. As it is, we only have three rooms. I'll have to let the guys out early. You and Sam will need to have separate ones since he's at risk. Then, she will need the last one. I don't think that's a problem, but where do we stop breaking the protocols we set in place for the carriers? Again, I'm not against this, I just want you to be certain that this is what *you* want."

"I hear you, and I understand." Dalton glanced back at Tala in the backseat. "Get it ready, please—and thank you, Clarisse."

She ran the test again and again. Clarisse knew it wouldn't come back any differently than the seven times before. She had to tell him now. She'd gone through every scenario, and there was just no other way. Dalton lay staring up at the ceiling. "Yes, Clarisse," he said, knowing she was staring at him. He could always feel her presence, no matter where she was. He didn't understand this, since he was a happily married man, but there it was.

"There's news," Clarisse said.

He knew something was wrong. She looked like she hadn't slept in days, even though she was in quarantine herself. Having operated on Tala, she confined herself to the lab. Her chestnut hair hung loosely down around her shoulders. He'd never seen it out of its tight bun.

"What is it?" Dalton said as he came to the window.

"Sam. He's been exposed."

"What do you mean?"

"He's not showing symptoms, but he's a carrier now," she said.

"Are you sure?" he asked in disbelief.

"Yes!" she said, and broke down. He'd never seen that happen before.

"God dammit!" Dalton yelled, thinking of Sam's now orphaned daughter.

"Does he know?"

Clarisse was still crying.

"Clarisse, does he know?" Dalton asked again.

"No," she answered, shaking her head. "I thought I should tell you first."

Graham carried Tala into the cabin carefully. They'd spent five days at the preppers' camp while Tala recovered from her injuries and the horrific ordeal. When she came to, Graham held her close while she cried.

He kissed her, "I love you, Tala. I'm so sorry this happened," he said. She held onto him, crying into his shoulder.

She had a fractured leg, and her right shoulder had been dislocated. Clarisse had examined her fully and then had a frank talk with her about how lucky she'd been in spite of what she went through.

The two women hit it off, and Clarisse said that she wished Tala had not been a carrier because she was someone she felt she could be real friends with. Tala felt the same, but was happy when they said it was time for them to go back, because she missed the children—and even Ennis.

Graham laid her down on the bunk, taking extra care to arrange her leg and arm, both in casts, carefully. Fully medicated against the pain, Tala smiled up at him. "I'm okay," she said.

He moved some of her hair out of her face. Then a very concerned Macy brought Tala a glass of water, pushing Graham out of the way. He gave the two some privacy, knowing Macy wanted to thank Tala for what she'd done for her. Tala hugged the girl, whose tears were streaming down her cheeks, then wiped them away for her and said to her in a strong voice, while holding her chin up, "I'm fine, Macy—really."

"I know they hurt you," Macy said as she began to sob even more.

Tala held the girl to herself, letting her cry. "Yes, they did, but there was no way I was going to let them take you, Macy, and no matter what they did to me, I know I did the right thing. Do you hear me? I love you as if you were my own child." Tala pulled Macy up to look her in the eyes again. "It doesn't matter what happened. What matters is that you were safe from them. You are the one who needs to go on. That's what is important to me."

"Thank you, Tala," Macy said.

"You don't need to thank me." Tala smiled at the girl and kissed her on her cheek.

Two weeks later, Sam and Graham tracked down two does through the deep snow in the east forest. Sam showed Graham how to rig up a carrier sled using boughs from the pine trees so they could easily pull the two kills along behind them, making it a lot easier than carting them manually back to camp.

"I've got a date in fifteen minutes, Graham," Sam said.

"Okay, Sam, see you back at the cabin." Graham watched as the quiet man went on his way.

Sam walked quietly across the frozen forest floor, breaking a deep snow path as it became necessary until he came to the rendezvous spot alongside the Skagit River, partly covered in ice. The sound of the rushing water was almost overpowering this time of year. He brushed the ice off a boulder and sat, waiting. He removed the small wood carving of the fawn he'd made for her this time, tossing it skillfully to land at the base of the pine across the river.

Soon he saw her coming, riding on Dalton's shoulders. Dalton had promised to take care of the girl as if she were his own. He sat Addy down on her feet, dressed in a pink snowsuit with her hands in gloves and her hat pulled down. She was well cared for, and Sam waved at his daughter as she waved back.

"Hi, Daddy," she said, shouting over the rushing water.

"Hi, darlin'," he said, wishing he could hold her in his arms; the ache was never ending. "I put a present by the tree," he said. Dalton pulled out the baggie and gave it to her, as usual. She ran over, excited to retrieve the gift. She knew to grab it through the baggie so Dalton could sterilize it before she could have it. The process would make the blond wood turn darker, but she didn't mind. She loved all the little creatures he made for her woodland collection.

"How was school today?" he asked her.

"It was good. I drew you a picture. I sent it to you," she said.

"I bet it's real pretty. I'll be sure to look at it as soon as I get back," Sam assured her.

"I love you, Daddy," Addy said.

"I love you too, baby. See you tomorrow."

Addy turned around, reaching for Dalton's outstretched hand. Dalton waved at Sam and he waved back, then Sam watched as they retreated back the way they came. When Sam could no longer see the pair, he turned and walked back to Graham's camp.

The Graham's Resolution series
On Wings That Travel - Prequel (coming soon)
The China Pandemic
The Cascade Preppers
The Last Infidels
The Malefic Nation

Perseid Collapse Kindle Worlds
Deception on Durham Road
Departure from Durham Road

Wayward Pines Kindle Worlds
Kate's Redemption

Bite-Sized Offerings
An Anthology Addition
Zombie Mom

Stand Alone
The French Wardrobe

Surrender The Sun
Book 1

A. R. Shaw, born in south Texas, served in the U.S. Air Force Reserve from 1987 through 1991 as a communications radio operator, where she was stationed at the Military Auxiliary Radio System (MARS) Station at Kelly Air Force Base, Texas.

Her first novel, *The China Pandemic* (2013), climbed to number 1 in the dystopian and postapocalyptic (SHTF) genres in May 2014 and was hailed as "eerily plausible" and with characters that are "amazingly detailed." Shaw continues to write the Graham's Resolution series.

Shaw lives with her family in eastern Washington State where, after the deep snow of winter finally gives way to the glorious rays of summer, she treks northeast to spend her days writing alongside the beautiful Skagit River.

Website and Blog: AuthorARShaw.com
Facebook Page: A. R. Shaw, Author
Twitter: @ARShawAuthor

Acknowledgments

No author completes a novel without the tremendous help from friends old and new. Here is a list of those whose brave souls aided in this series' creation.

Keri Knutson – Cover artist

Brian Bendlin – Editor extraordinaire

Gil Gruson – Radio Expert & Beta reader

Chris Barber – US Army soldier

John Barber – Trauma Surgeon

Mary Katherine Woods – Surgical Nurse

Thomas Shaw – Engineer & Beta reader and my HH

Ryan Chamberlin – Doctor & Beta reader

Steven Bird – Weapons Specialist, author & Beta reader

CDC – Patient with my many questions

Amos Barber – Hunting expert and my Dad

Ron Chappell – Blurb help

Gus O'Donnell – Second opinion on Blurb help

Sari Sandford and her father in Alaska – Ice fishing

Eric & Diana Tibesar – Cigars and smoking

Adam Shaw – Geology expert and my son

Will Moore – Police Officer & K9 expert

Steven Konkoly – Author & Sounding board

G. Michael Hopf – Also Author & Sounding board

Wendy Shaw – My constant sounding board and walking dictionary as well as my daughter

Oakley – My constant companion and your insight into Sheriff is invaluable to me

Made in the USA
Middletown, DE
31 May 2017